One Sweet Moment

One Sweet Moment

MAGGIE CRAIG

First published in Great Britain in 2009 by
Allison & Busby Limited
13 Charlotte Mews
London W1T 4EJ
www.allisonandbusby.com

Copyright © 2009 by MAGGIE CRAIG

The moral right of the author has been asserted.

A CIP catalogue record for this book is available from
the British Library.

10 9 8 7 6 5 4 3 2 1

13-ISBN 978-0-7490-7934-5

Typeset in 11/16 pt Sabon by
Terry Shannon

The paper used for this Allison & Busby publication
has been produced from trees that have been legally sourced
from well-managed and credibly certified forests.

PEFC
PEFC/16-33-111
CATO-PEFC-052
www.pefc.org

Printed and bound in Great Britain by
MPG Books Ltd, Bodmin, Cornwall

MAGGIE CRAIG is the author of six novels, three works of non-fiction, including a history of the women involved in the Jacobite rebellion of 1745, and numerous newspaper and magazine articles. She comes from a family where writing is considered an entirely normal thing to do, and which numbers among its forebears the weaver-poet of Paisley, Robert Tannahill.

*This book is dedicated to the late and much-lamented
Ian Somerville,
long-time Fiction Editor of* My Weekly *magazine:
a challenging editor,
an old-fashioned gentleman
&
a* superb *human being.*

Acknowledgements

I should like to express my appreciation of Jan-Andrew Henderson's *The Town Below The Ground;* Des Brogan, Frances Hollinrake and Alan J Wilson's *Hidden & Haunted: Underground Edinburgh* and David Hamilton's *The Healers: A History of Medicine in Scotland.*

I owe a huge debt to the late John Prebble's *The King's Jaunt* and I commend this meticulously researched and highly readable book to anyone seeking to know more about the historical development both of modern Scotland and the United Kingdom.

I am very grateful to the knowledgeable and helpful staff of the Central Library, George IV Bridge, particularly those in the Edinburgh Room.

I'd like to thank all the guides and others who have shown me round and allowed me access to the vaults under the South Bridge. I'd have been lost in there without Will and Sandy, who helped me get to grips with the lie of the land within this labyrinth of dark chambers – even if they did take an unholy delight in frightening me out of my wits in the process.

Will's subsequent input in terms of drawings, photographs and the readiness to discuss, work out and explain the layout of the bridge and its relationship to the surrounding buildings to the spatially challenged has been unstinting. He's like that.

On a special day in Edinburgh with my sister Kathleen and my late brother-in-law Brian Alexander, I was told tales of The Vennel and given a personal guided tour of Brian's old school, George Heriot's.

Thanks are also due to the very knowledgeable Martin Reid of Lothian & Borders Fire and Rescue Service and the fascinating Museum of Fire, Edinburgh.

The wonderful and wonderfully talented Patricia Bingham and Gillian Philip very kindly read and commented on the manuscript. Thanks for the *chiaroscuro*, Trish!

Lastly, this book would never have been born without the boundless initial enthusiasm of Ian Somerville and Harrison Watson of *My Weekly* magazine. I'll never forget that Monday night yomping around Broughty Ferry, nor those toasted sandwiches in Bannerman's in the Cowgate.

'To look over the South Bridge and see the Cowgate below full of crying hawkers, is to view one rank of society from another in the twinkling of an eye.'
RLS

PART ONE

Edinburgh,
Spring 1822

CHAPTER ONE

At first he was grateful for the heat. It crackled up from the hearth, warming his stiff legs and arms. His whole body was numb with cold and fatigue. How many chimneys had he clambered up over the course of this long week? His sister always told him how good he was at his numbers but he had lost count somewhere in the middle of this bitterly cold Saturday afternoon.

It was hours since he had last eaten and his belly ached with hunger. He tried once more to free his right foot, trapped by an awkward bend where one of the many chimneys in this grand house joined into the main shaft. Pain shot up his leg. Then, like a hundred jagged needles, it exploded into every corner of his skinny frame.

His master roared up at him. 'Get a move on, laddie! Or I'll put more coal on the fire!'

The boy had to wait for the spasms of agony to subside before he could speak.

'Ma foot's stuck!' he sobbed. 'I cannae move it!'

'Ye'll hae tae move it! Unless it's a roastit erse ye're wanting! Get on with it, ye wee bugger!'

The child tilted his head back, whimpering as the rough stone penetrated his hair and scraped his tender scalp. All he could see was a small rectangle of inky-black sky. The short winter's day was already over.

A narrow tongue of flame licked past his feet, searing his bare calves and singeing his tattered trousers. He yelled in pain and panic. Aware of freedom and fresh air a few tantalising feet away, he tugged again at his trapped foot. His scream of pain echoed up and down the chimney.

A moment later he heard a fierce, spluttering hiss. Realising the fire had been doused with water, he let out a panic-stricken moan. His master must ken fine what that would do. The child wet himself. As the warm urine coursed down his legs he found space in one corner of his mind to be ashamed of the fact. Only wee bairnies peed themselves. He was six years old and should be long past that.

Plump white tendrils of smoke snaked up from the grate. Two separate tentacles slid into the boy's mouth and nose, intertwining at the back of his throat. It was like having a fusty old blanket forced into his mouth. The acrid smoke rose further, stinging his eyes and the delicate skin that surrounded them like a swarm of malevolent wasps. Tears streaked the soot which coated his smooth young cheeks.

He began to cough, knowing that opening his mouth could only make matters worse. Breathing in smoke was what had killed his pal Davie last year. Once it had cleared, the boy had been dispatched up the shaft to push the lifeless body out onto the roof beside the chimney tops. Davie had been all floppy, like a grubby rag-doll staring up at him out of empty eyes. There were nights when the boy couldn't get that picture out of his head.

He wondered dimly if they would hack his foot off to make it easier to move him. He'd heard tales of things like that happening to other chimney boys.

His head was swimming, poisoned by the smoke which was slowly suffocating him. He couldn't breathe properly. Even with his bony little chest heaving and his heart hammering like a drum, he couldn't catch one decent breath.

Maybe he should stop trying. Close his eyes and allow himself to be spirited away. He sighed, allowing his mouth to fall open and admit the deadly smoke. He was feeling real hazy now, losing his awareness of where he was, even of who he was.

Yet a tiny window of lucidity remained. Pushing back the smothering grey curtains and his fading consciousness, it allowed a picture of his big sister Kate to flash into his head. Tears were streaming down her face. They had told her he was dead and she was weeping for him. Weeping sore and hard and moaning his name over and over again. *Andrew, Andrew, Andrew…*

His mind cleared and his determination returned. 'It's all right, Kate,' he muttered, gathering his strength about him. 'Ah'm no' deid yet!' All he had to do was free his foot. Clamber up the chimney to the outside world, freedom, life and Kate.

He braced himself, tugged harder on his trapped foot. Pain zigzagged once more through his small frame. He couldn't thole this, he really couldn't! Except that he had to. Kate would be so sad.

He yelled out another defiant 'Ah'm no' deid yet!', then screamed in agony. He tried to say the words again but his voice faltered and cracked before he was halfway through.

'Ah'm no…'

Maybe he was wrong. Maybe he was already dead. That was his last conscious thought. Although as everything faded, he could still hear his sister's voice, frantically calling his name.

Andrew, Andrew, Andrew…

CHAPTER TWO

'Ah'm no' deid yet,' he muttered, thrashing his small head from side to side in his anxiety to transmit that message to his sister. 'Ah'm no' deid yet, Kate. Dinna be sad. Please dinna be sad...'

'Andrew! Wake up, Andrew!'

His head stopped moving and his eyes snapped open. In her white nightgown and greeney-blue tartan plaid, the rippling waves of her auburn hair loose about her face, Kate was standing beside his bed holding a crusie lamp. She leant over him to place it in one of the small niches that dotted the chilly stone wall behind him. Low though it was, the vaulted ceiling that topped it was lost in the gloomy shadows above their bright heads.

Andrew stared up at her, blinked, and registered that the smell of smoke in his nostrils had been replaced by the stink of the fish-oil that fuelled the lamp. Coming up like the blade of a pocket knife being opened, he uttered an incoherent cry and threw himself into his sister's arms.

Five minutes later, Kate was still sitting on the edge of the narrow wooden bunk which formed her brother's bed, holding him close and murmuring the same reassuring words into his thick, soft hair. 'You're safe, Andrew. You're oot o' the chimney and you're never going back up one. You're far too big a laddie to climb up chimneys now. Far too big,' she repeated, knowing from heart-breaking experience those were the words which would soothe him the most.

She hadn't asked if it had been the usual nightmare. It always was. Four years on and her wee brother was still reliving the terror of that awful day. Sometimes he went for weeks or even months without the nightmares but sooner or later they always came back to torment him.

Unseen by him, her head over his shoulder, Kate wrinkled her nose and sniffed.

Aye, he had wet the bed again, but she would ignore that for the moment and sort it out later. He would go as red as his hair if she said anything: the same way he reacted when cruel people mocked his lolloping gait. He had escaped from the chimney by bending his leg as no leg should be bent. It had never recovered from the damage, leaving it badly wasted and, as a result, Andrew was lame.

Her arms tightened around him. At times like this, the memory of what he had endured – and seemed condemned to re-live, over and over again – made her so angry she could hardly breathe. He had been whole and sound and healthy before he'd been forced into working for that brute of a chimney sweep.

Kate's head snapped up. Well-oiled though the lock and hinges of the vault's gates were, she heard the whisper of sound as one was pushed open, brushing the straw that covered the earthen floor. She knew that sound too well. A tall and jagged shadow leapt onto the wall.

The man casting it emerged from behind a stack of whisky casks, ale barrels and bottles of claret. They were stored in a wooden framework that lifted them clear of the straw-covered floor. That protected them from the constantly rising cold and damp, an unpleasant fact of life for those who lived in the honeycomb of vaults and chambers inside the South Bridge.

It was a bridge with no river flowing through any of its nineteen arches. At right angles to the Royal Mile, spanning the long valley running behind Edinburgh's High Street, it linked with the North Bridge to create a straight and level road, which eased the passage of foot and horse traffic between the Old Town and the New. Almost as soon as the South Bridge was completed, lofty tenements had been built against both sides of it, closing its arches forever to daylight and fresh air. Only one remained open, through which the ancient thoroughfare of the Cowgate straggled.

Michael Graham's feet crunched in the straw as he drew nearer to Kate and her brother. Small tunnels erupted as startled mice scampered to the furthest extremities of the chamber. Kate narrowed her eyes in response to the abrupt increase in illumination. Trust him to be using a lantern with a good tallow candle inside it. Normally they saved those for The Pearl Fisher and its customers.

'In the name o' God,' he growled. 'Ah doot they'll can hear that blasted bairn oot in the Cowgate!'

Feeling Andrew's body tense, Kate shifted him so his head lay on her right shoulder, shielding him from their uncle. Michael Graham had always been too free with his hands: in more ways than one.

'He's all right now,' she said hurriedly. 'It's time tae get up anyway. Aunt Chrissie's got the porridge on.' She nodded in the direction of the grilled gates. The unmistakable aroma of simmering oatmeal was wafting up the underground close that gave access to the individual vaults of the bridge. With no natural light and precious few timepieces between them, it was one way this subterranean community knew morning had arrived.

Kate and Andrew slept in the second vault in from the street, where most of the valuable alcohol was stored. Their aunt and uncle had a room across the close on the ground floor of the building that sat on the corner of the Cowgate and Niddry Street. They did most of their living in the tavern, ready at any time of day to welcome the thirsty men who might step in from the Cowgate in search of refreshment.

There were plenty of thirsty folk within the South Bridge too, even if their purses were on the lean side. The next chamber up from The Pearl Fisher's two vaults housed a tannery, and the one beyond that an illicit whisky still. This wasn't a place where the law held much sway. Beyond the whisky still, in vaults subdivided by a few filthy sheets, lived a dozen individual families, evicted from their former homes when unemployment, illness or injury had thrown the main breadwinner out of work.

In the deepest recesses of the bridge lurked a rough lodging house, occupied by a shifting population of men and women with hard and shuttered faces. How any of them scratched a living was a question other folk who lived in here thought it wiser to leave unanswered.

Andrew had to pass all of these dark spaces on his way to work, heading for the top of the bridge by a succession of rickety wooden staircases, which rose through holes in the stone floors to give access to its three different levels. Hampered as he was by his lameness, Kate knew he was often nervous as he made his slow and halting way past them. That was always worse on the mornings after he'd had one of his nightmares.

'Want me tae walk ye up tae your work today?' She whispered the words into his hair but Michael Graham heard them all the same.

'Ye'll dae nae such thing, miss,' he barked. 'Are ye rearing a milksop here?'

For a moment Kate neither moved nor spoke. Within the protection of her arms, Andrew shifted. She knew he was struggling to get his courage up, forcing himself to tell her he could easily walk up through the bridge on his own. Lifting her chin from where it was resting on the top of his head, she turned and looked at their uncle.

Over-fondness for the food and drink dispensed at The Pearl Fisher had thickened his waist and coarsened his features but he remained a strong and powerful man. Much though she hated to admit it, she could see too that he retained remnants of roguish good looks. In his youth he must have resembled a handsome gypsy.

Watching his cronies and those he strove to impress respond to the ready smile and the immense affability he could adopt when he chose to, Kate had often wondered why so few of those folk seemed to register the air of menace he also carried about with him. To her it was always there. Sometimes she had the fancy she could see it, a great swirling cloak as dark as his black-hearted soul.

If it wasn't for him, Andrew's leg would be strong and undamaged. If it wasn't for him, Andrew would never have become a chimney boy in the first place. If it wasn't for him, Andrew wouldn't be tormented by these awful nightmares. If it wasn't for him— Anger broke over her like a storm-tossed wave.

'I'm walking my brother up tae his work.' She gave each word its full weight, positioning them like bricks in a wall: a defensive barrier between her and her uncle. 'It'll no' take me long.'

Her heart was pounding like a demented drum when, horribly, his hated features relaxed into a leering grin.

'Right fierce wee thing when ye put your mind to it, eh, Kate?'

She continued to hold herself erect, her face impassive. Concealing her emotions from him had become second nature.

'Ye'll be needing the key.'

'Leave it on my bed.'

'Take it from me.' He held out his hand to her and she leant over and grabbed the big key lying in his open palm. She wasn't quick enough to stop him from squeezing her fingers with his. The unpleasant smile curving his fleshy lips grew wider. He knew exactly what his touch did to her.

Kate wrapped both arms once more about her brother and waited for their uncle to go. When he did, leaving them with only the feeble glimmer of the crusie lamp, she listened as she always did until she heard the sound of his footsteps retreating behind the stacks of casks and barrels.

'Kate?' Andrew's voice was muffled. 'You're squashing me, Kate.'

Relaxing her grip, she stood up, let out a shaky breath and put a smile on her face for her brother. Kate had nightmares too. Only hers happened while she was wide-awake.

CHAPTER THREE

'I'm sometimes a wee bittie feart up here,' Andrew confided as he and Kate stepped off the final wooden staircase of their ascent. It was very quiet on the topmost level of the bridge, a place of criss-crossing passageways, dusty stone turnpike stairs falling away into blackness and a succession of locked doors.

You seldom saw a living soul in this part of the bridge but those locked doors told their own tale. They secured and concealed things some folk didn't want others to know about. As her brother tucked his hand into hers, Kate gave his fingers a reassuring squeeze. 'There's nothing here that need worry you, Andrew.'

'I dinna like all the doors.'

'I ken whit ye mean,' she said, as her lantern struck needles of light from the gleaming metal padlock that secured one of the doors. 'But it's your own imagination that's scaring ye. No' anything real. Try tae think o' it that way when you're feeling nervous. And here we are.' The workshop door stood ajar, allowing her to see that Andrew's master had lit the lamps within it. 'Ye'll be fine now.'

'Aye,' her brother agreed. 'On ye go, Kate. I'm no' wanting tae make ye late at the fish market.'

'A wee hug first?' she asked, bending forward and setting the lantern on the earthen floor. 'You're no' too big a boy for that?'

'I'll never be too big a boy for that, Kate.' He bestowed one of his big, beaming smiles upon her, although after a moment or two he issued a laughing complaint. 'You're squashing me again!'

Kate let him go and stooped again to pick up the lantern. 'I'll likely no' be able to get away tae meet ye tonight. We're aye real busy at eight o'clock.'

'I'll be fine, Kate. Honest. And ye're right. It is my ain imagination that frightens me. No' a few blootered folk I hae tae dodge on my way back doon. Even wi' my gammy leg, when they're fou I'm a hale heap quicker than them. And, aye,' he added with another smile, pre-empting the words hovering on her lips, 'I'll mind and lock up behind me.'

'You're too smart by half,' Kate said with an answering curve of the mouth. As soon as she heard him turn the key she wheeled round and hurried back down through the bridge. In theory, she could have walked along a corridor, mounted one of the turnpike stairs, gone through a close on the next floor up, stepped out onto South Bridge Street and been at the fish market on the other side of the High Street within minutes.

In practice, even supposing there weren't more locked doors barring her way, the thought didn't even occur to her. The worlds of South Bridge Street and the Cowgate were as distant from one another as the Earth was from the Moon.

The road that ran along the top of the bridge was home to the most exclusive shops in Edinburgh. Having deserted the Old Town for the New a generation before in search of air, light and space, the gentry returned for its education and to do its shopping.

The booksellers, stationers and publishers indicated the proximity of three esteemed seats of learning: the High School, George Heriot's School and Edinburgh University. Sharing the top of the South Bridge with them were hatters and glovers, shoemakers, dressmakers, drapers and the saddler's where Andrew worked.

Apart from a handful of adventurous shop assistants, publishers' clerks and students, few of those who worked or shopped up above would have dreamt of visiting the murky man-made canyon of the Cowgate. Fewer still would have contemplated investigating the mysterious and shadowy community that lived within the South Bridge.

Kate's own route to the fish market took her up the steep brae of Niddry Street. She kept to the lee of the buildings, picking her way round the piles of stinking rubbish that littered the causeway. They might be living in an age of change, great wonders happening all about them – or so one or two of the regulars at The Pearl Fisher were always telling her – but Edinburgh's citizens, at least here in the Old Town, continued to dispose of their household waste in the old-fashioned way.

At ten o'clock at night they opened the windows of their towering tenements and hurled it all into the street below: vegetable peelings, ashes from their fires and the contents of their chamber pots alike. Folk wending their way through the city at that hour had to hope the traditional warning cry of 'Gardyloo!' would be given in time for them to duck into the shelter of a nearby doorway. Early risers like Kate had to watch where they put their feet.

It took most of the night and well into the morning for the scavengers employed by the Town Council to clear up the accumulated nastiness that littered the narrow streets and closes. The people who lived in those gave the resulting heady mix of aromas a rueful nickname: the flowers of Edinburgh.

As she emerged onto the windswept ridge of the High Street, Kate shivered. There was a snell breeze blowing up from the Firth of Forth this fresh April morning. She pushed her two big wicker baskets into the crooks of her elbows and paused for a moment to adjust her plaid. Worn now like a shawl crosswise over her body, she pulled its ends more tightly through the thick brown leather belt that spanned her trim waist.

On the edge of South Bridge Street, she was obliged to stop to allow two early morning riders to trot past. She watched them go, the iron-shod hooves of their horses striking sparks from the few patches of clear cobbles.

She could never stand here without thinking of Andrew toiling away under the roadway, cutting and stitching leather in the saddler's basement workshop all day long. Summer and winter alike he worked by lamplight, buried alive within the innards of the South Bridge. His sister's mouth settled into a determined line. Not for much longer.

For Kate Dunbar had a plan, one that was going to get her brother and herself out of the South Bridge and away from their aunt and uncle for ever. All she needed now was the courage to put it into operation.

'Away in a dwam, lass? It's ower cauld tae stand still for ower long this morning, I'm thinking!'

Kate returned the cheeky smile the passing carter was throwing over his shoulder at her. Like most of the folk who were up and about at this hour, they knew one another by sight. 'You're no' wrong,' she called after him.

Her oatmeal-coloured skirt swirling around her calves, she zigzagged her way through the muck and rubbish and, with the ease born of youth and familiarity with her surroundings, plunged down the stinking and precipitous gully of Fleshmarket Close.

The steps brought her first into the meat market that gave the close its name. She hurried though the pens and stalls clustered below the North Bridge, glad they were empty. She didn't like to see the animals waiting to be slaughtered, especially the cows with their big sad eyes. She always thought they had sensed what was about to befall them and were sorrowfully resigned to their fate.

Something warm, furry and very alive streaked across her feet. Glancing down, she saw a striped cat with a silvery mackerel clamped between its jaws. A string of curses which would have made a sailor blush was being hurled after it. Kate grinned when she saw the tabby loup up onto a high wall far above the reach of human arms and settle down to enjoy her booty.

'If it isn't the bonniest lassie in Edinburgh come tae buy oysters from the ugliest auld fishwife!' Her weather-beaten face set off by the dazzling whiteness of her ruffled mutch, the woman who had called down the blood-curdling curses on the cat let out a great belly laugh. One of the fishwives up from Newhaven, she wore the same distinctive costume as every other woman selling her husband's or son's catch this morning: a white apron and short striped flannel skirt puffed out with several petticoats, topped by a dark shawl and that extravagant headgear.

The small linen cap that kept Kate's exuberant auburn tresses off her face was much simpler in style, although every bit as clean as the fishwife's, as was the capacious apron she wore tied around her waist. She liked to keep herself and her clothes as clean as possible, even if her skirts and bodices were always threadbare and well-mended before her aunt could be persuaded to put out the money for cloth to enable her niece to stitch new ones.

'You're no' really grudging one wee cat one wee fish, are ye?'

'Ach, we all hae tae eat,' came the philosophical agreement. 'Will your auntie be needing the usual today, dearie?'

Once the order was given and Kate's baskets piled high with oysters and herring and haddock, the woman reached up and pinched her smooth young cheek. 'A complexion like a bowl o' cream,' she pronounced. 'Ye'll be looking to get yourself a husband soon, young Kate. A fine rich merchant perhaps? Or a student at the University who's coming out to be a lawyer or a physician?'

'That'll be right,' Kate said, counting out coins into a palm the colour and texture of leather. She slid the draw-string purse from which they had come back into the big front pocket of her apron and batted a question back to the fishwife. 'But d'ye no' think a lawyer or a physician might be looking for a wife who's got some brains in her heid?'

'Having no book-learning doesna make you daft,' came the shrewd response. 'You'll make some young man a fine wife.'

'How about me then, Kate?' At the next stall, a lad in a rough tweed jacket and a yellow muffler took a break from stacking flat wooden boxes and batted luxuriant brown eyelashes at her. The fishwife shot him a withering glance and extracted a clay pipe from a pocket somewhere within the voluminous folds of her striped skirt. 'The lassie's no' that desperate.'

'She'd never go hungry,' he retorted. 'I'd aye keep her fed.'

'Aye, but with fish, ye great lummox. She's sick o' fish. We're all sick o' fish.' She winked at Kate. 'Ye'll find a better man than that, lassie.'

Kate took the banter with good grace. She would never marry, but they weren't to know that. Raising her head to prospect for a new customer, the fishwife offered a nugget of news to the departing one. 'Have ye heard, lassie? They say the king might be paying us a visit this summer.'

Kate raised her baskets and her eyebrows. 'Us?'

'Edinburgh,' supplied the young man behind the fish boxes. 'Seemingly he's tae mak a visit tae his northern capital.' The words were pronounced with cheerful sarcasm. 'Something for the gentry only, I'm thinking.' He flashed her a grin. 'No' for the likes o' us.'

'Aye,' Kate agreed. 'Somehow I dinna think His Majesty will be calling in for a wee refreshment at The Pearl Fisher.'

With the sound of laughter ringing in her ears, she made her way back towards Fleshmarket Close. A few moments later, on the point of turning the corner from the High Street into Niddry Street, she heard her name being called.

'Miss Catriona!'

That could be only one person. Kate pirouetted like a dancer on a music box, her laden baskets swinging out in response. Even as she turned, she realised she was now on the horns of an exquisite dilemma.

CHAPTER FOUR

Very few people addressed her by her full given name. Even fewer prefaced it with a polite *Miss*. She knew what most folk thought about lassies who worked in oyster cellars.

The lanky man emerging from the bookshop on the corner of South Bridge Street and the High Street treated everyone with respect – unless they happened to occupy an exalted position in society. Like many in his trade, Nathaniel Henderson held Radical political views. Stepping out of the path of a brewer's dray bowling along at some speed, Kate crossed the causeway and walked towards him. 'You're up betimes, Mr Henderson.'

'Mrs Henderson's brother from Peebles has been visiting us. He wanted to make an early start on his road home and we got up to see him off.' The bookseller brandished the newspaper he was clutching. 'Have you heard the news? It seems we're to be honoured with a royal visit.'

'Aye,' Kate said, 'they were talking about it at the fish market. But I'm surprised you're interested, Mr Henderson. I've never known you to hae much time for kings and princes.' Curious about that though she was, she was also playing for time. Should she take the opportunity of this chance meeting to broach the subject that had been occupying her thoughts to the exclusion of almost everything else for the past weeks and months?

Nathaniel Henderson peered at her over the narrow brass-rimmed spectacles perched on the end of his long nose. 'I'll be interested to observe the spectacle, all the same. Sir Walter Scott will be the master of ceremonies, I understand. He may be a great writer but I canna say I care much for his politics.' Tucking the newspaper inside the broad lapels of a shabby but still magnificent green and gold brocade dressing-gown, he put his hands behind his back and began pacing up and down.

Kate stood and watched him, ready to yell a warning should the bookseller's long strides take him and his full-skirted dressing-gown too close to an accumulation of nastiness piled up in the gutter. You aye had to keep an eye out for Mr Henderson when it came to things like that.

'It'll be bread and circuses,' he snorted. 'Hah! As if we can be won over to a morally bankrupt monarch and an outmoded system of government by public holidays and some jollifications—'

'Nathaniel Henderson! Will you stop speechifying? Does the poor girl not hear enough politics at her work?'

Peggy Henderson swept out of the shop like the tornado of energy that she was.

A foot shorter than her husband, her lack of stature had never stopped her from standing up to him or anyone else.

'Good morning, lass,' she said with a friendly smile. She was wearing a simple but elegant high-waisted dress in a red and cream print, her gleaming blonde hair piled on top of her head and threaded through with a narrow red ribbon. Hands on hips, she turned her attention to her husband. 'What are you doing traipsing up and down in your night-clothes like some old mannie who doesn't care any more?'

Nathaniel's mouth curved as he looked down at his wife. 'Och, Peggy,' he said, 'you're so bonnie first thing in the morning. As fresh as a wee crimson-tipped daisy.'

'Don't change the subject.' Even as the stern words were

uttered, Peggy Henderson was blushing in response to her husband's appreciative gaze. His smile deepened into a grin.

Feeling the familiar wistfulness as she watched them, a tug of longing for something she knew she would never have, Kate caught hold of two observations Nathaniel had made before his wife appeared on the scene. 'Public holidays?' she queried. 'Jollifications?'

Nathaniel tore his eyes away from his wife's face. 'Parades and music and fireworks. With everybody being expected to turn out to see all the money going up in smoke and yell huzzahs at that ridiculous man to whom we're all supposed to bow the knee,' he added scathingly.

'But the parades and music and fireworks will be great fun,' Peggy Henderson said, chuckling at the glower her comment provoked. 'D'ye not think so, Kate?'

'I suppose so. For those as gets tae see them.'

'That should be all of us, my dear,' Peggy responded. 'What with these proposed public holidays.'

'But those'll no' be for everybody, surely.'

Nathaniel waved the newspaper again. 'It's the patriotic duty of masters to free their workers to see the spectacle. According to this rag, anyway.' He looked with disgust at the venerable *Edinburgh Courant*. A regular reader and occasional contributor to the *Scotsman* – a mere stripling of a newspaper and one that wholeheartedly espoused the Radical view of politics – the bookseller read the *Courant*, so he had once confided to Kate, only because *it never hurts to know what the enemy is thinking*.

Personally she thought Mr Henderson read every piece of printed matter he could lay his hands on. He was a great reader, always talking about something he had learnt from a newspaper or a book. It was knowing that which had inspired Kate's wonderful plan.

She was going to ask the Hendersons if they would teach Andrew and herself how to read and write. She had it all worked out. If they agreed, they would come to the Hendersons on a Sunday, at a time to be mutually agreed. She would pay them, of course, had been saving up for months so as to be able to offer them two shillings per lesson. That seemed the right amount to offer, a shilling for her and a shilling for Andrew.

She already had nineteen shillings squirreled away, hardly able to believe she had managed to accumulate such a sum. Nineteen shillings was a small fortune – especially when you didn't actually earn any money.

Her aunt paid her no wages and made Kate give her any tips she received. Andrew, too, had to hand over his meagre earnings from the saddler's. It had taken Kate both courage and time to slip the odd penny or three penny bit into her apron pocket. One at a time so they wouldn't jangle. Only on occasional nights in case she had a guilty look on her face and gave herself away.

The coins were wrapped now in her spare chemise, it in turn tucked into one corner of the battered tin chest in which she kept her and Andrew's few clothes and possessions. She had set herself the task of amassing a guinea. It seemed an elegant sum.

She would hand it all over to Mr and Mrs Henderson and ask them to give her and Andrew a course of ten lessons. That would surely be enough for them to master the basics of reading and writing. The extra shilling could be used to pay for paper or slates or anything else their teachers might deem necessary.

Neither her aunt nor uncle gave a damn what she and Andrew did in their free time on a Sunday. They would never have to know: not until that glorious day when Kate took herself and her brother out of the South Bridge.

Once they were both able to read and write she was confident they could find themselves good jobs. As soon as they had secured those positions they could rent a nice little room somewhere – by that time she would have saved enough money for the first few weeks' rent – maybe even a couple of rooms if both of them were earning. Kate had lovely pictures in her head of her and Andrew in that little home, happy and comfortable and peaceful and free.

What she hadn't worked out was how she was going to summon up the courage to approach their prospective tutors. Ever since Mrs Henderson had started speaking to her and Andrew after the service at the Tron Kirk one Sunday, she and her husband had been kindness itself. Yet Kate still hesitated.

What if they thought it daft for a lassie who lived and worked in an oyster cellar to want some education for herself and her brother? What if they didn't think the Dunbars would be capable of learning to read and write? Kate had no doubts about Andrew's abilities but she was nowhere near as confident about her own.

'Are you all right, lass?'

'I'm fine, Mrs Henderson,' she replied, jumping as the bell of the Tron started to sound six o'clock. It made up her mind for her. She had waited so long for this and it made sense to give herself the best possible chance of success. Once she had her guinea she would ask them, and do so when she and Andrew were in their Sunday best – such as that was. 'Excuse me,' she said, flashing both Peggy and Nathaniel a smile, 'I'll hae tae be off.'

'I think she wanted to speak to us about something.'

Nathaniel slipped one strong arm about his wife's shoulders as they stood and watched Kate round the corner into Niddry Street. 'Then why didn't she? I hardly think she'd be shy of us now, my dear. However much she was when we first got to know her and young Andrew.'

'Although always determined,' Peggy countered. 'Do you remember how offended she was when I tried to give her that shawl of mine?'

'Said she wouldn't take it unless she could pay you for it and since she couldn't afford to do so she'd have to say thank you but no thank you.'

'I've never dared offer her anything since. Although I've often wanted to.'

'She has her pride.'

'And not much else, poor lass. Apart from her looks, of course. Although I sometimes fear those make her vulnerable. To the wrong kind of man, I mean.'

'She's quick-witted enough to see those kind of men coming,' Nathaniel said comfortingly. 'Sharp and shrewd. Not a young woman who's prepared to suffer fools gladly. Yet she has a warm heart too. If she'd been born into a different family...' For once he resisted the urge to make a political point, contenting himself with a heartfelt, 'The world's ill-divided, Peg.'

'It is that.' Peggy Henderson's eyes grew troubled. 'She keeps herself so clean too, in body and soul. That can't be easy where she lives.'

'You're right there, my love. Who knows what goes on in those stews under the South Bridge? Yet there are good people down there too.'

His wife shivered. 'And some gey wicked ones as well, Nathaniel.'

Kate stood on the threshold of The Pearl Fisher, blinking into the gloom. Feeling the customary pang at having to leave the bright day behind, she distinguished the angular figure of her aunt. Chrissie Graham was lifting the flap of the heavy wooden counter at the back of the vault. She came forward to stand in front of the bar, placed her hands on her hips and gazed sourly at Kate.

'What the de'il took you so long?' Her skirts rustled as she kicked something that stood at her feet: Kate's tin trunk. 'Ye'll explain this tae me, miss. Dinna even think o' playing the innocent.'

On the bar behind Chrissie Graham, visible to Kate now her eyes had adjusted to the gloom, was her spare chemise. A pile of coins spilt across it.

CHAPTER FIVE

Chrissie lunged forward and slapped her niece hard across the face. In sheer reaction, Kate dropped the baskets of fish to the floor, provoking a string of invective. 'Butter-fingered wee bitch. Stupid wee slut. Daft wee cow.'

Another sequence of slaps. One. Two. Three. Four. Each one hurt more than the last. 'Whit hae ye got tae say for yourself, eh?' Chrissie gestured towards the pile of coins. 'You been telling me lies aboot whit a'thing costs at the fish market? Cheating me, ye wee bitch?'

'I wouldna dae that, Aunt Chrissie! I havena stolen from ye. Those are my tips. No' all o' them, either.'

'*Your* tips?' Chrissie repeated, drawing the words out as though Kate had said the most ridiculous thing imaginable. 'And wha is that does the cooking in here?' She jabbed one thumb against her bony chest. 'Me. Like it's me wha has tae feed and clothe you two. Keep a roof ower your heids, forbye. I didna ask ye tae come here when that brother o' mine and his wife upped and died, did I now? It was yon interfering minister wha brocht ye. Yet your uncle and me agreed tae tak' the baith o' youse in. And this is how ye repay us?'

Fighting back tears, unable to speak, Kate found herself being gripped by both shoulders and shaken.

'D'ye ken where you and your brother would be noo gin your uncle and me hadna taken ye in, Kate Dunbar? Dae ye ken that?'

It always ended like this. Until she answered this question, the slapping and shouting wouldn't stop.

'We'd be in the puirshoose, Aunt Chrissie.'

'I canna hear ye. Look me in the eye and speak louder.'

Hating her aunt for making her do this, hating herself for giving in to her, Kate said the words again. 'We'd be in the puirshoose, Aunt Chrissie.'

'That's right. Ye'd be in the puirshoose.' Chrissie Graham spoke with grim satisfaction. 'You in one end and your wee brother in the other. If ye were lucky ye micht see him at the kirk on a Sunday but ye wouldna be allowed tae speak tae him or hae onything tae dae wi' him. Is that what ye want, miss?'

This was always the threat, the one Kate could not withstand. A life without Andrew would be a life not worth living. 'No, Aunt Chrissie,' she said. 'That's no' what I want.'

Her aunt peered into her face for a moment, grunted and released her. 'You'll be turning out your apron pocket every night afore ye go tae bed frae now on. Right,' she continued, holding out her hand, 'I'm needing my change frae the fish market. Wi' chapter and verse on whit it a' cost. Once ye've done that ye'll pit the fish away and get on wi' your work. We've a hale heap o' chores tae get on wi' this morning. They'll no' dae themselves.'

By the time Kate had finished stowing the fish away in the larder behind the bar, her nineteen shillings had disappeared. Obeying a curt instruction to put her chemise back in her trunk and return that to the foot of her bed, she spent the rest of the morning in a daze. She gutted fish, peeled onions and potatoes, scrubbed tables and chairs, spread fresh straw on the earthen floor of the tavern and transferred heavy cooking pots hanging over the fire from long brackets to shorter ones.

All she could think of was her lost nineteen shillings, and of what that loss meant to Andrew and herself. Throughout the long morning Kate struggled and failed to pull herself out of a pit of blinding despair.

She sat on the edge of her bed in the darkness. Outside the afternoon was warm and sunny. After the midday rush and the clearing-up that followed it she'd stood for a moment looking out into the Cowgate. Then she'd retreated in here.

Aunt Chrissie was in her room across the close, taking her afternoon nap. That would be her dead to the world for the next couple of hours. Kate presumed her uncle was where she'd last seen him, playing the genial host to the handful of drinkers who'd stayed on after the others had gone back to their work.

She crooked her elbow so her left forearm lay horizontally in front of her. With the thumb and forefinger of her right hand, she pinched herself, squeezing hard. She didn't have much spare flesh there. That made it hurt all the more. She deserved for it to hurt, as she deserved it that her face was still stinging from this morning's slapping. She was a fool. She had dared to dream.

Like the magic carpet in the tale a patron of The Pearl Fisher had once told her, she had allowed those dreams to bear her far, far away from reality. She had imagined Andrew being taken on as a message boy by one of the elegant shops on top of the South Bridge. He would do well, and in time work his way up to become a clerk or a cashier.

She had visualised herself becoming a seamstress in one of the same elegant shops. She sewed her own clothes. She was sure she could learn how to sew the fine ones ladies wore.

It seemed logical that a seamstress who sewed for ladies would be expected to dress like a lady herself. So she had allowed herself to imagine a Kate Dunbar – no, a *Miss Catriona* Dunbar – dressed in all manner of bonnie gowns: floaty white muslin, fine lawn or one of the newly popular cotton prints imported from the distant land of India. Mrs Henderson had a dress made out of one of those.

At night Kate and Andrew would go home to the nice, airy rooms they rented and she would prepare them a tasty meal and they would sit and talk. On summer evenings they would go out for a stroll, come home and sit by an open window and gaze out over Edinburgh. In the winter they would light the wall sconces and play cards or read to one another by the bright light of tall white candles.

The dream had become so real to her she had started dropping hints to Andrew about her plans for their future, had promised him the two of them were soon going to learn to read and write. What was she going to say to him now?

She took a fresh grip of her forearm, making herself gasp with the pain of it. She had failed her brother and that was no more than she deserved. She'd been stupid to imagine she could ever get them out of this place. Stupid, stupid, stupid.

When she heard the whisper of sound as the grilled gate was pushed open, she barely reacted. Maybe this was no more than she deserved too. He came round the stacks of barrels and bottles, lantern in hand, and sauntered across to stand in front of her. 'Ye're looking a bit doon in the dumps, wee Kate. Is that because ye lost your bit o' siller?'

She spoke without looking up at him. 'I suppose it was you wha tellt her where tae look for it.'

'Oh, aye. Spotted whit ye were up tae a month or two back.' He lifted a hand and smoothed her hair back from her face. 'Ye're really no' very clever, are ye? Stupid and skinny and reid-haired and wi' silly wee tits intae the bargain. Fit for nothing except tae lie on your back and spread your legs for me.'

'I have my monthly,' she said listlessly.

He shrugged. 'Makes no odds to me, pet. And it means ye dinna need tae mess aboot wi' rags and vinegar.' He drew his fleshy fingers down her face and neck to grip one breast, his touch greedy and rough as it always was. 'Now,' he said, his voice thickening, 'undo your laces, lift your skirts and dae whit ah tell ye tae dae, ye wee hure. Ye ken whit'll happen tae your brother if ye dinna.'

CHAPTER SIX

In a spacious bedroom in a house on the corner of Castle Street and Princes Street a young man yawned, stretched and opened his eyes. Reaching out to the night-table his mother insisted on covering in lacy mats and fussy little knick-knacks, his long fingers found his pocket watch. He had tossed it there when he had sneaked back into the house at some point during the wee small hours.

Half past ten. With a theatrical groan, Richard Hope threw himself back against a small hill of soft white pillows. Half past ten was the crack of dawn, especially on a day when he didn't have any classes at the university. He closed his eyes and tried to get back to sleep again but the argument he'd had with his parents yesterday evening kept swimming back into his head.

They were so fucking unreasonable! Did they expect him to spend all his time at his studies? Evidently they did, judging by the way his father had thundered at him last night. 'I give you a very generous allowance, young man! Seems to me the least you could do in return is to take life a little more seriously!'

His mother had been more concerned with Professor Steele taking Richard's lack of application to his studies as a personal slight. Richard groaned again. This time it was genuine.

It had never been overtly stated. Marjorie Hope would have thought talk of such matters immensely vulgar. All the same, her youngest son, the only one of her children still unmarried and living at home, was well aware of her hopes that he and Professor Steele's daughter would make a match of it. It was hinted at in a hundred subtle – and sometimes not so subtle – ways.

Richard had known Irene Steele since childhood and he liked her a lot. She was bright and intelligent. Certainly no simpering miss, she had a good – and often surprisingly broad – sense of humour. A bit of a blue-stocking, perhaps, but that was all right. Made her much more interesting to talk to than many young ladies he knew.

He could see how advantageous marriage to Irene could be. Her father was a fixture of Edinburgh's medical establishment. Like Richard's own family and as the old phrase had it, the Steeles were also *weel-connecktit,* beyond the medical world as well as within it.

Richard was interested enough in his subject – although in the set he was running with, it didn't do to show *too* much enthusiasm for anything that might remotely be construed as serious. A frivolous approach to life in general and in particular was the order of the day. As a youngest son, he was of course going to have to earn his own living. Becoming a physician seemed a congenial way of doing that.

Physicians diagnosed ailments. By and large they didn't soil their frilled shirt cuffs or green velvet coats by getting involved in the messiness of actual treatment. They left that to the surgeons, considering them the artisans and themselves the aristocrats of medicine. Many of their patients were real aristocrats, wealthy enough to express their gratitude in a most satisfactory manner.

Richard was related to several aristocrats in his own right but there was no denying that being the son-in-law of one of Edinburgh's most eminent physicians wouldn't hurt when it came to giving him a good start in his chosen profession. The trouble was, much though he liked Irene, she didn't make his heart beat faster.

A shaft of sunlight crossed his face. A breeze had stirred the dark blue brocade curtains that hung at the windows of his room. He sat up and swung his legs over the side of the bed. Then he buried his fingers in his wavy black hair and gave his scalp a vigorous rub.

Padding barefoot over soft rugs to the two floor-to-ceiling windows that overlooked Princes Street, he pretended to jump when he caught sight of his reflection in the cheval glass. 'Irene Steele wouldn't fancy me very much now, Mama,' he murmured. 'Nor her respected father either, I doubt.' He grinned at his dishevelled appearance, night-shirt rumpled and hair standing up on end. Yanking open the curtains, he gazed out at Edinburgh.

Standing sentinel on its rock as it had done for centuries, the castle was always magnificent. The vista made Richard's heart swell with pride, although he would have died rather than admit such an emotion to his sophisticated friends.

His eyes travelled to the Earthen Mound, a pile of soil, rubble and general debris heaped up in the valley at the foot of the sheer cliffs of the castle rock. It would, so they were promised, grow into a sweeping avenue which would form another link between the two halves of Edinburgh.

Directly in front of his window, what remained of the Nor' Loch – part of the castle's defence in the olden days – was now an unpleasant swamp. That would have to be drained and the area around it cleared. Some would regret the sweeping away of the two old physic gardens, where generations of medical students had studied the healing properties of plants. Richard himself had no truck with such sentimentality. The magnificent new botanical garden being established at Inverleith had rendered its predecessors redundant.

Behind the gully once filled by the stagnant water of the Nor' Loch rose the impossibly high tenements of old Edinburgh. Richard's eyes travelled up the tallest of them, the one in Parliament Square that was fourteen storeys high. Pity the ancient buildings were growing shabbier by the year, the Old Town fast becoming a haunt of rogues, thieves and vagabonds.

Walking backwards and forwards across the bridges to the university and the Royal Infirmary he had sometimes wondered how people could bear to live in such dirt and squalor. No wonder the poor were prey to every disease going.

One of his friends had suggested a meander through some of Edinburgh's seediest howffs and drinking dens this Saturday night. *A real debauch*. That was how Torquil Grant had put it. 'Who knows?' he had drawled. 'We might even get the chance to sample the more earthy delights they say these oyster cellars have to offer.' He had laughed, tapping the side of his nose in a knowing gesture.

Richard found the prospect both enticing and a trifle alarming. He didn't want to catch any nasty diseases. Yawning widely, he raised his arms, stretched and walked across to the colourful tapestry bell-pull that hung beside his glowing fire.

CHAPTER SEVEN

'Kate! There's men dying o' thirst over here! Mair claret, lassie!'

'In a wee minute!' she yelled back. Taking a swift side-step to avoid an arm heading for her waist, she banged her hip against a table. The pain brought quick tears to her eyes but she didn't have the time even to stop and rub the sore spot through her skirts. It was Saturday night and The Pearl Fisher was full, noisy and brilliantly lit too.

Flickering against the stone walls, sconces green with ver-de-gris and white with drips of old wax held the good tallow candles. More of those dotted the roughly hewn tables, stuck into the necks of wine and brandy bottles. They too were encrusted in wax.

Some of the drinkers were becoming raucous. Not to mention over-familiar. Those questing hands. The usual shouted requests.

'Give us a kiss, Kate!'

'Come and sit on my knee, Kate!'

The fiddler in the corner struck up a reel. With a shriek of pleasure, a young woman with painted lips and rouged cheeks leapt up from the lap on which she'd been perched, turning to extend a plump arm to her cavalier. As he rose bashfully to his feet, Kate recognised him for a widowed wheelwright who lived along the Cowgate on the corner of Blair Street.

In theory, his dancing partner helped Kate wait on the tables on busy nights. In practice, Ella Balfour was one of the prostitutes Michael Graham allowed to work The Pearl Fisher in exchange for a percentage of their earnings.

Roping in another two couples to make up a set, Ella kicked away the straw to create a space for dancing. One of half a dozen men clustered about a nearby table glanced up, mouthing a curse at the disturbance before his attention returned to the cards in his hand. They were playing a deep game tonight.

Lowering her tray onto another table, Kate began setting out bread, ale and two wooden platters of oysters. Apprentice printers both, the young men she was serving were talking politics.

'We're supposed to be grateful yon painted popinjay might deign to pay us a visit?' The speaker's voice rose in outrage. 'The man can hardly squeeze himself into his pantaloons, he's that puffed up wi' rich living and an exaggerated sense o' his own importance. And the way he treated the queen over the divorce was a damned disgrace.'

'Aye well, Caroline wasna exactly a blushing maiden...'

Kate's mouth tightened. The last thing she wanted to hear was yet another scandalous story about the late queen. 'Take your hands off the table,' she said to one of the young men. 'I canna get all this on otherwise.'

'Kate! Have we been ignoring you?' He reached for her own hand, raised her fingers to his lips and planted a smacking kiss on them. 'We apologise most humbly for not paying tribute to your radiant beauty.'

Kate snorted and retrieved her hand. As she continued to put out their food and drink, she reminded herself that this pair might have heads full of mince sometimes but there was no harm in them. Nor was the loss of her nineteen shillings their fault.

'Away and boil your heid and make soup wi' it, ye great daftie.'

Both he and his friend hooted with laughter, not at all put out by her response. Despite the flirting and hand-kissing and the occasional wandering hand, The Pearl Fisher's regulars knew there was no point in really trying your luck with Kate Dunbar. The man sitting a few tables away wasn't a regular.

'Would you be wanting something else?' she asked after he had gestured to her to come over. He'd already proved himself no mean trencherman.

He snapped a coin onto the end-on whisky barrel serving as a table and looked her up and down in a way that made her shiver inside. 'Depends what this shiny silver florin will buy me.'

'You've the wrong lassie. Ask one o' the other girls.'

'I could add a shilling to that florin.'

'There's no' enough money in the world to pay for what you want.'

'Every woman in a place like this has her price.'

'Not me,' Kate said crisply. 'And if there's nothing I can bring ye I've got work tae dae.' She cleared some tables on her way back to the bar and was scraping oyster shells into a bin when she felt her uncle's mouth against her ear. In a soft murmur and hideous, obscene detail he told her what he was planning on doing to her the next time.

She said nothing. Nor did she look at him. All she did was place the first emptied platter on the bar and slide it towards Andrew. Finished now with his week's work at the saddler's, he was kneeling on a high stool behind the bar washing plates and tankards in a big wooden bowl. Against the racket of the tavern she knew he would have heard nothing of what Michael Graham had said.

Beyond Andrew, Chrissie Graham was presiding over her pots like a smiling witch. She was aye in a good mood when she was cooking and The Pearl Fisher was full of folk paying for the fruits of her labours. Kate wondered what she would think if she knew what her husband was whispering into her niece's ear. She herself had learnt not to give him the satisfaction of a response, though she could not always stop the obscene threats from playing themselves over and over again in her head.

The fiddler was playing a slow air. It had a melody of heart-breaking beauty and it spoke of lost crowns and forfeited thrones and shattered dreams. Kate thought of her own shattered dreams and wondered bleakly if she was to live out her life at The Pearl Fisher. No choices, no money, no hope. She lifted her head, responding to the cheerful farewell a young man who worked in one of the local hiring stables was calling to her.

'There's a lot o' the regulars as are fond of ye, eh? Ever wondered if they would like ye as much if they knew what a dirty wee slut you are?'

She wanted to kill him. She had long since worked out how she would do it. She would take one of the big cooking knives and she would wait until the dead of night and then she would creep into the room where he slept, raise the blade above her head – But the pictures in her head always went blank at that point.

Nor did she ask who had made her a dirty wee slut. She knew what the answer would be. Nobody would believe the genial host of The Pearl Fisher could do such disgusting things to his own niece. Standing too close to her as it was, Michael Graham moved closer still.

'Respectable men,' he said, speaking as though he were imparting some great wisdom, 'dinna marry sluts wha work in oyster cellars. Especially ones wha dinna come wi' a maidenheid. Ye could fool one o' them aboot that, I suppose. A wee bit o' play-acting and a cup o' cow's blood, eh? And I daresay ye thocht a wee bit dowry might help too.'

Kate's busy hands stilled. If he knew her so little as to think she'd ever try to trick any decent man like that, he must be more stupid than she thought.

'If that's how ye think ye're going tae get oot o' here, ye can forget it. Try it again and I'll tell whoever your fancy lights on whit a hure ye are. There's new customers come in. Toffs by the look o' it. Go and be nice tae them and we'll see how much we can soak them for.'

She followed his gaze. Taking in the youth, the good clothes – they thought they'd dressed down to fit in with their surroundings, but they hadn't – and choice of tavern, she judged the newcomers to be well-off students, visiting the Cowgate for the thrill it seemed to give them. She'd met the type before.

There was the short one who would likely run to fat as he grew older. Standing back to allow the wheelwright and a giggling Ella Balfour to stumble out of the tavern, his eyes were fair bulging out of his head. There was the one who'd seen it all before. Languidly unbuttoning his black velvet jacket, he was smoking a slim cigar. Kate transferred her attention to the third young man, taken aback to find herself on the receiving end of an intense stare.

She registered dark hair, cut fashionably short and tousled, and a strong face with the high forehead that spoke of intelligence. She noticed he was taller than his friends and in possession of a wide and well-shaped mouth. It struck her as belonging to someone who found plenty in his world to laugh at. She noticed he was still staring at her.

Kate gave her sore hip a surreptitious rub. He'd better not be thinking of trying anything on. She was in exactly the right mood to deal with the likes of him.

* * *

Weaving between tables on her way back from the men who'd been dying of thirst, holding a tray of debris high to avoid bashing anybody on the head with it, snatches of conversation floated around Kate like ribbons in the wind.

Another of the prostitutes who found her clients in The Pearl Fisher was negotiating a price with a soldier down from the garrison at the castle. A man was listing the results of the races at Musselburgh. There was the clink of coins and the rustle of paper as bets were redeemed. She was surrounded by money, and had lost her own.

And it had been her money, fair and square, earned from the tips people left for her and nobody else. For a moment the injustice of it overwhelmed her, knocking her off-guard. A heavy arm snaked round her waist.

'One wee kiss. Surely that's not too much to ask. Not from a girl like you.' The man who had propositioned her earlier drew her down on to his lap. Encumbered by her tray, Kate struggled to free herself but succeeded only in making her captor more aroused. She could feel his response.

'Like to play that game, ye wee jade? So much the better.' He pressed his mouth against her own and she gagged at the taste of fish and ale. Twisting her face away, she felt his free hand close over one of her breasts. That was it. That was bloody it! Kate raised her tray as high as she could and tilted its contents over his head.

He jumped to his feet, upending her and the whisky barrel table. 'Bitch!' he roared. 'Trollop!' Face contorted with fury, he drew his hand up and back. It and its partner were pinioned within seconds.

Sitting with her legs drawn up on the straw of the floor, wiping her mouth with the back of one shaky hand, Kate found herself surrounded by a forest of fashionably clad male legs.

'Hand over the cove to us, Richard,' said a well-spoken and authoritative voice. 'We'll deal with him while you see to the girl.'

'Are you injured?'

He was bending over her, extending a solicitous hand. Like a gentleman to a lady. She saw the frill of a cambric shirt cuff and long white fingers. They looked like those of a strong and competent man. Dazed, she placed her own red and work-worn hand into that white one and raised her head to survey its owner. The blue eyes of Catriona Dunbar and the green ones of Richard Hope met, and locked fast.

CHAPTER EIGHT

'Are you injured?' he asked again. The high forehead was creased in concern, as though her answer really mattered to him.

He had a lovely voice, as mellow as a russet apple. Oddly breathless, Kate raised the hand not resting in his to smooth back the dishevelled auburn tresses threatening to obscure her view of his face. Her little cap was no longer on her head. It must have come adrift during the tussle.

Her searching fingers found the scrap of linen on the floor beside her. She should put it back on again but she needed two hands for the job. The young gentleman was keeping hold of one of them. He didn't seem to want to give it up.

He had the bonniest eyes. You could drown in those velvety green pools...

'I'm fine, sir. Thank you, sir.' Preparing to rise from the straw that had cushioned her fall, she glanced round to ensure she wouldn't collide with any of the other customers. She needn't have worried. Most of them had risen from their seats and gone out into the close. By the sounds of it, they were cheering on her rescuer's friends. Men aye seemed to like a fight, whether they were in the thick of it or merely spectators. She felt strong fingers close over her own, taking a firmer grip of her hand.

'Let me help you up. Then I think you should sit down for a minute.'

Kate scrambled to her feet. 'Ow,' she gasped, her sore hip protesting at the too-quick movement.

'You *are* hurt!'

'No,' she assured the young gentleman. 'No' really.' Tugging her hand from his warm grasp, she brushed straw from her skirt. 'I'll serve you and your friends and then I'll clear up this mess. Here they come now.' She bobbed a curtsey. 'I'm grateful to you, gentlemen.'

The shorter young man blushed. His companion raised an elegant hand. 'Think nothing of it. I doubt that scoundrel will trouble you again, Miss…?'

'Dunbar,' she supplied. 'Catriona Dunbar. But everyone calls me Kate.'

'Well, Kate,' he said, resuming his seat, 'permit me to do the honours in return. Torquil Grant at your service.' Kate tried not to look surprised. He had a very Scottish name but he didn't sound at all Scottish. 'On my right is Mr Archibald Dalrymple and on my left' – he indicated the young man with the black hair and striking green eyes – 'you have Mr Richard Hope.'

'Will you be wanting some oysters?' Kate asked, wondering why he was bothering to introduce them all. 'The partan bree is also very fine this evening.'

Torquil Grant wrinkled his well-bred nose. 'What in the name of Hades is *partan bree*?'

'Crab soup.' Richard Hope answered his friend's question without taking his eyes off Kate's face. 'Call yourself a Scotsman, Torquil?'

'Not usually if I can help it,' came the drawled answer. 'A Highlander, maybe.'

Richard Hope made a rude noise. 'Have you ever even visited your ancestral acres?' His concentration – and those eyes as soft as velvet – remained squarely on Kate, a circumstance of which she was very well aware. 'You really ought to sit down for a moment. That was a nasty upset you had.'

For a wild moment Kate was tempted to do as he suggested. She would take a seat and exchange the time of day with him, converse on the topics of the hour. Aunt Chrissie would love that. 'I'm fine,' she told him again. 'Now, what can I get you, gentlemen?'

After she'd taken their order and hurried away, Torquil Grant extracted a silver case from the inside pocket of his black velvet jacket. 'Seem to have lost my cigar somewhere in the midst of that little mêlée,' he observed to no one in particular, adding dryly, 'Close your mouth, Richard. You'll catch flies.'

Richard tore his eyes from Kate's retreating figure and refused the proffered cigar with a shake of his carefully untidy head.

'I will admit,' Torquil Grant said, offering the silver case to Archie, 'that young Kate is a rare filly. A veritable lily on a dung heap.' He sniffed the air. 'Have you noticed how fucking awful the stink is in here? Thank God for tobacco.' Lifting one of the tapers that stood next to the candle in the middle of the table, he lit up.

Richard's face bore a deceptively mild expression. 'Why is it that we may make free of her first name but she feels obliged to address us as *gentlemen*?'

'Good Gad,' put in Archie Dalrymple, lighting his own cigar, 'you're not turning into a Radical, Richard, are you? The Rights of Man and all that tosh about democracy?'

'Either that or he's smitten.' Casting a sly glance at Richard, Torquil Grant pronounced his next words through a haze of fragrant cigar smoke. 'I daresay you could have her if you wanted her. Probably for the same price as a plate of oysters. Or that outlandishly named soup she's bringing us.'

'Don't talk about her like that.' Richard's voice was sharp. 'It's obvious she's not that kind of a girl.'

'Works in an oyster cellar, don't she?' came the cynical response. 'Use your noddle, dear boy.'

'You're wrong. I know you are. Look how she reacted to that brute you two evicted.'

'I rather think it was the manner of approach she didn't like there. Not the approach itself.' A gleam of mischief stole into Torquil Grant's eyes. 'Like to put this to the test, Richard?'

Her aunt said nothing when Kate returned to the bar, merely threw her a black look as she filled a clean tray: three partan brees, one platter of oysters, bread, two bottles of claret and three pewter tankards to drink it from.

'Och,' she muttered. 'There's no' enough room on here for all o' this.'

'I'll carry something for you, Kate,' Andrew offered. 'I've no dishes to wash the now.' His expressive mouth quirked. 'As long as it's no' the soup. The way I walk, I'd likely spill that a' ower the place.'

'Take the oysters, then.'

He grinned at her. 'I'll try no' to empty them over anyone's heid.'

Kate pulled a face at him as she lifted the heavy tray. 'Very funny.'

'I thought so,' he responded cheerfully, and turned her wry grimace into a smile.

'Hull-oh!' called Archie Dalrymple as the little procession of brother and sister drew near. 'What happened to your leg, young fellow?'

'I got stuck up a chimney, sir.' Setting the oysters down, Andrew gripped the edge of the table for support, lowered himself to the floor and set about clearing up the mess of oyster shells and wooden platters.

'You were a chimney boy?'

'He would hardly have been shinning up a chimney for fun, Archie.' Richard Hope turned his dark head to one side, subjecting the boy's bare leg and foot to critical scrutiny. 'You can't put any weight on it? It looks whole enough.'

'The muscles in his leg are wasted,' Kate said. 'It makes it shorter than the other one. Are ye needing anything else?'

'Well,' Torquil Grant said, 'that depends what's on offer, young Kate. Although it's really our Mr Hope here who wants to know. He'd be willing to pay handsomely for the privilege. Got a little room somewhere nearby, have you?'

At Kate's feet, Andrew went very still.

CHAPTER NINE

She looked at all three of them in turn, ending with the one who had helped her up off the floor.

He'd be willing to pay handsomely for the privilege. More than the three shillings she'd been offered earlier? These young gentlemen were wealthy. You could tell that by looking at them. Aiblins this Mr Richard Hope might be willing to pay as much as four shillings to lie with her – not that it was ever going to happen.

Although he often told her he was sick of her and threatened to force her into Ella Balfour's profession, Kate knew Michael Graham regarded her as his exclusive property, and she knew why he wanted it that way too. He had told her often enough. He could have his way with her whenever he felt like it and run no risk of getting the clap or the pox. He had told her he would give her and her brother the thrashing of their lives if she ever went with another man.

She had never been tempted. Yet here she was turning the thought over in her mind, surprised by how calm she felt about the prospect. Then again, it wasn't as if she had her innocence to lose. Nor could any man do anything to her that she hadn't experienced before.

This was about money and nothing else. She had lost her nineteen shillings. She could recoup some of it by lying on her back and letting Richard Hope do what he wanted to do to her.

That couldn't happen here and now, of course. She would have to make an arrangement with him, maybe for tomorrow afternoon. Ella had a wee room along the Cowgate. She might let Kate take him there.

She wondered if he would be rough with her. Ella said some men were real gentle. Kate, who had known only roughness, didn't know whether to believe that or not. This Richard Hope didn't look like a man who liked to use his male strength to dominate and hurt but was that something you could tell from a man's face?

If she was going to do this, she'd have to swear Ella to secrecy. The thought of those beatings Michael Graham would dole out to her and Andrew didn't bear thinking about. Was it worth the risk? For four shillings, it might be.

Torquil Grant spoke, his voice a low and intimate drawl. 'Perhaps you might be willing to oblige us all, Kate. Not at the same time, of course.' He laughed again, opening his eyes wide in mock amazement. 'Although I'm wondering if I've hit upon a rather exciting idea there. What do you think, Archie?'

Staring at him, wondering if he'd said what she thought he'd said, Kate didn't see the thunderous glower Richard Hope was directing at his friend. 'Maybe we should ask Kate what she thinks,' piped up Archie Dalrymple.

Kate turned her attention to him. Fair bursting with excitement, he put her in mind of a puffed-up green puddock by the side of a pond. She glanced down at Andrew, still cleaning the mess off the floor – or pretending to. 'I think you're speaking in front of my young brother.'

'That's easily solved. Why don't you and our Mr Hope go and have a talk about this somewhere private? You can report back to the other two interested parties – who won't expect you to hurry, of course.' Torquil Grant's eyes travelled up and down her body, the sensation every bit as horrible as it had been when the man he'd helped throw out into the Cowgate had done the same. 'If you and Mr Hope haven't worn one another out and you're willing to take on the three of us, who knows how the evening might develop?' He drew on his cigar. 'We'd all have to agree a price, of course.'

It wouldn't be twelve shillings, then. She supposed even rich folk liked a bargain. Maybe they were going to offer her ten. She could make an arrangement with them for tomorrow afternoon and they would do what they would do and at the end of it she would have ten shillings. Ten shillings would pay for five lessons. Would she be able to look the Hendersons in the eye as she handed over money earned this way?

There were pictures in her head now. All three of them at once. Egging each other on. Doing whatever they pleased with her. To her. And all with her consent.

'Kate,' came an urgent voice. 'Miss Dunbar.'

He had seemed so nice. He had seemed truly concerned about her. She really must be stupid to think that had been genuine. There was only one reason why a young gentleman like him would take an interest in a lassie like her.

In that instant it was as though an unseen pair of hands threw a bucket of cold water over her, bringing her to her senses. What in the name of God was she thinking? Had she really been considering this? And how dare they sit there so calmly trying to strike a bargain with her before they used her?

'Miss Dunbar,' Richard Hope said again.

'It's ower late tae *Miss Dunbar* me,' she said scathingly. 'Leave the money on the table when you're done. Andrew, come wi' me *now*. We'll finish clearing up later.'

She realised only some time later that she hadn't told them what the reckoning was. Darting a glance across the crowded vault, she saw the three of them standing up, preparing to leave. The other two seemed to be remonstrating with Richard Hope. When he looked across at her, she turned her head away and willed them to go.

Five minutes later her uncle passed her between tables. 'The toffs must have liked you. Left enough tae pay for what they had mair than twice over.' He nodded towards the two bottles he was carrying. '*And* only took the neck oot o' the second o' these.' He leered at her. 'Hope ye didna let them hae a wee feel, slut.'

Five minutes later again, she was once more standing next to Andrew at his washing tub. 'Kate,' he said, his concentration carefully on the task in hand. 'See what those three young gentlemen asked ye tae dae…'

'Aye?' she responded.

'Ye wouldna ever dae it, would ye?'

'Never.'

That short but definite utterance brought his eyes up to her face. 'I wouldna like ye tae sell yourself, Kate.'

'I wouldna like tae dae that either, Andrew,' she said, and dropped a kiss on the top of his russet head.

Clearing the table where the young printers had been sitting, she found they too had left more than they owed, in their case a few coppers. They often did, thinking they were giving her a little something. They weren't to know she never got to keep it.

It took only seconds to lift one of the pennies and slide it down the front of her bodice, between her breasts. Against their softness and warmth, it felt cold and hard. Solid.

This was going to take months. So be it. This was how she was going to do it: farthing by farthing, bawbee by bawbee, penny by penny until she accumulated some money again – her money, honestly earned from the wee tips folk left her. This time she would find a better hiding place for it.

CHAPTER TEN

Somewhere in the dank gloom of Greyfriars Kirkyard an owl hooted. As if the eerie sound had been a signal, a smoky-silver moon chose that moment to sail out from behind lowering black clouds. Ghostly fingers of shimmering cold light touched tall granite obelisks, marble angels and ornate gravestones incised with the reminders of mortality.

Set above its crossbones, an eyeless skull flashed a grotesque grin. The sands of time ran relentlessly through an upturned stone hourglass. Lengthening in the moonlight, the shadows cast by the monuments spilt like flooding water across the soft green turf between the graves. A dark-clad figure knelt beside a mound of freshly dug earth.

'Get on wi' it, Graham,' the man growled. 'We're no' wanting the night watch to stumble upon us. If you hadna been late, we'd hae been up to Surgeons' Square and away by this time.' The man glared down at Michael Graham. 'Baith o' us already a few guineas the richer—' He broke off. Wooden for quietness, the dull thud of spade striking coffin was unmistakable. 'Are we through?'

'Aye. Take the spade and hand me doon the crowbar.'

'Careful, now. The medical gentlemen dinna like the merchandise damaged in any way. And mind and no' mak too much noise.'

'I ken my own business, man!' hissed Michael Graham, sliding the crowbar between two of the nails securing the planks that formed the coffin lid. It came away easily enough tonight, exposing the head and shoulders of the shrouded body inside the coffin. Once he'd pushed the splintered part of its lid upright, Michael Graham handed the crowbar to his accomplice before extending his own hand to be pulled out of the grave. He reached for the rope lying coiled like a snake beside it.

He didn't much care for what happened next but it had to be done. Hooking a rope under the corpse's arms and sliding it out of the coffin before hauling it up onto the grass was the only sensible way of going about this. Exposing the top half of the coffin rather than all of it meant less digging, less exertion and less time. In and out as quickly as you could. Much less chance of getting caught in the act.

Lying on his front with the other man gripping his ankles, Michael Graham lowered his head and shoulders down into the damp earth. Trying not to think about worms and rats and moles. Wishing the thought never crossed his mind that one day this man or whoever else was holding onto him might let go. Wishing his mouth and nostrils weren't being filled with tastes and smells he'd rather not have there. Trying not to see the waxy, dead face inches beneath his own, glistening in the cold blue moonlight.

He'd been too long at this work and he was beginning to dislike it more and more. It was damn risky, too, although a good earner. That was the trouble. Gave him a wee pot of money of his own which Chrissie didn't know about. She kept an awful tight hold on the purse-strings.

'Right,' he said, once the rope was around the body. 'Easy does it.'

Once the body was up out of its grave, the two men worked swiftly, covering up as much evidence of their night's work as they could. Stripping the body of its shroud and wrapping it in the rough grey blanket they'd brought along for the purpose, they lifted it into their handcart. Michael Graham threw the shroud back into the grave. If you were caught, it was said the courts were harder on you if you had taken the mort-clothes away. That was theft.

The two men lifted their wooden shovels and filled the grave back in. This work ought to be well-paid. There was enough bloody effort involved in it.

'What's up?' the other man said, lifting his head at the muttered curse. 'D'ye hear the watch?'

'No. Just thinking aboot something.'

'Dae it quietly, eh?'

Michael Graham grunted. There had to be an easier way of making money – and more than the bob or two he got out of Ella Balfour and the trollops he allowed to work The Pearl Fisher. Fancy those toffs paying so far over the reckoning tonight. Stupid of him tae tell the lassie. He might have pocketed the difference if he hadn't. She probably wouldn't even think of telling Chrissie but you never knew.

You never knew what that lassie might tell Chrissie. He wouldn't say he was beginning to worry about that, but she had grown bolder over the last year. She was less cowed, more likely to stand up to him. Well, he had done something about that last week, when he had told Chrissie about the wee slut's bit o' siller and then had his way with her. The memory was making him hard.

He had no conscience about his treatment of her. She had fallen into his lap like a juicy red apple falling off a tree and he had taken her as a bonus, to be used whenever and however he pleased. She and her crippled brother had a roof over their heads and food in their bellies, didn't they? Besides which, a man who worked as hard as he did was entitled to his comforts.

A man who worked as hard as he did was surely also entitled to an easier life. He'd aye had a notion to run a tavern on the High Street, move himself and Chrissie up in the world. They'd need a good bit of money to be able to make that leap.

'It's a fine morning, Kate.'

'It is that,' she agreed. Full basket in each hand, she paused to speak to the lad who'd jokingly offered to keep her well supplied with fish if she married him. He was stacking empty boxes, one on top of the other. 'Sold everything already?'

'Aye,' he said happily, 'I can get away hame for ma breakfast now—'

Seeing his eyes drift over her shoulder, Kate swung round to see what had caught his attention. Picking his way through the sea of striped-skirted fishwives, an elegant young gentleman was heading straight for her. She plucked his name out of her frozen brain. *Richard Hope.* The one who had seemed so nice and then turned out to be so nasty.

'Hoped I might find you here,' he said breathlessly. 'Only I slept too late. Had to run all the way and lost my top hat to a gust of wind on North Bridge!' He chuckled. 'It'll probably be in Norway by nightfall. How on earth am I to explain that to my mama?' He reached for her baskets. 'Give me those.'

Kate took a step back. 'Dinna be daft. You'd get the smell into your clothes.' And why, she thought, all too aware of the curious eyes turned in their direction, did you have to wear such fine ones? She supposed she should be grateful she'd been spared the Norway-bound top hat.

His cutaway coat was a discreet dark blue but there was no disguising the quality of the material. He might be wearing trousers rather than evening pantaloons but like his coat they were fashionably close-fitting and beautifully cut, nothing at all like the wide-legged corduroys favoured by working men like the ones in the fish market this morning.

'Say something,' Richard Hope pleaded. 'I need *some* reward for being up at this ungodly hour! Especially as this is the second day in a row I've been here! I was so proud of myself for working out where I might be able to find you and then I turned up yesterday and there was nobody here. Not a living soul!'

'You came here yesterday? On a Monday? Dae ye no' ken onything?'

'Well,' he said easily, 'I eventually worked out that since fishermen probably don't take their boats out on the Sabbath, there's unlikely to be any fish market on a Monday. Say something,' he said again.

'No' here.'

He was beside her, adjusting his long stride to her shorter step. 'May I not carry the fish for you?'

Prey to a confusing mixture of emotions, Kate marched on in silence through the meat market and towards Fleshmarket Close. Once she had gone up the first flight of steps, she stopped, set her baskets down and raised her face to his. My, but he was tall.

'Look,' she said. 'I ken fine what you want from me and ye might as well no' waste your time trying.'

He walked down a step or two and turned, allowing her the novelty of gazing down at him. 'What do you think I want from you, Kate?'

'What most men want from lassies who work in oyster cellars.' She could feel a blush creeping up her neck. That was ridiculous. 'What you asked me for on Saturday night and got sent off wi' a flea in your ear for. What you probably went and found somewhere else along the Cowgate.'

He shook his head. 'No. Not me, at any rate. I can't speak for my friends. We split up after we left the tavern where you work.'

She cast him down a curious look. 'Ye fell oot wi' them?'

'Yes. I was very angry with my friend for asking you what he did, and I told him so.' Richard Hope shook his windswept head as though trying to rid himself of a bad memory. 'That's not what I want from you, Kate. Honestly.'

She put her hands on her hips. 'Just as well. For ye're never going tae get it. I'm no' that kind o' a lassie.'

With a jolt of pleasure, she realised she was telling him nothing but the truth. Her uncle might have made a whore out of her, but given the choice, she had not made one out of herself.

'I could tell from the moment I first set eyes on you that you're no' that kind o' a lassie.' He threw her up a smile, acknowledging his use of the vernacular. So he did have a guid Scots tongue in his heid, even if he probably didn't use it very much.

'So what dae ye want?' she demanded. 'Why have you got up *at this ungodly hour*' – she mimicked the way he had said the words – 'and gone tae all this trouble tae find me? If you wanted tae see me you could hae come tae The Pearl Fisher.'

'Not if I wanted to see you privately.'

Kate tasted disappointment then, bitter as gall, and wondered why she should be surprised – or even care. 'So ye dae want what most men want from lassies who work in oyster cellars.'

'No!' The denial burst out of him. 'I want to get to know you better, that's all.'

'Och, Mr Hope!' she responded, exasperated with him. 'D'ye think I'm daft?'

'I think you're as smart as paint. And beautiful. And as fresh as the morning.' He dropped his eyes to the steps on which they stood.

As fresh as the morning. If only he knew. Yet her own eyes softened as she studied him. It was the sophisticated young gentleman who was blushing now. That was why he had lowered his head, trying to hide that reaction from her. When he looked up again he was all expectation, like a dog waiting for you to throw a stick for the umpteenth time, assuming she was going to agree to…whatever it was he wanted her to agree to.

'Look,' she said, wondering why she was feeling the impulse to soften the knock-back she was about to give him, 'you and me live in different worlds. And you dinna ken the first thing aboot mine.'

Two long strides brought him up the steps and gazing down into her face. 'Then show me your world, Kate. Please, show it to me.'

CHAPTER ELEVEN

She was looking at him as though he was a half-wit. He noticed the faintest sprinkling of freckles dotted over her nose, wrinkled now in enchanting perplexity. 'Ye want tae see the inside o' the bridge? And ye want me tae show it tae ye?'

'That's about it,' he agreed, and began demolishing any objections she might have to the idea. 'I understand you would want to be chaperoned— I beg your pardon?'

'Nothing,' she said.

'I could pay for my tour,' he went on eagerly. 'Would that help?'

'Oh aye,' she said, raising one russet eyebrow in a cynical gesture. 'Mair than likely that would help convince my uncle and aunt.'

'Does that mean you'll say yes too?'

She didn't reply but Richard felt sure she was weakening. She'd have told him to bugger off long since if she weren't. He decided to seize the initiative and her baskets. 'Lead on, Macduff.'

She still didn't speak, just kept looking at him.

'Oh, come on,' he urged, wondering what was going on behind the lovely face. 'Be a devil.'

'A tour, young sir? With my niece here as your guide?'

'Yes,' Richard said, repeating to them what he had said to Kate about her having a chaperone.

'Eh?' Chrissie queried, coming forward with a cook's knife in one hand and a large Spanish onion in the other.

'A chaperone, Chrissie,' Michael Graham said, swinging round to his wife. 'The lassie will require a chaperone.'

'Yourself perhaps, ma'am?' Richard said, hoping though he was that a chaperone might not be deemed necessary.

'Eh?' Chrissie said again.

'Young Andrew can do it after his work,' Michael Graham put in. 'Maybe tonight if we're no' busy.'

His wife was frowning at Richard Hope. 'Why do I recognise you?'

'I was here with my friends on Saturday night. When the unfortunate incident took place.'

'Which one would that hae been?' Chrissie countered sarcastically. 'There's a wheen o' unfortunate incidents in this place every day. Ach, I remember now.' Fat brown ringlets danced below her linen mutch as she pointed the knife at him. 'You had a bowl o' my partan bree.'

Richard made her a little bow. 'The nectar of the gods, ma'am, the very nectar of the gods.'

As her aunt preened at the bow, being addressed as *ma'am* and the extravagant compliment to her crab soup, Kate turned away, apparently seized by a coughing fit. When concerned green eyes settled on her bowed head another pair of eyes narrowed. Some very interesting ideas had just slithered into Michael Graham's head.

With a sternness from which Richard derived much private amusement, Kate instructed him to wear the oldest and shabbiest clothes he possessed for his tour of the bridge. Going one better, he borrowed some from the young man as tall as himself who'd recently come to work for his parents as an under-footman.

Hair crammed into a knitted cap, Richard sported a rough tweed jacket, baggy corduroy trousers and a red kerchief knotted rakishly at the throat of an open-necked shirt. Kate Dunbar's lovely blue eyes widened very satisfactorily indeed at the sight of him.

'No' that everyone winna ken ye're a toff as soon as ye open your mouth.'

He grinned, for some reason he couldn't quite fathom delighted by her acerbic directness. His good mood was further enhanced by the tussle she had with her uncle over the lanterns all three members of the party were to carry. On top of the florin Richard was paying for his tour of the bridge, Michael Graham tried to charge threepence extra for each of the fresh tallow candles required.

'Threepence is plenty for all o' them,' she said, handing back a sixpence and giving Michael Graham such a fearsomely black look Richard was forced to press his lips together so as not to burst out laughing. Miss Catriona Dunbar was growing more intriguing by the minute.

Hearing a footstep disturb the straw that lined the floor of the tavern, he turned. The boy ambling towards them was the same one who'd been there on Saturday night. Even if he hadn't already known he was Kate's brother, the blazing red hair would have proclaimed their relationship.

'How long ago did you damage your leg, young Master Dunbar?' Richard asked, a tug of professional curiosity taking him by surprise.

'Four years,' came the curt response. *What's it to you?* The boy didn't say those words, but he might as well have. Remembering what he must have overheard on Saturday night, Richard supposed he could hardly blame him.

He tilted his dark head to one side, subjecting the pale leg and bare foot visible beneath threadbare trousers to critical scrutiny. 'So you can't put any weight on it although it's whole enough,' he mused. 'If – as your sister said – somewhat wasted.' He glanced up at her. 'Yet fresh air and exercise can work wonders, you know.'

Now they were both looking at him as though he was a half-wit. 'Do you want to see the bridge or not?' Kate demanded.

Richard divided what he hoped was a winning smile between the two of them. 'I do indeed. What have you got to show me first?' He directed the question at the boy.

'The tanner's to start with,' Andrew said in a toneless voice. 'It stinks tae high heaven.'

'Because they soak the hides in horse piss? Oh!' Richard exclaimed. He clapped one hand over his mouth as if to stop the word which had already escaped it. 'Sorry,' he said to Kate. 'Forgot there was a lady present!'

His gaffe – or his apology – had made the boy laugh, an unaffected response that lit up the sharp little face, quite transforming it. The lightening of Kate's expression was more subtle, but it was there. All at once quite giddy with happiness, Richard allowed himself to be led into the murky innards of the South Bridge.

He had entered the caverns of hell: a murky maze of a dark underworld. As they penetrated ever deeper into the shadowy man-made spaces, Richard found himself longing even for the polluted air of the dingy and sunless Cowgate.

He could not only smell horse piss when they passed the tannery, he could see it too: ribbons of eerie green miasma rising from a huge round vat of softening hides. Pushing them under the noxious fluid with a wooden paddle, a middle-aged man with barely a tooth in his head called out a greeting to Kate and

Andrew. They returned it, introducing Richard as a cousin from the country, newly come to Edinburgh to study at the university.

'Safer to call ye that,' Kate murmured. 'Folk here dinna much care for outsiders. And there's plenty o' poor students, am I no' right?'

Following his guides up the increasingly steep slope of the underground close, Richard was horribly aware of being confined, enclosed by thousands of tons of masonry and shut away from the light and air of the outside world. He laid an experimental hand on the wall to his right. Slimy water trickled down the stones in a multitude of greasy rivulets. Was nothing clean in here?

He glanced up. Standing like a beacon at the top of a short flight of stone steps, Kate was holding her lantern aloft, positioning it to light them as brightly as possible for him. 'Be careful, they're a wee bittie worn.'

As crumbly as stale cheese and unpleasantly spongy underfoot would have been Richard's own description. 'Where do you keep your things?' he asked as he climbed up to her.

'My things?'

'Your clothes. Don't they get awfully damp?'

'I dinna hae many clothes. Anything I'm no' wearing I keep in a tin trunk. My hairbrush and my spare caps and things. That keeps the damp oot. And the mice.'

His eyes went to her head. 'Do you always wear a cap? Never just a ribbon?'

'Sometimes just a ribbon. The last one I had wore out. Broke in two,' she explained further, presumably responding to a look of incomprehension from him.

'Why don't you buy a new one?' The moment the words were out of his mouth he wanted to kick himself. Expecting another acerbic response, his heart sank when he saw the dominant emotion his tactless question had provoked was embarrassment.

She can't afford to buy herself a new ribbon when the old one wears out. Oh, fuck. What can I say to make her feel better about that? Nothing. Nothing at all.

He was almost grateful when his nostrils begin to react to a new witches' brew of aromas, giving him a chance to change the subject. 'Something to see here?'

She indicated the archways ahead of them, diminishing in height as they came up against what had once been the valley wall. 'Shine your lantern in that direction.'

'*Good God...*' he breathed. This vault was full to the gunwales. Men, women and children presented themselves to his horrified gaze. Although few of the adults reacted, some of the children looked up at the sudden increase in illumination.

The chamber was dotted with a few feeble crusie lamps, pinpricks of sickly yellow light in the Stygian gloom. The place stank to high heaven, the fetid stench of human sweat and waste mingling queasily with cooking smells and the pungent fish-oil that fuelled the lamps.

'Oh!' The exclamation was surprised out of Richard by the sight of the cadaverously thin man who had materialised, as though out of thin air, between himself and Kate. He was reminded of the skeleton that dangled in macabre fashion in the corner of one of his lecture theatres.

'A young man studying at the university, you say? Interested in how we unfortunates live?' A bony hand was proffered. 'Alan Gunn, sir. At your service. And my family.'

Richard glanced down. Three skinny children clung to their father's coat tails, an older girl and two younger boys. Kate was bringing oatcakes out of her apron pocket and handing them round. Guiltily aware that his interest in the South Bridge had everything to do with Kate Dunbar and nothing whatsoever to do with the plight of Edinburgh's poor, Richard cast about for a safer topic of conversation. 'From your manner of speech you hail from the far north, Mr Gunn. How come you to be in Edinburgh?'

Alan Gunn was clearly too down on his luck and too weary to pull any punches. 'We were put off the land to make way for the landlord's sheep,' he said in his soft accent. 'Encouragement to leave being offered by the factor and his men slaughtering our cow and firing our thatch.'

Richard felt the hairs stand up on the back of his neck. He'd heard rumours of such things but had dismissed them as wild exaggerations, put about by the Radicals to stir up trouble. Besides, you couldn't allow a few tenant farmers to stand in the way of progress. Could you?

'My wife was near her time when they burnt the house.' The steady voice trembled. 'I carried her in my arms for ten miles, the bairns trailing behind us. She was confined the following day but she died. And the babe with her.'

Richard struggled to find words. What possible consolation could he, who had never suffered anything worse than boredom, offer to a man who had suffered so much? He looked down again at the Gunn children. 'These little ones must miss their home.'

'Aye,' Alan Gunn sighed. 'We thought we were poor there, sir, but we were rich. We had sunlight and fresh air, land to work and feed ourselves from. We were rich,' he repeated. Squaring his pitifully thin shoulders, he swallowed. 'I should not presume on so short an acquaintance but if you were to hear of a position, perhaps when you are in and around the university... I suspect there's but little call for crofters in Edinburgh,' he said with another cadaverous smile, 'yet I believe I could learn another trade. I am neither a stupid nor an uneducated man, sir.'

'Indeed no, Mr Gunn. I can tell that merely by speaking to

you.' Hoping he didn't sound like a condescending young pup, Richard stuck out his hand to shake the older man's once more. Once they were well out of earshot, he turned to Kate. 'Perhaps I *can* do something for him—'

She cut him off, rattling out a question. 'Shall we get going? There's a lot more to see.' Confused by her abrupt change of mood, he stood gazing after her.

'She'll get annoyed if we dinna keep up wi' her.'

'Will she?' Richard asked, swinging round to find himself the target of the unsmiling gaze of Andrew Dunbar. 'Where are we headed for now?'

The boy pointed heavenwards. 'Where I work.'

'What do you do?'

'Make saddles and bags and tack. Mend them too.'

'Do you enjoy that?'

The boy shrugged. 'It's all right. I dinna like being inside all day, though.'

'What are your hours of work?'

'Six in the morning till eight at night.'

Richard's mouth fell open. 'You work fourteen hours a day?'

Andrew Dunbar shrugged again. 'We'd best ging efter Kate noo.'

'Hang on.' Richard dug into his pocket for the sixpence she had refunded. 'Take this as your payment for the extra work in showing me around.' He threw the coin to Andrew, who caught it but made no move to pocket it.

'I canna be bought,' he said flatly. 'Nor can my sister, either.'

Winded, feeling as if he had lost his footing and fallen into a deep pit, it took Richard a moment to reply. 'I don't want to buy your sister.'

The boy's critical scrutiny of him hadn't faltered. 'What dae ye want from her, then?'

'Only to be her friend. Yours too, if you'll let me.'

Andrew Dunbar grunted. It was a distinctly non-committal sound.

'Please keep the sixpence. It's a wee gift from me to you. That's all. Nothing more and nothing less.' He made a hopeful suggestion. 'It's rude to refuse a gift.'

When, after a moment, the child put the sixpence in his pocket, Richard's face broke into a relieved smile. 'Friends? You and me, I mean?'

'We'll see,' Andrew Dunbar said. 'We'll see.'

CHAPTER TWELVE

Kate was waiting for them where the passageway appeared to come to a dead end. As he drew closer, Richard spotted a flight of wooden steps disappearing into the shadows above her head. 'There's a lodging house in there,' she whispered. 'Gin ye want a quick look?'

Richard didn't swing the lantern too high, picking out a jumble of bodies and faces. Pale as a ghost, a woman scowled and spat at him. A man with a wooden leg lay slumped against a wall, a bottle in his hand. He raised it to his mouth, tilting his head back to garner the last drops of alcohol.

'Move,' Kate urged. By the time the drunk swore and hurled the empty bottle against the wall of the close, all three of them were on the wooden staircase, safe from the shattering glass. They emerged into another passageway, much quieter than the one they had left.

Richard had expected the interior of the bridge to be as straightforward as its exterior. He'd been wrong. Many of the vaults were subdivided and had narrower passageways within them, some darting off at odd angles. The darkness of the shadows beyond their lanterns made it difficult to work out where you were in relation to the main arches. The occasional glow of another moving light round a corner somewhere gave the whole place an unpleasantly sinister atmosphere.

There were lots of doors and passageways up here. Some of

those must surely lead out to the street. Then again, which level were they on? It should be the middle one, but they had climbed quite a bit in the lower passageway. Perhaps they were closer to the top of the bridge than he realised. He spun on his heels, trying to get his bearings. 'It's like a labyrinth. Any minute now I expect to have to defend you both from the Minotaur.'

'The what?' Andrew demanded, wrinkling his small nose in a gesture very reminiscent of the one his sister had made yesterday. Well, the boy might be unnervingly fierce but it was clear he had a natural curiosity and an enquiring mind.

'It's one of the myths of Ancient Greece. The Minotaur was a ferocious beast with the body of a man and the head of a bull. It was imprisoned within a labyrinth.'

'And this is a lab-y—,' Andrew took a run at it. 'A labyrinth?'

'In a way. It's all twists and turns and passageways, isn't it?'

'Did the Minotaur ever get out of the labyrinth?'

'No, it was slain by the bold Theseus.' Seeing the interest in his bright eyes, Richard posed a question. 'You don't have any schooling at all?'

'I canna even read.' There was no mistaking the wistfulness in the boy's voice.

'You could learn—'

'He works fourteen hours a day.'

Sitting with her legs dangling on what might have been designed as a high stone work-bench, Kate was rubbing at the indentation the chain of the lantern had left on her palm. The lamp itself stood next to her, bathing her in soft yellow light.

'So I've learnt.' Richard found a projecting wooden beam from which to hang his own lantern, flexed his fingers, thrust his hands into his trouser pockets and propped himself against the wall. 'That must make it difficult for him to do sufficient walking to strengthen his leg.'

'Aye,' Kate said, and added a dry observation. 'It's as well no' tae make empty promises. D'ye no' think?'

Richard returned her unflinching gaze. 'I shall do what I can for Mr Gunn. You have my word on it. Aargh!' He recoiled as something leapt at him from the overhanging beam. It coalesced into a ginger and white cat. The rat swinging from its jaws had to be dead, although it hadn't long shuffled off this mortal coil. Richard could feel the warmth of its body as it passed his face. Using his shoulder as a stepping stone, the cat reached the floor and scampered off, the rat still clamped between its jaws.

'Jack!' yelled Andrew. 'Clever boy!' He set off in uneven pursuit of the cat, his lantern bobbing about like a fishing boat in a stormy sea.

Richard laughed as he watched them go. 'Jack being the bridge's resident mouser, I presume. Andrew's right to congratulate him. Rats carry all manner of diseases.'

'I know.'

Once more blue eyes met green. *I know better than you do. Because I live with all of this. Because I may have no education but I'm not stupid either.* Richard wondered if that was what she really wanted to say. Kate crossed her legs and he caught a glimpse of striped stocking. Red and white, spilling over the top of sturdy, if rather battered, laced ankle boots. They looked dainty on her feet.

He wanted to walk over there, hoist himself up beside her and talk to her for hours. He wanted to find out everything about her. What had happened to her and Andrew's parents? Was she happy to live here? She couldn't be. He wanted to know what her hopes and fears and dreams were.

He stepped forward, and saw wariness slide across her face. How many times a week did she have to defend herself against unwanted male attention? Small wonder if she was sometimes prickly. He resumed his casual stance, picking some fluff from the under-footman's jacket.

Kate's stern expression didn't waver. 'You just gave me your word. About Mr Gunn.'

'You don't believe I really will do anything to help him though, do you?'

'No. I dinna.'

'You think I'm a bored young gentleman who'll have forgotten all about the South Bridge and everyone in it by this time tomorrow?'

'That's about it,' she agreed.

'Well, Miss Catriona Dunbar,' Richard said, 'I'm clearly going to have to prove you wrong, am I not?'

It was late. Chrissie Graham had taken herself off to bed and her husband had locked up The Pearl Fisher for the night. Now he was following Kate and Andrew along the underground close to the vault where they slept. Standing back to allow him to unlock the grilled gate, Kate laid her hands on her brother's shoulders. He was sleepy, barely able to keep his eyes open. 'Soon be in your bed now.'

He let his head fall back so he could look at her and mumbled a question. 'Can I get washed in the morning, Kate?'

It was Michael Graham who answered him. 'Aye. Away to your bed now. I'm needing a word wi' your sister.'

Half asleep though he was, Andrew continued to gaze up at Kate. She squeezed his shoulders and gave him the little nod which meant *I'm all right. On you go.* 'You take the crusie lamp,' she said, handing it over to him. 'Careful with it, now.'

Kate watched as he and the flickering light disappeared behind the stacks of whisky barrels and claret bottles, aware that her uncle was hanging his lantern from a projecting iron bracket on the wall of the close. So it was more than a word he needed with her – but she had already known that.

She'd been anticipating this conversation all day, ever since she'd come back from the fish market with Richard Hope. Waiting for it had made her edgy, which in turn had made her rather sharp with Richard. She was feeling a wee bit guilty about that now. His good humour hadn't failed, nor his good manners either.

Fancy him apologising for saying *piss* in front of her. *Sorry! Forgot there was a lady present.* She was no lady and he knew that as well as she did. It had been sweet of him, all the same.

'Nice wee game ye're playing wi' young Mr Hope, Kate,' her uncle said softly. 'Maybe ye're no' as daft as I think ye are.'

'I'm no' playing ony games wi' onybody!' she said, startled.

'So ye just happened tae bump intae him this morning? At the fish market? No' exactly his usual stamping-ground, I'm thinking. Or a usual time in the morning for him to be up and about. Come off it, lassie. And tell me right now when and where ye've arranged tae meet him again.'

'I havena arranged tae meet him anywhere,' she protested. 'Like I didna arrange tae meet him today. He came looking for me.'

'So when will he be back?'

'I dinna ken that he will.'

'Did he tell ye he would?'

'Aye,' she said reluctantly.

'What else did he tell ye?' Michael Graham laid his hand on her neck, digging his fingers into her smooth skin.

'That he's going to try and find a job for Mr Gunn.'

The fleshy fingers relaxed, and the black brows shot up. 'Did he, by God? You've really got him by the balls, eh?' His face darkened. 'I trust that's only in a manner o' speaking, ye wee hure.'

She wasn't going to dignify that with a response. Bracing herself in anticipation of the back of his hand striking her face, Kate saw his expression change. He was turning something over in his mind. Catching her studying him, he clicked his tongue against the back of his teeth, his features settling into a sneer. 'Dinna hae the brains ye were born wi', dae ye?' He shoved her through the gates and pulled them to. 'Get tae your bed, slut.'

By the time she was behind the wine and whisky racks he had locked up and was reaching for the lantern. An uneasy Kate stood and watched its bobbing light grow ever more dim as he went back down the underground close.

CHAPTER THIRTEEN

However much he disapproved of Sir Walter Scott's politics, Nathaniel Henderson had to admit the man was a damn' fine writer. Engrossed in the famous novelist's latest offering, the bookseller lifted his head with some reluctance when the bell on the back of the shop door jangled. The identity of his new customer had him blinking in surprise.

Laying Sir Walter on the dark wooden counter behind which he was perched, Nathaniel slid off his high stool and walked forward. 'What can I do for you this noontide, young Andrew?'

'I-want-tae-buy-a-book.' The words were rattled out, the boy's skinny shoulders heaving. 'For-Kate's-birthday-next-week.' He took a great gulping breath.

Nathaniel laughed. 'Slow down, laddie. Slow down. Come and sit here and catch your breath. Now,' he said, waiting till the boy had wriggled up onto the stool he himself had just vacated, 'what's the great rush?' Folding his arms across his unbuttoned yellow and white striped linen waistcoat, Nathaniel surveyed Andrew over the brass spectacles which sat, as usual, on the end of his long nose.

'Well,' the boy began, 'a birthday present's got to be a secret, aye? So I thought I'd juke up through the shop and across the road while my master's away having his meridian. But we're no' supposed tae leave the workshop during the day and sometimes he comes back early tae check on us, so I'll hae tae be quick. I've got sixpence,' he informed the bookseller, thrusting out a fist and uncurling his fingers. Resting in his grubby palm, the coin glinted in the spring sunshine pouring in through the tall and narrow leaded casements that flanked the door to the street. 'Mr Hope gave it to me.'

'And who might Mr Hope be?' came a female voice.

Andrew peered round Nathaniel to his wife, emerging from the stairs which gave access to their rooms above the shop. 'A young gentleman who fancies our Kate, Mrs Henderson,' he said, a quick frown creasing his forehead. 'He says he only wants tae be her friend but he fancies her really. Ye can tell by the way he looks at her. I think he's maybe all right, though.'

Over the top of Andrew's head, Peggy and her husband exchanged a different kind of look.

'Right then,' Nathaniel said, slapping his hands together. 'A whole silver sixpence. I'm sure we can find you an excellent book in exchange for that. What'll it be, young man? A tale of high romance and exciting adventures? A handsome volume with coloured plates of flowers and animals? A selection of the poems of Mr Robert Burns?'

Like a watchful heron poised on a river bank, Nathaniel tilted his head to one side and regarded Andrew with an expectant air.

'I didn't know Kate could read,' Peggy Henderson said.

'She canna. But she's wanting tae learn. We baith do.'

As both the Hendersons gazed at him, the puzzled look on Andrew's face cleared. 'The poems. Kate aye loves it when somebody sings Mr Burns' songs at The Pearl Fisher.'

'Another satisfied customer!' Having ushered Andrew out with a grand flourish, Nathaniel closed the door behind the boy, put his shirt-sleeved arms behind his back and turned to face his wife. She was wearing a high-waisted brown and cream striped gown topped by a short brown velvet spencer. A pretty bonnet in the same colour and material was a perfect match for the little jacket, as was the drawstring reticule dangling from her wrist.

His wide mouth curved. 'You're a sight for sore eyes, Peggy. Off to one of your ladies' meetings, I take it. More good works?'

She nodded, and walked forward to stand in front of him. 'You've been known to do some of those yourself, Nathaniel Henderson,' she said fondly.

Looking down at her with equal affection, Nathaniel arched his eyebrows.

'I can't think what you mean, Peg.'

Lifting one small gloved hand, she poked him in the chest. 'I know the price of all the books in this shop as well as you do. That rather fine edition of Mr Burns' poems sells at one shilling and sixpence.'

He pulled one hand from behind his back and struck himself on the forehead. 'Really? I must have forgotten.'

Peggy frowned. 'I don't like the sound of that young gentleman Andrew mentioned.'

Nathaniel transferred both hands to his wife's trim waist. 'His interest may be honourable, my dear. Let us not worry about Miss Catriona unless and until we have to. Off you go to your meeting. The sooner you're away, the sooner I'll have you back.'

'You haven't forgotten the soirée in the New Town this evening?'

'Must we go? I'd far rather stay at home with you.'

'We have to show our faces. My good works, as you are pleased to describe them,' – Peggy yelped as her husband took a firmer grip of her – 'rely heavily on the patronage of the ladies of the New Town. A circumstance of which I know you disapprove but that's the situation and we have to work with it.'

'I could never disapprove of anything you do, Peg. You have a heart which overflows with love and kindness. My only regret in life is that I haven't given you the children on whom you might have lavished that love and kindness.'

'Aiblins I haven't given them to you. Aiblins we should also not yet give up hope, Nathaniel.'

'Not even after twelve years of marriage, Peg?'

'We are young yet. I certainly don't think we should give up trying.'

'I'm all in favour of that,' came the enthusiastic response. 'In fact, I could close the shop for a wee while and we could retire upstairs now.'

Peggy blushed. 'Nathaniel Henderson! What an idea!'

'Personally, I think it's one of my better ones.'

'And I think I have a meeting to attend. Are you going to let me go?'

'Only if you pay the forfeit,' he murmured. 'And you ken fine what that is, bonnie lass.'

Peggy smiled, coiled her arms around his neck and raised her face for his kiss.

A closed fan struck Richard's wrist a glancing blow. Propped against a white marble pillar around which gilded grapes and glistening vine leaves coiled, he came back to reality with a jolt – he'd been wondering if it was actually physically possible to die of boredom – and found himself meeting the laughing brown eyes of Irene Steele.

'Dear me, Richard,' she complained, 'are you so reluctant to take supper with me that I must hunt you down?'

Elegant in black evening jacket and white pantaloons, he made her a deep bow. Across the room, brilliantly lit by wall sconces and dangling crystal chandeliers, he saw his parents gazing approvingly at him. That made a nice change. He offered his arm. 'I'm afraid I was lost in thought, Irene. Shall we proceed to the supper room?'

Hearing voices nearby raised in argument, his companion turned her head towards them. Tonight she had her gleaming brown hair piled on top of her head, only a few little trailing curls allowed to escape. The style suited her, showing off the graceful sweeping lines of her face and neck and the pale-green gown she wore offered a tantalising glimpse of curving bosom.

'Nathaniel Henderson,' she murmured.

Following her gaze, Richard saw a thin and lanky man, taller even than himself. He recognised him vaguely, remembered buying a book or two in his shop on the corner of South Bridge and the High Street. That shop didn't deal in medical textbooks, so he hadn't often found the need to visit it.

'Bit of a Radical, isn't he? Got himself into trouble with the authorities during the troubles of two years since, I believe. Attended the trials of the leaders of the insurrection and spoke out at all of them?'

'James Wilson was hardly the leader of an insurrection,' Irene said scornfully. 'And to have hanged a man of his mature years was a disgrace. As for what was done to Baird and Hardie at Stirling—' She shuddered. 'One might have thought that beheading them after they were cut down from the scaffold was an unnecessary barbarity in a country that considers itself civilised. Like something out of the Middle Ages.'

Richard shot her a surprised glance. He had never imagined a young lady would have taken an interest in such frankly revolting matters.

'The Radical bookseller said his piece on that occasion too, didn't he? Got himself arrested?'

Irene nodded. 'Locked up in the guard-room at Stirling Castle for several days.'

'That is his wife standing next to him? Somewhat comically shorter than her excessively tall husband? His extreme opinions must pose difficulties for her.'

'Perhaps she shares them, Richard. We women are permitted to have political opinions, you know.'

'I most humbly beg your pardon for assuming otherwise, Irene. What is the bookseller arguing with those other gentlemen about?' Even though the voices were raised, it was hard to catch more than a few disjointed words over the general hubbub of the soirée. Irene tilted her head and listened. 'The king's visit, I think,' she said after a second or two.

'Most of Edinburgh is discussing that.' Richard raised his eyebrows. 'In my mother's case, *ad nauseam* as far as I'm concerned. Even the most ancient of my professors are growing enthusiastic about it. La, 'tis quite touching to see how excited the poor old souls are becoming.'

'You might even be getting quite excited about it yourself,' Irene hazarded, 'were it not so much the fashion among young gentlemen like yourself to pretend to be interested in or moved by nothing. Your highest aspiration is to suffer from ennui, is it not?'

Irene continued without giving him the opportunity to respond to that sally, which was probably just as well. Since last Saturday he had found himself more interested in Kate Dunbar than he could ever remember being interested in anyone or anything in his entire life.

'I suspect Mrs Hope is not questioning the carrying-out of the visit itself.' Irene's lovely face grew troubled. 'Or, indeed, questioning the king's right to wear the crown and occupy the throne.'

'The bookseller is not the only one to have somewhat ambivalent feelings towards our monarch,' Richard murmured.

'Indeed,' Irene said in correspondingly low tones, 'but it is not always wise to express such views too forcefully. Especially when the objection is not only to the personage but to the existence of the monarchy itself. 'Tis a somewhat dangerous opinion to espouse when memories of the recent troubles remain so vivid.'

Even as she spoke, Richard saw the bookseller's wife lay an admonishing hand on her husband's sleeve. He looked down at her and the dangerous political argument ceased as they excused themselves and joined the crowd flowing like a broad river through to the supper room.

'Seems the fellow also has the bad taste to be in love with his own wife and not care who knows it,' Richard said flippantly.

With a deft flick of the wrist, Irene Steele unfurled her fan and fluttered it in front of her face, surveying him over the top of it. 'Was it thoughts of love that were occupying you just now, Richard? Thoughts perhaps of a special young lady?'

'Perhaps it was yourself, my dear Irene,' he said, and bestirred himself to be charming. That wasn't difficult. His supper companion was not only extremely attractive, she was vivacious and entertaining too. As ever, her conversation tonight was both amusing and wide-ranging, although they both avoided any more talk of politics. The subject had always bored Richard, anyway.

Having presented him with such perfection, it wasn't Irene Steele's fault if his thoughts kept drifting back to the picture he was carrying in his head of a girl in a homespun skirt and heavy boots, a great mass of auburn hair tumbling about her face.

Where that lovely girl was obliged to live appalled him. Even a privileged young man who had grown up in the rarefied atmosphere of the New Town could hardly be unaware of how much poverty there was in Auld Reekie – and crime and disease too. The latter was why Edinburgh had acquired such a reputation for the study of medicine, after all. There was illness a-plenty to practise on.

Then there were the veterans of the wars against Bonaparte and the French, all those men with wooden legs begging in the streets.

Sometimes you gave them a penny to salve your conscience and at others you contrived not to see them, your eyes sliding past to the newest grand building being put up in the New Town. Vaguely pitying of the poor and the lives they led, up until now Richard had not allowed himself for long to be moved by their plight.

Down there in the dark vaults of the South Bridge, there had been no escape, no way of averting his eyes or transferring them to something more pleasant. Everywhere he had looked there had been dirt and filth and degradation.

What he had observed and experienced – ye gods, the smells alone! – on Tuesday evening had been a revelation to him. He'd had no idea people in Edinburgh were living in such conditions, his fellow citizens of the Athens of the North. That grandiose name seemed a poor joke when he thought of the gloomy interior of the South Bridge.

A girl like Catriona Dunbar shouldn't have to live there. A girl like Catriona Dunbar should spend her days in a flower-filled garden.

After supper, freed once more from the need to make conversation, Richard allowed himself to imagine what Kate would look like with that abundance of hair piled up on top of her head, her feet shod in dainty slippers and her body clothed in a beautiful gown. Shamelessly ignoring the efforts of the rather good pianist who opened the second half of the evening's programme, he gave himself up to this new vision of her. That current fashion dictated ladies' evening gowns should be both close-fitting and low-cut was an added bonus.

He pondered which colour would suit her best – eau-de-nil such as Irene was wearing, perhaps. The pale shade would offer a dramatic contrast to Kate's auburn waves. Then again, those would look equally wonderful against a dress of a darker hue. Unable to decide, he came to the conclusion that she'd be the equal of any girl in this room – any girl in Edinburgh – whatever colour of dress she wore. A slow smile spread across his face as he mentally corrected himself. She would surpass any of them.

He realised now he might have offended her by his insistence on seeing inside the South Bridge. She'd thought he'd come to gawp, as people in his grandparents' time had toured the madhouse near Greyfriars Kirk to laugh at the bizarre behaviour of its unfortunate inmates. What he'd said about helping Alan Gunn must have sounded like the emptiest of promises from an over-privileged young man, bored and seeking distraction. Propped once more against the marble pillar, Richard's mouth set in a determined line. He was going to show Catriona Dunbar there was a lot more to him than that.

First he had to get through the rest of this interminable evening. He wondered how many other people here were bored. Irene was right. It was an attitude many people affected. To suffer from ennui was fashionable.

How spoilt we all are, Richard thought. There's wonderful food and wine on offer here, pretty girls and handsome men dressed in the finest of clothes. A pianist giving his all. Wit and sparkling conversation. He and his kind had so much and people like Kate Dunbar and her brother so little.

He thought of Alan Gunn and his children. What a sad story they had to tell, and now they had ended up in that awful place. Damp. Dank. Dangerous. Shut away from fresh air and sunlight. The Gunns shouldn't have to live there either. Nobody should.

His thoughts drifted back to his idea of Kate in a flower-filled garden. Gardens. There was something in his mind about gardens. What the hell was it?

That was when it happened. Like every candle in the Assembly Rooms being lit at the same moment, a quite breathtakingly wonderful idea exploded in Richard Hope's head.

CHAPTER FOURTEEN

'Good morning.'

Whirling round at the sound of his voice, Kate was startled by the rush of pleasure she felt. That reaction sharpened her voice, making her sound not very welcoming in the bright April morning. 'I didna think I was going to see you again.'

Wearing the clothes she'd last seen him in a week before, he might have been standing on the corner of the North Bridge waiting for a workmate. Until he pushed himself away from the dressed stone blocks, tugged off the knitted cap and pulled himself up to his full height. 'Will you come somewhere with me, Kate? Please,' he added. 'It's not far and I promise you'll be quite safe. We'll go this way so nobody you know at the fish market will see you.'

She drew in a long breath. 'Do you give me your word that I'll be safe with you?'

'I give you my word,' he said, and reached out to take her baskets from her. He led the way, down through Carrubber's Close to the valley between the Old Town and the New, the one she'd climbed up from only a moment or two before. When they got there she followed him onto the rising ground against which the waters of the Nor' Loch had once lapped.

They passed through drying and bleaching greens, laundresses already busy pegging out sheets and shirts which flapped in the warm breeze. Skirting the forest of wet linen, going in under the soaring arches of the North Bridge, Kate found herself in front of a walled enclosure screened by bushy and untidy trees. Setting down her baskets, Richard Hope extracted a jangling keyring from the deep pocket of his shabby jacket, selected one long-shanked key and put it into the lock of an elaborate but dilapidated wrought-iron gate.

He turned it, withdrew it and pushed the gate open – or tried to.

'It's blocked,' Kate said, squinting through the iron railings and curlicues. 'There's a hale heap o' leaves and mud behind it.'

'Some brute force and ignorance required, then.' Richard gave it a hefty shove. The gate squealed its protest, but opened.

'Needs oiling,' she observed.

'Mr Gunn should be able to deal with that, don't you think?' Richard Hope's smile was as dazzling as the morning sun.

'You've found him a position?' she queried, the words rushing out on a gasp of pleasure.

'It's only temporary,' he warned. 'A few months at most. But yes,' he said, that dazzling smile still in place, 'I've found him a position. Come and see.' He ushered her through and she ran in front of him along a gravel path, one of several which converged on an ornately carved stone fountain.

Reaching it, Kate whirled round, her short skirts and petticoat spinning out around her. 'It's a garden!'

'The Old Physic Garden,' Richard confirmed. He placed the baskets under the shade of an ancient pear tree espaliered against the wall next to the gate. Closing the gate – grimacing as it screeched again – he walked towards her. 'We don't use it anymore. It's probably going to be built over. Funny,' he said.

'What is?'

'Right at this moment I feel quite sad about that. It's never bothered me before.'

Kate threw him an uncertain little smile before continuing to take in their surroundings. She saw flowerbeds, overgrown but tinged with the colours of the first spring blooms; a sundial in one corner and a statue in another; a wooden summer house in a dilapidated state of repair; a small pond at the other end of the garden. 'If this is all going to be built over, why would there be work here for Mr Gunn?'

'You'll have heard the king might be visiting?'

She turned to him, lips twitching. 'Is onybody in Edinburgh talking aboot onything else?'

'No,' Richard agreed. 'My mama, for one. Morning, noon *and* night. My professors at the university are almost as bad. Although that's worked to our advantage. Apparently one of the king's personal physicians trained in Edinburgh,' Richard laughed and ran a hand through his hair, making it stand up on end, 'oh, about a hundred years ago, and he has a sentimental attachment to this place. He wants to see it again, so somebody will have to do some tidying-up before he gets here. Therefore,' he said triumphantly, 'there's a position for your Mr Gunn.'

Kate clasped her hands together like a pleased child. 'Och, Mr Hope! That's wonderful. Thank you!' She threw him a questioning look. '*We* don't use it any more? *Your professors at the university?*'

'I'm a medical student.'

'Studying to be a physician?'

'Ah-hah!' he said. 'Light dawns. You thought I was nothing but a well-off wastrel, didn't you?'

'Aye. I mean—' She stopped, covered in confusion by having given him that instinctively honest answer.

'Don't worry.' His eyes were dancing with amusement. 'Medical student or not, I think I am nothing but a well-off wastrel.'

'No' if you're going to be a doctor,' Kate protested. 'That must mean you want to help folk. That's a grand thing to do. A fine thing.'

'You think so?' All at once his voice was very dry. Although she shot him a sharp look, she made no comment, changing the subject to ask how he had secured the position for Mr Gunn.

'Asked the professor who mentioned it in the first place. He's been away. Only came home last night. That's why there's been a delay – I could only call on him yesterday evening. Told him I knew exactly the man to tidy up the garden here.'

'You've gone tae a lot o' trouble.'

'Not really,' he demurred. He seemed to be looking at her a little oddly, as though he were studying what was round her face rather than her face itself. 'Moreover, I've been very glad to do it. Shall I come with you now and we can tell Mr Gunn together? I can't wait to see his face when he hears the good news... Will you please take your little cap off?'

Not knowing why she obeyed him, Kate removed her cap and slid it into the pocket of her apron. His voice dipped to a soft murmur. 'Your hair is so beautiful this morning. It must be because the sun's behind it. It really is your crowning glory. Like threads of copper and gold and red glowing in the morning sun. It's beautiful. *You're* beautiful, Kate... Why have you gone all stiff?'

'Because you shouldna be saying these things tae me, Mr Hope.'

'*Mr Hope?*' he queried with a quizzical smile, taking two steps towards her. 'Call me by my first name, Kate. Call me Richard.'

'I dinna think that's a very good idea, Mr Hope.'

When she folded her arms across her chest, his smile grew wry. She was doing her damnedest to keep him at a distance and he knew it. 'But we're friends, aren't we?'

'Ye think so?'

'I think you like me. I think you're quite intrigued by me.'

Kate's chin went up. 'Gey sure o' yoursel', are ye no'?'

'Not at all sure of myself.' He took another step towards her all the same.

'Thank you for arranging the job for Mr Gunn. When is he tae start?' Her eyes went to the pocket of the shabby jacket. 'Maybe I should take the key wi' me now, Mr Hope.'

'Not *Mr Hope*,' he pleaded. 'Richard. *Do* you like me, Kate? Even a little bit? As much as this wee flower, maybe?' He stooped and plucked one of the bluebells growing in a clump at the edge of the path.

'Och,' she said reproachfully. 'Now it'll die.'

'Not if you press it in a book. Then you can keep it for ever.' Three final steps and he was there, holding the flower out to her. 'It's the same colour as your eyes, Kate.' His beautiful voice was low and husky. '*Ca-tri-o-na*.' He gave each letter of her name its proper value, transforming it into the lilting rise and fall of water trickling over stones on a riverbed.

She thought he had a lovely name too. *Richard Hope*. Or was it to be simply *Richard*? She gazed at him as he was gazing at her. She saw luxuriant waves of hair gleaming blue-black in the sunlight; neatly trimmed sideburns accentuating strong cheekbones; a humorous and determined mouth.

She knew this could lead nowhere, except perhaps to heartache for herself. Wordlessly, she held out her hand and received the flower from his.

CHAPTER FIFTEEN

Their fingertips were touching. Her warm skin against his warm skin. Excitement coursed through his veins. He wanted more. He *needed* more.

'Got hold of the wee flower?' He slurred the words, stumbling over them as though he were drunk. Maybe he was, intoxicated by Catriona Dunbar and the beautiful morning and being here in the Old Physic Garden with her. Its overgrown and abandoned beauty and air of wistful melancholy made it impossibly romantic, the sort of place about which poets penned dreamy verses. Richard pulled himself together and repeated his question.

When she nodded in reply he drew his long fingers down her hand to encircle her wrist, tugging her towards him. Seeing her eyes widen, he murmured a few words of reassurance. 'Don't be scared, Kate. There's no need for you to be scared.'

'You promised I'd be safe with you.' She sounded as dazed as he felt.

'You are safe with me. All I want to do is kiss you. Let me do that, Kate. Oh, please let me do that!'

She was still scared. But he could see something else in those beautiful blue eyes. She wanted this as much as he did. She wanted him. A second explosion of pleasure tumbled through his veins. *She wants this. She wants me.*

Be gentle. Hold back. Don't frighten her. As she turned her face up to his, he fought to keep faith with those self-issued commands. He brushed his lips against hers, breaking the contact almost as soon as it was made. *Be gentle. Hold back. Don't frighten her.*

When he felt her thread the fingers of her free hand through his hair and pull his mouth back down onto hers, he stopped thinking at all.

As his eyes fluttered shut, he gave himself up to sensation. The softness of her lips beneath his. The taste of her mouth. The scent of her warm skin. Clean and...lemony, that was it. Her skin smelt of lemons. With neither conscious thought nor intent, he slid his arms under the rough wool of her plaid and around her waist. Instinct took him there.

His long fingers curved to hold her safe and secure in his arms. Through her thin bodice and the equally thin chemise beneath it, he could feel the warmth and firm softness of her body. Such a wonderful feeling. *Such...a...wonderful...feeling...*

Somewhere in the Old Physic Garden a thrush began to sing its song to the morning. A soft breeze ruffled his hair, and hers. Even with his eyes closed, he fancied he could see as well as feel those warm auburn tresses as they curled under his chin and coiled against his neck. He had a mermaid in his embrace. Or perhaps the Lorelei, sitting on her rock in the Rhine and enticing poor sailors to their doom.

Pleasure surged through him. Excitement mounted within him. Desire rose, his body reacting to the closeness of hers. With a little moan of pleasure, he took an even firmer hold of her and deepened the kiss, his lips coaxing hers apart, his tongue flicking along her teeth— And found himself being thrust backwards as she wrenched herself out of his arms.

'Kate?' Blinking – surely the sun was ten times stronger now than it had been a moment ago – he reached out for her. Evading his grasp, she retreated, walking rapidly backwards away from him and towards the gate. He started in pursuit, and saw that her eyes were once more wide and alarmed. She was scared. She really was scared.

If he'd had any doubts about her innocence, they evaporated in that moment, a great wave of tenderness swamping desire. 'Och, Kate. Don't look so worried. Please don't look so worried!'

She continued to back away from him, her hands by her sides and curled into fists which rested on the firm folds of her skirt. As he watched, she straightened her fingers and stretched them. Readying herself to pick up her baskets. Readying herself to leave the Old Physic Garden. Readying herself to leave him. The bluebell dropped onto the pebbles at her feet.

'I have to go.' The words were breathless and rushed. 'My aunt will be wondering where I am.'

'Let me come with you so we can both tell Mr Gunn about the position. You wouldn't deprive me of witnessing his pleasure, would you?'

'Folk will talk if they see me wi' someone like you.'

'Someone like me?' He put a droll expression on his face and glanced down at himself. 'I'm not dressed like *someone like me*, am I?' Taking encouragement from what looked like indecision on her part, he pressed the point. 'I'll carry your baskets and we'll be a lad and a lass walking together through the town. Just Richard and Kate walking through the town. There's nothing wrong with that, surely. No impropriety there.'

Judging he might now be able to join her at the gate without causing her to dart through it like a startled kitten, he walked forward. Crouching down to pick up the little blue flower, he sprang back to his feet. 'Won't you take this with you?'

'I've nothing to put it in.' She still sounded breathless. She still sounded scared.

'I do.' He dug into the pocket of Jamie the under-footman's old jacket and brought out a small notebook. 'I brought this with me in case I missed you and had to leave a note at The Pearl Fisher.'

'That wouldna hae done much good. I canna read.'

'You can't?' He couldn't keep the surprise out of his voice and her chin went up in response to it.

'Dinna ken much about how other folk live, dae ye?'

'That would seem to be the case,' he agreed, hearing the defensiveness and regretting he had been the cause of it. Tearing a sheet out of the notebook, he placed the bluebell on it, folded it in half and offered it to her for the second time. He experienced a sharp stab of pleasure and relief when she took it, sliding it into her apron pocket. 'I put it inside a book?'

'Inside the back cover. Leastways, I think that's how Irene Steele does it. A heavy book is best. Or you can pile other books on top of the first one.'

'Who's Irene Steele?'

Richard cursed himself for a fool. What sort of an idiot spoke about one young woman when he was making love to another? If that was what he was doing. 'Just a girl I know. Do you have a book to put that flower in?'

'Aye.' Her voice was stronger now, and warmer. 'Andrew gave me one for my birthday.'

'When's your birthday?'

'Today.'

'Oh, Kate,' he exclaimed, seized by dismay, 'if I'd known that I'd have brought you a present. Och, I wish I'd known that!'

Some of the tension left her then, and she offered him a cautious smile. 'You did give me a present, in a way. Andrew used the sixpence you gave him to buy my book.'

'What did he choose?'

'The poems of Robert Burns.'

'I *love* those. But what are you going to do with them if you can't read?'

'Learn. Andrew and me baith. As soon as I can find the money to pay for a tutor.'

'I know plenty of students at the college who're always looking for ways to earn a few extra pennies. There's a notice board where I could advertise for you, if you like. Happy birthday, by the way. What age are you?'

'Nineteen. What age are you?'

'Twenty-two.'

For a moment they stood by the gate in silence, looking at one another. Then Kate patted the pocket of her apron. 'You've given me another present, now I come tae think o' it.'

'Did you thank me for it?' Folding his arms, he looked down his nose at her, deliberately arch. 'I don't think you did, you know.'

His play-acting was working. She was relaxed again, enough to hold her heavy skirt out to one side and bob him a curtsey. 'Thank you, Mr Hope.'

'Thank you, *Richard*,' he corrected, urging her to use his first name for what seemed like the umpteenth time. 'Please say it. Please, Kate.'

'Dinna gie up easily, do you?'

'I think you've made that observation before. *Thank you, Richard*,' he prompted again.

She heaved a theatrical sigh. 'Thank you, *Richard*. What's the matter wi' you now?'

For he had tilted his head back and allowed his eyes to flutter shut. He opened them again and beamed at her. 'It was hearing you say my name at last.'

'It made you feel ill?'

'It made me feel wonderful.'

'Are ye sure?' she enquired, and in her air of mock solicitude she was every bit as arch as he had been a moment before. 'Ye look like some poor body who's no' quite right in the heid.'

Richard whooped with laughter. 'You're f-funny,' he spluttered. 'You're really funny!'

And as he grinned at her and she laughed with him, Richard was aware he had never felt so alive as he did here, in an overgrown garden hidden under the North Bridge, talking to a girl wearing a homespun skirt and a plaid. He was also aware that the second most brilliant idea he'd ever had in his entire life had leapt into his head.

'Tell me,' he said. 'Is The Pearl Fisher open for business on a Sunday?'

Her mouth quirked. Oh God, but she had such a lovely mouth...

'Depends who's asking.'

'Me. I want to know if you have any spare time on a Sunday.'

'Some. Why dae ye want tae ken?'

'Because,' he said, 'I could come to the Cowgate on a Sunday afternoon and teach you and Andrew to read.' He was excited again, the blood fizzing through his veins. 'What have you got to say to that, Miss Catriona Dunbar?'

CHAPTER SIXTEEN

Kate had nothing to say to that. All she could seem to do was stare up at him, notice how the breeze tugged at his black hair, think how handsome he was, how full of life and vitality.

'I've nae money,' she said at last. 'I couldna afford tae pay ye.'

'I wouldn't want you to pay me!' he exclaimed. 'I wouldn't want a penny piece for this! Not so much as a brass farthing!'

'Nor payment in kind, neither?'

'Dammit, Kate,' he said with a quick frown, 'what sort of a cad do you think I am?'

'So ye dinna want tae lie wi' me?'

'I didn't say that.' His voice softened. 'But there would be no charge for the lessons, Kate. Not in any way, shape or form. No price you'd have to pay. I'd love to teach you and Andrew to read. And write, too,' he added. 'If you would like.'

I would like, she thought. I would like that so very, very much. If only she didn't know that there would be a price to pay and both of them might be required to pay it. If only she didn't know she ought to tell him to go away and never come anywhere near The Pearl Fisher ever again.

'Come on,' he urged, stooping to lift her baskets. 'We'll talk about this while we walk.'

She gasped at his cheek. 'You're assuming I'm going to let you walk me back to The Pearl Fisher?'

He raised his eyebrows at her. They were as black as his hair and much straighter than her own. 'I'm assuming you've too kind a heart not to. If I come with you now I'll have the pleasure of seeing Mr Gunn's pleasure. With a bit of luck, I might also stand a chance of sneaking back home before my mother and father see me dressed like this and start quizzing me as to what I've been up to. Out you go, Kate, and I'll lock up.'

'You'd get a raging from your parents?' she asked as he set her baskets down again while he secured the gates from the outside.

'A *raging*?' he queried, flashing her a smile. 'That's a good word. Yes, I'd be in trouble. And I'm in enough hot water as it is.'

'Why's that?'

'Lots of reasons. Right then. Off we go. Dare I wager that by the time we get up to the High Street I'll have convinced you to let me teach you and Andrew how to read and write?'

Now. She should tell him now. *Go away, Richard Hope. I don't want to see you again.* She'd be lying, but it would be for his own good – and hers. It was unfortunate that the words seemed to have a mind of their own, were refusing to pass her lips. Aiblins that kiss had cast an enchantment over them.

A memory flashed into her head – her mother telling her the tale of Thomas the Rhymer, how he had met the beautiful Queen of Fairyland and been spirited away by her on a bonnie white horse to her secret kingdom. He returned to the world of mortal men and women after what seemed to him like a few days, only to find he'd been away for years.

He'd been left with a legacy of his time in Fairyland too. Forever afterwards, whenever he'd opened his mouth he'd been incapable of speaking anything but the truth, giving him the gift of prophecy and the title of True Thomas. In Kate's case the enchantment seemed to be working the opposite way, stopping her from saying what she knew she really ought to say. She found herself pointing to her baskets. 'By the time we get up to the High Street you'll be out o' puff. Gin I were you, I'd save my breath tae cool my porridge.'

'This Miss Steele,' Kate said as she and Richard Hope crossed the High Street a few moments later.

'What about her?' Annoyingly, he didn't sound in the least out of breath. It seemed he was stronger than any young gentleman of fashion had a right to be. Only he was more than a young gentleman of fashion, wasn't he? He was studying to be a physician. Overawed by the realisation that she was walking through the town with someone who would one day be a doctor by her side, Kate heard herself ask another question. 'Is she pretty?'

He stopped dead and wheeled round, a gleam of unholy mischief in his eyes. 'Why would you want to know that, Kate?'

'No reason,' she said loftily. Leastways, she hoped that was how she sounded. 'You'd be as well to bide where you are and have a wee rest now afore we go doon Niddry Street.'

'A weakling as well as a cad, eh? Rest assured, Miss Dunbar, that a wee rest will not be required.' Slanting him a glance as they walked together down the brae, Kate saw that he was still mightily amused. 'Irene Steele is very pretty. Clever, too, and a really nice person. Funny and kind and warm-hearted.'

'Are you affianced to her?' Kate asked, hearing how stiff she sounded and exasperated with herself because of it. Why in the name of God was she quizzing him about this Miss Steele? She wished the young lady no harm but she was of no possible interest to her. Her bewitched mouth was at it again.

'No. Although my mother would like me to be.'

'Is that one of the reasons you're in trouble at home?'

'It could be. My turn to ask a question now. Do you really think I would have kissed you if I were engaged to another girl?'

Kate threw him a cynical look as they rounded the corner into the Cowgate, sadly wasted because his attention was elsewhere. 'Ah, here's your uncle.'

Kate stiffened. Fortunately, the attention of the two men she now stood between was on one another.

'Why,' Michael Graham exclaimed, 'if it isn't Mr Hope. You're up early, young sir.'

'Indeed, Mr Graham. I trust I find you well.'

'Capital, Mr Hope, capital. Can I do aught for ye this morning? Take the baskets from the young gent, lassie.'

'No need. Show me where they go and I'll deposit them there. You can indeed do something for me, Mr Graham. You and your good lady. 'Tis a proposal I have to put to you both in connection with Kate and young Andrew.'

Michael Graham's eyes widened. 'Indeed, sir? Then kindly step inside.'

'It wouldna cost us anything?' Chrissie Graham asked.

'Absolutely nothing, Mrs Graham. It would be my pleasure to do it.' Glancing across the trestle table and up at a hovering Kate, Richard wondered why she now seemed so much less confident than she had before. He also wondered why she didn't sit down, next to her uncle, who was sitting directly opposite him.

Chrissie Graham had lowered herself onto the bench seat on Richard's side of the table. He was glad he had turned down her offer of a cup of warmed ale. The interior of The Pearl Fisher still smelt of last night's drinking and eating, not to mention an undercurrent he could only attribute to the unwashed state of many of the tavern's clientele. It would be all too easy to imagine oneself a trifle queasy. 'As I've already told your niece, I'm not prepared to take a penny piece for this.' Once more he glanced up at Kate. 'Not so much as a single brass farthing.'

'Uncommonly generous of you, young sir. Uncommonly generous. I think it's a splendid idea. Young Andrew could do with some schooling.'

'Miss Dunbar too,' Richard put in.

'Who?' demanded Michael Graham. 'Oh,' he said, slapping his forehead as though in comic realisation and swinging round to look at Kate. 'Miss Dunbar too. Aye, of course. When would you be proposing to give these lessons to Miss Dunbar and Master Dunbar?'

Richard divided a smile of enquiry between Kate, her uncle and her aunt. 'We had wondered – I mean, I had wondered – if Sunday afternoons might be a convenient time.'

'I think Sunday afternoons might do very nicely. Would ye no' say so, Chrissie?' A look passed between Michael Graham and his wife, confirming Richard's impression that Kate's uncle was a lot keener on this idea than her aunt was.

Thinking she might be concerned about the proprieties, he hastened to offer reassurance. 'We would of course conduct the lessons within The Pearl Fisher here.'

'You'd be better outside o' it. Gin the weather's fine.'

Richard made Michael Graham a little bow, relieved for two reasons by that suggestion. Even out in the Cowgate the air would undoubtedly be sweeter than in here and they would also be there in the quiet of a Sunday afternoon. With a bit of luck, he might get to spend some time alone with Kate.

'Then,' he said, 'if that's agreed, I fear I must reluctantly take my leave of you all.' He gazed up at Kate, and knew it must be clear to everybody which one of them he was most reluctant to leave.

'No' afore you've seen Mr Gunn,' she said.

'No, indeed,' he agreed. 'Although I shall have to make haste after that.' For two pins he'd stay here all morning, help Kate with her chores or something – not that he would have the faintest idea where to start. But the sooner he got home the less likely it was his parents might catch him in Jamie's old clothes and give him that *raging*. Richard thought again what a good word that was.

'I'll go and fetch Mr Gunn now,' Kate said, leaving him to explain to his host and hostess why she was doing that. After that story had been told Michael Graham asked if he should procure some slates for the scholars.

'Eh, yes,' Richard said. Until this moment he had given no thought at all as to how he was going to instruct Kate and Andrew. 'That would be most helpful. I shall bring some other...eh...materials with me on Sunday.'

Hellfire. What would his parents say if they could see him now, sitting in a malodorous oyster cellar at half past six in the morning, conversing as politely as though he were in one of the best parlours in the New Town?

The situation, he realised with a spurt of amusement, would be entirely outwith his mother's experience, comprehension or imagination. He wasn't so sure about his father, having a shrewd suspicion that Edward Hope might have had some adventures of his own in his youth. Seeing Michael Graham's head lift, Richard turned. Alan Gunn was standing behind him.

CHAPTER SEVENTEEN

'I thought he was going to shake my hand off,' a sombre Richard said as, under instruction from her uncle to 'See Mr Hope on his way now, lassie!' Kate walked with him along the Cowgate.

'He's very grateful to you.'

'I didn't do very much.'

'Aye, you did.'

'He had tears in his eyes.'

'I noticed,' she said. 'Although I pretended I didna.'

'I've done a good thing then, have I?'

'You've done a good thing.' They had reached the corner of Niddry Street and she knew full well what she ought to say to him now but the right words wouldn't come. Others did. 'I suppose you'd best be off home afore ye get into any mair trouble wi' your parents.'

'What about your parents? Are they dead?'

Kate nodded. 'Four years since. Of the typhus.'

'I'm so sorry,' he responded. 'Lucky you had relatives who could take you in. Will you please come round the corner with me?'

'Mr Hope,' she began, tucking a wayward strand of auburn hair behind one ear. 'Richard.'

'That's better,' he said with a deep curve of his wide mouth...but she was doing her utmost not to think about his mouth, those firm yet gentle lips that had kissed her own. 'Come round the corner with me,' he said again.

'All right,' she said, thinking it would give her the chance to say what she had to say to him.

'What a reek!' he exclaimed a moment later, his hand shooting up to cover his nose and mouth. For there was a team of scavengers busy now in Niddry Street, making their way up the brae with a cart and shovelling the mounds of nastiness into it. The vigour of the scaffies' spade-work was stirring up a hideous mix of smells.

Kate couldn't help but laugh, pulling on his sleeve to draw him into the first open close at the foot of the slope. 'It might be easier on your delicate nose if we stand here for a wee minute. I dinna suppose ye hae this in the New Town.'

'No, thank God. That smell is *vile*! Why do we put up with such a primitive method of disposing of our waste in any part of Edinburgh – Scotland's capital city – in this day and age?' he demanded. 'More importantly,' he continued, gazing down at her in the gloom of the close, 'how is it that you always smell of lemons?'

'Because I rub my skin with a cut lemon to get rid of the smell of fish. What else are you in trouble with your parents about?'

'They think I'm not paying enough attention to my studies.'

'Are they right?'

He made a balancing gesture with his right hand. 'Perhaps.'

'D'ye no' want tae be a doctor?'

'No. I mean, yes. I do want that.'

'Then ye'll hae tae stick in, get your heid doon ower your books. Your parents wouldna be too happy if they knew where you were now, would they? Or that you're planning to take time away from your studies tae teach Andrew and me?'

'Probably not,' he allowed. 'But let me worry about that.'

'Maybe I can't do that,' Kate responded. 'And maybe this is

no' such a good idea after all. For you tae teach Andrew and me, I mean.'

'But you really want to learn how to read and write, don't you? And for Andrew to learn how to read and write? If you want to do that and I want to teach you I don't see what the problem is. Your uncle's all for it,' he added eagerly.

She opened her mouth to speak – and closed it again without saying anything.

'Och, Kate,' he said in that lovely mellow voice, 'I meant what I said about there being no charge, you know.'

He had misunderstood her concern. There was no way he could have realised what was really worrying her: that the only reason her uncle had received him with such apparent friendliness was because Michael Graham was planning on relieving him of some of his money.

There were horrible pictures in her head of Richard Hope being jumped on in some dark close somewhere by a couple of her uncle's cronies, left lying bruised and bleeding on the cobblestones. Wanting only to make those pictures disappear, she responded to what the unsuspecting young man standing gazing so warmly at her had just said.

'So if I tellt ye there would be nae mair kissing that wouldna change your mind about wanting tae teach Andrew and me?'

'No.' He raised black eyebrows over sparkling eyes and sent Kate's see-sawing emotions swinging off in an entirely different direction. 'As long as you'll allow me to try to change your mind about the kissing. When we were in the Old Physic Garden I had the distinct impression you were enjoying it as much as I was.'

'That's n-not the p-point,' she stuttered, all at once uncomfortably warm.

'Isn't it?'

Despite her embarrassment, she could not stop her eyes from

finding his mouth. That kiss. Oh, that kiss… She couldn't think what to say next so she leant out of the close and squinted up the hill. 'Ye'll can go now. Ye micht even hae a clean causeway tae walk ower. The scaffies are nearly up at the High Street.'

When he didn't move, she drew her head back in and looked at him.

'I can't wait until Sunday to see you again,' he said. 'Why don't I come back this evening? Or better yet, this afternoon?'

She folded her arms and tried her best to scowl at him. 'Do ye no' hae classes at the College this afternoon?'

'Yes, but I could cut them.'

'You'll do nae such thing. Have we no' just agreed ye hae tae stick in at your studies?'

He laughed. 'Och, but you're stern, little Miss Dunbar.'

'Dinna be sae impertinent. And go. Now.' She hesitated only for a few seconds. 'I'll see you on Sunday.'

'So I am allowed to come and teach you and Andrew?'

'Aye, I suppose so.' Och, but she sounded so grudging and ungrateful! She did want him to teach them. She wanted that more than anything in the world.

'May I please not come tonight?' he asked, seeming not at all put off by her attitude. 'Or tomorrow afternoon, when I don't have any lectures? Or tomorrow night? Or Thursday night? Or Friday or Saturday night? Even the most conscientious of my fellow students don't study then.'

He was hard to resist. She was fighting a smile as she shook her head at him. 'No' tonight or tomorrow afternoon or any other night, either. I'll see you on Sunday, as arranged.'

'May I at least do this, then?' Bending forward, he dropped the lightest of kisses on the corner of her mouth before pulling back to see her reaction.

'Seems tae me ye've already done it.' She pointed to the

opposite corner of her mouth. 'I'll no' be able to walk straight gin ye dinna gie me one there an' all.'

'Your wish is my command,' he murmured, leaning forward once more to bestow the kiss she had – so much to her own surprise – requested. His lips were as light as a feather: like a butterfly fluttering around her mouth. When he raised his head, the two of them stood for a moment just looking at one another.

'There,' he said after a moment. 'Now you won't be off-balance. But I thought there was to be no more kissing.'

'There isn't. Ye're dreaming these ones. Now, dae as ye're tellt and go.' She gave him a little shove in the right direction.

'Only if you stand in the street and wave to me all the way up,' he said as he stepped out onto the causeway. 'I'll walk backwards.'

Kate's lips twitched. 'I wouldna recommend it. Likely ye'll trip and end up clarted up wi' all the flooers o' Edinburgh. They canna lift everything into their wee cairtie. Get up that road, Richard Hope.'

He laughed again, and went at last. When he turned at the top, Kate was still standing at the foot of the brae. Tugging off the little knitted hat he'd only that moment put back on, he made her an extravagant sweeping bow. Laughing back up at him, she made shooing gestures with her hands and mouthed 'Go on!'

When he blew her a kiss, she raised one hand in admonition but pretended to catch it all the same. He grinned, gave her one last wave, about-turned and disappeared from view. She stood for a moment holding the imaginary kiss and gazing up at the ridge of the High Street. Then she raised her hand, uncurled her fingers and spread them wide. It was as though she were freeing a wee bird.

* * *

'You're no' too stupid tae ken whit he's really efter, are you?' Her eyes adjusting to the gloom, Kate found herself being looked up and down with the air of contempt at which Chrissie Graham was so practised. 'Or stupid enough tae gie it tae him? Dinna come running tae me when ye get yoursel' in trouble, that's all. Gin yon one plants a bastard in your belly, I'll pit baith you and the wee cripple oot the door.'

'Chrissie,' Michael Graham said. 'Dinna be like that. Kate's no' daft. Are ye, pet?'

The endearment made her skin crawl, unease bobbing once more to the surface. He had Richard Hope in his sights. She knew he did.

'Ye'll watch yersel, Kate, eh? This'll dae us some good too, Chrissie.'

'How d'ye work that oot?' his wife demanded.

'Well, if the wee one gets himself a bit o' education he'll aiblins be able tae get a better job. Bring a bit mair siller back tae ye at the end o' each week.'

'Ye think so?'

'I'd say it's a distinct possibility. The bairn's got a gammy leg but there's nothing wrang wi' his heid. There's some brains in there. Am I no' right, Kate?'

She looked from him to her aunt. Chrissie Graham's expression had already lightened. Money. That was all she cared about. They were a right pair.

'Am I no' right, Kate?' her uncle asked again.

She hated to agree with him about anything, but she wanted to see Richard Hope again. Michael Graham had the power to help or hinder that.

'You're right,' she said, and moved away from them to get on with her work.

She should have sent him away. Whether he had offered to teach Andrew and her to read and write or not, she should have thanked him for getting the job for Mr Gunn and then she should have sent him away. She should never have encouraged him in the first place, should never have agreed to show him the inside of the bridge, should not have gone to the Physic Garden with him this morning.

She should definitely not have allowed him to kiss her while they were there. Nor should she have kissed him back, or asked him for another kiss when he had taken his farewell of her at the foot of Niddry Street. Why had she done that? Oh, but she could still feel his mouth at the corner of her own, feel his breath warm against her skin...

Her head was filled with pictures of him. She saw him over and over again in her mind's eye. Standing waiting for her on the corner of the North Bridge. His handsome face lit up with pleasure when he told her how he had secured the position for Mr Gunn. Handing her the wee bluebell. Smiling down at her in the dimness of the close at the bottom of Niddry Street. Sweeping her that daft bow from the top of it.

All through the long day and the ones that followed, Kate hugged the pictures of Richard Hope to her and kept the memory of his kisses on her mouth.

CHAPTER EIGHTEEN

He supposed he deserved it. No, he knew he did. His initial interest in the unfortunate souls who occupied the dark vaults under the South Bridge had been almost entirely spurious, nothing more than an excuse to spend time with Kate Dunbar. The flash of inspiration that had impelled him to offer to teach her and her wee brother to recognise and form their letters had sprung from exactly the same motive.

And where had his oh-so-brilliant idea led him? Why, to being the unlikely dominie of a gang of miniature ragamuffins. He had arrived at The Pearl Fisher on Sunday afternoon to find the Gunn children waiting for him too – and for the last hour had been rewarded for his efforts with only fleeting glimpses of Kate as she darted backwards and forwards at the beck and call of her aunt and the few drinkers in the tavern.

April had newly given way to May and although there had been a torrential downpour this morning, the day had turned out fine and warm. The long table at which Richard was to preside over his pupils had been carried outside so they could all benefit from the fresh air and sunshine.

In observance of the Lord's Day, there was little work being done. So the Cowgate, like the rest of Edinburgh, was quiet. There were few people about and no horses and carts and the noxious cargoes the latter often pulled.

The Sabbath or not, The Pearl Fisher was open for business.

The Kirk might disapprove but Richard didn't think there was any actual law forbidding the opening of taverns on Sundays. Although its more respectable and God-fearing customers were absent, there were enough thirsty men about to make it worthwhile keeping the place open.

Hearing Kate's light step – already so heart-stoppingly familiar to him – Richard looked up. 'Some refreshment for the scholars and their tutor,' she announced across the big round tray she was carrying. 'Or am I interrupting you too soon?'

'Not at all,' he said, indicating to the children they should clear their slates out of the way to allow her to set the tray in the middle of the table. 'I suspect the scholars have had more than enough for one day.' He surveyed his charges. 'Am I right?'

'We have liked your lesson fine, Mr Hope,' Rebecca Gunn told him shyly. 'May we please come back next week?'

'Of course,' he said, touched by the look of gratitude on her face and wondering what he might bring with him for the second lesson which would offer Alan's Gunn's children more of a challenge than they'd had today. The three of them already could read and write. Simply copying out the letters and words he was showing Andrew wasn't going to be enough.

Kate's brother was soon going to need something more challenging too. He was soaking it all up like a sponge. He was grinning hugely now, first at Rebecca Gunn and then at Richard. His initial suspicion of him seemed to have evaporated completely over this past hour. 'Aye,' he agreed, 'we've had a rare time, sir. But we're looking forward to our walk to the Old Physic Garden too.'

For Alan Gunn had invited Richard to do that with them all after the lesson, when he had also handed over a silver threepenny bit to pay for his children's lesson. 'Will a penny per head be sufficient for the moment, Mr Hope?' he had asked. 'It's precious little, I know. Once I have been working for a week or two I shall of course be able to pay you more.' The horrified words of refusal that sprang to Richard's lips had stayed where they were when Kate had trod – very firmly – on his foot.

Pretending to cough, she had covered her mouth, turned away from Alan Gunn and mouthed a few urgent words. 'He *needs* to pay you.'

Thinking about that now, he smiled up at her as she set out a plate of buttered oatcakes, a pitcher of milk for the children and a tankard of ale for him. During the week he would use the silver threepenny to buy some sweets and fruit for the children, and would bring those treats with him next Sunday.

Richard was in the sunniest of moods, relieved that his pupils had enjoyed their lesson despite his own obvious shortcomings as a teacher. He would prepare a much better one for next week. He was relieved about something else too. When the subject of the walk to the Old Physic Garden had been broached, he had thought Kate's uncle was not going to allow her to go along.

Then Michael Graham's grim look had relaxed, and he seemed now to be all for it. With Mr Gunn and all the children on the walk, presumably he had realised his niece would be well chaperoned. Damn it.

'Will you join us?' Richard asked Kate. 'It must be less busy in there by now. Lots of people have come out while we've been sitting here. You are supposed to be having a lesson too.'

'Och, I'm no' sure it's worth your while trying to teach me.' One hand rose to rub the back of her neck, under the thick waves of her hair. 'I don't see I'd be any good at forming my letters.'

He gave her a brisk answer to that. 'You have no evidence to support that belief, Kate. Why don't we start with your own name?'

'Aye, Kate,' Andrew said. 'You'd like fine tae be able to write your name, have you no' aye said that?'

His sister smiled at him. He'd finished his milk and it had left him with a white moustache on his upper lip. 'I have,' she admitted. She sat down beside Richard, taking the space her brother had vacated. 'Go on, then. Show me how to write my name.'

'First, watch how I do it.' His eyes flickered up to the children as they rose from the table, Rebecca Gunn gathering up the spare slates. He was torn between being glad to be left alone with Kate and wishing they had taken longer over their milk and oatcakes. Responding to a chorus of *thank you, Mr Hope,* he waited till they had gone back inside before applying himself once more to the slate and writing her name out on it.

'That looks gey complicated.'

Turned sideways now on the bench, leaning in to him so she could see the letters chalked on the slate, she was very close to him. He could smell her hair, warm and clean. She was so fresh and sweet and neat. Living where she did, he couldn't figure out how she managed it. The lemons, of course. They helped. A picture slid into his head of Kate naked, washing her arms and neck and throat and rubbing a cut lemon over her soft and creamy skin...

'Richard.'

'What?'

'You're staring at me like a daftie. That no' quite right in the heid look again. Or is it that you've gone tae sleep wi' your eyes still wide open?' She was laughing at him, and it made him feel so good. Kate Dunbar was laughing at him. She was happy in his company. Relaxed. So he had to keep her that way. Allow her to call the shots. Which didn't mean he wasn't going to ask for what he wanted.

'Let me come here one afternoon or evening during the week.' Every afternoon and evening during every week, he thought.

Every waking moment. I want to spend them all with you.

'No.'

'Why not?'

'Because you should be spending your afternoons and your evenings studying. Will ye no' be having examinations coming up soon? Tell me why my name looks so complicated.' She was peering at the slate again. Richard sighed, and for the moment resigned himself to play the dominie.

'Because I've written it out in full. C-a-t-r-i-o-n-a,' he said, spelling it for her. '*Catriona.*'

That earned him a raising of her lovely blue eyes to his face. 'I love the way you say my name,' she told him with delightful shyness. 'But I think you'd better start off with teaching me how to write Kate.'

'All right.' Under *Catriona,* he wrote out her name in its shorter form. 'There. Now you try. I've left space for you to do it below where I've written.' He looked up and found her laughing at him again.

'You've made a mistake, Mr Schoolmaster.'

'No, I haven't.'

'Aye, you have. I may not be able to read yet.' She stretched out her hand and traced the first letter of her name with her index finger. 'But I can see that's a different letter from the one you wrote Catriona with. That was like a curl. This one's like somebody kicking out their leg.'

'You're absolutely right,' he said, delighted by the accuracy of those observations. 'But Catriona and Kate do begin with different letters.'

'That doesn't make sense.' Placing the tip of her index finger on her chin, she adopted a look of comical perplexity. '*Catriona. Kate.* They must begin with the same letter. They sound exactly the same.'

Oh, God, but she was so lovely... I'm enchanted by you, he

thought. *If I am awake with my eyes wide open, I'm having the most wonderful dream. And I don't want to wake up from it.* He spoke, and it was as though some other young man was saying the words.

'That's a very logical observation, Kate.'

He placed one hand on his chest and made her a little bow. Having discarded Jamie's old jacket because of the warmth of the day, he was in his waistcoat and shirt sleeves. The plain black waistcoat had belonged to Jamie too. The linen shirt was Richard's own. He'd undone the cuffs and folded them back, allowing the sun to get at his wrists and forearms. 'Kate, also known as Catriona,' he pronounced, hardly knowing what he was saying. 'Miss Logical.'

She propped her elbows on the table and her chin on her fists. 'So you have made a mistake?'

Giving himself a mental shake, he tapped the end of her pretty little nose with the slate pencil. 'No. Your observation may have been logical. Unfortunately the English language isn't. Especially when it comes to pronunciation. Catriona starts with a C, Kate starts with a K.'

'That's daft.'

'Maybe. But that's the way it is. Now, are you going to copy out your name? If I'd known you were going to be such a troublesome pupil I'd never have offered to teach you.'

'Oh aye, ye would,' she murmured, the gleeful look on her face metamorphosing into something altogether warmer, lazier and more intimate.

'What did you say?' he demanded.

'Nothing,' she said instantly, and straightened up from the relaxed posture in which she had been sitting, laying her hands flat on the table in front of her.

'Oh, Kate,' he said, 'don't do that!'

'Don't do what?' she queried, her voice colourless.

'Withdraw from me,' he said, and laid one hand over one of hers too quickly for her to withdraw from that, too. 'And there's no need to look so worried. There really isn't.'

Kate bit her lip and looked away from him in favour of studying Jack, the South Bridge mouser. The big ginger and white tom was lying on the warm cobbles in front of them, taking the air and occasionally bestirring himself to wash his massive paws.

'It's all right, Kate,' Richard said gently. 'It's all right for you to tease me. I rather like it, in fact.'

She stopped studying the cat, slid her hand out from under Richard's, and gave him a cautious little smile. 'You going to get on with your work, Mr Schoolmaster?'

Even after only a few days in gainful employment, Alan Gunn had grown greatly in confidence. Showing them around the Old Physic Garden, pointing out the difference he'd already made in the weeding of the flowerbeds and vegetable patches and the start he had made on repairing the paths, his bony face was alive with the pleasure of it all. His enthusiasm was infectious.

'Are you to renovate the summer house too, Mr Gunn?' Richard asked. 'It's quite dilapidated at the moment, is it not?'

'There are to be carpenters coming in for that and after them painters to freshen it up, inside and out.'

'What's it like inside?' Kate asked.

'I'll show you,' Alan Gunn said, selecting one of the keys from the ring he now wore at his belt. 'Don't go in, though, Miss Kate, for the floorboards are rotted and not safe to stand on.'

Kate looked in, Richard casting a glance over her shoulder. A bench ran along the back wall and half-a-dozen ancient and battered cane chairs were stacked one on top of the other. Otherwise, the old summer house was littered with the detritus you would expect to find associated with a garden: broken plant pots, piled up troughs and seed trays.

'This is all to be refurbished too.'

'Lest the king's physician take it into his head to have a wee sit down?' Richard suggested.

Alan Gunn nodded as he shooed the children back from the door of the summer house. 'Indeed, Mr Hope,' he said, closing and locking the door again. 'I understand the specification is for a *pleasant garden parlour*.' His smile was wry, perhaps even sardonic.

'The royal visit is proving to be expensive to Edinburgh.'

'Aye,' Alan Gunn agreed. 'But in that it is providing much work for people like myself. I am very grateful for that, young Mr Hope. Please don't think I'm not.'

'I did very little,' Richard protested. 'I am only glad to have been able to have been of some small assistance to you and your family.'

'Some *small* assistance?' There was nothing sardonic in Alan Gunn's expression now. 'You underestimate yourself and your kindness, Mr Hope. What you have done for me and my family—' He broke off, and when he spoke again his voice was husky. 'I find I cannot put it into words, young sir. But please know that you will always have my heartfelt gratitude. If there is ever anything I can do for you – though I cannot imagine what that might be – you have but to say the word.'

Deeply moved, not sure if he could say anything without unmanning himself, Richard offered Alan Gunn his hand. The firm handshake that followed was interrupted by a shout.

'Father! Come and see these wee beasties we've found!'

Dividing a smile between Richard and Kate, Alan Gunn sped off towards his children and Andrew. Wasting no time, Richard took her by the wrist and pulled her round the back of the summer house. 'This rule of yours about no kissing,' he murmured. 'Are you very firm about it?'

CHAPTER NINETEEN

Too short a time later, Richard strolled across the North Bridge. 'Dragging my feet like a schoolboy who doesn't want to go to school,' he muttered, grimly amused at himself and the state he was in. Weak as a kitten. His knees turned to jelly. Not wanting to leave the Old Town. Not wanting to leave her. Not allowed to see her again until next Sunday. God Almighty, next Sunday was an eternity away!

The afternoon sun was warm on his face and hands. Funny how the day should have turned into such a beautiful one when the morning had been so wet and miserable. He didn't need the additional warmth of the wee knitted hat but he felt more at ease wearing it. It might afford him some sort of disguise if he should encounter anyone he knew on his walk home.

Gazing at the Firth of Forth in the distance, he wondered if Kate had really meant it when she had told him not to come back to The Pearl Fisher until next week. A slow smile spread across his face.

No kissing. She certainly hadn't meant that. Not if those precious few moments in the Old Physic Garden were anything to go by. How odd. He was about to walk over the top of it, nestling as it did under the bridge. As she had nestled in his arms, surrendering herself to his mouth and his hands. Oh, God. The remembered sensations swept through him, stopping him in his tracks. *Oh God, oh God, oh God...*

He stepped over to the parapet of the bridge, propped his arms on top of it and lost himself in the vista and the intense hazy blue of the Firth of Forth. He had surrendered to Kate every bit as much as she had surrendered to him. What he wanted to do now was run back over the bridge, hurtle down to The Pearl Fisher and beg her to allow him to do it all over again.

Do what? The obvious, of course. The desire to make love to her, lose himself inside her, was well-nigh overwhelming. Yet at the same time, he was acutely aware of her innocence. Touched by it, as she was completely untouched. He was sure she was still a virgin. Much though that realisation was moving him, it was doing nothing to dampen his current state of arousal. Quite the reverse. Hot, burning desire and overpowering tenderness. It was a devastating combination, one he knew he'd never experienced before.

To date, he'd exchanged kisses and caresses with a few adventurous girls of his own class and had three full-blown and intimate love affairs with young women outside it. No, he thought, narrowing his eyes as he gazed at the distant Firth, *love* wasn't the right word. *Dalliances,* perhaps. Two of those had been with sophisticated women a few years older than himself. He'd never been the kind of young man who took advantage of his parents' housemaids. He despised that kind of behaviour.

The two older women – not so much older than himself – had been actresses appearing at the Theatre Royal, which he would pass as he crossed over to the other side of the North Bridge. Just as soon as he regained the ability to walk.

Both young women had been treading the boards in successive winter seasons at the theatre and had made their interest in him clear. On each occasion, it was they who had made the first move. Flattered and excited, Richard had for a few heady weeks fancied himself in love. Both young women had laughingly told him not to be such a moon-calf and he had parted from them on good terms.

Later there had been the girl to whom Torquil Grant had introduced him at a party in Union Street, off the top of Leith Walk, where the assembled company had been somewhat louche to say the least. She had certainly been very advanced in her views and her manners: fun to be with, flirtatious in the extreme, and very accommodating.

Two weeks into the *affaire,* Richard had been happy to help out when she had found herself 'temporarily a little strapped for cash, Richard dear' and struggling to pay the rent on the rooms where she lived alone save for her maid. Three months in, bad-timing on her part led to a chance meeting on the stairs of her building with another young gentleman of Richard's acquaintance.

Comparing notes, the two of them had realised they were being played for fools. Furthermore, that what on their side they had fondly imagined to be an *affaire de coeur* was to her nothing more than a commercial transaction.

Mulling it over now as he stood leaning on the parapet of the bridge high above the Old Physic Garden, Richard wasn't sure he had ever actually been in love. There had been an innocent and unspoken passion for one of his cousins when he had been fourteen or so. That had faded away in its own good time. Now when he met the girl he enjoyed her company but wondered what he had seen in her in the romantic sense.

A seagull landed on the parapet. Turning his head, he saw it was surveying him out of its unblinking and beady eyes. 'Don't look at me like that,' Richard told it softly. 'Do you think I've got any idea what I should do about this? I think I'm in love, seagull. I really do. Don't bother your shirt telling me she's a girl who works in an oyster cellar and who speaks the broadest of broad

Scots. I know that. And I don't care. I really don't. In fact, I rather like it— Hey!'

For he had been doused with cold water, splashing against the backs of his legs. Whirling round, he saw a landau bowling past him, its wheels whirling through a deep puddle left by the morning's rain. The water rose up and wet the front of Richard's legs. 'Hey!' he shouted again. 'You've soaked me!'

The driver looked over his shoulder at him, laughing. Richard froze. It was Torquil Grant.

CHAPTER TWENTY

How in the name of fucking Hades was he to explain why he was walking across the North Bridge on a Sunday afternoon dressed like this?

He needn't have worried. As he and the carriage moved on, Torquil's eyes flickered over Richard in contemptuous amusement and without the least sign of recognition. 'Of course I've soaked you,' he sneered. 'That's what I was aiming to do, you great booby. Can't you take a joke? Such a pretty splash I made!'

Turning to face forward again, laughing with the two girls and other young man in the carriage, he cracked the whip he held in his right hand and drove off, leaving Richard staring after him in disbelief. Torquil Grant. His friend Torquil Grant. How the *hell* could he not have recognised him?

Richard looked down at his wet trousers, plucking the thick corduroy free from his knees, where the water had plastered the heavy cloth flat. The clothes, he supposed. That was why Torquil hadn't realised who he had soaked. Richard's mouth tightened.

Being dressed as a working man or a poor student had obviously not only rendered him unrecognisable but also made him fair game as the target of a mindless prank – unworthy of an apology, too. *Manners maketh the man. Fine feathers make fine birds.* And often don't.

Richard shook his head and let out an exclamation of disgust.

As he set off again, crossing the bridge before taking a circuitous route back home, he was thinking about his old nurse. She had been full of those sorts of proverbs.

There had been a picture book from which she had read them to him. That must still be in the nursery at the top of the house, along with the rest of his childhood library. He would look some of the books out and take them with him next Sunday.

Kate had no fine clothes but she had manners, which, when it came down to it, were all about kindness and consideration for others, like the way she had taken an interest in the old summer house when Mr Gunn had shown it to them today. Mr Gunn and his children had manners too. Real courtesy.

Yet they were condemned to live in those dank chambers within the South Bridge. It couldn't be healthy. Or safe. Not with all those drunkards in there. Thieves and vagabonds too, he'd wager.

If Alan Gunn did well at the Old Physic Garden there might well be a permanent position for him at Inverleith, a house too, probably. That was a nice thought. But it still left Kate and her brother in that awful place.

With a swift glance around him to make sure no one was watching, Richard slipped down the lane at the back of his home. An idea flashed into his head. It came as a series of pictures.

Kate in some nice, airy rooms somewhere, preferably with a view towards the Firth of Forth. He was sure she would like that. Wearing pretty dresses and reading books and walking backwards and forwards with Andrew to school every day. The boy was as bright as a button and that's what he ought to be doing.

The coachman had one of the horses out in the mews, grooming her. Brendan O'Sullivan clearly had no difficulty in recognising his master's youngest son, his craggy face breaking into a grin. 'Well, now,' he said in his soft Irish brogue. 'Would you be wanting to tell me what you've been up to dressed like that, Mr Richard?'

Richard placed one long finger against his lips. 'Nothing now. My adventuring is over for the day – apart from getting up to my room without anyone seeing me. I can rely on your discretion, Brendan?'

'Away with you,' the older man said fondly. He had been with the Hope family since before Richard was born, set him on his first pony, helped him school every other one since. 'Say a quick good-day to my fine girl first.'

'With pleasure.' Clapping the mare on her big, warm neck, Richard disappeared into the house. He was in luck. At this time on a Sunday afternoon, all was still, and he took the deserted back stairs two at a time. Once he was in his room, he peeled off his damp clothes and laid them over the back of a chair in his dressing-room to dry out. Then he shrugged into his favourite Burgundy coloured dressing gown and walked across to the window which gave him the view of the castle and the Old Town.

How nice it would be to stand here with Kate. That was a complete impossibility and he was not so blinded by his feelings for her that he couldn't recognise that. He allowed his eyes to travel up the buildings on the other side of the gulf which separated one half of Edinburgh's inhabitants from the other. But maybe he could stand at another window with her.

Outside in the mews, the mare had grown restless, moving from one foot to another and whinnying. Brendan the coachman murmured soothing words and stepped out into the cobbled lane, knowing even before he heard the sound of footsteps that someone must be walking along it.

The stranger raised a hand in greeting. 'I fear I've taken a wrong turning here,' he called. 'Mind you, I see the detour might have been worth it!' As he gave the mare the once over, Brendan recognised the unmistakable signs of a fellow horse-lover.

'That,' Michael Graham pronounced, 'is a magnificent animal!'

CHAPTER TWENTY-ONE

'What are you up to?' Kate asked, coming back to the counter and finding Andrew bent over the very end of it.

'I'm practising my letters,' he explained without looking up. 'For Mr Hope next Sunday.'

'You're keen.'

'Well,' he said, 'I'm no' going tae hae much time during the week. Although I've decided I'm going tae dae a wee bittie every evening.'

'Let me see what ye're doing now, then.'

'My name,' he said proudly, pointing to it, and then, with a quick, apologetic glance up at her, 'My letters are gey big.'

'Your name fills the whole slate,' she agreed. 'Is that bad?'

'Mr Hope says I've no' tae worry aboot it. That the mair I practise the neater I'll get. Kate, can I get the book o' poems oot o' the tin trunk sometime and hae a look at it?'

'Of course you can. But I dinna think ye'll be able tae read Mr Burns' poems yet, Andrew.'

'I will soon,' he told her with cheerful determination. 'And I thocht I might already be able tae recognise some o' the letters. I want Mr Hope to see I'm willing tae work hard, Kate. So he'll keep wanting tae teach us. You and me and Rebecca and the wee ones.'

His face was alight with pleasure. She lifted one hand to the back of his head, smoothing its riotous auburn disarray. 'You enjoyed his lesson, then?'

'It was rare. Did you like your lesson too, Kate?'

'Aye,' she said. 'Very much.'

'Why don't you practise your name?' He glanced round the tavern. 'Naebody's wanting ye right now. I've got your slate here.' He reached under the counter and brought it out.

Catriona. Kate. Underneath Richard's neat printing was her own clumsy attempt at her name. She grimaced.

'Practice makes perfect, Kate. That's what Mr Hope says.'

'All right,' she said. 'I'll give it a go.' Three attempts later, hoping she wasn't fooling herself the third was an improvement on the first, she looked up and found her brother watching her. 'Are you laughing at me, Andrew Dunbar?'

His reply was threaded through with affectionate amusement. 'Your tongue was poking out o' the corner o' your mouth. Like you were really concentrating.'

'I was. What d'ye think?' She turned the slate towards him.

'Nae bad. But—'

'Practice makes perfect?'

'Exactly.'

Brother and sister grinned at one another.

This rule of yours about no kissing. Are you very firm about it?

She had proved to be anything but. It had been a matter of seconds before she had given in, succumbed, allowed herself to be putty in his hands.

Och, his hands... The feel of them on her waist, travelling up her back, those long, smooth fingers sliding into her hair... *Och, his hands...* Not to mention his mouth. The feel of his lips on hers. Warm yet cool. Gentle yet firm. Seeking a response. One she had given him in full measure, her own hands reaching up to explore the cool skin of his face and the warm depths of his thick, lustrous hair.

Heading for the rickety wooden steps that led down into the middle level of the bridge, Kate paused for a moment. Placing her lantern on a protruding flat stone, she tucked her hands in under her arms and allowed her eyes to flutter shut.

She hadn't walked Andrew up to the saddler's basement today because her wee brother had needed her to – he hadn't had one of his nightmares – it was she who had needed the extra activity. She was restless, full of pent-up energy – and longing to see Richard again.

Richard. She shouldn't have given in to his pleas to address him by his first name. She should have stuck with *Mr Hope*. There were so many things she shouldn't have done, like accepting the little skein of hair ribbons he had brought out of his pocket while they were round the back of the summer house at the Old Physic Garden.

'All the colours of the rainbow,' he'd said gaily. 'That's what I asked for. Will you take them, Kate? As a late birthday present?'

She had taken them, too touched and delighted by the wee gift not to. She was wearing a lovely dark green one today. She was off her head. There could be no future for her and him, and there could be only one reason why someone like him would be interested in someone like her.

Yet that wasn't what it felt like on Sunday in the Old Physic Garden, nor last Tuesday when he had first taken her there. He had held back, even allowed her to order him about. In an odd sort of way, he'd seemed to enjoy that.

'I can't see you again till next Sunday? That's cruel, Kate. Really, really, cruel.' Now she was wondering why she had imposed that restriction. Next Sunday was an eternity away. She was perplexed too, wondering how a girl who had endured what she had could be filled with such longing for the touch of a man's hand and the pressure of a man's mouth on her own. Oh, but it wasn't just any man she was thinking of, it was Richard—

Kate's eyes snapped open. Shocking in the silence of the quiet shadows in which she stood, she heard a distinctive sound: well-oiled wheels rolling quietly across a stone floor. The hairs stood up on the back of her neck as she peered through the gloom to the source of the sound. She could see the light of a lantern now, bobbing ever closer through the blackness of one of the closes that fed into the underground passageway.

Well-oiled wheels rolling quietly across a stone floor. Well-oiled wheels which would otherwise have creaked and squealed under the burden they bore: a dead weight.

The long and narrow barrow came into view first, emerging out of the close into the main passageway. A small metal lantern, enough to light the way and no more, hung from one corner of the cart. Wrapped in a rough grey blanket, the shape of the cargo it bore was unmistakable. The man manoeuvring it around the corner came into view. 'Well, well, well,' said Michael Graham. 'Look who's here.'

CHAPTER TWENTY-TWO

'No' for much longer,' Kate said, unable to stop her eyes drifting down the body in the blanket: a man by the height and shape of it. She had long suspected Michael Graham might be involved in this foul trade. There had been the occasional overheard snatch of conversation, the witnessing of covert exchanges of substantial sums of money.

'Shift your arse,' he said. 'I need tae get the merchandise safely stowed away. The daylight overtook us.'

'I dinna want tae ken.' What a way for anybody to end up, being manhandled about by someone like him. Dug up out of your grave, brought in to one side of the bridge, stowed away here till night fell again and then hurtled along Infirmary Street to Surgeons' Square, where the anatomists had their houses and lecture theatres. Somebody's husband, somebody's father. Now merely *merchandise*.

'I dinna suppose it occurs to you that young Mr Hope might end up cutting into this?'

It hadn't. The thought brought Kate up short, long enough to find herself on the wrong side of the barrow and her way blocked by it. 'Let me past,' she said tightly. 'I've tae get tae the fish market.'

'The fish market'll still be there in another ten minutes. I'm needing a wee word wi' you.'

He pushed the barrow forwards, forcing Kate to backtrack

along the passageway. Angling it to allow her no possibility of escape, he unlocked the padlock on the door next to him. It was the shiny new one she had noticed the last time she had walked Andrew to his work.

'I didna ken ye had a store-room up here.'

'Well, ye ken noo.' Michael Graham jerked one thumb towards it. 'Get in there.'

'No,' she said, shaking her head in emphasis of her refusal.

Dodging under the barrow with an agility that belied his bulk, he grabbed her by the shoulders and flung her against the door. It fell open and she stumbled into the room, her momentum carrying her to the brick wall on the other side of it. Pain shot through her back as she struck it, and her head swam.

In the few seconds it took her to see straight again, her uncle had the body and the barrow in the room and the door closed and bolted from the inside. He walked across to where she stood against the wall. 'How much dae ye ken aboot Richard Hope?'

'Nothing I'm going tae tell you.'

That answer earned her a slap across the face. 'Then hold your tongue and listen tae me.'

Kate blinked back tears of pain. 'How could someone like you ken onything aboot someone like him?'

She was asking for another slap. She got it, along with a growled, 'Shut your mouth, ye wee hure. I'll no' tell ye again. Your new friend Mr Hope lives in a fine big hoose on the corner o' Castle Street and Princes Street wi' his mother and father and a wheen o' servants. He's kin tae all manner o' important folk, forbye. The Earl o' Hopetoun, for one. Young Mr Hope's no' just weel-off, wee Kate. He's gentry.'

She stared up at him. 'How dae ye ken all o' this?'

'I followed him hame last Sunday. Efter you lot went on your wee jaunt tae the Old Physic Garden. Saw you and him juking round the back o' the wee hoosie in there. Letting him growp ye up, were ye, slut?'

She hardly heard any of that, her mind occupied with what he had said about Richard and his family.

'Once he went intae his fine big hoose, sneaking in through the tradesmen's entrance, I may add, I managed tae fall into conversation wi' the coachman. He was oot in the lane seeing tae one o' the horses. Bonnie big handsome mare. They've eight horses a'thegither.'

Kate's blood was running cold. A big house. Servants. His family rich enough to have their own coachman and eight horses. Kin to the Earl of Hopetoun. Not just well-off but gentry. Too rich a prize for Michael Graham to be able to resist.

'You leave him alone,' she said hotly.

'My, my.' Michael Graham affected a look of swooning rapture. 'Dinna tell me you've lost your heart tae him. Dinna tell me you think he really cares aboot you.' His face was full of amused contempt. 'Who'd care aboot a dirty wee trollop like you?'

I think you're as smart as paint. And beautiful. And as fresh as the morning. As the words flew into her head, Kate lifted her chin. 'I'm no' listening tae any more o' this.' When she attempted to pass her uncle, he grabbed her and thrust her back against the wall, laying one hand on her throat to keep her there.

'Ye'll go when I've finished wi' ye and no' before. Ye've made a good start by making him work for it. Telling him no' tae come back till Sunday.'

Kate tried to shake her aching head and felt her hair catch on the crumbling bricks of the wall. 'I've tellt ye afore. I'm no' playing games wi' him.'

'Oh, aye you are. And here's the first rule o' this game. Gie him a little o' whit he fancies and nae mair. Keep him dangling, like.

In a perpetual state o' frustrated desire. The lad'll no' be able tae think straight if he's aye got an itch in his britches.'

She couldn't bear him talking about Richard like this. It was like watching someone pull clean laundry off one of the ropes strung high above the Cowgate and trample it into the dirt and glaur of the street.

'Ye've nothing tae lose, pet. Efter all, ye are damaged goods. Although, assuming it's no' too late – and it had better no' be,' Michael Graham said, his voice edgy with menace, 'for the meanwhile it'd be wise tae let the young gentleman think ye're as pure as the driven snow. Shouldna be too difficult. I dinna think he's very bright.'

'He's real clever! Any fool can tell his heid's stuffed fu' o' brains!'

'Brains is one thing. Kenning whit's what is another.' The hand on her throat flexed, the fleshy fingers digging into her smooth skin. The smell of dank, damp earth rose off them, as it did from the dead man lying mere feet away from her.

Not a man any more. Now merely merchandise. She had something in common with the corpse. She was *damaged goods.*

'Listen tae me,' Michael Graham said. 'The plan's simple. Even a stupid wee slut like you should be able tae understand it. Keep him dangling for a wee while and then let him have you – allow yourself tae be persuaded, like. At which point ye'll mak sure ye've got that wee drop o' cow's blood wi ye. Then I'll discover the baith o' ye and tell him he's ruined you. I'm guessing he'd pay a pretty penny for me no' tae tell his parents he's taken some poor wee lassie's maidenheid.'

Kate stared at him in disbelief. She had feared he was planning to have Richard set upon in some dark close and robbed. That would have been bad enough. This was a hundred times worse.

'You and me'll have tae set it up beforehand, of course. I could fair look forward tae seeing you being ploughed by the young gentleman. In fact,' the rasping voice thickened, 'mebbe I'll no' discover you on the first occasion. Aiblins I'll wait till the second or the third.' He pressed himself against her, forcing her to feel his arousal. 'Take masel in hand while he stuffs it up ye.'

Struggling to keep her face away from his, Kate spoke in a cracked whisper. 'I'll not do this. *I will not do this!*'

'Oh, aye, you will.' He stepped back, the better to power the blow he struck her. It knocked her head once more against the unforgiving wall. This time when her vision cleared she saw a look she knew only too well on Michael Graham's face.

'Looks like you're needing a wee reminder on which side your breid's buttered. On your knees, slut.'

His free hand was already at the buttons of his trousers.

CHAPTER TWENTY-THREE

Gagging and retching, on her hands and knees at his feet, Kate spat what was left in her mouth onto the earthen floor. She needed water. Gallons and gallons of it. Over her and in her and swilled around her mouth and spat out again a hundred times over. Her dark-green ribbon had come off; it was lying there in front of her, wet now with her spittle, and worse.

Only his legs within her line of sight, she saw Michael Graham take a step back. 'Look up at me.'

This at least she could deny him, even if it did cost her a clout on the side of the head that made her ears ring. Then he hooked his fingers under her chin, forcing her obedience to his demand. He drew his free hand down himself before transferring it to her face, smearing her mouth and cheeks.

'Ye'll dae whit ah tell ye tae dae, cunt.' He put his thumb on her bottom lip and pressed hard. She opened her mouth in an involuntary response and he slid his fingers in. When her retching would have forced them out again, he pushed her once more hard against the brick wall. 'You'll reel the young gentleman in. It'll be a long game, mind. So you'll keep your legs tight shut till I tell ye otherwise. Understood?'

His eyes flickered to the corpse. 'And here's something ye mebbe dinna ken. The medical gents are aye looking for bairn's bodies.' His voice was silky with threat. 'Pay by the foot and inch for them.'

He pulled his fingers out of her mouth and wiped them once more over her lips. 'Terrible the accidents that can befall brats in this toun, eh?' He stepped back and began fastening his trousers. 'Now get up and bugger off. I need this place locked.'

She couldn't think about what he had just said. Not right now. If she did, she would never be able to summon up the strength to stand up and walk out of here. So Kate focused on the moment instead.

She had grazed the back of her head. She could feel blood oozing through her hair. Her back and shoulders ached. It was going to hurt to stand up. She knew he was watching her, revelling in her humiliation.

She looked again at her hair ribbon, reached for it and scrunched it into a ball. Scrambling to her feet, she stumbled out of the room, Michael Graham's laugh following her.

Early though it was, a maid she knew was at the well in the High Street, fetching water for the house where she worked.

'Can I borrow one o' these for a wee minute?' Kate already had hold of one of the girl's leather buckets, her own baskets set down on a clean patch of cobblestones. Lifting it above her head, she poured half its contents over herself, gasping as the cold water splashed over her face. She had washed that before she had left the The Pearl Fisher but she still felt dirty, as filthy as the street around her.

She set the bucket down again and used her two hands to rub the water in. Everywhere that he had touched. Her hair. Her face. Her throat and the top of her breasts. Then she poured the water that was left over herself again.

'Are you a' right, Kate?' the girl asked, clearly bemused.

'Half-asleep, that's all.' Somehow she managed to put a smile on her face. 'Needed tae wake masel up.' She raised the leather bucket. 'Can I refill this for you?'

Kate went round the fish market in a daze, although she didn't think anyone noticed. She was still walking and talking and responding with automatic little smiles to the chat and the jokes. Only when she was almost at the top of Fleshmarket Close did she set her heavy baskets down, squeeze her eyes shut and put her back to the wall.

She began to tremble then, shaking so much the only way she could ground herself was to tilt her sore head and press it hard against the rough stone behind it. When the pain became too much to bear she slid down the wall, hunkered down onto her heels and wrapped her slim arms about her bowed head. Huddled into a small ball of fear, misery and self-loathing, she stayed like that until she heard the sound of footsteps coming up the close.

Poised to slice an onion, Kate found herself staring at the knife she held. It was viciously sharp, kept that way by regular grinding. The blade shone, bright as a well-polished mirror. She could see herself in it, even if the image was distorted, her eyes and forehead disproportionately large. She turned the blade first one way and then the other but the distortion remained.

She looked stupid, like one of the poor dafties you saw around the town and felt sorry for. Still studying her reflection, she wondered who she was to feel sorry for anyone. She was stupid. Worthless, too, and of no value to anyone. Why else would Michael Graham do what he did to her if she wasn't worthless?

Kate turned the blade of the cooking knife the other way and wondered what would happen if her hand were to slip—

'That'll no' slice itself, ye lazy wee bitch,' came her aunt's voice. 'Stop dreaming and get on wi' your work.'

In the early afternoon, knowing Chrissie Graham had gone off for her nap and her uncle was playing host to the few customers left in The Pearl Fisher, Kate stood at the rough bench in the other vault which provided her and Andrew with a makeshift wash-stand.

It held a cracked pink porcelain jug and a mismatched cream basin. To one side of those she laid down the lemon and small knife she had brought along from the tavern. On the other side of the jug and basin, next to one of the three sweet-smelling cakes of soap Mrs Henderson had given her on her birthday, sat the ribbon Kate had left there this morning. It was dry and crusty now, half its width, crumpled-up and twisted. Spoilt and ruined.

Richard Hope had been so happy when he'd given her the ribbons, so light-hearted. It had been almost as though he were courting her. Lad to lass. Man to maid. For one sweet moment he'd made her feel like an untouched girl again, innocent and carefree and clean.

Kate leant forward, gripped the edge of the rough bench and allowed one raw sob to escape her lips. *Stop dreaming.* She'd barely been given the chance to start.

She couldn't leave the ribbon where it was in the state it was in. Andrew might notice it. She should throw it out. So she hooked it up with her little finger, ready to do that, but it slid off and fell into the wide and shallow china basin. As it landed in the small drop of water that lay in the bottom, the fabric relaxed and began to smooth out.

Kate stared at it for a moment, observing the process. She pressed the ribbon with the tip of her index finger, allowing more of it to get wet. Then she drew in a breath, raised her head, lifted the pink jug and poured out enough water to immerse the whole ribbon, before picking up the soap Mrs Henderson had given her.

Once the ribbon was washed and rinsed, she changed the water, hung the ribbon to dry over to the top of the pink jug and washed her face. She cleaned her lips hard, drawing two soapy fingers over and under her teeth and gums before rinsing her mouth out yet again with clean water. Loosening her bodice, she washed her neck and throat and breasts.

She cut a couple of slices of the lemon and rubbed them over her skin, slid a third slice into her mouth and sucked hard. It was sharp enough to make her shiver.

Holding it in her mouth, she brushed her hair and, after a moment's hesitation, crossed the vault to her tin trunk and pulled out another of the ribbons Richard had given her, a black one this time. Once she had tied her hair back with it, she stepped out into the close, spat the slice of lemon into one of the slop buckets that stood to one side of the entrance to The Pearl Fisher, and turned towards the sunshine streaming in from the street.

A shadow fell across the brightly lit opening. As the late customer stepped towards the doorway of the tavern, Kate saw who it was, and blinked hard.

CHAPTER TWENTY-FOUR

'Kate!' he said. 'I almost didn't see you there. Good afternoon.'

She should say something, but wasn't sure that she could. With the sun behind him as he stepped into the shady interior of the underground close, he looked in that instant as though he were on fire, displaced sunshine blazing out around his tall frame. Like an angel, Kate thought, a burning, burnished, black-haired angel.

'I know you told me not to come till Sunday but I couldn't keep away. It was hard enough waiting until today. This was as long as I could last.' He took another step forward and lost the halo of fire. The buckled strap of a tan leather satchel crossed his chest. Although he was smiling, there was something in his eyes which hinted at uncertainty, even nervousness. How could that be?

Someone like him surely could never be unsure of himself, confident he would receive a welcome wherever he went. Not just well-off but gentry. Kin to the Earl o' Hopetoun. Lives in a big house in the New Town. One with a stable at the back of it with eight horses, a coach and a coachman in it. It was surely impossible for someone like her to possess the power to make someone like him nervous – especially someone who felt as bad about herself as she did today.

Her mouth was dry. Obliged to lick her lips before she could speak, finding the taste of lemon still on them, she found herself rattling out a couple of belligerent questions.

'Have you come frae the College?' Her eyes ranged over him. He seemed to be wearing a mixture of the shabby clothes and his own, as though he had taken pains to look more like a poor student than a wealthy one. 'I thought it was Wednesday afternoons you had off.'

'I don't have any classes on a Tuesday afternoon either. I've been to my morning ones.'

'Then you should be at your books now. Studying for your examinations. You shouldna be here.'

'Are you not pleased to see me, Kate? Do you want me to go away?'

'Mr Hope,' came her uncle's voice. 'Come to give my niece another lesson, have you, young sir?'

'If she would like that, Mr Graham,' Richard said, his eyes not leaving Kate's face. 'But I'm not sure if it's convenient.'

'Guid sakes!' Michael Graham blustered as he came out of The Pearl Fisher. 'Of course it's convenient. Give me a hand and we'll carry a table outside. The lassie's needing some fresh air. She's been working hard all morning.'

She hated him. Hated the way he was pretending to be concerned about her. Hated the way he smilingly beckoned her out into the Cowgate as though he really was what an uncle should be. Hated the way he bustled back into The Pearl Fisher to fetch two slates. Hated the flourish with which he handed them over to Richard Hope.

'There now. Anything else you require, young sir? A tassie o' claret, perhaps? A tankard of ale or a bite to eat?'

'Nothing, thank you, Mr Graham.'

'Then I'll leave you two scholars alone. Wouldn't want to stand in the way of learning!'

Darting a glance at Richard Hope, Kate saw that he was hovering at the end of the table. He was stooping too. If he was doing that to try and make himself look less tall, it wasn't working.

'Are you no' going to sit doon?'

'Not until you do.'

Why was he treating her like a lady? Why was he pretending she was something she wasn't? If he knew what her uncle had done to her this morning, if he knew what Michael Graham was planning to do to him— Oh, God... *If he knew what her uncle had done to her this morning.* Kate sank down onto the bench.

'Mind if I take my jacket off? It's rather warm today.'

'Why would I mind?' That snapped response earned her another uncertain look before he swung the jacket off, laid it over the end of the table and sat down next to her.

'Lemons again. Such a clean smell.'

His smile faded when she didn't respond to it. He picked up the slate. 'Shall I write out your name again for you to copy? Or would you prefer to learn something new? Maybe you and Andrew have been practising.'

'We have been practising.' She could see Andrew now in her mind's eye, so happy to at last be learning how to write. I want Mr Hope to see I'm willing tae work hard, Kate. So he'll keep wanting tae teach us. You and me and Rebecca and the wee ones.

'New words today, then?'

'Please yourself,' she said, her voice dull. 'Write what you like.'

'Kate...' His free hand came over her left hand, resting on the table in front of her.

Her fingers flexed beneath his. 'Please don't do that.' She wasn't clean. She could wash herself as much as she liked but she would never be clean. If he knew how dirty she was he wouldn't want to touch her.

'Kate,' he said again.

'Write some words on the slate.'

There was a tiny pause before he began writing, copying out three words and saying them out loud as he did so. '*Table. Bench. Ale.*'

He tapped the index finger of his left hand against his top lip. She had noticed him doing that last Sunday too. She wondered if it was a typical gesture for him, a repetitive and unconscious action that helped him to think. Like the way he ran a hand through his hair when he was nervous and seemed not to realise he had done it.

When he was nervous. She had to be wrong about that. Once more, the litany began to play through her head.

Young Mr Hope's no' just weel-off, wee Kate. He's gentry.

Dinna tell me you think he really cares aboot you? Who'd care aboot a dirty wee trollop like you?

You'll reel the young gentleman in. Understood?

The medical gents are aye looking for bairns' bodies. Pay by the foot and inch for them.

'*Dress*,' Richard Hope said. 'How about *dress,* Kate? An odd selection of words, to be sure, but I suppose a young lady such as yourself might like to know how to spell *dress.*'

'I'm not a young lady. I've never worn a dress, either.' She hardly knew what she was saying, using the words only to try to block out the other ones echoing around her head.

Richard Hope looked up. She knew enough to know that the way his hair was cut, windswept though it looked, was carefully contrived. Fashionable. A young gentleman of fashion. He was all of that and more.

'You've never worn a dress?' She saw the mischievous comment hovering on his lips. 'Oh, I see what you mean. Always skirts and bodices, is it? Would you *like* to wear a dress?' He gestured with a lift of his chin towards South Bridge Street, far above their heads. 'A pretty one made by one of the dressmaker's up there?'

She shrugged. 'I'm never likely tae get one, am I?'

The amusement vanished from his face. 'What's wrong, Kate?'

'Nothing's wrong.'

'Yes, there is. Won't you tell me what I've done wrong so I may try to put it right?'

'You havena done anything wrong. Write out another word,' she commanded. 'You've still got space.' Carefully not looking at him, she didn't miss another highly charged pause before he spoke again.

'What word would you like?'

'I don't care. You choose. Just do it.' An adjustment of her gaze brought her a view of his left hand and uncovered forearm. When he had discarded his jacket, he had unbuttoned and rolled back the ruffled cuffs of his shirt. Despite his colouring, he had only a light dusting of hair on his forearms. His skin was very fair: a gentleman's skin, nothing like as dark as that of the working men she was used to, who routinely rolled up their sleeves or stripped to the waist when they worked in the open air and all weathers.

His shirt wasn't as shabby as the rest of the clothes he had elected to wear today. It was made of the best linen. It smelt so fresh, newly laundered, and starched too. Some maid in his parents' house would have done that, or maybe a washerwoman who came in to do the heavy laundry work.

Kate's eyes travelled from his rolled-up sleeves to his hands. Those hands had held her waist and roamed over her back and buried themselves in her hair. She had loved the feel of his long, slim fingers, craved their touch. And this morning other fingers had buried themselves in her hair, yanked her forward, forced her to… Bile rose in her throat, and her hand flew to her mouth.

Richard looked up. It was he who broke the silence that followed, his deep voice very gentle. 'It's you who's got that no' quite right in the heid look on your face now, Kate.'

She tried to laugh at the way his well-bred tones had softened into broad Scots, but the sound refused to come out. Instead, she dropped her hand and a little sigh born of something very close to desperation escaped her lips. It drew his attention to her mouth, his eyes dropping to it.

'Kate,' he breathed.

'Richard,' she heard some lassie whisper in response. Not until their lips were almost touching did she realise the lassie had been her.

CHAPTER TWENTY-FIVE

She slid away from him, along the bench, her desire to put distance between them all too evident. 'Do you cut up deid bodies?'

Richard jerked back. 'What sort of a question is that?'

'One as I'm needing an answer to. Do you cut up deid bodies?'

He surveyed her for a moment. If you were part of the medical world in Edinburgh, you never discussed this subject with anyone outside it. There were various reasons for that, the most important being also the most unpalatable.

Even if you had no direct evidence of it – went out of your way not to, in fact – you knew that practically all the bodies that appeared in dissection rooms had arrived there as a result of the night-time activities of the resurrection men. However much you tried not to, you also knew some of those gentlemen were your fellow students.

Those who were obliged to fund their studies by working as assistants and demonstrators to the professors of anatomy couldn't afford to be too nice about what such assistance involved. Nor could they afford to worry that some of the things they did ran counter to the law, morality and public sensibility.

It was impossible to explain to outsiders the hideous compromises required so medical students could learn about the human body. You knew they simply wouldn't understand, that you were wasting your breath if you tried. Richard opened his mouth and attempted to explain it to Kate.

'I haven't personally done any cutting up yet,' he said, adding a light: 'No such luck. Although I have attended dissections, of course.'

'No such luck?' He heard both the incredulity and the distaste and was aware of the unexpected desire to get her to change her mind.

'The human body is fascinating, Kate. Endlessly fascinating. The way all our organs and bones and muscles are positioned and connected to one to the other. The way everything works. Studying it in depth is a crucial aid to understanding it. Especially, as it were, from the inside out. We know a lot already but there is so much we still have to learn if medicine is to progress and continue to help us medical men care for and heal our fellow human beings. To put it succinctly, examining dead bodies helps us cure diseases in live ones.'

He'd surprised himself by coming out with that little speech. Until now he hadn't realised he felt so strongly about the subject.

'And grave-robbing?' she demanded. 'You think it's all right for folk tae dae that?'

'I think it's a vile thing to do!' he said forcefully. 'But until we can persuade people to make it known they'd be happy for medical schools to have their bodies after their deaths, I think it's a vile thing we're going to have to keep on doing. I'm sorry about it – really, truly sorry about it.' He shook his head, trying to rid himself of some very unpleasant mental pictures. 'I can only imagine how distressing it must be for people's relatives if they find out it's happened.' He gave that some thought. 'It must be absolutely bloody awful. Excuse me for swearing in front of you.'

She made a sound halfway between a laugh and a sob, a reaction he wasn't sure what to make of. Whatever she was thinking, she looked a little wild – and fierce, if beautiful with it.

Like a warrior queen. As he was wondering how the devil they had travelled from almost kissing one another to this gruesome subject, she changed it to another. A question was fired at him.

'Where do you bide?'

'In the New Town.'

'Whereabouts in the New Town?'

'In a house on the corner of Castle Street and Princes Street. In fact,' he added, 'I have a great view of the castle from my bedroom window.' If he'd been hoping that additional piece of information might lead the conversation off into more peaceful waters he was out of luck. Folding her arms across her breasts, she knitted her auburn brows. The reddish-brown linen bodice she wore today over a black cotton skirt was an exact match for them and her hair. That was tied back with one of the ribbons he'd given her, a black one.

'It'll be a fine, big hoose, is it?'

'It's a nice house,' he agreed. 'It's not *that* big, though.'

'Depends what you're used to, I suppose.'

'I suppose it does.'

'I daresay you've got relatives wha live in far bigger hooses.'

'I do, as a matter of fact. One of them lives in what you could only describe as a palace.'

'Would that be the Earl o' Hopetoun?'

'How did you work that out?'

'It's no' very difficult. Considering what your surname is. Folk like us dae gossip aboot oor betters, ye ken.'

He was beginning to get a little angry with her now. Could he help being born into his station of society any more than she could help being born into hers? Was it something he was supposed to feel ashamed or embarrassed about? Reaching for a weapon with which to retaliate, he found one. 'Is that the only reason you're interested in me, Kate? Not because of who I am but because of *what* I am? A well-off young man, with even more well-off relatives? With an earl for an uncle? Are you only interested in me because you think you might be able to get something out of me?'

She gasped, stared at him for a few unforgiving seconds, then flew to her feet. Even though it was only her light weight that had left the bench, the speed with which she had moved made it rock and shake. 'If that's what you think, maybe you should just take yourself off! Right now!'

'I'm sorry,' he said immediately, rising to his feet too. 'Kate, I really didn't mean to insult you!' He reached a hand towards her. She was edging between the bench and the table and he thought she meant to go back into the tavern. 'Don't go, Kate. Please don't go!'

The rippling waves of her hair danced as she tossed her head. Definitely Queen Boudicca now. No doubt about it. The warrior queen with the hair like flame was in the Cowgate and she was throwing lightning bolts at him with her eyes. 'What about why you're interested in me?' she demanded. 'Am I no' just a bit o' fun as far as you're concerned?'

And then, in the blink of an eye, her demeanour changed. 'I'm sorry,' she said, both hands flying up to her mouth. 'I shouldna have said that! I dinna ken whit I'm saying the day!'

'Well, you've said it!' he yelled back at her. 'The words are out now, Kate! You can't call them back! A bit of fun?' he repeated, bracing himself with the heel of one hand on the edge of the table. 'Do you think I'm finding this fun? Discussing dissection with you? It wouldn't have been my choice of conversation. Would I have come on Sunday and given the children their lesson – which took some preparation, I'll have you know – if I was only after a bit of fun? I've already done masses of prep for next Sunday's lesson. Would I be going to all this trouble if I was only after *a bit of fun*?' He howled the words at her. 'Is that really the sort of person you think I am, Kate?'

'I don't know!' she shouted back, angry again. 'I really dinna ken the first thing aboot ye!'

'You seem to know quite a lot about me,' he retorted. 'And you seem to have me down as a well-off young man who's only out for what he can get. How dare you say that to *me*, Catriona Dunbar! How dare you judge me like that!'

She blinked, but came back at him with another question. 'Why else would someone like you be interested in someone like me?'

'You want to know why I'm interested in you? You really want to know?'

'Aye! I really want to know!'

'I'm interested in you because I—' He stopped himself. 'Would you believe me if I told you I want to be your friend?'

'So you'll be inviting me to take tea wi' your mother in the parlour o' that fine big hoose on the corner o' Princes Street and Castle Street sometime real soon, will ye?'

Richard's lips twitched. 'Probably not, but it's a lovely idea.' He straightened up, removed his hand from the edge of the table and rubbed at the heel of it with the thumb of his other hand.

'Your mother would likely have a fit.'

'Undoubtedly.'

'Is your hand sore?' The question was a solicitous one; the tone of voice in which it was put anything but.

'Nothing to speak of. It's already wearing off. Will you sit down again, Kate? Please?'

'Why would I do that?'

'Because if you sit down again and don't pick any more fights with me I'll answer your question properly. The question as to why I'm interested in you. Please, Kate,' he said again. He sat down too, drew the slate towards him and rubbed it clean. Then he wrote three little words on it.

'If your hand's no' sore I'd like fine tae ken why it's shaking,' she said brusquely.

'My hand is shaking because of the words I've put on the slate.' He turned it towards her.

'I canna read them.'

'Try.'

'I can make out an *e*. At the end o' the middle word. The same letter there is at the end o' *Kate*. Apart from that I dinna recognise ony o' the letters.'

Richard swallowed hard. 'Maybe you can hazard a guess as to what the words are, Kate.'

She raised her eyes to his face. What could he read in there? Anger, certainly. Was it born of fear? Did she really believe his interest in her was only that of a wealthy and spoilt young man towards a girl who had taken his fancy? That he would help himself to what he wanted and discard her as soon as he'd done so?

She wasn't the only one who was scared. He was absolutely bloody terrified. When he had told the seagull on North Bridge he thought he was in love he'd been light-hearted, thinking perhaps of a summer-long flirtation. When he'd picked up the slate and written on it, he'd been in deadly earnest.

Please God, he thought, please God let her feel the same way about me as I do about her. *Please God...*

Somewhere very close to them, someone coughed.

CHAPTER TWENTY-SIX

As one, the two of them turned their heads towards the bottom of the table. A not very tall, fashionably dressed woman in her mid-thirties was standing there, cradling a parcel tied up with brown paper and string. Kate rose to her feet. Watching her as he also stood up, Richard saw that her colour was high.

'Mrs Henderson. We didn't see you there.'

She was trying so hard to sound cool, calm and collected. The girl who served ale and oysters in a low tavern was maintaining her composure as well as any fine lady he had ever known.

The fashionably dressed little woman didn't reply other than with a swift nod of the head but the word *evidently* hung in the air. Richard had recognised her immediately. The Radical bookseller's wife. Judging by the way she was looking at him, not to mention the stiff way she was holding herself, she had recognised him too. The stance and the stony look seemed to indicate she remembered where she had last seen him to have been a long way from the Cowgate.

When she turned her attention from him to Kate, Richard took the opportunity to clean the slate of its betraying words and heard Kate ask politely, 'Can I do aught for you, Mrs Henderson?'

'Perhaps you might introduce me to your friend, lass.' Hearing every last nuance in that ostensibly neutral statement, Richard decided there was nothing for it but to put his faith in the old saying that honesty was the best policy.

'Perhaps I can introduce myself, Mrs Henderson.' He made her a little bow. 'Richard Hope, at your service.'

'You have the advantage of me, sir.'

'I don't think so,' he said pleasantly, wondering how it was that women of all ages and classes could manage, when they put their minds to it, to sound so haughty and dismissive. 'I believe we were both at a soirée held recently in the New Town, ma'am. I have also purchased the occasional book from your shop. I may be back there again soon, searching for material for my voracious scholars.' He half-turned, indicating the long table with a sweep of his linen-sleeved arm. 'This is my schoolroom. I was here last Sunday teaching Kate, her brother Andrew and some other young friends to read and form their letters. As I shall be this coming Sunday also.' He wasn't looking at Kate, but his final comment was for her. 'And, I hope, for many Sundays after that.'

Damn, damn, damn. He should have said Miss Dunbar, not Kate. Peggy Henderson's reaction to that familiarity sprang into her rather lovely eyes – lovely, but with a gaze every bit as direct and clear-sighted as Kate's. 'Indeed, sir? That is most commendable.'

It was phrased as a compliment; the frosty politeness with which it was delivered made it anything but. Richard was relieved when Kate posed a question. 'What's in your bundle, Mrs Henderson?'

The little woman swung round to her. Richard could still feel the waves of disapproval wafting towards him. 'Nathaniel's second-best coat.' She gave Kate a smile. 'Since I bullied him into buying a new one, his third-best. There's a lot of wear left in it and I wondered if Mr Gunn might be able to make use of it. I met him at the kirk last Sunday morning and he told me his wonderful news.'

'Och, Mrs Henderson!' Kate exclaimed, 'that's real kind o' you! He'll want to give you something for it, of course.'

'There's no need for that.'

'You'll hae tae tell Mr Gunn that yourself, Mrs Henderson,' Kate replied, her russet brows settling into a frown.

'Not if you tell him I'll be mortally offended if he offers me so much as a brass farthing, Kate.'

Not so much as a brass farthing. He'd said that to her too. It was clear she hated to be the object of anyone's charity, or to accept charity for anyone else she knew who felt the same way as she did about it. Unfortunately for Kate, the little woman seemed possessed of a determination equal to her own.

'I won't take any money from Mr Gunn, Kate, and there's an end to it.'

'All right.' The reluctant response and the frown gave way to an apologetic smile. 'Dinna get me wrong, Mrs Henderson. It's real good o' you tae think o' him. I'm sure he'll be able to make use o' the coat.' She turned to Richard. 'Do ye no' think so, Mr Hope?'

Mr Hope. She shouldn't have called him that. Since he had referred to her by her first name, she should have addressed him by his. Since he had gone to some trouble not to look like the wealthy young man he was, there was nothing wrong with him calling her Kate, and nothing wrong with her calling him Richard.

On the other hand, he had admitted to the bookseller's wife – possibly when he needn't have done so – that he had been a guest at a party in the New Town. Since she knew about Alan Gunn's new job, it was more than likely she knew who had secured the position for him, although that didn't necessarily mean this little Mrs Henderson knew quite how far away Richard Hope was from being an impoverished student. He ran a hand through his hair. This was all so bloody complicated.

On the other hand, why the devil *shouldn't* he be sitting here talking with Kate Dunbar? They weren't doing anything wrong and he didn't see why he should be made to feel as though he was up to no good here. He lifted his chin. 'I'm sure Mr Gunn will appreciate a smart coat,' he said, mentally kicking himself for not having thought about that. He could surely have found Mr Gunn a smart coat. 'I believe he is to be presented to the king's physician at some point during the royal visit.'

'You are *au fait* with the plans for that, sir?'

'Isn't everybody?' he asked with a smile. *Try charm, Richard. It doesn't often fail you.* 'The news-sheets have been full of it ever since it was announced.'

Charm had failed him this time. Peggy Henderson's eyes were as full of suspicion as the news-sheets were of the plans for the king's visit. Kate's eyes were troubled, and he thought he could see a plea in them.

'Do you want me to go?'

He felt desolate when she nodded but if that was what she wanted there was nothing else for it. It was pretty clear the bookseller's wife wasn't going anywhere in a hurry.

'Mrs Henderson,' he said, making his bow to her before offering the same courtesy to Kate. 'I shall see you and Andrew and Mr Gunn's family this coming Sunday as arranged, I hope?'

Kate didn't answer, only continued to look at him with that mute appeal in her eyes. Did she really want him to go? Torn, he looked again at Peggy Henderson.

'Mr Hope,' she said, her voice very cool. 'Please do not let us further detain you.'

Richard was passing the Theatre Royal and almost over the bridge before his brain cleared. Why the fuck had he allowed himself to be dismissed like a servant? And what fucking business was it of the bookseller's wife if he and Kate Dunbar were seeing one another? How dare she assume, as she obviously did, that his intentions were dishonourable?

Damn Mrs Busybody Henderson's eyes. Damn them a hundred times over. He was honest enough to allow another thought to form. The bookseller's wife's right to interfere derived from Kate herself. It was obvious she cared what the little woman thought of her, valued her good opinion. So if he wanted to keep seeing Kate, he had to make his case to her mentor and self-appointed guardian.

If he wanted to keep on seeing Kate.

He hadn't planned on writing what he had on the slate. The words had spilt over out of the argument. No, that was wrong. The words had spilt over out of his emotions. They were what he genuinely felt. He was in love. He really was in love – with a girl who worked in an oyster cellar. Bloody hell.

As if that wasn't enough, he'd fallen in love with a virtuous girl. Pure and innocent. A virgin. She wasn't going to agree to become his mistress. Not in a million years.

This had to be one of the most stupid things he'd ever done in his entire life. Standing in front of the Theatre Royal, other pedestrians grumbling because they had to walk around him, it occurred to Richard that he and Kate hardly knew one another. They had first met only a couple of weeks ago. How the hell could he be feeling like this about a girl he barely knew?

He glanced up at the theatre's elegant neo-classical frontage. Maybe he was fooling himself, as he had done with the two actresses. Maybe for the sake both of Kate Dunbar and himself he should keep walking and hereafter, as much as humanly possible, avoid the Old Town, do his best never to see her again.

Then again, maybe he should stop breathing.

CHAPTER TWENTY-SEVEN

Peggy Henderson slid onto the high stool behind the counter just as the bell on the shop door jangled. 'Mr Hope,' she said, pronouncing his name in that cool tone of voice to which he was already becoming accustomed. 'How may I help you?'

He'd been rehearsing a little speech on his brief journey back across the North Bridge. The clever words flew out of his head in the face of Peggy Henderson's all too obvious hostility.

'There are things I w-want to do for K-Kate,' he stammered. 'Will you p-please help me d-do them?'

'Things you want to do for Kate?'

He was in no state to watch his words. 'I'd like to rent her rooms somewhere. Buy her some nice clothes. Get her—'

Get her and her brother out of those foul vaults under the South Bridge. That was what he'd been going to say. He wasn't given the chance.

Sucking in a breath, Peggy Henderson slid off the stool, lifted the flap at the end of the counter and marched round to stand in front of him. 'Do you know what I'd like, Mr Hope? For you to leave these premises forthwith. I think you've mistaken what kind of business I'm in.'

'Mrs Henderson—'

She spoke over him, as though she hadn't heard him. 'I'd also like you to leave Kate alone. Not see her again. I don't suppose you've given any thought as to how much damage you might be doing to her reputation?'

She had pulled herself up to her full height during this little speech. That wasn't very impressive but she was: quite daunting. Only he couldn't allow himself to be daunted. He had to stand his ground.

'Mrs Henderson.' He had removed the little knitted hat as he had come into the shop. Now, thinking how best to phrase this, he ran a hand through his hair. 'Mrs Henderson, have you never said the wrong thing?'

'Many times. But you said exactly what you meant there, I think.' Leaning past him, she pulled the shop door open, allowing the sounds of the street to float in. The rumble of carriage wheels on the causeway. A snatch of conversation as two women walked past. 'Please leave, Mr Hope.'

'Mrs Henderson, you don't understand.'

'I think I understand only too well.'

Richard kicked the door shut with his foot. 'Excuse me, Mrs Henderson, but I know you don't. I realise how what I said a moment ago must have sounded.'

'Do you?'

'None better. But you did not let me finish what I was saying. I mean Kate no harm. I do not want her to be damaged or hurt in any way by her association with me. Quite the opposite. I want to help her. And Andrew.' His smile flashed briefly. 'The two of them go together, do they not? I am also doing everything I can not to damage Kate's reputation.' He drew one hand down his tall body, indicating his clothes. 'That's why I dress like this when I go to see her.'

'Och, Mr Hope! Are you really so naïve as to believe that a mere change of apparel will disguise who you are and what you are?'

'It has served me pretty well thus far,' he told her earnestly.

'Even one of my closest friends did not recognise me in these clothes. I am coming to believe that how we are dressed makes a huge difference to how other people treat us.'

''Tis an interesting observation,' Peggy Henderson allowed. 'Although I still wonder how long it will be before the people around Kate become curious and make it their business to find out something about you. At which point you will damage her reputation merely by being who you are. When a young gentleman of fashion manifests an interest in a girl occupying a much lower station in life than his own, conclusions are drawn and tongues wag. You must know that.'

'As well as my garb when I visit Kate, I am also doing my utmost not to draw attention to myself as a *young gentleman of fashion.*'

The little woman's eyes narrowed. 'You say those words with some distaste.'

'Meeting Kate and her brother and Mr Gunn and his family has given me much pause for thought. Made me think about a lot of things.'

'Such as?' Peggy Henderson demanded.

'About how ill-divided the world is, for a start. About how unfair life is.'

'You should talk to my husband.'

'Should I?'

'Aiblins. Mr Hope, if you have recognised how ill-divided the world is, you must see that it is impossible for you and Kate to meet on anything approaching an equal level. That you have by far the upper hand in any relationship you have or might have with her.'

'I would not have it so.'

'But it *is* so. What is there between Kate and you?'

'Nothing improper.'

'What, then?'

He lifted his gaze, looking over her head towards the back of the shop. Feeling a tug on his sleeve, he looked down again. The bookseller's wife pulled him round so their positions were reversed, him standing now with his back to the interior of the shop.

'I saw what you wrote on the slate,' she murmured.

He felt the blood drain from his face. Through the window in the door he observed the people who at that moment were walking past the shop. An elderly man raised his top hat in greeting to someone on the other side of the road. Behind him, out on the cobbles of South Bridge Street, an open carriage drawn by a pair of handsome greys trotted past. For a few seconds the clip-clop of the horses' hooves filled the bookshop. As the sound diminished it was replaced in Richard's ears by the rustling of skirts. His interrogator was adjusting her stance.

'You have gone quite pale, Mr Hope.'

'I know it.' Looking down once more into Peggy Henderson's face, he wondered if he was imagining a gentler tone of voice.

'Is that because you know how sacred those words are which you inscribed upon the slate? Words which should never be written or spoken unless they are genuinely felt and meant? Sincerely, and from the bottom of one's heart. Never to be used cynically by privileged young men who always get what they want and have no conscience as to how they do so?'

'All of that,' Richard replied. 'And because I have scared myself by writing them and meaning them. Terrified myself, in fact. But I do sincerely feel and mean them, Mrs Henderson. From the bottom of my heart.' His voice had grown husky. 'I suppose you are going to tell me I cannot possibly feel this way about Kate when I have known her for such a short length of time.'

'I would be a hypocrite if I did.'

'You and Mr Henderson had not known one another long before you fell in love?' he asked eagerly.

'Love at first sight,' Peggy confirmed. 'I never believed in it until I met Nathaniel. Do you think Kate returns your feelings?'

'I hope she does. Oh God, I really hope she does!'

'I should think if you really cared for Kate you would hope the opposite. Nothing honest or decent can come of this and you have just told me you know that. Och, Mr Hope, I am so sorry.'

Richard raised one hand and wiped away the tears that had sprung to them. The bookseller's wife laid one small hand on his sleeve. There was no mistaking the gentleness in her voice now.

'Must I?'

'Yes.' She gave his arm a little shake. 'For Kate's sake, you must.'

'If that is how it must be,' he replied, 'then at the very least I should like to leave her with a good memory of me. And her and Andrew both in a better state than I found them. I had thought perhaps to buy him some special shoes.'

'Special shoes?'

'One of them built-up,' he explained, 'to take account of the shortness of his right leg, so he might walk more easily. There is a shoemaker I know through the university who does such work. But there is something even more important I should like to do for him – and for Kate too.'

'Which is?'

'Given the opportunity, I am sure they will progress well in reading and writing. Both of them are intelligent. I do not see why it should not be possible for Andrew to apply for a bursary which would allow him to attend George Heriot's. They take some poor boys each year, as I am sure you know. They must be either orphans or the sons of widows.' His head snapped up. 'What was that noise?'

'Nothing. Go on with what you were saying.'

'You will think I am suggesting this as an excuse to allow me to continue to spend time with Kate. Maybe I am at that. But, Mrs Henderson, I believe that if I continue to play the part of tutor over the summer I can make a real difference to both her and her brother's life. A few months, madam, that is all I am asking for. Until the end of the summer. Mrs Henderson,' he pleaded, 'between us both might we not contrive to do some good here?'

Peggy Henderson's eyes flickered to one of the tall bookcases behind Richard's back, which projected into the centre of the shop, forming a bay.

'I think you had better come out now, lass.'

CHAPTER TWENTY-EIGHT

As she emerged from behind the bookcase, Richard turned and looked at her. 'You heard all of that, Kate?'

She nodded, not trusting herself to speak. She had not only heard it, she had seen it too, peeking through the gap between the tops of the books and the next shelf up. Although his back had been to her, she had watched his hand go up to wipe his eyes, observed Mrs Henderson comforting him.

Awed by this evidence of how deeply his feelings for her ran, she was aware of a wild impulse to run across the bookshop floor and fling her arms about him – and knew that could only make matters worse than they already were. Och, but when he spoke, he sounded so sad.

'I've made even more of a hash of this than I thought. I don't suppose you're going to allow me to buy you so much as a handkerchief. Although you might let me kit Andrew out. If it's for him, you'll put your pride in your pocket, won't you?'

The words ran off her tongue before she could stop them. 'I like the sound o' these special shoes. I like the idea o' him going to school even more. You really think it might be possible?' Oh, in the name of God, why was she asking him that? None of this was going to happen – not with the plans her uncle had. Och, but it was a dazzling prospect all the same!

'Let us sit down,' Peggy Henderson said. 'I shall make some tea and we shall discuss this like civilised people. Mr Hope,' she added, 'you might like to know that when I brought Kate up from the Cowgate she was very anxious to impress upon me that I should not think badly of you. She has told me – as did Mr Gunn himself – how you secured the position at the Old Physic Garden for him and how you have worked hard to prepare lessons for the children and herself. Kate also tells me you have not taken advantage of her in any way, that you have attempted neither to cajole nor coerce her into doing anything she does not want to do.'

Richard blushed and stammered something about respect. Peggy Henderson surveyed him with a steely eye. 'It's a good word. Whilst I am making the tea, leaving the two of you alone here, I expect you to continue to show that respect to Kate. Is that understood?'

'Of course.' Watching as his face grew even rosier, Kate allowed herself to be ushered into one of the chairs set around the large square table that occupied much of the middle of the floor. Richard was invited to sit down on the opposite side of it. In the midst of her distress and confusion, Kate found it within herself to see the humour in the situation. Mrs Henderson was putting them well out of reach of one another.

'I shall not be long,' that lady said as she glided towards the back of the shop. 'And I would further point out that a customer may step in from the street at any moment.' As she disappeared, Kate and Richard gazed at one another across the piles of books that separated them.

'What does she think we're going to do?' he asked, running a finger along the inside of his shirt collar.

'I canna imagine,' Kate said, and asked another question she knew she should not ask. 'What did you write on the slate?'

'You must know by now.'

'Mrs Henderson turned you round when she asked you about that.'

'So she did. But I'm guessing there's nothing wrong with your hearing.'

'There's not,' Kate agreed. She should let this go. She knew she should. It would be so much better for both of them if these words were not said. It would be much better for both of them if these words were *never* said.

'Scared to ask?' Richard enquired, his lovely voice very gentle.

Kate nodded. He could not know just how scared she was to ask. He could not know all the reasons why she was so scared.

'I was scared to write it,' he confessed. 'I'm even more scared to say it.'

'I wouldna have thought someone like you would be scared o' anything.'

'Oh, I'm scared of lots of things, Kate.' Miles away from her on the other side of the big table, he looked like a starving man who could see food mere tantalising inches beyond his reach. 'Most of all at this moment, I'm scared that when I walk out of here I'm never going to see you again. I can't bear the thought of that, Kate. I really can't!'

'Och, Richard...' she breathed, 'I canna bear the thought o' no' seeing you again either!'

In an instant the two of them were on their feet. Yet when they met a split second later, halfway round the table, she put her hands against his chest and held him off. 'No,' she said breathlessly, 'we mustn't do this! And you mustn't kiss me, Richard, you really must not kiss me!'

'I can't *not* kiss you!' he cried. 'If I don't kiss you right now I'm going to explode! Or shrivel up and die,' he added huskily, his eyes fixed on her face. 'It's that serious, Kate. A matter of life and death.'

'Och, Richard,' she said again, but could not find it in herself to resist when he put his fingertips under her chin and raised her face to his. His kiss was gentle, seeking a response but not forcing one. How like him to allow her to make the choice about what happened next, always supposing any of this had ever been a matter of choice. As the hand wrapped around the two of hers loosened, her fingers relaxed against his chest and her lips parted beneath his.

'Lemons,' he said when the lingering kiss at last ended. 'You even taste of them.'

She stared at him. Then her eyes filled up with tears. He drew her close and pulled her head onto his shoulder. 'Cry if it helps,' he said gruffly.

'Tears don't help,' she sobbed. 'Tears dinna do anything!'

'They're a release,' he said. 'A sort of cleansing. So cry if you want to. But don't worry about any of this. We'll find a way to be together, Kate, I know we will.'

'Just because you say so?' she managed.

'Just because I love you. That's what I wrote on the slate, Kate.'

'I'm not worthy of you, Richard.'

'You've got that the wrong way round, Kate. It's me who's not worthy of you. It's me who's at your feet. Whatever the world or society thinks.'

She buried her wet face in his jacket and wondered what he would say if she told him what she had really meant. 'You said something,' she mumbled. 'Something about renting rooms for me.'

'It's seemed like a nice idea at the time,' he said with a wry laugh. 'Mrs Henderson's spiked my guns there, I fear. Or maybe it's you who's done that.'

Kate lifted her head, not understanding, and raised one hand to rub away the tears that were preventing her from seeing him properly.

'Allow me,' he murmured.

Her eyes fluttered shut. 'There,' he said when he was done. 'As my nurse used to say, now you have a nice clean face.'

A nice clean face. Tears are a release. A sort of cleansing. She allowed all of those words to travel around her mind. Then, without opening her eyes, she asked, 'Would you wipe my mouth, too?'

'If that is your desire,' he murmured, and drew his fingertips across her top and bottom lip in turn. 'And now you have a nice clean mouth.'

She opened her eyes and gazed up at him.

'You've never lain with a man, Kate, have you?'

Her face flamed. He frowned, muttered, 'I beg your pardon. That was coarsely put,' and rephrased the question. 'What I mean is, Kate...am I your first sweetheart?'

'Does it matter so much to you?'

'Yes,' he said, his voice laced with a mockery she guessed with sudden insight was directed against himself, 'and no. Will you answer my question?'

She could not drop her gaze. Do that and she might as well tell him the truth. Give him an honest answer and she didn't doubt that this would end right now. He would be shocked and disgusted and he would recoil from her. And what would Michael Graham do if she allowed a prize like Richard Hope to slip from her grasp? *A matter of life and death.* Those words too were echoing inside her head, wrapping themselves around a vision of her wee brother, piercing her heart with fear.

Yet that wasn't why she gave the young man studying her so intently the answer she did, and when she spoke she told him nothing but the truth. 'Yes, Richard,' she said, 'you are my first sweetheart.'

'Then I'm honoured.' He took his hands from her face,

stepped back and with formal courtesy raised her hands to his lips and pressed the lightest of kisses on the back of each one. 'I love you, Kate.' He gave a soft laugh. 'There. That's me said it twice. It's getting easier each time.'

Despite the laugh, despite the relieved words, she felt him tense. He was, she realised, waiting for her to give those three little words back to him.

What was it he had said about it being impossible to call words back once they were spoken aloud? She had never expected to say these words to any man. Saying them would take her into the unknown, carry her out onto an uncharted ocean, and him along with her. There were dangerous rocks ahead. Since he must remain unaware of them, it was only her who could steer their fragile little craft safely past those reefs.

She had no idea how she was going to achieve that remarkable feat. She was pretty certain that sooner or later the two of them were going to have to walk away from one another. Could she make the inevitable heartache any less if she stopped this from going too deep now, hope that when he was an old man he could look back with a smile on the summer he had spent with a lassie who worked in an oyster cellar?

And what about the heartache he would feel if Michael Graham forced her into betraying him? What would happen then? Could she put paid to her uncle's callous plan if she simply agreed with Richard that he could rent rooms for her? It would get her and Andrew out of the South Bridge and away from The Pearl Fisher, out of the dark underworld through which her uncle walked like a malevolent shadow.

Mrs Henderson's spiked my guns there, I fear. Or maybe it's you who's done that.

She realised now what Richard had meant. He thought she was an innocent, still an untouched maid, and that he could not therefore ask her to become his mistress.

'Kate,' he said, transferring his hands to her shoulders and pushing her far enough back that they could see one another clearly. 'Say something. If it's not going to be the words I want to hear then at least put me out of my misery. Tell me there's no hope. Tell me you don't want to have anything more to do with me. Tell me it's impossible for us to continue to see each another. Tell me to go and jump off the North Bridge if you like, only for pity's sake tell me something!'

He looked more thirsty than hungry now, as though she were a long cool drink of water and if he didn't drink it, he would die. Kate gulped in a breath and threw fear, shame, common sense and caution to the winds. 'I love you, Richard. Och, I love you too!'

Coming through into the shop a moment later, Peggy Henderson was obliged to take six steps backwards, lift a spoon from her tea tray and throw it onto the floor.

CHAPTER TWENTY-NINE

'Until the end of the summer?' Peggy queried.

The three of them were sitting around the table, Richard and Kate together on one side of it and Peggy presiding over the tea tray at the top.

'Yes,' Richard Hope said. 'I shall continue to teach Andrew and the children – ' his voice softened ' – and see Kate – until the end of the summer.'

'By the end of the summer you mean when you resume your studies at the university after the long vacation?'

'Exactly,' he said, taking the cup and saucer she was holding out to him and placing them on the table.

But will it not make it so much more difficult for you two to part the longer you continue to see one another? The question hovered on her lips – and stayed there, unspoken.

The young man raised his cup to his lips, blew on it, and took a sip of Peggy's finest Darjeeling. He was using his left hand to do so but she was pretty sure he wasn't left-handed. She had not only seen what he had written on the slate, she had also seen him rub the words off it.

His right hand was currently not available to him because it was holding Kate's. The two of them thought they were concealing that from her by means of the folds of Kate's black skirt but the angle of their arms made it impossible for an observant woman not to realise what they were up to.

Sweet. Very, very sweet. But sad too. This love affair was doomed. How could it be otherwise? Something else hadn't escaped Peggy's notice. Kate had lifted her own tea only after she'd darted a few glances at both her hostess and Richard Hope and seen how it was done. Peggy had realised too late that this was probably the first time in her life Kate Dunbar had drunk tea. 'Twas a beverage rather too expensive for the poor.

The lass could learn how to drink tea. She could be dressed up in a pretty gown. She could be encouraged to mind her *p*s and *q*s when she spoke. Peggy Henderson didn't doubt she would be clever enough to pick up all of these accomplishments and more. But her family background would remain what it was. There was a gulf a thousand miles wide between these two young people and no engineer had yet come up with the plans for a bridge which could cross it.

'You really think Andrew could go in for a bursary at George Heriot's?' Kate sounded awe-struck by the very idea.

'I'm sure he could,' Richard said warmly. 'Especially if we can get his reading and writing to a good standard before he even applies.'

Kate turned to Peggy. 'Do you think so too, Mrs Henderson?'

'He is a very bright boy,' Peggy replied. 'But would you find it difficult to reconcile your aunt to doing without the wages he earns at the saddler's?'

She regretted the words the instant they were out of her mouth. They made Kate bite her lip and dimmed the light in her bonnie eyes. So Peggy decided not to mention the second problem that had occurred to her – that Heriot's probably set some store by the respectability of their scholars and those scholar's homes. She doubted a vault in the South Bridge with an aunt and uncle who kept an oyster cellar would qualify.

'Your uncle will be an ally,' Richard said. 'He has been very happy to help with our little Sabbath School, has he not?'

Kate said nothing in response to that, only gave her would-be lover a swift little smile. Peggy's mind was still running on unbridgeable gulfs. Education could be a bridge, for a boy at any rate. A woman might marry her way up the social scale but never when the divide was as wide as this one.

She suspected Richard Hope's parents already had a suitable bride picked out for him. As, despite his obvious feelings for the lass whose hand he was holding, she suspected he himself was too much a product of his class for it to even cross his mind that he might marry a girl like Kate.

She didn't blame him for that. Like her husband, Peggy Henderson held Radical political views. As Richard Hope himself appeared to have but recently discovered, she knew very well that the world was ill-divided. She believed the laws, social divisions and attitudes of that world needed fundamental and wide-ranging reform.

Betrayed though they might have been, she believed too in the principles of the French Revolution. Liberty. Equality. Fraternity. A practical and far-sighted woman, she also knew it was all going to take generations to achieve.

She was acquainted with two people who had, as society saw it, married beneath their stations, one a man and one a woman. In Peggy's own view, each of them had made a huge, quixotic gesture in the name of love. Ten years on in one case, five in the other, one of those marriages was strong and loving, the other as unhappy as a marriage could be.

Cut off by his family and former friends, neither he nor his wife received at any of their social gatherings, the husband in that partnership had become bitter and angry. Even in the first case, where the wife was of a much higher social class than her husband, there were problems, Peggy knew. One of the young woman's sisters visited her from time to time but that was the only contact she now had with her family.

The girl often looked so wistful, not to mention worn out, small wonder when she was running a house and caring for four children without the army of cooks and maids and nurses who had helped bring her up. Her own mother spoke proudly of her other grandchildren, but never of these four. There had been an awful incident when the young woman had taken them to see their grandmother and been kept standing on the doorstep before being refused admittance to what had been her childhood home.

Kind-hearted Peggy, who longed so much for children of her own, had struggled to comprehend the cruelty of that. How could a mother refuse to receive her own daughter and grandchildren? Rigidity of belief, she supposed, an absolute conviction that society was ordered along God-given lines and anyone who crossed those threatened the stability of the whole structure.

Kate Dunbar and Richard Hope stood at much more extreme points of the social scale than the couples of whom Peggy was thinking, so extreme that even to contemplate marriage between such a pair was ridiculous. Besides which, fierce though it was, it would seem this fire had flared up only recently.

Aiblins it would burn itself out. Aiblins she would be better advised helping it do so by putting no obstacles in its path rather than in trying to persuade them to part now. Absence might only make the heart grow fonder. Adversity might only make them more determined to continue seeing one another.

Feeling for the young couple sitting sipping her tea, Peggy gazed sympathetically at them. Responding to that, Richard Hope was all youthful and handsome eagerness. She could quite see why Kate had lost her heart to him. 'You will help us, Mrs Henderson?'

Peggy lowered her tea cup from her lips and came to a decision. 'On one condition, Mr Hope.'

'Anything, madam. Absolutely anything that you stipulate.'

'That's a very rash statement, Mr Hope,' Peggy said with a wry smile. 'You do not yet know what my condition is.'

'I don't care. Tell me what you require of me and I shall do it.'

Out of the corner of her eye, Peggy was aware that he had taken a firmer grip of Kate's hand, the folds of the lass's skirt adjusting themselves in response. 'Very well,' she said crisply. 'What I require is a solemn promise that when you and Kate part at the end of the summer, she will – in your own words – be in no way damaged by her association with you. That you will not leave her in a worse state than you found her.'

'Mrs Henderson!' he protested. Funny how strait-laced the young could be sometimes, in speech if not in action. Kate was blushing. So was he.

'We all know to what I am referring. Do I have your promise, Mr Hope? Your solemn promise?'

His blush was already fading, leaving him grave and composed. 'If she will only allow me to do so, I promise – in my own words – that I will leave Kate in a better state than I found her.' He smiled. 'She will surely also allow me to buy her a pretty gown or two.'

'No, I won't,' came the immediate response.

'Oh.' He tilted his head back. *Coupe sauvage*. That was what you called the style in which his hair was cut. It was the very height of fashion. 'But you will permit me to buy these special shoes for Andrew?'

'I'd love it gin ye did that, Richard.' Kate's voice was thick with emotion. 'It would mak' such a difference tae him if he could walk more easily.'

'He could also do with some smart clothes if he is to apply for a bursary at Heriot's. Wouldn't you say so, Mrs Henderson?'

'I would.' Peggy perked up. Richard Hope had just injected a blessed note of humour into this poignant conversation. She could see exactly where he was going. Putting her brother first as usual, Kate clearly couldn't.

'You really think he might stand a chance of getting in?' she asked, her eyes shining.

'I do. Especially if I give him extra tutoring during the week as well as on Sundays. Would he be too tired for me to come to The Pearl Fisher after he finishes work? Let us say on two evenings each week?'

Kate shook her head. 'I'm sure he wouldn't be but The Pearl Fisher's maybe no' the best place. It's gets gey noisy in the evenings.'

'We'll find a quiet corner somewhere. I'm really looking forward to seeing him in his new shoes and clothes. You won't know him, Kate. He'll be quite the fine young gentleman.'

'He's going to look so smart,' she agreed.

Amused by how such a shrewd girl wasn't seeing this one coming, Peggy was diverted enough to bat the ball back to Richard Hope. 'Everyone's beginning to talk about how Edinburgh should be smartly turned out for the king's visit. Everyone as well dressed as they can afford to be. Am I not right, Mr Hope?'

He angled his head so Kate couldn't see one side of his face and winked at Peggy. Aye, she could definitely see why the lass had fallen for him. 'Perfectly right, Mrs Henderson. There are to be parades and festivities for all. I should think Andrew will enjoy those, wouldn't you, Kate?'

'Oh, aye. They say everyone is to be let off work so they can be out and about for the parades and things. Everyone in their Sunday best—' She stopped short, realisation dawning at last.

Richard Hope threw his tousled head back, laughed, and seized the prize. 'You'll want to be out and about with him, Kate, won't you? If he's wearing smart new clothes you'll have to be dressed to match. Wouldn't you agree?'

She narrowed her eyes at him. 'Think you're *so* clever, don't you?'

'Modesty forbids my replying to that question, Miss Dunbar.' He bathed her in a smile that would have melted the stoniest of hearts. 'Does this mean I get to buy you at least one pretty gown?'

'I dinna have anywhere tae keep a pretty gown.'

Watching them, Peggy Henderson saw more here even than young love and physical desire. There was a growing affection too, fond and teasing and deepening before her very eyes. The poor things.

'You may keep your new gown here, Kate. And if you wish, Mr Hope, and if Kate's aunt and uncle agree, you may tutor Andrew in the bookshop in the evenings.'

Now both of them were looking at her as though she were their fairy godmother. The poor things, Peggy thought again. The poor wee things.

CHAPTER THIRTY

Until the end of the summer. This afternoon in the bookshop he had plucked the words from somewhere deep within his frozen brain. Sitting up late in his bedchamber that evening, Richard tried saying them out loud.

'Until the end of the summer.'

Was that a long time or a short time? He wasn't sure. The days were warming up now, but it remained chilly enough when the sun went down on these May evenings for him to need a fire in his bedroom. He was sitting in front of it now, in his nightshirt and flowing wine-red dressing gown, his long legs stretched out to the dying embers.

He was musing about the difference between his and Kate's lives. Late though it was, she was probably still serving customers at The Pearl Fisher. Since he'd left her there this afternoon he'd done very little. Endured a formal dinner with his parents and too many guests. Had a bath. Thought about Kate.

He stood up, walked across to the long windows that looked out over Princes Street and drew back the curtains. Above the dark and brooding bulk of Edinburgh Castle the stars were unusually brilliant tonight. Fewer fires burning in the Old Town, he supposed. Now that spring had arrived, the poor at least would be economising on fuel.

He wondered if Kate might have finished her work and be out in the Cowgate gazing up at the stars as he was. Seconds later he was telling himself he was a bloody idiot. Of course she wasn't. Her aunt would have her clearing up and wiping tables and then she'd be packed off to bed, only to rise at the crack of dawn tomorrow morning and start all over again. God, but the woman got her pound of flesh from her niece. He wondered how much she paid Kate. He was pretty sure it wouldn't be much.

When he had accompanied Kate back down to the Cowgate to put the new proposal forward, Michael Graham – affable man that he was – had been all for it. His wife had wanted to know how much this extra tutoring was going to cost. When Richard assured her he didn't want any recompense for it, she had immediately raised another objection.

'How are we supposed tae manage withoot the bairn helping?'

'It's only two evenings,' Kate had said. 'I can easily do his work as well as my own.'

Not happy about that at all but realising there probably wasn't any alternative, Richard had forced himself to bite his tongue. She had already asked him not to mention the prospect of Andrew going to George Heriot's. He presumed that would be another battle she would have to fight with her aunt.

Richard gripped the edge of one of the brocade curtains. It wasn't right that a girl like Kate should be buried down there under the South Bridge working like a slave, while he who did so little lived in this beautiful house and led such a comfortable life.

He had this spacious bedchamber, for a start. She must sleep in one of those gloomy vaults she and her brother had guided him around. God Almighty. As dark and as chilly as the grave. Probably infested by mice. She had spoken of protecting her things from the creatures. With not even a tiny sky-light for her to look out of and dream her dreams gazing up at the stars as he was doing now, wishing on the brightest one he could find.

He wished he could have her with him now. She could have a

bath. She'd enjoy that. She liked to be clean. He had a hip bath which was filled by pitchers of hot water carried up to his dressing room every evening. It took several servants and two or three runs up the back stairs by each of them to fill it. He had to sit in it with his knees drawn up. There would be a lot more space when it was only occupied by Kate.

He would help her wash herself. Oh, but that was a lovely thought…and an arousing one. Smoothing a soapy cloth over the curve of her breasts, raising bubbles, making her laugh by dabbing those bubbles on her nose, making her sigh by rubbing them over her nipples, watching those stand up against her creamy skin, making her sigh again by sliding his warm and soapy hand between her legs. Making himself sigh. *Oh… And oh again…*

When she'd had a long enough soak, he would lift her out, wrap her in a warm towel and carry her to his big, comfortable bed and make love to her. He'd have to leave the towel beneath her, because of the blood. She was pure and untouched and when he made love to her for the first time she would bleed. He was a medical student. He knew the theory. He understood the mechanics.

This was the first time he'd thought about the reality of a girl losing her virginity. It filled him with a strange mixture of emotions. There was passion and desire, of course, raw and hungry. There was huge tenderness too, though, and a real awe. It was such a big step for any woman to take, and an irrevocable one – and he had as good as promised not to try to persuade Kate to take it.

A tear slid down his cheek. Blotting it with his fingertips, he stared at them for a moment. He had shed tears this afternoon too, in front of the bookseller's wife. Before today he hadn't cried since he was a boy, upset by the breaking of some toy or other.

Little amuses bairnies, and littler gars them greet.

That had been another of his nurse's proverbs. She'd had as many in Scots as in English. Only what he had wept over today wasn't little. He loved Kate Dunbar. She loved him. She too had wept today. Practical, no-nonsense Kate had shed tears. And they could be together only until the end of the summer?

He drew in a breath, found the brightest star again and wished with all his might for what he knew he could not have. Lowering his gaze, he directed it towards the unseen corner of South Bridge Street and the High Street. 'Why did I agree with you, fierce little Mrs Henderson? Why did I agree with you that I can't have Kate?'

Was it any consolation that he could at least feel noble about this? Not bloody much. *Until the end of the summer.* It wasn't enough. A lifetime wouldn't be enough. There had to be a way for Kate Dunbar and him to be together, there simply had to be.

Nothing was sure. He knew that. The road in front of them was rough and muddy, full of twists and turns. Yet somewhere deep inside him a fierce and glorious fire blazed into life, warming him to his very bones. She loved him. *Kate Dunbar loved him!*

Michael Graham had sent his wife to bed with the assurance that 'me and the lassie'll soon tidy up' and Kate had taken the key to the vault from its hook under the bar and handed it to Andrew along with a crusie lamp and told him she'd be along in a wee minute. Now she and her uncle were alone together in the tavern, him on the outside of the bar and her behind it.

'Like tae tell me whit the *fuck* you were playing at this efterneen?'

Kate lifted a cloth and wiped a tray she'd already cleaned twice before she spoke. 'It worked, didn't it?'

'You trying tae tell me ye provoked that wee *contritong* ye had wi' him? A lovers' quarrel tae make him even keener on ye?'

'Aiblins I'm no' as daft as ye think I am.'

'So ye've seen sense?'

'I suppose ye could say that.' She'd been readying herself for this all evening, and now she was going to direct this conversation where she wanted it to go. 'It'll hae tae be a long game, though. Like ye said. Maybe a month or twa.'

'So the bairn'll get his lessons and you'll likely get some wee folderols along the way?'

Kate shrugged. 'Anything wrong wi' me wanting something for masel oot o' this?'

She got no answer to that, only another question. 'Whit aboot yon Mrs Henderson? Where does she come intae this?'

'She's trying tae protect my virtue,' Kate responded, her voice expressionless.

'That's a good one.' Michael Graham let out a guffaw. 'Did ye no' tell her that horse bolted lang syne?'

'I'd hardly dae that. She can be useful tae us too.' God forgive her. God forgive her for speaking like this about the woman who'd been so kind to her today, who'd been so kind to her and Andrew every other day she'd known her.

'How dae ye work that oot? I dinna think she's likely tae help ye become Mr Hope's hure.'

Kate let his words wash over her. The time was coming when she would no longer have to put up with his foul coarseness and the vile names by which he invariably addressed her. 'She'll no' ken aboot that until it's ower late tae prevent it. And me being able tae meet him at the bookshop's going tae help. I canna gie in tae him straight away, can I? He'd smell a rat gin I did that.'

'So the young gentleman does think ye're pure and innocent? That's another good one. So,' he continued expansively, 'once this month or twa is by, ye'll succumb tae his blandishments?'

'That's aboot it, aye.' She met dark eyes which gleamed with malice and greed. 'In my ain time and where I choose for it tae happen. You'll no' be there.'

Michael Graham inclined his head to one side, and his voice grew dangerously low. 'Dae ye tell me that, wee Kate?'

'I do tell ye that.' The rags of this plan had begun to form in her head while she was still in the bookshop. Now she had it all worked out. By the time this month or two was past, she and Andrew were going to be out of this place. They'd both be able to read and write by then and there must be a way she could get herself a better job. Mrs Henderson would help her do that, she was sure of it. The bookseller's wife had been so kind today, so very, very kind. Kate lifted her chin.

'I've something else tae tell ye. You'll leave me alone from now on. Like I'll keep the key tae the vault from now on.'

It took him a moment. Then he lunged across the bar at her. She stepped back in the nick of time and the arm reaching for her hit the wood with a crack that made her eyes water as much as his. She waited till he had worked his way through a string of curses.

'Were ye no' listening tae me this morning?' he growled. 'When I said whit I did aboot your wee brother?' Her uncle was cradling one arm with the other now, his face etched in lines of pain. Yet there was triumph there too. He thought he had hit her weak spot.

He was wrong. Andrew was her strength. Kate lifted the big cooking knife she had laid on the bar in readiness. She'd been rehearsing this moment in her mind all evening too.

'Ye wouldna *bloody* dare!' scoffed Michael Graham.

'I wouldna use it on you.' She spoke quietly, and she was very composed. 'Gin onything happened tae Andrew there would be nothing mair you or onybody else could dae tae me. I'd turn this knife on myself then. Dinna think I wouldna. Ye'd hae nae bait tae catch Richard Hope then. Forbye which, once folk started asking questions aboot why I'd ta'en my ain life – and they would – it wouldna be long afore ye were twisting in the wind along in the Grassmarket.'

She had shaken him, she could see that. When this thought had flown into her head a few hours ago it had shaken her too. Yet she knew he wouldn't give in easily and was unsurprised when he came at her from another direction, his voice a vicious hiss.

'Let me tell ye something, ye dirty wee slut. If I want ye, I'll have ye. Where I like and when I like and how I like. Up your cunt or up your arse or on your knees with my cock in your mouth like ye were this morning.' He drew his tongue around his lips. 'Can ye still taste me, pet?'

She was instantly back there, reliving everything to which he had subjected her this morning, pictures and sensations exploding in her brain. She could taste it, smell it, feel it. Used and misused as he pleased. Shamed. Humiliated. Degraded. Sullied.

Then a very strange thing happened. A different set of pictures and sensations poured into her head: Richard offering her the little skein of ribbons, announcing so cheerfully that he had asked for *all the colours of the rainbow*; Andrew bent over his letters, lost in learning; Mrs Henderson handing her a cup of tea and Kate sipping it, enjoying the hot refreshing taste on her tongue; Richard wiping her tears away, kissing her and telling her that he loved her. Cleansing her with her own tears and his gentle fingers.

And for the first time, Kate felt in her heart what she had always known in her head. The shame of all she had suffered at Michael Graham's hands over the past four years belonged to him, not her. So she did not drop her head before his leering gaze or his vile and obscene words. Instead, proud as a queen, she looked him in the eye. 'You'll no' touch me again. Not ever.'

'Says who?' came the contemptuous response. 'Your gentleman friend? The one who's daft enough tae think you're pure and innocent?'

Not daft enough. Sweet enough. Whatever she said now meant nothing, the words merely a means to an end. 'I'm the only one as can reel him in. Gin I tell him tae go away, he'll dae it. And you ken better than me how wealthy his family is.'

She could see the calculations going on behind Michael Graham's eyes as he weighed up the loss of his freedom to use her as he pleased against the prospect of easy money. She laid the blade once more against her neck. 'I keep the key. You dinna touch me again.'

Somewhere out in the Cowgate a church clock began to chime midnight. Kate hadn't heard it toll any of the previous hours but it was quiet in The Pearl Fisher now, that strange silence which settles on a place usually full of noise and activity.

Michael Graham was staring at her. She tilted the knife, felt its steel cold against her warm neck, counted the peals of the bell inside her head and waited for him to speak.

Twenty minutes later she sat on the edge of her bed in the darkness, holding the big iron key to the vault between her two hands. Greed had won. Tonight, for the first time since she had come to this awful place, she would sleep safe and she would sleep sound. The price for that was the devil's bargain she had struck with her uncle. Then again, she had no intention of keeping her side of it.

The key was warm now, heated by her hands. She slid it under her pillow and placed those warm hands on her knees. She heard

Andrew stir in his sleep but could tell from the rhythmical rise and fall of his breathing that he would not wake. Unless his nightmares disturbed him, he was a heavy sleeper. Thank God.

It was during the night, with Andrew sleeping only a few feet away, that her uncle had first raped her. She had been startled out of her own sleep by the weight of his body pressing down on hers, his brandy-laden breath spitting into her ear all the ways he would hurt her brother if she didn't let him do what he wanted to her. Afterwards he had washed her roughly with a vinegar-soaked cloth, told her she would be doing it herself the next time – *it's no' the man's job tae clear up the mess* – and left.

Her legs covered in blood and her brutalised flesh quivering in searing agony, robbed in a few horrific moments of the only treasure she possessed, Kate had bitten back the tears of shock and pain until she was sure Michael Graham had gone. They were the one thing she could refuse him, the only part of herself she could withhold. Even when she did weep she had done it quietly, so as not to waken Andrew.

She never did cry until after the man who took such fiendish delight in brutally forcing himself on her had gone. Then came the night when she did not cry at all, the night she realised tears would not get Andrew and herself out of the South Bridge – that maybe nothing would. Yet hope never completely died. It was hope that – eventually – took her to the kirk, seeking there something good and true to counter-balance the degradation of what her life had become.

She had been terrified when she and Andrew first walked into the Tron, sure the tall, thin-faced minister in his black Geneva gown could see right through her, would know how sullied she was, how unworthy to enter the house of God. All through the service she kept waiting for him to stretch out his long arm and condemn her as a slut and a whore.

It had not happened. The minister had preached Jesus's message of love, forgiveness and kindness, spoken of how important it was for Christians to follow those teachings with everyone they met, and not only on the Sabbath. A few Sundays later, the Hendersons had begun speaking to Kate and Andrew.

Slowly and cautiously, in fits and starts, Kate had dared to believe that maybe she and Andrew could get away from their aunt and uncle and that she could make a different and better life for them both. Now she was daring to believe she could see the pathway unfolding in front of them – but she knew the nightmare would not really be over until they were out of this place.

She might have done that today. If Richard had asked her if he could set her up in rented rooms somewhere before Mrs Henderson had become involved in their argument, Kate knew she would have been sorely tempted to say yes.

Yet that could not happen now. They had both made that promise to Mrs Henderson. Richard himself was now convinced Kate was still a virgin, innocent and untouched. She could never let him know the truth. He would be so hurt, so disappointed.

Until the end of the summer. She wondered what was going to happen then. If they kept their promise to Mrs Henderson they would have to part. Oh God, how could she bear that? And how could she be feeling like this about a young man whom she hardly knew?

Yet in an odd way she felt as though she had known him forever. Even from the beginning, there had been a sort of recognition between them. Somehow she had also known there was much more to him than the wealthy student and young gentleman of fashion.

And he loved her. He really did love her. The knowledge warmed her to her very bones. Kate slipped beneath the covers of her bed. Within minutes she was sound asleep.

PART TWO

Summer, 1822

CHAPTER THIRTY-ONE

'You've been working hard for the past two hours, Mr Medical Student. D'ye no' think it's time ye had a wee break?'

He looked up, blinking. She was standing on the other side of the long table, holding an empty wooden tray flat against herself. She was wearing her rust-coloured bodice and black cotton skirt, her hair secured only by one of the satin ribbons he had given her, black to match her skirt, and she was a sight for sore eyes.

'I lost track of time.'

'Well,' she said, with a delightfully prim air, 'I'm right glad to see you sticking in at your studies but I'm thinking ye're maybe in need o' some sustenance. What can I get you?'

'I've got all the sustenance I need right now. As long as you stay where you are and keep smiling at me.'

'Och, you!' she said. She was always relaxed and happy in the afternoons. Richard suspected that might have something to do with her aunt taking her nap then. Kate's uncle too seemed to make himself scarce at this time of day.

'Mr Geikie's been drawing you,' she announced, laying her tray down and transferring the pewter tankard and soup plate which Richard had pushed away from his books and papers some time before. 'And ye didna even notice. Young Mr Chambers was here too, doing some more investigating for yon book he's writing aboot Edinburgh. Ye've missed him as well.'

Walter Geikie was sitting at the end of the table, his sketch pad propped up in front of him. He went nowhere without it. A well-kent figure around the Old Town, he could neither hear nor speak, a childhood illness having robbed him of both faculties. As though in compensation for the cruel trick fate had played on him, he was a gifted artist.

His subjects were the ordinary people of Edinburgh in their customary surroundings: a group of children playing in the street, women fetching water from one of the city's wells, an old couple sitting on their doorstep in the sunshine. Standing up, he tore the page from his sketch book and placed it with a flourish in front of Richard.

'It's me,' he said, looking from the paper to Walter Geikie in admiring amazement.

'Let me see.' As Kate leant over the table, the artist turned the paper towards her. 'Och, it really is you! That's a grand picture! Ye've caught him perfectly.' She laughed. 'All studious and bent over his books.' Whether Walter Geikie understood her words Richard didn't know. He was getting the enthusiasm, all right. Beaming with pleasure, he made Kate a little bow and proffered the sketch to her.

'I think he wants to make you a present of it, Kate.'

She pointed towards herself. 'For me, Mr Geikie? Am I tae tak the drawing?'

He nodded and she took it and gave him a little bow in return. 'Thank you, Mr Geikie. Thank you very much indeed.'

'He should sign it, Kate.' Richard lifted his hand and wielded an imaginary pencil and Walter Geikie took the drawing back and added his signature before returning it to her.

'Thank you,' she said again. Holding the drawing in one hand, she imitated the action of drinking with the other. She rubbed her fingers together to indicate money before passing her hand through the air in a gesture of denial. 'On the house, of course.'

The young man shook his head, drew his watch from his waistcoat pocket and pointed to it. He gathered up his belongings and took his leave of them, more smiles and bows being exchanged on all sides.

'He's a nice man,' Kate said as they watched him go.

'I'd say so. So talented too. Though why you'd want a picture of yours truly is beyond me.'

'I'd tell ye but it would only puff ye up wi' ower great a sense o' your own importance.' She indicated the two books lying open on the table and the loose sheets of paper on which Richard had been taking notes from both of them. 'What's this you're working on?'

'I've to give a talk to my fellow students. Comparing and contrasting these two books.' For her condition for allowing him to visit the The Pearl Fisher almost every afternoon was that he had to devote at least some of the time he spent there to his studies.

'What are they?'

He lifted them, keeping his place with his thumbs, and presented their covers to her. 'You tell me, Miss Reading Student.'

Kate's eyes flickered from one to the other before she struck a pose and pointed an accusing finger at him. 'You thought you could catch me out, didn't you? Well, I might no' be able to read the first word but I can read the rest of them. They're the same on both books. Why are you studying two books that are exactly the same?'

'They're not exactly the same. They're different editions. One's a hundred years old and one was only published this year. I'm looking at what's changed.'

'Because doctors know more now than they did a hundred years ago?'

'That's the idea, at any rate,' Richard said with cheerful

cynicism. 'Whether it's true or not might be open to debate. And prove it,' he challenged.

'Prove what?'

'That you can read most of the words.'

She sounded out the ones she knew. 'Something of the Roy-al Coll-ege of - what's that next word?'

'Physicians,' he supplied.

'Oh, aye, of course. Something of the Royal College of Physicians of Edinburgh.'

'Very good. Nine out of ten. And the first word of the title?'

She wrinkled her nose, the way she always did when she was either perplexed or concentrating hard on something.

'I love it when you do that,' he murmured.

'Do what?'

'Never mind,' he said, not wanting to make her self-conscious about a gesture that so enchanted him. She didn't spend nearly enough time out in the fresh air for his liking. All the same, her creamy skin had begun to respond to the summer sun. The ribbon of freckles that now danced across the bridge of her nose enchanted him too.

'P...' she began, sounding the first letter out. 'h...' He waited, and was not disappointed. 'Och no, that's wrong. 'When you put *p* and *h* together they make an *f* sound, don't they? Like physicians.'

'Exactly like physicians.'

'*Phar-ma-co-*' She looked up. 'How do you pronounce the last bit?'

'*-paeia*,' he supplied. 'The whole word's *pharmacopoeia*.'

'Say it again.'

When he did, splitting it into its syllables, she repeated it after him, rolling the word around her mouth as though she was enjoying the feel of it.

'Very good. Take a stab at what it means.'

'It sounds like pharmacist. It sounds Latin.'

'It is. The medical profession loves to use Latin.'

'So us ordinary folk winna understand what ye're all talking aboot?'

Richard laughed. 'Partially that, I think. So what do you think *pharmacopoeia* might mean?'

'Everything tae dae wi' physic?'

'Correct. Today you are my best pupil.'

'Today I am your only pupil.'

'You're still the best one. Come and sit next to me for a wee minute.'

She laid the drawing of him on the table and slid onto the bench, her mouth curving. 'You're beginning tae speak the same way we dae doon here.'

'I know. I mean, *I ken*. It helps me fit in. Am I no' right, lassie?' he queried.

'Aiblins,' she teased. 'Ye certainly dinna seem tae have much trouble finding that Scots tongue that was hiding somewhere in your heid. Can I have two pieces o' paper to put this drawing between?'

'My grandparents were very broad in their speech,' Richard said, giving her what she'd asked for. 'On my mother's side, at any rate.'

'How about your mother herself?'

'My mother has worked very hard not to sound too much like a Scotswoman.'

He had puzzled this out on one of his walks across the North Bridge. Listening to Marjorie Hope now, he could hear the occasional betraying pronunciation, the little slip-ups that indicated she too had once been broader in her speech. Now he came to think of it, he could remember her rebuking his nurse for teaching him some old sayings and proverbs in Scots. His nurse had gone right on doing it, of course.

'What's making ye smile now?'

'I was thinking about my old nurse. It was her who made sure I had a guid Scots tongue in my heid. Told me I might need it one day. Looks like she was right.'

'You need it to be able to understand Robert Burns,' Kate pointed out. 'Does your mother no' like his songs and poetry?'

'That's the odd thing. My mother and her friends love Robert Burns. His songs are really fashionable at the moment. Even if they're being mangled by someone with marbles in their mouth,' – he grimaced, remembering several such occasions – 'most of them are in Scots. Curious,' he mused. 'I wonder if there are other countries in the world where people of a certain social status mark that by affecting to despise their own mother tongue, then nod in smiling approval when someone sings in it. Bit of a dichotomy there.'

'Bit of a what?'

He explained to her what the word meant. She took it in, thought about it for a moment and came up with another question. 'Micht ye also say your mother and ladies like her listening to someone wi' bools in their mou' mangling Burns but no' wanting your nurse tae speak tae you in Scots is a wee bit *ironic*?' The russet brows knitted in anxious enquiry. 'Would that be the correct use o' that word?'

'Perfectly correct.'

The worried look relaxed. 'Would you like to practise your talk on me?'

'You wouldn't mind?'

'Of course I wouldn't. I'll aiblins learn something too.' She pulled a face, mocking herself. 'What I can understand o' it.'

'Don't say that. You're a very intelligent person. This

conversation we're having proves that. Not that this might be much of a compliment but I happen to think you're a lot cleverer than I am.'

She looked doubtful. 'Maybe aboot some things.'

'The things you need to know to live here, you mean? About which you think I'm a bit of a neep-heid? But I didn't mean only them. Not by a long chalk.'

He was beginning to babble; small wonder when he was being so distracted. Their conversation was exercising his brain. Her sitting so close to him was appealing to other parts of his anatomy.

He could smell her clean skin, perfumed as always by that tang of lemons. He was aware of everything about her. Her beautiful blue eyes. Her freckled nose. Her wide mouth. Her glorious hair. Her high round breasts, small but shapely. He wanted to take her in his arms, burrow his hands under her clothes and gently stroke those breasts, kiss and caress her for hours.

Those moments in the Old Physic Garden each Sunday and in the close at the foot of Niddry Street when he left The Pearl Fisher in the late afternoon weren't enough. Even though the kisses and caresses she now permitted were growing ever more passionate, they absolutely weren't enough...

'Richard.'

'Aye?' he asked, lost now in how wonderful he still found it when she addressed him by his first name. Wondering too what the chances were of persuading her to spend time alone with him somewhere private and secluded – somewhere like the Old Physic Garden. There had been two sets of keys to the place and Richard had handed over only one to Mr Gunn.

So all he had to do was work out if he could trust himself not to try to make her go farther than she wanted to, persuade her to meet him there at dead of night – she being at work in The Pearl

Fisher during the evenings and Alan Gunn being at work in the Old Physic Garden during the day. Nothing too difficult, then, which didn't stop him from indulging himself in a vision of meeting her there by moonlight among shimmering paths and rustling trees and sweet-scented flowers.

'You've got that no' quite right in the heid look on your face again.'

'Do you blame me? I'm looking at you.'

She tapped his papers with her index finger. 'Get on with rehearsing your talk.'

He could see a smile lurking in the corners of her mouth. 'I'd really like to kiss you.'

'Ye canna do it here. Anybody might see us. To your work.'

'Your wish is my command, madam.'

'You *are* a neep-heid. A complete daftie.'

'Aye,' he agreed, and began his talk.

CHAPTER THIRTY-TWO

'Well? What's the verdict?'

She was gazing at him with what looked remarkably like admiration. 'It's very good. You're very good. At explaining things, I mean. You make it all very clear. Easy to understand.'

'You're not just saying that?'

She shook her vibrant head. 'No. If you'd have been awful, I'd have tellt ye. Maybe you should go and teach at the College once you get your degree.'

'I've never contemplated doing that,' he said, startled.

'Have you no' tellt me one of the professors o' anatomy is so boring he sends you all tae sleep? The one who reads out from the notes his grandfather wrote? If you've got a gift for teaching you should use it. D'ye no' think so yourself?'

'Aiblins,' he said, mentally disputing with himself that he might have any kind of a gift while at the same time enjoying himself watching serious Kate. 'What about *your* gifts?'

She snorted in derision. 'What would those be?'

'Well, you're beautiful, for a start.'

'So you say.'

'So everyone with eyes says. Like I said earlier, you're clever too. Not to mention kind-hearted.'

She dipped her head, darted a shy glance back up at him. 'D'ye really think I'm clever?'

'As you just asked me, d'ye no' think so yourself?'

She danced the fingers of one hand along the table. 'There are so many things I dinna ken aboot.'

'What sort of things would you like tae ken aboot, Kate?' he asked in affectionate mimicry.

'All sorts o' things. Everything there is tae ken.'

Richard laughed. 'There's nothing like being ambitious.'

'You think I couldna learn things?'

'I think you could do whatever you set your mind to. You already have done, Kate. I'm amazed by how quickly you've come on with your reading and writing.'

She smiled, clearly pleased by the compliments but not sure whether or not to believe them. For a moment the oddness of their situation struck Richard. How was it that the two of them – so separated by class and status as they were – were sitting here in the Cowgate conversing so earnestly?

His initial attraction to Kate had been purely physical. He had seen a pretty girl and he had wanted her – but no, that wasn't exactly how it had been. Even when he had first set eyes on her, there had been something more there, a *frisson* of excitement and something else he couldn't quite put his finger on. In an odd way, there had been a sense of recognition, a feeling that somehow and somewhere he had known this girl before. In another life, maybe. Didn't the Hindoos of India believe something like that?

'Dinna tell me,' he said, watching her expressive face. She wasn't like that with everyone, he had noticed, and wondered if he was flattering himself to think that while she opened up a little while in the Hendersons' company, she only fully dropped her guard when she was with him or her brother. 'I'm looking no' quite right in the heid again.'

'Away wi' the fairies,' she said blithely. 'What were ye thinking aboot?'

'I'll tell you another time. We're still talking about how you're going to learn about everything. You're aiming to be like Mr Henderson, then?'

'He does seem tae ken everything aboot everything. Whatever you ask him, he's never stuck for an answer.'

'Fount of all knowledge,' Richard agreed. He had come to know the bookseller a little over the past few weeks, talking with him before and after he gave Andrew his lessons. He had even twice attended the Midweek Club, the convivial discussion group which rendezvoused at the bookshop on a Wednesday evening. They were all a bunch of bloody Radicals, of course, but their conversation was damned interesting.

They discussed everything and anything: religion and science, poetry, painting and the latest novels; the recent and more distant history of Scotland and of the British Isles; the political situation in Europe; the war currently raging in the Peleponnese as the Greek people fought for their freedom from the Ottoman Empire; the consequences of the abolition of slavery, if only in the British Empire, and of the long struggle of the campaign led so tirelessly by Mr William Wilberforce to achieve that noble aim. Richard was finding it all fascinating.

It had made him think, too. He agreed that black slavery was a terrible evil. Pondering that had set him thinking about Andrew's fourteen-hour-day, of how hard Kate worked, and of what he had learnt from Nathaniel Henderson about the conditions endured by the coal-miners who toiled under the ground a mere few miles from Edinburgh and, for that matter, in the coal-fields throughout Britain.

Richard had discovered Scottish miners were little more than serfs, they and their children bound for life to their masters, the coal-owners. Shocked, he had heard himself advance the idea that there were forms of slavery in Scotland which ought also to be addressed.

'How do you think Mr Henderson manages to know everything?' he asked Kate now.

'Reads a' his own books?'

'Exactly. I'm sure he'd let you read them too. He's said as much. Mrs Henderson too. She says they've got enough customers who treat the place like a library that one more would be neither here nor there.'

'I couldn't go into the bookshop.'

'Why not? Ladies do go into bookshops, you know,' he said, wishing Irene Steele could hear him. 'There are even one or two who attend the Midweek Club.'

'I'm not a lady.'

'I'm not so sure one of those who comes to the Midweek Club is either. Technically speaking.'

Kate shot him a curious look. 'What d'you mean by that?'

'Nothing. Anyway, I think you are a lady. A natural lady.'

She snorted again. 'I dinna look much like a lady, do I?'

'You would in a fashionable gown.'

Kate sighed. 'We've been over this a hundred times, Richard.'

'High time you agreed to let me buy the gown, then. Andrew will have his new clothes and shoes soon. You'll want to go out with him when the king comes. Don't you want your wee brother to be as proud of you in a nice new dress as you're going to be of him in his smart new clothes? Go on, Kate,' he urged. 'Say yes. It would make me so happy if you said yes. You must be tempted. You like pretty things.'

He had brought her some of those pretty things over the past few weeks. A new hairbrush. A little fan painted with pink and white rosebuds to keep her cool as the weather grew warmer. A tiny nosegay of fragrant flowers. Boxes of sweets and baskets of fruit. Whenever he saw pretty little fripperies he thought of her.

He never brought her scent, though. He liked the smell of lemons too much.

'Richard, of course I'm tempted—'

'Then say yes.' He reached for her hand. 'Please say yes.'

She raised the hand he wasn't holding to his brow, pushing back a stray lock of his black hair. 'Can't resist my good looks and charming manners?' he asked hopefully. 'Say yes, Kate. Say, *yes please, Richard, I'd really like you to buy me a pretty gown.*'

'Never give up, do you?'

'Does that mean you are saying yes?'

'Richard, I dinna ken aboot this, I really dinna.'

Some instinct told him not to press the point. 'I'll ask you again later, then. You're not going to send me home yet, are you?' There was a little frown between her brows. He wanted it gone.

'You always talk as though I'm in charge o' this.'

'You are.' Raising the hand he held to his mouth, he planted a kiss on it and released her. 'Want me to hear you read now?'

The frown smoothed out. 'Can we do one of the poems from my book?'

'As long as you don't cheat by reading out one of the songs you know off by heart.'

She giggled, and the tension between them relaxed. 'Had you fooled for a moment.'

'You did. Go and fetch Mr Burns then.' He pulled his satchel towards him, dug into it and brought out a book. 'After which I shall introduce you to another great poet. A gentleman by the name of Keats.'

Returning in no time with her precious collected poems of Robert Burns, she resumed her seat on the bench next to him, set the book down and flipped it open with such enthusiasm that she turned it over, revealing a small piece of folded paper inside the back cover.

'That's never the bluebell I gave you that morning in the Old Physic Garden.'

'It is.' She opened the paper and showed the little bloom to him.

'You kept it?'

'Of course I kept it. You gave it to me.'

His heart turned over in his breast. 'I love you, Catriona Dunbar.'

'I know,' she replied, adding shyly, 'I love you too, Richard Hope. Are you going to listen to me reading one of these poems?' She began to leaf through the book and hesitated at one page.

'Maybe not that one,' he said, glancing at it: *Ae fond kiss, and then we sever; Ae fareweel, and then for ever?* Definitely not that one. Her next choice brought the most rueful of smiles to his lips. *O my luve is like a red, red rose...* 'Maybe not that one, either.'

'Och, but I really like it! Do you not, Richard?'

Too much, he thought. I like it too much, and it's another one that always makes me think of you. 'Pick a different one.'

She looked at him. 'I think an awful lot of these poems make you sad.'

'I think you might be right. You could always cheer me up by agreeing to have the dress.'

'That would make you happy?'

'That would make me very happy.'

'All right,' she said after a moment. 'But don't mention it to my aunt or uncle.'

'If you don't want them to know about it yet, of course I won't.'

'I don't want them to know about it at all,' she said, and returned to leafing through the book of poetry. 'How about "My Heart's in the Highlands"?'

'Fine,' he said, and watched her as she read. It was debatable how much safer this poem was. *My heart's in the Highlands, My heart is not here.* He'd never been to the Highlands but he'd always wanted to go. Now he was dreaming of making that journey with Kate, being with her when they both saw the lofty mountains and the tumbling waterfalls and the deer running through the heather for the first time.

He was helpless, an unarmed and defenceless prisoner of his love for her. She really was in charge of this. She had all the power – and was completely unaware of it.

CHAPTER THIRTY-THREE

Nathaniel Henderson gave his wife one long, last, lingering kiss, eased himself out of her and rolled over onto his back. 'The cloth?'

'Please, my love,' she said, watching the long shape of him in the darkness as he sat up, swung his legs over the side of the bed and lifted the square of linen from the nightstand. It was already folded into a thick, soft wad. Adjusting her position as little as possible, Peggy allowed him to place it between her legs. He got back into bed, pulled the covers up over them and turned into her, one arm coming to rest around her waist.

'I love you.'

She kissed his forehead. 'I've rather gained that impression over the years.'

She felt the curve of his smile against the top of her arm. Within minutes, she could hear from the steady rhythm of his breathing that he had fallen asleep. She did not grudge him his rest. Now that the sensations aroused by the fierce tenderness of their love-making were beginning to fade, she knew though that sleep wasn't going to come easily to her tonight.

There had been so many nights when she had lain awake in this bed. By a Highland mile, on most of those it had been the same old thought, prayer and wish that had filled her head. *Let this be the night on which I conceive my husband's child. Please God, let it happen tonight.*

They had tried everything. Herbal remedies. Sea bathing. Following a specific regimen when it came to what they ate. Putting a pillow under her hips when they made love so Nathaniel's seed would have no difficulty in reaching her womb.

Unbeknownst to Nathaniel – a true son of the Enlightenment and of the rational and scientific approach to just about everything – Peggy had tried all manner of superstitions too. Touching stones and pebbles and rocks said to be imbued with power, keeping other tiny ones in her pocket and under the mattress of their bed. Dipping strips torn from one of her petticoats under magical springs in hidden groves and tying them to the surrounding trees. Drinking from holy wells whose water was supposed to guarantee conception.

Nothing had worked. They still adhered to the procedure advised by one physician they had consulted and which they had followed tonight, allowing his seed to remain inside her throughout the night. It couldn't hurt, but she knew neither of them now had much faith in the practice.

She often pondered the irony. She was lying back, moving as little as possible, giving Mother Nature as much help as she could. How many women all over Edinburgh were at this moment doing the opposite – washing and douching themselves with vinegar and moving about as much as possible, hoping and praying they wouldn't conceive?

Peggy's restless thoughts leapt to Kate Dunbar and Richard Hope, making a very uncomfortable connection. Had the promise she had exacted from that young man been like trying to command the incoming tide to go back out when it so desperately wanted to come in?

Poor Kate. Poor Richard Hope. Peggy was coming to know him a little, and she had to admit she liked what she saw. He had an easy and friendly way with him, and was beginning to treat

Andrew Dunbar like a younger brother. He was thoughtful too. Tonight he had given his young pupil some money, with instructions to pay Rebecca Gunn for the work she was doing in The Pearl Fisher on Tuesday and Thursday evenings.

'Only,' he'd admonished, 'your big sister's not to know. All right?'

Peggy knew all this because Andrew had come to her about it after Richard had left, troubled by the idea of keeping any kind of secret from Kate; troubled too because Rebecca had volunteered to do the work for nothing.

'Out o' the goodness o' her heart,' as the boy had put it so earnestly to Peggy. 'But I ken fine she could really be doing wi' the money. That's the problem, Mrs Henderson.'

Peggy had given him a glass of milk and a piece of gingerbread, sat down with him and discussed his problem. They had come to the mutual conclusion that there could be such a thing as a good secret, and this was one of them.

Andrew Dunbar was a nice child, touchingly solemn and vulnerable at times but a real boy at others, high-spirited and full of fun. A son of whom any parent could be proud. How sad that his own had been taken so early. From the way Kate spoke of them, they had been loving and caring.

A gardener and a laundress, they had been respectable but humble. Could they have ever imagined their son might one day become a scholar at George Heriot's? How proud they would have been of him.

Peggy released a soft sigh into the darkness of her bedchamber. That Andrew Dunbar would win a place at Heriot's was by no means a foregone conclusion. It was also going to be some leap. First the aunt had to be persuaded. A bit of a harridan, it was obvious Chrissie Graham was also a miser. Persuading her to forego his wages – paltry enough though Peggy imagined them to be – would be no easy task for Andrew's sister to accomplish.

There were the simple practicalities too. Kate did very well but turning her brother out smartly dressed and ready for school each morning wasn't going to be easy for her. She had asked if Peggy could keep his new clothes, which would mean Andrew coming to the bookshop each morning and evening to change into and out of them.

Kate would probably want to accompany him to school, at least to begin with. Given how much that would cut into her morning, her aunt undoubtedly wasn't going to like that either. Taking care not to dislodge the cloth, Peggy shifted her position. She hated lying on her back. When Nathaniel murmured a protest in his sleep, she laid her hand on the warm arm curled protectively around her waist and gave it a reassuring pat.

Perhaps Kate would let Peggy get him ready for school and walk him there. She'd be more than happy to do that, and to meet him afterwards too, if required. She'd enjoy that, hearing about his day and his teachers and his fellow pupils. For a moment, Peggy lost herself in happy reverie, imagining herself in that role.

She really should try to get to sleep, though. A busy day lay in front of her tomorrow. Most of her days were. They'd be busier still if she were going to walk Andrew Dunbar to and from school, although it wasn't as though Heriot's was very far away. Nor was she contemplating an irksome or tedious task. Taking this on would be a joy, something that would add so much pleasure and sparkle to her daily round. She closed her eyes.

Seconds later, they shot open. There was a question in her head. Richard Hope's voice was asking it. *Between us, might we not contrive to do some good here, Mrs Henderson?* Peggy's eyes opened wider still.

CHAPTER THIRTY-FOUR

Kate stood in the Henderson's bedroom in her chemise and a considerable amount of embarrassment, entirely unused to being the focus of so much attention. Both Mrs Henderson and the dressmaker were fussing around her. It was the former who had decreed she would ask the latter to come to Kate, rather than the other way round.

'It will be more suitable, lass,' she had said. 'More *comfortable* for you.' Kate had realised immediately what she meant. Even if her chemise was on the plain side, she supposed one girl in her underwear was much like any other, a young woman not so easily distinguishable from a young lady. Dressed in her usual calf-length skirts and bodices, she looked too much what she was to have stood much chance of being welcomed into any of the dressmaking establishments on South Bridge Street.

That the dressmaker – a shrewd-eyed and attractive woman somewhere in her late thirties – seemed inclined to gossip was unfortunate. Not knowing how to deal with the woman's obvious curiosity about her, Kate had been relieved to find Mrs Henderson was more than equal to the task of diverting the conversation into safer waters than her own background, where she lived and who she was related to that the dressmaker might know.

Mrs Henderson had described Kate as a friend of the family and steered the conversation towards the royal visit and the preparations being made for it. Thank God this gossipy lady doesn't know who's paying for my dress, Kate thought, feeling a little faint as she always did when she realised all over again who Richard was. *Not just well-off but gentry. Kin to the Earl of Hopetoun.*

'You'll soon be getting busy, I suppose.'

'We already are,' responded the dressmaker, giving Kate a red face by measuring round her breasts. 'We're making a number of court dresses for ladies who are to be presented to the king.'

'Those presentations will take place at the Palace of Holyroodhouse?'

Noting down Kate's bust measurement, the dressmaker nodded. 'There are to be two levees, as they call them. One for the gentlemen and one for the ladies.'

'Only those who are considered truly to be ladies and gentlemen, I expect,' Mrs Henderson said lightly.

'All the gentry,' the other woman agreed.

All the gentry. Oh, God. She was being bought a dress by a young man who was probably going to meet the king. For a moment the enormity of it took her breath away.

'Are you all right, my dear? You look a wee touch pale.'

Peggy Henderson looked anxious, the dressmaker curious. Kate put a smile on her face. 'I'm fine, Mrs Henderson. Just grand.'

She was relieved when Peggy once more changed the subject, asking the dressmaker if everyone was taking on extra seamstresses to cope with the flood of work.

'Some,' the woman said. 'Although only those who know what they're doing. None of us has the time at the moment to instruct anyone who doesn't. And those who've been taken on will likely be let go again at the end of the royal visit. Even the gentry's purses are going to be lean after all this expenditure. It'll be back to old clothes and cold porridge for everyone, I'm thinking.'

Kate shot her a quick look at that, but little more was said after the seamstress acquired a mouthful of pins and the conversation perforce became more sporadic. When the woman's work was done, Mrs Henderson's offer of a cup of tea was declined on the grounds of her being expected elsewhere.

'But you'll stay and take tea with us, lass.' The words were said so firmly that Kate, flattered by the invitation anyway, saw there was only one possible response. 'I'll show you out,' Peggy said to the dressmaker, throwing a smile over her shoulder as the two of them left her bedchamber, 'and I'll leave you to get dressed and come downstairs in your own time, my dear.'

When Kate walked down to the bookshop a few moments later, Nathaniel Henderson was standing behind his counter waiting for her. He looked nervous. Why on earth would Mr Henderson be nervous of her?

'Miss Catriona,' he said with grave courtesy. 'There is something Mrs Henderson and I should like to discuss with you. Will you be so good as to listen to what we have to say?'

Walking back to The Pearl Fisher some time later, Kate found herself taking the long way round, crossing the South Bridge before doubling back into Infirmary Street and down Robertson's Close to the Cowgate. Some of the shops on South Bridge Street were beginning to decorate their windows and frontages in readiness for the royal visit: the blue and white Scottish Saltire, the red and white cross of St George, the Union flag in which both were represented, lengths of ribbon and swathes of tartan fashioned into rosettes or draped to hang in graceful curves.

The excitement surrounding the impending arrival of King

George IV was mounting with each passing day. Seized by a fit of patriotism, likely also nagged into it by his wife and daughters, Andrew's master had declared he would go further than releasing his workers for the individual parades and events. For the duration of the royal visit, the shop and workshop would close at noon.

Everyone's pay would be cut too, of course. No employer was going to pay his employees for hours they weren't working. Since Andrew handed over his entire wages to his aunt, that made no odds to him. He was overjoyed by the prospect of so much free time, quite dazzled by it.

He was going to be even more dazzled when Kate told him what the Hendersons had just suggested. Her own head was spinning with it.

Emerging into the Cowgate, she spotted Richard, sitting at the long table outside The Pearl Fisher. There was a book open in front of him but he wasn't reading it. His head was up and he was staring into space. Focusing on her as she crossed the road towards him, he stood up and came round the table to greet her.

'I saw you walking past a few moments ago,' he said, gesturing up above their heads to the one exposed arch of the South Bridge that spanned the Cowgate.

'Is that when you stopped reading? What's the book?'

'Your copy of Burns. Your uncle fetched it for me.'

'He had no right to do that,' she said hotly.

Richard lifted his hands, palms outward, in a placatory gesture. 'He was only trying to be helpful, Kate.'

She gazed up at him. There had been times over the past couple of months when she'd been aware of a wild impulse to tell him everything, throw herself at his feet and beg him to understand and forgive – and to rescue her.

Rescue me, Richard. Please rescue me. Those were the words she longed to say to him. Yet she could tell him nothing unless she told him the whole truth and that she could not do. He would be shocked and appalled. Disgusted. What decent man wouldn't? Particularly a man like Richard, whose upbringing had been so different from hers.

He would not understand how she could have allowed it to go on for so long, would not understand why she could not have told her aunt, would not understand why she had not taken Andrew and herself and run away...would not understand that she'd had nowhere else to go.

No money. No other family. No way of earning a living and keeping a roof over her and Andrew's heads and food in their bellies. No alternative except the poorhouse, which was no alternative at all.

Richard would not understand any of this but she did not blame him for that. He was older than her but he was a boy. Carefree. Or had been till he had met her. Right at this moment, he did not look very carefree.

'Which poem were you reading before I walked over the Cowgate and distracted you?' She leant forward across the table. Richard's hand went to the book but too late to turn the page. She glanced up at him and for a moment they stood motionless, each the prisoner of the other's gaze.

'Let me see,' she said, and he took his hand away. She began to read the poem out loud. He always made her do that. Because that way they both knew she was getting it right. Because, so he always said, she read the Scots in which the poems were written so very beautifully.

'*Ae fond kiss,*' she began, '*and then we sever...* Oh. It's that one. You are making yourself melancholy with it. That's foolish.'

'I am foolish.' He shrugged. 'And melancholy enough already. Even before I read what the Bard of Alloway has to say about parting.' He quoted it to her without having to look at the printed words, and his voice was not quite steady.

Had we never lov'd sae kindly,

Had we never lov'd sae blindly,

Never met – or never pairted,

We had ne'er been broken-hearted.

Kate looked at him. 'I cannot wish we had never met, Richard. And the summer is no' over yet, ye ken.'

'It's August, Kate,' he said despairingly. 'Soon it'll be September and then it'll be October and after that I'll be going back to the university to do my final year.' He reached for the book, flipped it over, opened the back cover and the folded piece of paper that lay there. One long finger rested with infinite gentleness upon the pressed flower. 'Will you always keep this?'

'Until my dying day,' she said. 'Until my dying day, Richard.'

Closing the paper over the little blue bloom, he shut the book and sank down onto the bench in front of the table. 'There must be a way, Kate. There must be a way for us to be together!'

Kate swallowed hard as she joined him. 'Richard, Mr and Mrs Henderson have just asked me something.'

'Kate, I don't want to talk about the Hendersons. Not right now!'

'It's important,' she insisted. 'Richard, Mr and Mrs Henderson have asked Andrew and me to go and live with them.'

CHAPTER THIRTY-FIVE

He shot up from the despairing slouch in which he'd been sitting. 'But this is wonderful news, Kate. Surely this is the best of news!'

'More than I could ever have hoped for. Mr Henderson has promised that whatever happens about Heriot's, Andrew will definitely go to school. If I allow him to go and live with them, of course.'

'But you will, Kate, won't you?' All melancholy fled, Richard's handsome face was alive with enthusiasm. 'You'll go too, of course.' He waved towards The Pearl Fisher and the South Bridge. 'Get yourself out of this place. I don't suppose your aunt's going to be very happy about losing you but, hey-ho,' he said gaily, 'your uncle will have to persuade her. He will surely see what a marvellous opportunity this is for you and Andrew.'

Kate's stomach lurched. How was she to explain to him the conflicting hopes, fears and emotions the Hendersons' offer had unleashed inside her head? They were jostling for position in there like a tangle of fankled ribbons. She plucked out one of them at random.

'Richard,' she said, 'the Hendersons dinna hae a big hoose, only a couple o' rooms over the bookshop. To have me staying wi' them as well as Andrew would be a bit o' a squeeze. Besides which, they're no' wealthy folk. To expect them to gie me my bed and board as well as Andrew isna fair.'

'Come on, Kate! If they've asked you to go and live with them they must have worked out they can afford to do it. If you feel the need to repay their kindness could you not do so by helping in the shop? You'd like that, surely.' He laughed. 'You could read all the books and learn about everything there is tae ken.'

'Och, Richard!' she said in exasperation. 'Me serving in the shop wouldn't earn the Hendersons any more money, would it? If I could secure myself a position as a seamstress I might be able to pay them for my board at least. I used to think I might be able to do that but now I dinna think it's very likely. Nobody's going to have much money to spend at the dressmakers' once the king's visit is past.'

'Work as a seamstress?' He frowned. 'Slaving away with a needle and thread from morning till night and ruining your eyesight into the bargain? It is not what I would want for you, Kate.'

Her mouth set in a mutinous line. 'I could not bring myself to let the Hendersons feed and clothe me as well as Andrew.'

'Then allow me to do it. I could easily afford to pay them for your board and lodging.'

'Do you really think Mr and Mrs Henderson would agree to that? And could you do that and no' want to see me in return? And would I no' want to see you when you'd be walking past the bookshop nearly every day on your way to the university? Even if Mrs Henderson would permit us to keep seeing each other, how could we expect her and Mr Henderson's friends and customers no' to notice what was going on? Or for that no' to get back to your family?'

She had no doubt her aunt could be persuaded to let her and Andrew go. Give Chrissie Graham some money to compensate for the loss of their labour – a guinea or two would do it – and she wouldn't even bother to wave them goodbye.

It was, Kate thought, a price the Hendersons might be willing to pay. Or she could ask Richard for the money. She knew he would give it to her. But a few guineas would not be enough to satisfy Michael Graham. He'd hardly spoken to her over the past weeks but she was aware of his growing impatience. As she was aware of the anger she had provoked in his black heart by standing up to him.

Unable any longer to hide her feelings from Richard, she turned a troubled face towards him. He slid along the bench towards her and she saw that he intended to take her in his arms. 'Not here,' she whispered, having to reinforce that plea by placing her hands on his chest. 'There are people about.'

'Dammit, Kate,' he growled, 'there are always people about! How can we talk about any of this when we can never be private with one another?'

'We made a promise to Mrs Henderson,' she said. 'Which included our agreement to part at the end of the summer.'

'I'm not willing to do that, Kate,' he said grimly. 'Are you?'

She looked into his eyes, remembering the first time she had done so and how she had thought she might drown in those velvety green pools. *Might* drown? She had long since raised her arms and sunk below the surface.

'No,' she whispered. 'I'm not willing to do that either.'

He went very still. 'Spell it out for me, Kate. Tell me what you are thinking so there can be no danger of my misunderstanding your meaning.'

'Do I have to?' she asked with a tiny smile.

'You want me to do it?' When she nodded, he drew in a long breath. 'You are agreeing to become my mistress? To let me set you up in rooms somewhere?'

She nodded again.

'You are worried that Mr and Mrs Henderson will disapprove, Kate?'

'Of course. But I do not think either of them would try to stop me from seeing Andrew on that account. They would not be so cruel.'

'Nobody could stop you from seeing Andrew.'

'No,' she agreed. 'I do not believe so.'

'But if you are seriously considering this, might I not suggest that I simply install both of you in those rooms?'

'You ken fine what's wrong wi' that idea.'

'Andrew,' Richard said, nodding his head. 'Who once told me his sister wasn't for sale.'

'Aye. And also because o' something Mrs Henderson said about George Heriot's prizing respectability in its scholars and their families.'

'You think none of them have any skeletons in their cupboards?' came the cynical response.

'Mrs Henderson said something about that too. About boys in receipt of a bursary being scrutinised more closely than the others. *Scrutinised*,' she said. 'Is that the right word?'

'It's the right word,' he confirmed, adding with deceptive mildness, 'Mrs Henderson says more than her prayers, I think.'

'She's only trying to help me do the right thing. She's a good person, Richard.'

He sighed. 'I know she is. But, Kate, couldn't we between us work out some way we could do this without anyone else having to know?'

'Folk gossip, Richard. And there is something I must ask you afore I even consider doing this. What would happen when you grow tired of me? Or when you marry Miss Irene Steele?'

CHAPTER THIRTY-SIX

'Grow tired of you? Marry Irene Steele? Kate, I love you! Don't you know that by now?' He leapt to his feet and straddled the narrow bench. 'God Almighty, Catriona Dunbar, is your opinion of me really as low as that? And,' he demanded, 'your opinion of yourself? You are not some muslin to be picked up and discarded at will by me or any other man! Hellfire, Kate, how can you even think of yourself that way?'

He glared down at her. Her chin and bottom lip began to tremble. 'Come with me,' he said. 'Come with me *now*!'

He didn't care who might see them but he knew she did. So he did not grab her by the hand and pull her into his arms until they were standing together inside the close at the foot of Niddry Street. Once they had reached that protection from any inquisitive eyes, he told her again that he loved her, that he would never grow tired of her, that he wasn't going to marry Irene Steele.

'If you agree to do this I would regard myself as your husband, Kate. This would be like a marriage to me.'

She raised her face from his chest. 'Och, Richard!'

'Would that be Och, Richard, yes, or Och, Richard, no?'

She continued to gaze up at him, but gave him no answer.

'You're feart,' he pronounced.

The word earned him a quick smile. 'Aye,' she agreed. 'I'm feart.' Of much more than he knew.

'You need time to think about all of this?'

'I dinna ken time's going tae help ower much. Right at this moment I dinna really ken whit I should dae aboot anything. Except that Andrew has to go and live with the Hendersons.'

'Of course he does. It's a marvellous opportunity for him. You could always make it a condition of him going and of your continuing to see him regularly that what you choose to do with your own life is your own affair.'

'Could I?'

'Of course you could. But I think you need to think it over first.' He wrapped his arms more tightly about her and his wry laugh stirred the waves of her hair. 'I may well die of desire and longing for you in the interim but I'd say you should take as much time as you need to do that.'

'People dinna die o' desire and longing.'

'You so sure of that?'

'No,' she said, expelling the words on a sigh. 'I'm no' so sure o' that.'

'We'll find a way, my love. Why has that made you smile?'

'Because you always think that just because you want something it's going to happen.'

'And you're the opposite. You think you're never going to get the things you want.'

'Maybe,' she conceded. 'Can we please talk about something else now?'

'Of course we can. Tell me what happened with the dressmaker. Did you find it a diverting experience?'

'A wee bit embarrassing, tae tell ye the truth. Standing there in my chemise with her measuring me.'

'Wish I'd been doing the measuring,' he murmured in response, laughing when she hit him on the chest. 'Tell me what else happened.'

'The dressmaker had brought wee patches o' material with her. Samples, she called them. So I could choose the colour and pattern I wanted. I liked that bit o' it.'

'Am I to know which colour and pattern you have chosen?'

'Certainly not.' She was regaining her composure with every word. 'No' till you see me in the dress.'

'Very well, madam. I look forward to that occasion with considerable impatience. I shall, however, endeavour to curb my natural desire to see you garbed in the height of fashion.'

'You've gone all hoity-toity again.'

'So I have. I can keep this up for hours, you know. Whether it's the real me is another matter entirely.'

She was calm now, if rather grave. 'Thank you, Richard. Thank you for my dress.'

'It is my pleasure to buy it for you, Kate. My very great pleasure. I trust shoes and a spencer and a pretty bonnet are also being purchased, as per my instructions to Mrs Henderson?'

'You're very generous.'

'No. I'm very selfish. This is all for my own gratification. To provide me with a feast for my eyes. A pretty gown and a beautiful girl inside it.'

'I dinna ken aboot that,' she demurred. 'But the gown is going to be beautiful. The loveliest thing I've ever worn, Richard.'

'I love you. You do know that, don't you?'

'I know it,' she said. 'And I love you too.'

When their lips met, he found himself remembering his silent instructions to himself when they had first kissed back on that fresh April morning in the Old Physic Garden. *Be gentle. Hold back. Don't frighten her.*

He knew she really was *feart*, and scared of more than gossip or of how the Hendersons would react to her becoming his mistress or how that might be accomplished without Andrew having to know – forlorn hope though that probably was.

She was scared of the physical side of it too, of love-making and of losing her virginity. That was natural and only to be expected. When the time came he would be so very gentle with her. When the time came. He refused to say *if*.

He wanted this more than he had ever wanted anything in his life. He wanted her beside him for the rest of his life, as his lover and as his companion: like a wife.

CHAPTER THIRTY-SEVEN

'Richard, have you heard a single word Miss Steele or I have exchanged over the past ten minutes?'

'Of course, Mother. You're talking about everything you need to do before the king comes to Edinburgh.'

Marjorie Hope looked a little mollified. 'You had an alarmingly distant look in your eyes, my dear. Isn't it possible for you to work up some small amount of enthusiasm for the royal visit?'

Elegant in formal day clothes – his favourite dark blue cutaway coat and close-fitting buff pantaloons, Richard toyed with the crumbs of cheese on his plate and found himself exchanging a smile across the table with Irene Steele. She was a guest for lunch today at the Hope family home. Richard's father had been there too, but had excused himself half-an hour since on the grounds of having to attend a meeting of one of the innumerable committees on which he sat.

'If you absolutely insist, Mama,' Richard drawled.

'Richard,' she said again, although this time the reproach was uttered in more affectionate tones. Having emerged from this penultimate university year with flying colours and a glowing report, he was currently more in his parents' good books than he had been for some time. Although how long that was going to last was a moot point. He knew he hadn't been as attentive to Irene Steele over the course of this interminably long luncheon as his mother would have liked.

He'd been preoccupied with thoughts of Kate, of course. When he wasn't actually in her company, he usually was. He did have some space left in his head for thinking what a fuss was being made about the impending royal visit.

Come next month, it would appear half the population of Scotland was preparing to decamp to the capital. As his father had privately put it to Richard, raising his eyebrows in exasperated amusement: 'Astonishing how many people have suddenly remembered they have friends and relatives in Edinburgh who might be able to put them up for a night or two.'

Not that everyone was going to be welcoming His Majesty King George IV with unqualified enthusiasm. The briefest of attendances at the Midweek Club was enough to confirm that. Curiosity, a feeling of gratitude to the Hendersons for how they were prepared to help Andrew and Kate and, perhaps, the need to keep in with them, had sent Richard back on several occasions.

He'd found himself enjoying the cut and thrust of impassioned political debate more than he could have imagined. He had listened to Nathaniel Henderson describing the trials of the Radicals who'd gone to the gallows two years before and the bookseller's own involvement with those events, and found himself moved. Whether you agreed with what they had done or not, Baird, Hardie and Wilson had died for what they believed in. There was something inspiring about that.

He'd been moved too when Alan Gunn had spoken to the Midweek Club about his experiences of being evicted from his croft in Sutherland. He hadn't been the only one. You could have heard a pin drop in the bookshop on that occasion.

What was being discussed over the lunch table today was a lot less gripping. Richard was dimly aware that his mother and Irene Steele had been talking about clothes. It would appear that a multiplicity of new garments had to be bought, sewn and worn for the king's visit.

It wasn't only females who were getting exercised about that. *Dear Sir Walter* – as Richard's mother invariably referred to their neighbour who lived further up Castle Street – had suggested gentlemen not in the military should, despite that, wear a sort of uniform. The Wizard of the North had gone so far as to design one.

It was described in the little booklet he had written giving advice to Edinburgh's citizens as to how to dress and behave during the king's visit. *Hints Addressed to the Inhabitants of Edinburgh and Others in Prospect of His Majesty's Visit – by an Old Citizen* – had seldom been out of Marjorie Hope's hands since she had purchased it. Richard was almost at screaming point with having extracts from it read out to him. He was horrified by the suggestion in Sir Walter's *Hints* that every man in Edinburgh should appear in public wearing tartan at least once during the royal visit.

The idea struck him as absurd in the extreme. If you had Highland blood in you and were proud of the fact, fine. If you were someone like his own father, who never spoke of the Highlands but with a shudder at the memory of his only visit there and pained references to barbaric mountains and tumultuous waterfalls, it struck Richard as being hypocritical in the extreme and quite risible into the bargain.

Yet Edward Hope, albeit at the behest of his wife, seemed set on swathing himself in the stuff. Judging by many of the conversations to which he'd been half-listening throughout July, Richard was horribly afraid that lots of people were going to be swathed in the stuff.

What a stupid, unnecessary fuss. Those who had more clothes than they knew what to do with were to get more, while a girl like Kate was so appreciative of one pretty gown and the little bits and pieces that went with it. He was longing to see her in it.

So he supposed he did have some interest in clothes, although only in those Kate Dunbar might wear. Or not wear. He longed to see her in her new dress and he longed to see her wearing not a stitch. As he longed to make love to her every night, fall asleep with her and wake up with her again every morning...although if she did agree to him renting rooms for her, he would be able to spend the night with her only occasionally. His parents could never know what was going on.

Like a husband. That was how he had described it to her, trying to convince her how deep his feelings for her were. He would be almost a husband, offer her almost a marriage. Only what sort of a marriage would it be if he had to keep her and his visits to her brief and secret? Kate deserved more than such a clandestine arrangement. She deserved a lot more—

'Richard!'

'Aye?' he enquired absently, before wondering what the hell he had done now. His mother was looking at him as though she were the sheriff on the bench and he the miscreant who had committed some heinous crime.

'*Aye?*' She queried. 'Did I bring you up to say *aye*, Richard? I don't think so.'

He looked at her for a moment, knowing what line was assigned to him now. He should apologise, tell her he'd forgotten himself – only he found he couldn't.

'It's a word, Mama. It means *yes*. As I'm sure you know. Since it's a very ancient word – they still use it in the Houses of Parliament in London, Mama – I don't see why you object to it so much. It's also a good Scottish word, and I believe one of the main purposes of the royal visit is that the king should see Scotland and experience some of our history and traditions. The

Scots tongue is part of that. Indeed, your own parents – my grandparents – spoke good Braid Scots, had a *guid Scots tongue in their heids.* As you yourself may well have had when you were a *wee lassie,*' he added, pronouncing the words with exaggerated precision. 'Is that not so, Mother?'

He had silenced her. Glancing from her to Irene Steele, he saw a mixture of sympathy and reproach in the younger woman's eyes. Looking back at his mother, he saw hurt and embarrassment. He was in no mood to allow himself to be stopped by that.

'It's all nonsense,' he said shortly. 'All this stuff about how you speak, who you're connected to by marriage or by blood. That's not what matters. It's your character that signifies your true merit, how you treat your fellow man and woman.'

He stood up so abruptly the under footman had to leap forward to prevent his chair from falling over. Richard turned to him. It was Jamie, the young man from whom he had bought the rough jacket and trousers he had worn on his first visits to the Cowgate.

'Thank you,' he said before swinging back round to the table. 'If you'll excuse me, Irene. Mother,' he said formally. 'Oh, and by the way, I absolutely refuse to dress up like a toy soldier or wrap myself in tartan.' Giving both women the stiffest of nods, he wheeled round and strode from the room.

As he marched through the front lobby of the house, the senior footman materialised out of nowhere, racing to beat Richard to the front door.

'Dammit,' he yelled. 'I'm perfectly capable of opening the bloody door!'

'Richard,' came a soft voice from behind him. 'Will you please wait a moment?'

'Why?' he demanded, and saw male eyebrows that had already

risen at his snapped comment – the young master never normally behaved so boorishly – rise further at this less than mannerly response to a young lady's request. Grudgingly admitting to himself that none of this was Irene Steele's fault, Richard waved the senior footman away.

She glided across the black and white tiles of the hall to stand in front of him. 'You've met someone,' she said. 'Haven't you?'

CHAPTER THIRTY-EIGHT

'Met someone?' The disdainful repetition of an unwelcome question had often knocked the questioner back in the past. He might have known the technique would cut no ice with Irene Steele.

'A girl. A young lady.' She studied him thoughtfully. 'Or perhaps a young woman. Someone who is beneath your own station in life. Or in some other way not quite worthy of you.'

'Beneath my own station in life? Not quite worthy of me? Do you ever wonder who we think we are, Irene? To consider ourselves so far above other people?'

'I think,' she said, 'that it is very difficult for people of our rank in society to think otherwise.'

'Until our eyes are opened.'

'As yours have been?'

'As mine have been.' Yet he was as bad as those whom he was castigating. He had offered Kate *almost a marriage,* told her he would be *like a husband* to her.

Did he really expect her to be grateful to him for such a shabby proposal?

'I shall not ask you for details, Richard.'

'That's good, because you'd be wasting your breath, Irene. This is my own private matter.'

'She's so special to you? Lucky girl.'

He folded his arms, propped one shoulder against the front

door and gazed impassively at her. 'Was there something else, Irene?'

'Before you hurtle out of the house, you mean? Leaving your mother close to tears? You know, Richard,' she went on, 'I do not think Mrs Hope can help how she is. Forgive me for speaking so plainly to you.'

'You're forgiven,' he said flippantly, although that reference to his mother being close to tears had hit home. 'Go on.'

'As I understand it, your mother's family is an old and honourable one but in comparison with your father's a relatively humble one.'

'Gentlemen farmers on one side and sea captains on the other,' Richard agreed. 'Not titled, nor related to anyone with a title.'

'Indeed. I think your mother found it most acceptable to want to marry your father. The fact he is of the gentry was very attractive to her.'

'That's one way of putting it.'

Irene Steele laid a hand on his arm. 'Do not judge your mother too harshly, Richard. We all make choices in life. Sometimes those choices are forced on us by circumstances or upbringing or by what we are trying to escape from.'

He looked at her curiously, bounced out of his absorption with Kate by the shrewdness and perspicacity with which Irene Steele was speaking. 'Is there something from which you wish to escape, Irene?'

She took a deep breath and looked him in the eye. 'Marriage, Richard.'

'I thought all women wanted to marry.'

She arched her beautifully shaped eyebrows at him. 'Did you?'

'You want never to wed?'

'Perhaps when I am quite old,' she allowed. 'When I am in my forties or thereabouts. Always assuming I can find someone who shares my intellectual interests. Although I might equally find such companionship with a member of my own sex.'

'What?'

'Nothing. There can be more to life for a woman than marriage, you know. Have you any idea what it feels like to be expected to follow a path laid out for you merely because you have been born a member of one sex rather than the other?' She tapped him on the shoulder with her fan. 'I shall lend you a book by an author called Mary Wollstonecraft, which takes as its subject the rights of women.'

'The rights of *women*?' he queried, unfamiliar with both the phrase and the concept – the rights of man, yes, but not those of the other gender. 'This is a new book?'

Irene laughed. 'It was first published thirty years ago. It remains a most stimulating text.'

'Then I shall enjoy reading it,' he said with grave politeness, and earned himself a smile.

'If you ever get round to it. You have no idea how much I envy you, Richard. To be able to study at the university as you do is a privilege I long for.'

'But you would not want to become a physician.'

'Not personally, although I know there are women who do. Do you not think many members of my sex would prefer to be treated by a female physician?'

It was not something he had ever considered. He did so now. 'For modesty's sake, you mean?'

'That's one reason. But it is too late now to discuss this subject.'

All at once, he felt a surge of affection for her – and an appreciation of the brain which lay behind the lovely face. 'Yet I should like to discuss it with you, Irene. That is—'

'If I do not misconstrue your interest in me,' she supplied. She laid a hand on his arm. 'Oh, my dear Richard, you do not need to fear me. Since my mama is long dead, I have no designing mother for you to fear either. So may the two of us not now be able to relax in one another's company and simply be friends?'

'This is a rather extraordinary conversation for us to be having, Irene.'

'Not really. You and I should be friends, Richard. Nothing more.' She reached up and kissed his cheek. 'But also nothing less.'

'You,' he pronounced, 'are a most unusual and interesting young woman.'

'I'm glad you've realised that, Richard. Now I think you should go and apologise to your mother.'

'Yes,' he agreed. 'So do I.'

Marjorie Hope was still sitting at the luncheon table, Jamie standing beside the sideboard opposite her and staring at the space above her head. He was not yet old enough to have learnt how to school his face into the bland and impassive mask of the upper servant. There was a woman crying a few feet away from him and he was distressed by it.

How sad. How absurd. Two people in a room. One in need of comfort but unable to accept it, the other afraid to offer it. 'Go,' Richard mouthed to the other young man, giving him a swift clap on the shoulder by way of reassurance before crossing the dining room to kneel at his mother's feet. He had made his mother cry. What sort of a son made his mother cry?

'I'm sorry, Mama,' he said, lifting the hand that rested in her lap. 'I'm so sorry I spoke to you like that. Can you ever forgive me?'

She raised her free hand and brushed back the lock of black hair that had fallen across his brow. 'I only want what's best for you, Richard.'

'I know that, Mama,' he said gently. 'I am a very ungrateful son.'

'You are a very loved son, Richard.'

'You and my father have never left me in any doubt of that, Mama. *Can* you forgive me?'

'Do you even need to ask that question?'

Richard smiled up at her, raised the hand he held, and pressed it to his lips.

CHAPTER THIRTY-NINE

It was the middle of August, and Edinburgh was thronged with people, bursting at the seams. They had come from all over the country: the Highlands, the Borders, Fife, Perth, Dundee, Aberdeenshire and Moray. The chance to see the king and the pageantry surrounding his visit was not to be missed. Despite the traditional rivalry between Scotland's two largest cities, people of all ages and classes had flocked to the capital from Glasgow and the west of Scotland too.

There was a joke going the rounds that the western city must be completely empty at the moment, its entire population having decamped to Edinburgh. Judging by the number of Glasgow accents Richard was hearing as he shouldered his way up the Earthen Mound this Monday morning, that vision of the normally bustling streets of Glasgow as quiet and empty wasn't so far from the truth.

He threw a question over his shoulder to Brendan, the coachman. 'Do you think everyone here knows where they're going to be sleeping tonight?'

'Not our problem, Mr Richard,' came the wryly amused response as Brendan drew level with him. 'We certainly can't squeeze any more folk in.'

'Indeed not. I doubt there's a room to be had in the whole of Edinburgh.' All the grand hotels on Princes Street were filled to capacity, as were the numerous coaching inns spread throughout the city and dotted around its outskirts. More humble lodging houses were doing a roaring trade too, accommodating the servants and retainers of the great and the good. Anyone anywhere who had a room to let was doing so.

Those who had so fortuitously remembered they had friends and relatives in Edinburgh were being welcomed by those friends and relatives with varying degrees of enthusiasm. The Hope household was full to capacity, both above stairs and below it.

'Too many women in one kitchen,' Brendan had confided morosely to Richard late last night as the two of them stood in the mews chatting for a few moments.

'Too many women in one drawing room,' Richard had confided in return. 'I never knew I had quite so many aunts or female cousins. Or that they were capable of talking quite so much. All at the same time too.'

'If they're anything like the ones twittering about the kitchens at the moment, usually nothing's decided at the end of it either,' Brendan had replied.

He and Richard had caught one another's eye this morning during one such interminable discussion taking place in the first floor drawing room to which the coachman had been summoned. The king had been expected to be safely in Edinburgh in good time for the city to celebrate his birthday this Monday – August 12th – but stormy weather out at sea had delayed him.

Now everyone was wondering if the first pageant planned for the visit would go ahead today or not. This was to be the ceremonial transfer of the Honours of Scotland – crown, orb and sceptre – from Edinburgh Castle to the Palace of Holyroodhouse, where they would remain for as long as the king did.

George IV wasn't actually going to be staying at Holyroodhouse. Neglected for so long, in a part of town that had become down-at-heel and unfashionable in the extreme, the palace had been deemed too shabby to house the person of the reigning monarch. That was a mere detail. Richard could see the symbolism behind the handing over of the Honours of Scotland quite clearly.

Whilst in Edinburgh, the King of the United Kingdom was taking custody of the ancient markers of Scottish monarchy and nationhood. You could say what you liked about Sir Walter Scott and his High Tory politics – and many of the people Richard had met over this summer at the Hendersons' bookshop did – but the writer was a very clever man.

He'd been the prime mover behind the royal visit and he'd organised every last detail of the planned events. Firmly of the belief that Scotland's future lay in the political union with England and the other countries of the British Isles, his aim was to reinforce that union. The tools he was deploying were much less tangible but potentially much stronger than laws and treaties.

There was the shared history, even if for hundreds of years that had seen Scotsmen lining up on one side of a battlefield and Englishmen on the other. Despite that – in largely fruitless attempts over the centuries to prevent it – the royal families of both countries had intermarried on more than one occasion. Genealogists and print-makers in Edinburgh were doing a roaring trade in charts that showed how inextricably linked the royal houses of the two countries were.

Scotland had no royal house of its own now, the Stuart line having more or less died out. The Jacobite Cause, which had sought to put that dynasty back on the throne, had shattered in bloody carnage at Culloden, almost eighty years since. For a long time after that, any mention of Jacobitism had been seen by those who governed as rank sedition, as dangerous a cause to espouse as Radical politics were today.

As the man once known as Bonnie Prince Charlie had slid into a drunken old age, the threat posed by the Jacobite Cause had guttered out along with him, fading into a harmless and even romantic twilight. It had become safe to laud the highlanders who had made up so much of his army back in 1745 and '46 as gallant, if misguided, warriors, loyal to a fault.

Over the past forty years, many of their descendants had demonstrated that loyalty to the British crown, playing their part in wars in America, Europe, India and elsewhere around the globe. Warriors needed wars. Warriors needed leaders, kings and princes for preference. Aye, Sir Walter Scott was a clever man, all right.

When he had been summoned to the drawing room, Brendan had reported that the man himself had gone past the end of the mews first thing this morning in his coach and four heading for the Mound. The procession was to assemble there before proceeding first to Edinburgh Castle to collect the Honours of Scotland and thence to Holyroodhouse to deposit them there.

The trouble was, there was now such a guddle of coaches and horses and people at the top of the Mound it was impossible to see what was going on. It didn't look as though the procession had started moving, but who could tell? Would it keep to its original route of coming down the Mound and along Princes Street, or might the decision be taken for it to go straight down the High Street?

Unable to stand the fruitless speculation any longer, Richard had suggested he and Brendan walk up the hill to see if they could find out what was happening. Using copious polite repetition – *Do excuse us, can you please let us through?* – coupled with ruthless use of his height, Brendan's bulk and their combined shoulders and elbows, they had fought their way to the top of the hill.

On the way, they discovered that two incidents had delayed the commencement of today's big event. One was the unanticipated arrival of a Highland chief who felt he had been slighted by not being asked to ride at the head of the procession. The other was that there had been a problem with Sir Walter's horses. Excellently trained animals though Brendan knew them to be, they had become nervous and unmanageable in the face of such a crowd and such confusion.

'Not the beasts' fault,' the coachman stated with vehemence, defending all members of the equine kingdom as he invariably did.

'Any animal might become nervous in this crush,' Richard agreed. 'Hang on,' he continued, 'that fellow over there's saying something about the procession.' He cocked his head, listening for further information. Both he and Brendan heard it.

'Still in the castle, expected out at any moment,' the coachman supplied.

'And going down the Mound as planned. They'd better clear the way—' Richard's head jerked up. 'What the *hell* was that?'

Brendan was already striding up the unforgiving slope that led up past Ramsay Gardens to the Castle Hill. 'Wood cracking, Mr Richard.' He threw the next, chilling words over his shoulder to a pursuing Richard. 'And people screaming.'

CHAPTER FORTY

Lungs bursting, Richard ran out onto the Castle Hill. Only because he had seen it a few days before did he know what he was looking at: one of the viewing platforms that were being constructed all over Edinburgh to enable as many people as possible to see the king and the parades and processions that were to take place during his visit.

This platform was nothing now but a mess of ropes and planks, men already swarming over the debris and attempting to lift it clear. The people buried beneath it were calling and yelling for help. All of the voices sounded young. Boys, mainly.

Oh, God, no! Frozen for a few seconds by the sheer horror of the thought that Andrew Dunbar or either of the Gunn boys might be buried under this, Richard felt a dunt in his back.

'We can help too, Mr Richard.'

'Of course.' Striding forward, his arms reaching out towards one of the planks, he felt Brendan seize him by the elbow.

'We'll all be doing more harm than good if we don't do this carefully. Dislodge the mess and perhaps hurt these poor souls even more. Order and method, Mr Richard. That's what's required here.'

'You're right, Brendan.' Richard ran a hand through his hair. 'You're absolutely right. Tell me what to do. I'll take my lead from you.'

Over the next forty minutes, Richard worked as he was

directed, not only by Brendan but by the handful of other men who seemed to know what they were doing. Sweating and straining, he put all of his strength into the job. At first, he was aware that he was repeating a frantic prayer inside his head. *Please God. Let Andrew not be under all of this. Nor any of the Gunn children.*

When he realised he didn't want anyone to be under all of this, he found a strange calm settling upon him. He would be no use to any of those lying injured under these rough planks and dusty ropes if he didn't calm down. Calm down, do what he could, help whoever he found here.

It was early afternoon before he left the Royal Infirmary. He went, of course, to The Pearl Fisher. As ever, he stood for a moment at its entrance, blinking into the gloom. He was almost knocked off his feet when Kate came rushing forward.

'Hey!' he protested, taking an involuntary step backwards even as his arms settled around her.

'You're safe!' she cried against his chest. 'You're safe!'

'Of course I'm safe. Och, Kate, you weren't worried about me, were you?'

'Of course I was worried about you! We heard aboot the accident. That it was mainly boys and young men who were hurt. Naebody was talking o' onything else when they came in for their meridian. I wanted to go straight along to the Royal Infirmary but Aunt Chrissie wouldna let me, so Andrew and Rebecca went but they were sent away at the door because everyone was so busy. I was going to go back there a wee minute ago but Andrew said you might come here as usual and then you might be worried aboot us. So now he and Rebecca have gone up to the bookshop to see if Mr and Mrs Henderson know onything.'

The torrent of words ceased as she pulled back out of his embrace, and he saw her eyes widen. 'Richard, you're hurt! Come and sit doon and let me hae a wee look at ye!' She gestured wildly towards the front of his shirt and in obviously increasing alarm at both of its sleeves.

'I'm not hurt,' he replied, hastening to reassure her. His own eyes adjusted now to the gloom of the tavern, he glanced down at himself and saw what she saw, a filthy, dusty shirt with streaks and smears of blood on it. He had long since discarded his coat, making it into a pillow for a young lad whom he had lifted into a cart that had taken some of the injured to the military hospital within Edinburgh Castle.

'It's not my blood, Kate. I was helping other people who'd been hurt. They took some of them up to the castle and the rest went to the Royal Infirmary.'

'You went there too?'

'Aye. Although I wasn't much use. It was the surgeons most of the injured needed.' He bowed his head and pinched his nose with his thumb and forefinger. 'People have lost arms and legs, Kate. Most of them young lads.' He laughed a mirthless laugh. 'Too adventurous, that was the trouble. They were told the viewing platform wasn't complete, told not to climb up it. But they did it anyway. As far as I know, two of them have been killed. That's not what they expected when they woke up this morning, is it?'

Kate took his hand from his face and wrapped her own fingers around it. 'Come and sit doon and I'll fetch you a wee restorative.' Ushering him into a smoke-blackened settle in the corner of the tavern close to the bar, she hovered over him as he dropped down into it. 'Whit aboot your mother and father, Richard? Will they be worried about you too?'

'No.' His speech slurring as emotion and exhaustion began to catch up with him, he explained as she went behind the bar that Brendan had been with him. 'Once we were sure we had everybody out, he went back down the hill to let my parents know what was happening and that I'd accompanied some of the injured to the infirmary. Thanks,' he added, taking the pewter tankard into which Kate had sloshed a generous measure of claret. 'Come and sit next to me?'

As she slid in beside him, he placed the tankard on the table in front of him and put one arm around her shoulders. 'I shouldn't do this. I'm filthy.'

'You need to do this,' she countered. 'And, forbye, I'm no' exactly averse to you putting your arm aboot me.'

'That's nice to know,' he mumbled. 'I felt so useless this morning, Kate.'

'I dinna see why. Sounds tae me like you really helped those poor folk.'

'I'd have gone in there like a bull at a gate if Brendan hadn't told me to be careful. Done more harm than good.'

'So you've learnt a lesson from your coachman. Too proud tae dae that?'

'No, of course not!' He pulled back a little, the better to look at her. 'Brendan set me on my first pony. Brendan... Well, he's Brendan, that's all.'

'And that's a lot?' she queried, gazing back at him.

'Aye. That's a lot. There were other men helping too,' he said. 'All kinds of men. Gentry and common men and shopkeepers and carters. Mr Henderson was there. He was also one of those as knew what to do. Cool head in a crisis. I expect he's telling Andrew and Rebecca all about it right now. Settle down again,' he instructed. 'I wasn't much use at the infirmary, either.' Pulling her back into the embrace of his arm, he tilted his head to one side and rested it against hers.

'So why did ye bide there so long?'

'Because I was sitting with the injured. Administering laudanum. Trying to reassure them while they were waiting to go under the knife. Doing my best to convince them they were in safe hands. It's often shock that kills patients undergoing an amputation.'

'Did ye reassure them? Make them less shocked?'

'I think I succeeded in calming them down a bit.'

'Then you helped them. I'd jalouse you probably helped them a lot mair than ye ken. Are you hungry?'

'Starving. Although I didn't realise that until you brought the subject up. Can you feed me, Kate?'

'Cullen Skink all right?' Disentangling herself from him, she rose to her feet.

Richard smiled up at her. 'Cullen Skink is perfect.'

He left an hour later, Kate walking with him to the corner of Niddry Street as usual, although they did not slip into the close to kiss and caress as they normally did. Instead, Richard bent forward and pressed a long, cool kiss against her forehead. There was no one about, the street deserted. 'When do you get your dress?'

'Thursday morning. In time for us to watch the king go up the High Street from Mr and Mrs Henderson's window.'

'Are you excited about it? The dress, I mean.' He pulled a comical face. 'Seeing the king too, I suppose. Although I'd never admit to feeling excited about that.'

'I *was* excited about it. Until this awful thing happened today.' A frown creased her creamy forehead. 'Would I no' be a very—' She paused, searching for the right word. 'Would I no' be a very *shallow* person gin I were still to be excited about something like a dress, when other folk have lost their lives?'

'I do not think so,' Richard said, gravely considering her question. 'In a way, does it not do a disservice to those who suffered today if we become gloomy and sad? Far better to see if there is something practical one can do for them. For example, I shall call past the castle's infirmary and the Royal tomorrow and see how the survivors are doing. If it has not already been thought of, I shall suggest the starting of a collection to help those who might need financial support,' he added, the idea at that very moment occurring to him.

'That would be a fine thing to do.' Kate's eyes softened. 'You're a good man, Richard Hope.'

'Me? I'm nothing but a well-off wastrel.'

'You are nothing o' the sort. Richard,' she went on, 'some folk are saying the accident is a bad omen—'

He placed his fingertips against her mouth – his hands, at least, he had washed at The Pearl Fisher – and stopped her words. 'I don't believe in bad omens and neither should you. In fact, I forbid it.'

Her face lit up with laughter. 'You *forbid* it? Who do you think you are, my husband or something?'

The word brought them both up short. He hadn't offered her marriage, he had offered her almost a marriage. Promised he would think of her almost as a wife and himself as like a husband. Once again he could see that from her point of view it wasn't much of a bargain. Not secure, not respectable, not honourable. Yet he couldn't stop himself from saying what he said next.

'You haven't given me an answer yet, Kate.'

She raised one hand and drew it down the side of his face. 'Soon, Richard,' she said. 'You'll have your answer very soon.'

'Then I must be content to wait until I receive it.' They kissed, and he headed off up Niddry Street, turning within a few steps to look back down at her. 'See you on Thursday, then?'

'Aye. Although aiblins ye'll no' recognise me in my fine new gown.'

'I don't think I'll have a problem,' he said, still walking backwards up the hill. 'You'll still be my Kate even when you're dressed like a fine lady, won't you?'

'Of course I will,' she called up. 'Of course I will.' A smile curved her mouth. Such a smile it was too: tinged by the sadness of what had happened today, yet mischievous and loving as well. 'Dinna keep walking backwards. Ye might fall over.'

'What,' he called back, thinking how much he loved this girl, 'and get my clothes dirty? That would never do.'

Kate stood and watched as he turned, strode to the top of Niddry Street and turned again to wave and blow her a kiss as he always did before disappearing from view. That would be him heading for the North Bridge and his road home.

You'll still be my Kate even when you're dressed like a fine lady, won't you?

She'd been touched by the question and by the look on his face when he had asked it. His Kate. That's what he wanted her to be.

Somewhere nearby a church bell chimed the hour. Three o'clock. Early yet. Aunt Chrissie wouldn't rise for another hour. There was time to stand here and think.

Going back over the events of the day, something else Richard had said came back to Kate. *That's not what they expected when they woke up this morning, is it?* Life was like that. You never knew what might lie in front of you: tragedy round one corner; more happiness than you had ever dared to imagine round the other.

If you had the courage to pay the price.

CHAPTER FORTY-ONE

'I almost look like a young lady,' Kate said, standing in some bemusement in front of the cheval glass in Peggy Henderson's bedchamber.

Peggy laughed and patted her on the shoulder. 'You do look like a young lady, Kate, and a very lovely one at that.' Her busy hands rose to the puffed sleeves of Kate's dress, plucking at the material until she had it standing out to her satisfaction. 'You were absolutely right to go for this material. The gold and silver fabrics were striking but this is much more *à la jeune fille*. It's perfect for you.'

'You helped me choose it, Mrs Henderson,' Kate said, continuing to gaze at the dress, the background colour of which was a rich creamy buttermilk and which was printed with pretty little sprigs of blue flowers with delicate green stems.

'I only confirmed your own opinion. You have a good eye for colour, lass.' Raising one hand, Peggy described a circle in the air. 'Turn around so I may check if the skirt is hanging properly.'

Obeying her, Kate threw a shy smile at their combined reflections in the mirror. 'The material feels lovely too. It's so nice to wear long skirts. Och, there's a word for what I mean but I dinna ken what it is!'

'Luxurious?' Peggy suggested.

'Luxurious,' Kate repeated. 'Aye. *Lu-xur-ious,*' she said again, allowing the consonants and vowels to roll around her mouth and enunciating the word with such relish that both women laughed.

'You've learnt a lot of new words this summer, haven't you?'

Having completed the requested turn, Kate's hand went to her hair, piled up on top of her head and threaded through with one of the ribbons Richard had given her, a blue one that exactly matched the colour both of her eyes and the flowers on her dress. 'Like *à la grècque*, you mean?' She glanced at her mentor of all that was modish. Seeking reassurance that she's pronounced that correctly too, Peggy thought. She had. The girl was a quick study.

'Perfectly pronounced. And your skirt is hanging beautifully. Why do you frown, my dear?'

This time the anxious glance was being cast in Andrew's direction. Perched on the edge of a carved wooden chair set at the open window of the bedchamber, he was engrossed in what was happening in the street below. A hum of excited voices rose from it.

Despite his obvious absorption in what was going on outside the window, Kate spoke softly. Raising one hand, she laid it against the front of her bodice. There wasn't much to that, scoop-necked as it was and ending not very far below her breasts, as its empire line style demanded. 'This is not immodest?'

'Not at all,' Peggy said. 'It is the very height of fashion. And, you know, my dear Kate, it is not cut *so* very deep.' She too lowered her voice. 'Wait till you see how some of the ladies who have come with the royal party are dressed. One of my friends lives in Picardy Place. She says that when the procession came up from Leith last Thursday, her husband confessed he was not sure where to look!'

For the much anticipated arrival of King George IV in his Scottish capital had happened at last, delayed by bad weather though the royal flotilla had been. He had now been here a week, holding levees and audiences at Holyroodhouse and dining with Sir Walter Scott and other notable citizens. Today it was the turn of the ordinary people of Edinburgh to see their monarch.

The king was to progress up the High Street from the Palace of Holyroodhouse to Edinburgh Castle. Once again, the symbolism was evident to anyone who cared to look for it. Over the centuries so many Scottish kings and queens had also undertaken that short journey, conferring on the narrow thoroughfare which linked the two royal residences its other name of the Royal Mile.

Today's event had been put in jeopardy by the rainy weather that was dogging the visit. It had been reported that Sir Walter had felt it necessary to issue an apology to the king over that, telling him a funny story about the old worthy who, finding himself in a similar position, had hastened to assure an important visitor that there was nothing *personal* in the continuing downpours.

From his post at the window, Andrew had announced a few moments ago that it looked as if everything was all set to go ahead. Certainly the folk congregating on the High Street with their umbrellas above their heads seemed to think so.

'What about you, young man?' Peggy called. 'What do you think of your sister?'

'I think she looks braw.' Sliding off the wooden chair, Andrew came across the room to join them. Watching him, Peggy found there was a lump in her throat. It was heartening to see him walking so much more easily.

'What do you think of yourself in your fine new clothes?' she asked, making a sweeping gesture with her arm to indicate that he should come and stand next to his sister in front of the cheval glass.

'I think I look braw too. The shoes are the best bit,' he told both women, his eyes dropping to his feet. 'Forbye I'm still a wee wobbly on the built-up one.' He pulled a face. 'I'd have loved tae have gone up Calton Hill last week tae see the king coming up from Leith but Kate was feart I might fall over and get trampled on.' The rueful grimace changed to one of tolerant amusement for his big sister's fears.

'Aiblins you'll be used enough to your new shoes to go up there when the king leaves,' Peggy comforted. 'Mr Henderson wouldn't let me go either, Andrew.'

'Because he doesna approve o' the king?' Kate asked.

'He said that was the reason. A matter of principle, he said. I said it was a matter of principle not to be rude to a guest, whether or not you agreed or disagreed with them and the position they occupy. And since the king was coming as a guest to Edinburgh, we both ought to go and greet him.'

'What did Mr Henderson say to that?' Andrew queried, his face alight with interest. He didn't yet know he was going to be joining the Henderson household, a stipulation Kate had made. When Peggy had asked what would happen if he didn't want to come and live with them, Kate had laughed. 'He'll want to. Dinna worry about that, Mrs Henderson.'

'And you, Kate?' Peggy had asked. 'Will you be coming to stay with us too?'

'I'll tell you that very soon, Mrs Henderson,' Kate had replied. 'There's something else I have to think over first.' Then she had changed the subject, leaving Peggy horribly afraid she knew only too well what that *something else* might be.

'Mr Henderson,' Peggy said now, answering Andrew's question, 'confessed that what he was really worried about was that the two of us might become separated in the crowd and someone might knock me off my feet. Not see me.'

'Because you're no' very tall?'

'Exactly. So it was only because he was worried about me. Although I still wish we had gone. By all accounts it was a bonnie sight, all the ships of the royal squadron together, riding at anchor off Leith.'

'I'm going tae see them on Sunday afternoon. Wi' Mr Gunn and Rebecca and the others. We're going out in a boat and we're going tae sail round them all!'

'How thrilling. How has this come about?'

'Och, in all the excitement I almost forget to tell you,' Kate said, her eyes shining as brightly as her brother's. 'Mr Gunn has secured a permanent position at Inverleith.'

'At the new botanical garden? How wonderful!'

'Aye,' Kate said. 'There's a wee house goes with the job too. Seemingly they're real pleased with the work he's done at the Old Physic Garden—'

'Did he meet the king's physician?'

'He did,' Andrew put in. 'It's him wha's hired the boat. A wee thank you to the citizens of his native city, he told Mr Gunn. He was giving out tickets for the boat trip and he gave one to Mr Gunn and then asked if he had ony children wha might like tae ging too—'

'And Mr Gunn didn't tell any lies,' Kate put in. 'All he said was he knew of four children who would love to go on a boat trip!'

'Only he forgot to ask for a ticket for you, Kate,' Andrew said regretfully.

'I'd likely be seasick, Andrew. You go with the Gunns and enjoy yourself. He already knows the names of all the ships in the royal flotilla, Mrs Henderson.'

'I know,' Peggy said, pride in her voice as there was in Kate's. 'Let's hear them, Andrew.'

He reeled them off, beginning with the stately sailing ship on which the king had sailed north – the *Royal George* – on through the private yachts and Royal Navy ships and finishing with the two steamships that were also part of the dozen-strong royal flotilla. *The Comet* and the *James Watt*, so he informed Peggy and his sister, were there lest the seas had been so choppy the king might have had to board one of them in order to make better progress north.

Peggy Henderson looked admiringly from him to Kate. 'How does he know all this?'

'Andrew always knows things like this. Makes it his business to find them out.' She laughed. 'He's no' so different from Mr Henderson in that respect.'

Then he'll fit right in here. The words weren't said out loud but the thought passed between Peggy and Kate. The two women smiled at one another before Peggy looked at Andrew again, so smart in a blue jacket, black trousers and dazzling white linen shirt fastened at the neck by an elegantly simple cravat.

Her boy. So very soon to be her boy. With Kate's permission, of course. The lass had made that very clear. This arrangement would require her initial and ongoing permission. She'd been nervous when she'd said that but determined. Peggy pointed towards Andrew's cravat. 'I'm amazed by how quickly you've learnt to tie that.'

'Mr Hope's a good teacher,' Andrew told her. 'About how to tie a cravat as well as how to read and write.'

Mr Hope. Mr Richard Hope who was waiting for them in Peggy's parlour, last seen cooling his heels in an obvious fervour of impatience as he anticipated his first sight of Kate in the pretty new gown he had bought for her. Oh dear. The young man was smitten enough as it was. When he saw Kate dressed like this...well, Peggy wasn't quite sure what would happen when he saw Kate dressed like this.

The lass had always had an air about her but over the summer she had grown so much in confidence, acquiring a womanly poise. Because she knows she is loved, Peggy thought, remembering the same blossoming in herself after she and Nathaniel had found one another.

Their path had not been smooth. Her father had been horrified by Nathaniel's political opinions, Nathaniel too passionate about those to be able or willing to conceal them. With the support of Peggy's brother, her father had at last been reconciled to his daughter marrying the man she had chosen, though his relationship with his son-in-law still wasn't an easy one.

All the same, Peggy and Nathaniel *had* found their path and been able to walk along it together, side-by-side. They were husband and wife, partners in the honourable estate of marriage. Peggy couldn't see how Richard Hope could offer the same kind of respectable partnership to Kate.

Kate herself must know that. The lass was no silly girl with stars in her eyes. Yet could it be she was delaying in giving Peggy a decision as to whether she too was coming to live above the bookshop because she was hoping against hope that her lover might yet ask for her hand in marriage? Or, as Peggy feared, was she trying to make up her mind as to whether she was going to accept a less honourable proposal?

'Should we go through, Mrs Henderson?' Kate asked. She laid one hand flat on the front of her gown. 'Butterflies in my stomach,' she confessed. 'About meeting the assembled company. I'd like to get that part o' it over with!'

Peggy laughed. 'Don't worry about them. All they'll want to know about is your opinion on this, that and the other. Usually related to politics. Not to mention,' she added, reaching out and tweaking one of the waves of Kate's hair, 'that there are a few of them who wouldn't want any too searching questions put to them about their own backgrounds.'

Radicals to a man – and woman – though they were, a group of the Hendersons' friends and most loyal customers had eagerly accepted the invitation to watch King George IV progress up the High Street of Edinburgh. The first floor windows of the Hendersons' flat were ideally positioned to give everyone an excellent view of the monarch whom they despised personally for his excesses, extravagance and cruelties to the late queen and whose position as hereditary ruler they fundamentally and continually questioned.

For some reason she didn't care to examine too closely, Peggy had thought it might be better if Richard Hope first met this new Catriona Dunbar in company. When she saw his face as he turned in response to the opening of the parlour door, she realised she might as well not have bothered. As far as Richard was concerned, there were only two people in the room – himself and the girl he was gazing at with such love and longing in his eyes.

CHAPTER FORTY-TWO

'Have I rendered you speechless?' Kate asked *sotto voce* half-an-hour later. As Richard had picked up some of her ways of speaking, so she had acquired some of his turns of phrase. They were standing together in one of the corners of the Hendersons' parlour, as far away as they could get from the windows and the rest of the company.

'You look beautiful,' he murmured. 'And you must know you do. Haven't you noticed the way every man in this room has been gawping at you?'

'Aiblins,' she said, dipping her head in delighted embarrassment. 'Apart from Mr Henderson, of course. He's only ever got eyes for Mrs Henderson. Quite a few o' the gentlemen are also giving yon Miss Drummond the eye.'

'Ah, well,' Richard said, throwing a swift glance at the young woman Kate had mentioned, who was perhaps not quite so young as she looked. It was all very skilfully done but a seasoned observer could see the artifice. 'They might be getting rather a lot of encouragement to do that from Miss Drummond herself.'

'Och, Richard,' Kate protested, 'she seems really nice. She's certainly not one of those silly, coquettish women.'

'No,' he agreed. 'She's much too professional for that.'

Kate looked at him for a moment. He looked back at her, the familiar gleam of mischief stealing into his green eyes.

'You canna possibly mean what I think you mean.'

'Can't I?'

'No!' Kate said, expelling the word in disbelief.

'Yes.' Low already, he lowered his voice further still. 'Miss Amelia Drummond and your Ella Balfour follow the same profession.' The mischievous gleam grew brighter. 'The oldest one, that is.'

'But she seems so well-bred. Although friendly too.'

'I'll say.'

Kate's eyes widened again. 'How... What...' She paused, wondering how best to phrase the question.

'She propositioned me,' he murmured. 'On a previous occasion. As you would say, I sent her off with a flea in her ear. Politely, of course. Told her I was spoken for.'

'I'm very glad to hear it.'

'Let's talk about us,' he said hungrily, his beautiful voice low and husky. 'Have you any idea how jealous it's making me to see all these men looking at you?'

Teasing words sprang to her lips. They remained there when she saw the depth of emotion in his eyes. 'You don't need to be. Och, Richard, you really don't need to be!'

'Prove it,' he urged. 'Meet me on Sunday at the Old Physic Garden. Please, Kate.'

She had just told him about the boat trip Andrew and the Gunn family were taking on Sunday afternoon. He had just told her about the spare set of keys to the Old Physic Garden.

'We could spend a couple of hours together. The two of us. With no one else to bother us. We could talk. There are things we need to talk about. Things for which we need privacy.'

'What if it rains on Sunday afternoon?'

'We'll go into the summer house. Does that question mean you'll come?'

'I didn't say that. Did the summer house no' need a new

door? That surely means it's got a new lock too.'

'No, it doesn't.' He shook his head. Bowing to pressure from his mother, he'd had his hair cut the previous week. Kate had told him acerbically she hoped he hadn't paid too pretty a penny to his fancy New Town barber. He still looked as if he'd only just got out of bed. She hadn't told him how much she loved the tumbling disarray of the dark, shining waves of his hair. Wild and windswept and free.

'Apparently the lock was sound, so they decided to economise. There's a novelty, eh? Mr Gunn told me.'

'Isn't it wonderful that he's got a permanent position at Inverleith? Although Andrew's going to miss them all when they move.'

'It is wonderful. And the children will surely be able to visit each other. Especially when Andrew becomes a schoolboy and is living here with the Hendersons.'

'You're so sure he's going to get into George Heriot's?'

'I couldn't be more sure. But we weren't discussing Andrew or the Gunn family. We were discussing what time you're going to meet me at the Old Physic Garden on Sunday afternoon. The earlier the better as far as I'm concerned. Shall we say one o'clock? Please, Kate,' he pleaded. 'We've hardly seen each other over the past week. It's not going to get any easier while the king's in Edinburgh, either. We really do need to talk. You know we do.'

She raised her eyebrows. 'So all you want to do is talk?'

'I didn't say that.' She saw him relax, drank in the slow smile that was curving his lips and the teasing promise that was lighting up his handsome face. 'Although I promise you nothing will happen we don't both want to happen.'

'What about the things we both *do* want to happen?'

Watching as that penny dropped, she saw desire slide into his eyes. 'Oh, Kate,' he moaned. 'D'you mean you might permit me to...' He paused before settling for '...permit me to take a few liberties?'

'Dinna get carried away,' she warned him darkly. 'For I'm no' planning to.' That was already a lie. A wave of desire for him was breaking over her. She was thinking of the last time they had stood together in the close at the foot of Niddry Street.

His hands were caressing her. His lovely voice was soft in her ear, telling her how much he longed to touch her and be touched by her without the barrier of clothes between them. Now he was murmuring about how he longed to see her beautiful breasts...her lovely legs...and, he always added, with the lazy smile that turned Kate's insides to butter...everything else in between.

'Oh, Kate.' He gave a funny little moan. 'How carried away do you think you might get? I'd love you to tell me. In as much detail as you like.' He drew in a breath deep enough to make his shoulders rise. 'Ooh, now I come to think of it, I'd *really, really* like that!'

She'd really like that too. She knew she would. Feeling her body respond to the very thought of it, she saw his gaze drop to her breasts. His voice was warm and intimate. 'Where will you permit me to touch you, Kate?'

'I haven't agreed to meet you yet. And lift your eyes, Richard Hope.' She was horribly aware it wasn't only her face that was growing rosy.

'No. I'm enjoying the view far too much. Do you have any idea how much self-control I'm exercising so that I don't touch you now?'

'Wheesht,' she whispered. 'Someone will hear you.'

'Not a chance. They're all too busy waiting for the king to appear.' He threw a glance over his shoulder, confirming that.

Following his gaze, Kate saw a skinny young man leaning at an impossible angle out of one of the casements, everyone else crowded around him.

'And you're no' bothered because you've already seen him? You haven't told me about that yet. Is it true he wore a kilt with flesh-coloured pantaloons below it?'

'Aye. He looked quite ridiculous. But wheesht yourself for the moment. If this company knew I'd been at one of the levees at Holyrood, they'd likely hang me from the nearest barber's pole. Not that I caught more than the briefest glimpse of the king through the crush. Especially when all the ladies had so many ostrich feathers pinned to their hair. Irene Steele said she felt like a horse at a funeral—' He stopped himself. 'You've no need to be jealous of her, you know.'

'I didn't say I was.'

'The look you gave me spoke volumes. Irene and I are good friends. That's all. I think you'd like her, too. I think she'd like you.'

'You're very possibly right. Although we're never like to meet one another, are we?'

'I think that's them coming now!' came a shout from the window.

'Damn,' Richard muttered. 'And bloody blast. And Hell's bloody bells into the bargain. Sunday afternoon, Kate. We'll talk about all of this. Say yes. Please say yes.'

'Wheesht,' she urged again, and led the way over to the window. An anticipatory silence had fallen on the Hendersons' parlour, and on the crowds of people lining the High Street, quiet enough for Kate to hear the wail of bagpipes in the distance. The sound had become a familiar one in Edinburgh over the past ten days as the city had filled up with Highland chiefs and their tails: bands of followers dressed in belted plaids or tartan trews and bearing all the accoutrements of Highland warriors of old – broadswords, targes, dirks, feathered bonnets, bagpipes and all.

As Peggy and Nathaniel began to open up all the windows, the skinny young man who'd been acting as look-out pulled himself back in and offered up a joke. 'Know what the definition of a gentleman is? Someone who *can* play the bagpipes, but doesn't!'

'I like the sound of the bagpipes,' Kate protested under cover of the laughter that followed.

'So do I,' Richard murmured in her ear. 'Let's get you the best possible view of the proceedings. You too, Andrew,' he said, turning to the boy who'd that moment appeared at his elbow.

'Hey,' protested the skinny young man as Richard elbowed his way in. 'Oh,' he said, catching sight of Kate. 'I beg your pardon. Didn't realise you had the young lady with you.' He moved to one side. 'Please. Take my place.' His eyes were travelling appreciatively over Kate.

'Uncommonly civil of you, sir,' Richard said, and swiftly put himself and Andrew on either side of Kate, obliging the skinny young man to move along to the next window. How sweet. How funny. She had never seen this side of Richard before.

'Are you laughing at me?' he demanded.

'Would I dare?'

'Oh, you'd dare all right.'

'Here they are!' cried Andrew. 'Och, Kate, Mr Hope, look at this!'

Obeying that excited command, Kate yelped in alarm. Her brother was half in and half out of the window. Lunging forward, she caught the back of his jacket and a face full of rain. The weather didn't seem to have dampened the spirits of the crowds lining the High Street. They'd grown noisier again, eagerly anticipating the procession.

'Come back in a wee bit.'

'I'm fine, Kate. I'll not fall.'

'You might. And you're getting wet. Your nice new clothes will be drookit.'

'Leave him alone,' Richard said amiably. 'He'll not fall and his clothes will dry out. Here we are! They're coming up the hill now!' Sophisticated young Mr Hope sounded as excited as the would-be schoolboy.

'Look at that bonnie black horse,' Andrew said. 'Who is the gentleman riding it?'

'The Knight Marischal, Andrew. Sandy Keith of Ravelston. His mount is indeed a magnificent animal.'

'What does Knight Marischal mean?'

'It's an hereditary office. An honour conferred on the Keith family by one of the Scottish kings.' Richard looked to Nathaniel Henderson for confirmation. 'I'm telling the lad the truth, I trust.'

Nathaniel nodded. 'Although the original title was *Earl Marischal*.'

'Weren't the members of that family strong in the Jacobite Cause?'

'Enough to have to go into exile,' his host confirmed. 'One of them ended up as a close confidant of Frederick the Great, which may or may not have compensated for having lost the Earl Marischal title as a result of choosing the wrong side in the dispute between the House of Stuart and the House of Hanover.'

'So reviving it is another of Sir Walter's little touches?' asked Amelia Drummond.

The skinny young man was giving Richard an odd look. 'You know the Knight Marischal well enough to call him Sandy rather than Alexander?'

'Not to his face.' Richard laughed. 'He's as old as Methuselah, for one thing.'

'Old enough to know better than to get himself up in those clothes,' Nathaniel Henderson snorted. 'Did you ever see anything like it outwith the pages of a book of fairytales? What would his illustrious and gallant forbears have thought of him?'

The Knight Marischal wore a flowing cloak of red velvet. When he adjusted his hold on the bridle of his horse, the white silk lining of the cloak showed. Two men walked on either side of his black horse. They wore rose-pink satin coats and white breeches.

'Oh, I don't know,' Peggy Henderson said, 'is not much of this costume authentic to its period? Look, Kate,' she called. 'They've even got white roses on their shoes!'

Nathaniel Henderson was snorting again. 'It's absurd. Completely absurd.'

'The horse is wearing clothes too,' Kate observed.

'Aye,' Richard said. 'Definitely what you would describe as *richly caparisoned*.'

'Richly *what-ed*?' she demanded, turning a laughing face up to him.

'I'll spell it for you later,' he promised. He laid his hand on her shoulder. 'Look. You don't want to miss this. It's the Scottish crown.'

'Being carried by the Duke of Hamilton,' Peggy Henderson said. 'Who would appear to be dressed in the style of the Merry Monarch and his cavaliers.'

'The Merry Monarch?' Kate asked, gazing down at a rider wearing a huge white lace collar over a black satin doublet, the full sleeves of which were slashed to show their white satin linings. The precious cargo he carried in front of him made her mouth drop open.

The Scottish crown. She, Kate Dunbar, was looking at the Scottish crown. *A cat may look at a king*; and a girl who works in an oyster cellar may look at a crown and wear a beautiful dress and be loved by Richard Hope. If I were to die now, she thought, this very minute, then at least I'd have lived...

'Charles II,' Peggy said in answer to her question. 'Who was, I think, the last reigning monarch to visit Edinburgh. Am I right, Nathaniel?'

Kate lost Mr Henderson's answer, entranced by the beauty of the Scottish crown. Set on its own cushion, the blue velvet of that darkened and deepened by the rain, the crown was wet too, its glorious gold and sparkling jewels glistening in response. 'It's beautiful,' Kate breathed. 'So very, very beautiful.' Richard's fingers squeezed her shoulder in agreement.

'One of the oldest crowns in Europe,' he told her proudly. 'Built up from a simple gold circlet worn by Robert the Bruce himself. Here come other gentlemen bearing the sceptre and the orb, completing the Honours of Scotland. And all of them lost for two centuries until Sir Walter discovered their hiding place in the castle. Oh, and that other rider is the Lord Lyon, King of Arms.'

'A red cloak for him,' Peggy said, peering through the window. 'Over a green coat.'

'A green coat lined with gold,' Kate supplied. 'Embroidered with...' Leaning forward for a better look, she felt Richard's hand bunch up the cloth at the back of her dress. 'Leave me alone,' she told him in an amused murmur, the words for his ears alone. 'I'll not fall. Thistles,' she announced in a louder voice. 'Gold thistles.'

For a moment everyone in the Hendersons' parlour stood in silence, watching as the rainbow of colours of clothes and heraldic tabards, velvet and gold caps and bright tartans splashed bravely across the grey background of the wet and dismal day.

'When would the High Street of Edinburgh have last seen an event such as this?' asked Amelia Drummond.

'At the final riding of our own parliament over a hundred years ago,' Nathaniel Henderson replied morosely. 'When a corrupt Scottish nobility took English gold in exchange for voting Scotland out of existence. *The end o' an auld sang.* That's how Fletcher of Saltoun put it. The people of Scotland did not want the Union. On the day it came into force, the bells of St Giles played "Why am I So Sad on my Wedding Day?"'

Kate threw him a glance over her shoulder. He sounded so sad too. 'Och, but Mr Henderson, we might not have our own parliament any more but Scotland does still exist!' She waved a hand towards the window. 'Does all of this not prove that? We still have the crown our kings and queens wore. We still have lots of the things that make us who we are. The Honours o' Scotland. The thistle as our symbol. The tartan the Highlanders are wearing. We want the king to see all this. We want him to know that we're different. I ken you think this is all bread and circuses but there's something magnificent about it. Is that not true? We're all standing here watching it and enjoying it. Maybe that's part of being Scottish too. That we do all enjoy this.'

She stopped, realising too late that every head in the room was turned towards her. Nathaniel Henderson threw her the wryest of looks. 'Some acute observations there, Miss Catriona. Very acute indeed. And,' he went on, generous in defeat, 'I'd have to admit Sir Walter's management of this is also inspired. Whatever you think of what he's doing, he is indeed doing it magnificently.'

'Reconciling Scotland and the House of Hanover,' Richard suggested. 'Associating Scotland's history with its own.'

'Which it is,' Peggy Henderson observed. 'There's no getting away from that. The royal houses are intertwined through marriage and subsequent ties of blood.'

'That's why a republic might be an excellent idea,' someone said.

'Won't ever work,' Amelia Drummond replied. 'As Miss Dunbar has pointed out, people enjoy the tradition and pageantry that goes with having a monarchy.'

'Especially when the tradition and pageantry comes complete with handsome Highland warriors,' Peggy said, gazing once more down into the High Street. 'They are magnificent too, are they not? All with their swords and targes. Kilts and plaids lend such an air to men as tall as these.' She glanced apologetically at her husband. 'One cannot deny that, Nathaniel.'

'I do not deny it, my dear. I might only observe that in the wake of the Jacobite Rising of 1745, the wearing of tartan was forbidden by law for a good forty years. Back in '45 or '46 there might well have been folk watching from this very window who would have been terrified by the sight of so many fully armed and tartan-clad Highlanders marching up the High Street of Edinburgh. But it would appear we're all Highlanders now.'

'Indeed,' Richard said with some feeling. He'd just spotted Torquil Grant among the massed Highlanders. That really was ironic. His one time friend had been brought up in London, spoke like an upper class Englishman and despised everything that was Scottish – everything except an Edinburgh medical training, that was. Richard knew Torquil planned to head back to London as soon as he got his MD, to set up in a lucrative private practice.

'Oh, look!' Andrew Dunbar cried. 'Is this the king coming now? The fat mannie waving the great big hat?'

'That's him,' Richard confirmed, laughing at Andrew's description of His Majesty, King George IV.

Kate glanced at Mr Henderson. He felt so strongly about the king. She knew Mrs Henderson had extracted a promise from her husband that he would not call out or do anything that might get him into trouble with the authorities. There was, she had observed, a platoon of soldiers lined up in front of the bookshop door, which was probably no accident.

Nathaniel Henderson was determined all the same to get a good look at the man of whose person and position he so disapproved. As his coach passed under the window, the king turned his head. The eyes of the monarch and the subject who denied his authority met. In the midst of a sea of cheers, there was a moment of silence. The king nodded to Nathaniel and the royal procession moved on.

CHAPTER FORTY-THREE

It was all over. Refreshments had been offered and enjoyed. A spirited discussion had taken place, not only on the events of the day and the king's visit but on the dizzying prospect that Scotland might one day get her parliament back. Kate had found herself once more offering an opinion. If the democracy that the Radicals advocated really was only a matter of time, then if the people of Scotland wanted their parliament back they could surely achieve that aim.

'We have to find our courage again,' Mr Henderson said darkly.

'Not to mention our confidence,' Amelia Drummond added, smiling at Kate. 'Have confidence in yourself and you can move mountains.'

As the party in the Hendersons' parlour broke up, the skinny young man spoke to Kate. 'So you enjoy spectacle, Miss Dunbar?'

'I do,' Kate said. 'Very much.'

'May I then ask if you have yet viewed the illuminations that bedeck the New Town? I should be happy to escort you and your young brother around them, if you would like. Perhaps tomorrow evening, when hopefully it will not be raining so heavily as it is now?'

She felt Richard's breath, warm on the back of her neck. 'Very kind of you to offer, but Miss Dunbar and Master Dunbar are viewing the illuminations with me tomorrow night.'

The skinny young man held up both hands, palms outward, as though finally offering his surrender. 'Can't blame me for trying, sir. No offence.'

'None taken,' Richard said smoothly. 'Although there damn well is,' he muttered as the other young man retreated. 'Who does he think he is, asking you to go and view the illuminations with him like that?'

'I might ask you the same.' Kate spoke with some asperity. 'I might also ask *when* you asked Andrew and me to go and look at the illuminations with you. I canna recall the occasion.'

'I'm asking you now.'

'Dinna look down your long nose at me,' she scolded. 'And dinna be so daft. How could Andrew and me walk round the New Town with you?'

'Put one foot in front of the other and try not to bump into any of the new gas lamps?'

'Very funny. You ken fine what I mean. You live in the New Town. Your family lives in the New Town. Lots o' other folk you know, too. All those aunties and cousins you've got staying with you at the moment. What if one o' them sees you with Andrew and me?'

'What if they do?'

She looked at him. He looked at her. Then: 'We'll go tomorrow night once they're all safely into the ball at the Assembly Rooms.'

'Are you no' going to that?'

'You need a ticket. There weren't enough to go round.' He didn't tell her he'd been sent one by the Earl of Hopetoun's secretary but had passed it on to a cousin, swearing the girl to secrecy. Tickets for the ball were like gold dust. The last thing he needed was for his mother to find out he hadn't accepted what was both an invitation and a mark of favour from his most grand and aristocratic relative.

He didn't think there was too much danger of his absence being noticed. The need for a ticket notwithstanding, he suspected there would be as much of a crush at the Assembly Room as there had been at the levees at Holyroodhouse. He'd be surprised if anyone found the space to do any dancing at this ball.

'Say you'll come and let me show you the illuminations, Kate. How about I rendezvous with you and Andrew here tomorrow night at half past seven? Will you both wear your new clothes?'

There was another little pause. 'I'd have to persuade Aunt Chrissie she could do without me for one evening.'

'You can do that. Ask Ella Balfour to remain vertical rather than horizontal for one evening.'

'Richard!' she said reproachfully.

He grinned at her. 'Have you noticed we're all alone in this room now?'

She had noticed that. The Hendersons were downstairs seeing their visitors out through the bookshop and it hadn't escaped Kate's notice that Peggy had swept Andrew up with her when she had left the parlour, allowing Kate and Richard some time alone together.

'What will you permit me to do when we meet on Sunday afternoon, Kate? Will you maybe let me touch you here?' He brought his hand up to the front of her gown and began to run one finger around its square neck. Swiftly down from her shoulder. Slowly across the front of it. The rest of his hand brushing across one breast and then the other.

Kate's eyes fluttered shut. 'You shouldn't have done that.'

'Your reactions are telling me otherwise. Want me to do it again?'

'No. Yes.' Her face was glowing now. She could feel the heat. As she could feel how her breasts had responded to his touch. 'What if someone comes back up?'

'We'll hear them on the stairs long before they get here.' Taking a step closer to her, he issued a soft command. 'Move back. Into the corner of the room.'

'No,' Kate said, but did it anyway. His hands rose again to her breasts, his palms resting on their gentle swell and his fingertips dancing along the smooth and creamy skin exposed by the low-cut bodice of her gown.

'I love you in this dress,' he murmured. 'But I'd love to see you wearing no dress at all.'

'You shouldn't say that either.'

'I just did. Turn around.'

'Why?'

'Dae as you're tellt, woman. You're going to like this.' One arm came round her neck, warm and possessive. His free hand he slid down the front of her bodice, in over her breast and underneath it to cup it in his fingers. 'Aah,' he sighed. 'That's better. Don't you think that's better, Kate?'

'I don't know what the correct word is to describe what I think about this.' Not sure how she'd managed to formulate a coherent sentence, within seconds she found herself breathless, barely able to speak at all. He seemed to know that.

'There comes a point,' he murmured against her ear, 'when words are superfluous. If it feels good just give me some sort of an indication of that.' When he moved his fingers to stroke her breast, a little moan floated out through Kate's parted lips. 'So this does feel good, Miss Dunbar?'

'Aye,' she said, the word floating out on a sigh of pleasure. 'Does...this...feel...good...to...you...too?'

'It feels wonderful to me. You feel wonderful to me.' He

brought his thumb up. Kate moaned again and allowed herself to fall back against him.

'Very nice,' he said softly. 'Very, very nice. Pity we're going to have to stop soon.'

She uttered a wordless protest at that.

'What's this?' he asked. 'Careful Kate not being careful any more? I'm going to turn you around now and kiss you, and you're going to kiss me back. Only tell me one thing first. What time will you meet me at the Old Physic Garden on Sunday?'

The time for hesitation was past. 'Two o'clock,' she murmured. 'That's the earliest I can get there.'

His warm hand stilled, and he swung her round so they could look at one another. 'You're saying yes?'

'Aye.' Loved and loving, she gazed up at him. 'I'm saying yes.'

CHAPTER FORTY-FOUR

'Your eyes are huge, Andrew!'

'They have to be big, Kate. I'm not wanting to miss any of the illuminations.'

Over his head, she mouthed a few amused words to Richard. 'He's so solemn.'

Richard nodded, not sure he was capable of speech. With each passing moment he was growing more excited, his blood tumbling and fizzing through his veins. Being with her over here in the New Town was risky. He knew it was. As he also knew that he was revelling in the awareness of that risk.

He'd been so careful all summer. Now the summer was drawing to a close and he was tired of being careful. He was in a dangerous mood tonight. Reckless. Not caring if someone he knew did see him with Kate and Andrew. He managed a question to her. 'Are you enjoying the illuminations too, Kate?'

'More than anything. More than anything I've ever seen in my entire life!' She laughed at her own enthusiasm. 'I'm not wanting to miss any of them either.' Suiting the action to the words, she looked away from him in favour of gazing about her at the brilliantly lit splendour of the New Town.

They had started in Queen Street. Meeting Kate and Andrew at the Hendersons' as arranged, Richard had led them there first, through St Andrew's Square and down the hill. He'd had a mental tussle with himself about that, wondering if he should have been bold enough to head for George Street. Perhaps running the risk of being seen by a friend or relative on their way to the ball in the Assembly Rooms was exactly what he ought to do. He wasn't ashamed of either of the Dunbars, was he?

He glanced at the two of them. How could anyone be ashamed of this pair, especially tonight? They both looked so good in their new clothes. Taking in the illuminations, they both looked what they were, bright and intelligent and interested in the world around them. In the end, though, knowing Kate was nervous about them bumping into someone who knew him, he had plumped for Queen Street as the starting point for their tour of the illuminations.

The façade of almost every house was lit up. The lights were created by a combination of etched glass panels with lamps, candles or the new wonder of gas lighting placed behind them. There were flags everywhere, a mixture of the blue and white of Scotland's St Andrew and the red, white and blue of the Union Jack. There were pictures of the king on his throne, with columns of tartan-clad Highlanders respectfully approaching him.

There were pictures of Edinburgh's landmarks too: the castle, the High Kirk of St Giles, Holyroodhouse, John Knox's house. There were thistles galore, sometimes on their own, sometimes intertwined with the rose of England. There were angels and cherubs, birds and butterflies and patriotic slogans.

Welcome to the land of your ancestors!

Scotland welcomes her king!

A Health Unto His Majesty!

On one house in Queen Street, a female figure carried a ship in her arms. Above her head a motto blazed out. *Let Glasgow Flourish!*

'Guess who's lodging there?'

'Might it be the Lord Provost o' Glasgow?' Kate asked.

'Correct. Not to mention most of his magistrates. If we go up this way we'll come to Charlotte Square and then we can walk along George Street.'

'Everyone who's going to the ball will be there now?'

'Bound to be. There's lots to look at in Charlotte Square too so it'll be a wee while before we're in George Street anyway.' He laid a hand on Andrew's shoulder. 'How's your foot, young man? Not getting sore with us doing all this tramping about?'

'Not a bit, Mr Hope, sir. Oh,' Andrew breathed as they emerged into Charlotte Square, 'this is rare!'

More flags. More Highlanders in flowing tartan and shining broadswords. More flattering representations of King George IV. More thistles and roses.

Richard was impressed too. He was even more impressed by the effect the illuminations were having on Kate. There was the way the light they cast spilt over her face. There was the way that lovely face lit up in response to each new picture she saw. She looked bewitched. Spellbound. 'Which one do you like best?' he asked gently.

'Och, I don't think I can say. Every one's better than the last!' She turned her bright, happy face up to him. 'How about you?'

'I like the picture I'm looking at now,' he murmured, knowing Andrew was too absorbed in the illuminations to be listening to him. 'The one of a red-haired girl with beautiful blue eyes.'

When she smiled at him, he felt his heart melt. It was he who was bewitched, falling more under her spell with every passing moment. He could not bear to give her up. He did not think when they met tomorrow at the Old Physic Garden she was going to tell him they must part, but how could he know? For her to become his mistress, she was going to have to sacrifice a great deal. Would she think he was worth it? Tears pricking behind his eyes, he looked away from her and pretended to survey the crowd.

Judging by the voices and snatches of conversation he was hearing, it was made up of people of all ranks of society. It was harder to discern who was who when everyone was wearing their best clothes. One of his visiting cousins had observed that the common people of Edinburgh had been remarkably well turned-out and remarkably well behaved throughout the visit. There had been little disorder and few obvious signs of drunkenness. Richard's cousin had ventured the opinion that being well dressed might have inspired people to be on their best behaviour too.

He had made an observation for himself this evening. Kate and Andrew still spoke with their own warm, soft accents, but they had adjusted them a little, minding their *p*s and *q*s more than he'd ever heard them do. Just as he adjusted the way he spoke when he went down to the Cowgate. It worked both ways, then. People with a good ear and sensitive to their surroundings and nuances of behaviour and speech could fit in anywhere.

Gazing along George Street, thinking they had probably best walk along the opposite side from the Assembly Rooms, he gave a little start.

'Something wrong?' Kate asked.

'Not a thing.' Taking a firm hold of her hand, he tugged her towards him. 'Andrew. We're going this way now.'

'Where to, Mr Hope?'

'Across George Street.' Would she know which side the Assembly Rooms were on? He hoped not. Once they got closer to them, she could hardly fail to notice the coaches tailed back from the front of the building: coaches that weren't waiting for their owners to come out but had yet to deliver them to the ball. It was Andrew who spotted those first, lifting his sharp little chin to indicate the landaus and sociables clogging up the broad and graceful avenue. A crowd had gathered to watch all of the arrivals.

'Would folk not have been better to have used Shank's mare?'

'Undoubtedly. Especially those folk who only live a few hundred yards away from the Assembly Rooms. But it's important to make an entrance, you see. Excuse me.' Applying his tried and tested technique of combining politeness with the ruthless use of his height, shoulders and elbows, he cleared a path through to the edge of the thoroughfare for himself, Kate and Andrew.

She went along with it. Given that he had such a firm grasp of her hand, Richard supposed she didn't have much choice. 'Look,' he said, with an idea in his head that if he could stop her from uttering a protest everything would be all right. 'That's the Duke of Atholl going in. Oh, and there's the Duchess of Buccleuch.'

Kate gave him one of her looks. 'I thought you said everyone would have gone in by now.'

'I suppose this congestion has delayed them.' He had known it would. Dammit, he could surely admit that now, even if only to himself. He had wanted this to happen.

He was still holding her hand. When it tightened around her fingers, she posed a quiet question. 'Who's coming now, Richard?'

'Is it the king?' Andrew asked excitedly.

'Not the king,' Richard said, his height allowing him to scan the next half-dozen carriages progressing at a snail's pace along George Street. 'Someone I want you to meet. Come with me, Kate. You too, Andrew.'

He was no longer thinking about this, no longer trying to work out what he was going to do or say when he reached the open landau for which he was heading, the one which was carrying his mother and Irene Steele.

CHAPTER FORTY-FIVE

It was his mother who spotted him first. 'Richard! What on earth are you doing out here?'

'Showing some friends the illuminations, Mama,' Richard said firmly. 'May I have the honour of presenting Miss Catriona Dunbar and her brother, Master Andrew Dunbar? Miss Dunbar,' he said, turning to Kate. 'Please allow me to introduce you and Andrew to my mother.' His eyes were flashing her a message but she wasn't sure how to interpret it. She was even less sure what he wanted or expected her to do now.

With similar formality, he introduced her and Andrew to the young lady sitting opposite his mother in the open carriage – and Kate found herself being introduced to Miss Irene Steele. Irene Steele. The girl his mother wanted him to marry. Kate looked up first at Mrs Hope and then at Miss Steele, and couldn't think of a single word to say to either of them.

With a quick glance at Richard, Irene Steele took Kate aback by smiling at her with what seemed like genuine friendliness. 'Are you enjoying the illuminations, Miss Dunbar?'

Responding to the open attitude, Kate relaxed. 'Och, they're grand! Real bonnie!' You're real bonnie too, she thought, seized by an enormous wistfulness. You seem like a nice person too. He probably will marry you. If his parents want him to, then you must be suitable for him in every possible way. You'll come from the right sort of family and you'll probably have money too, and you'll be the sort of woman who'll know how to encourage him to make the best o' himself—

Mrs Hope's eyes had narrowed. 'You are surely not here without a chaperone, Miss Dunbar?' There was a very slight emphasis on that *Miss*, but not so slight Kate wasn't instantly aware of it. She might look the part of a young lady tonight but she knew she hadn't sounded like one when she had responded to Irene Steele's question.

'Richard and Miss Dunbar have perhaps become separated from Miss Dunbar's chaperone in the crowd, Mrs Hope.'

'Actually no, Irene. Miss Dunbar's chaperon is here.' He indicated Andrew. 'Her brother. Who is shortly to become a pupil at my own old school.'

Marjorie Hope's eyebrows shot up. 'George Heriot's?'

'Master Dunbar has secured a scholarship, Mama. He is a very clever young man.'

'Is your mother a widow, then, *Miss* Dunbar?' Again there was that faint emphasis or, more exactly, a reluctance to address her as a young lady should be addressed.

'My mother and father are both dead, Mrs Hope.'

'Who are your people, then? With whom do you reside?'

Her people. A tavern keeper and a grave robber. She could hardly tell his mother that. Kate turned in mute appeal to Richard. At exactly same moment, he swung away from her, responding to something the coachman was saying to him. Kate turned back to Mrs Hope and for a moment the two women simply looked at one another.

There were so many emotions passing across his mother's face. She was doing her best to hide them from Irene Steele but they were all there. Anger. Embarrassment. Fear. *Fear?*

'Brendan is being signalled to move on,' Richard said. 'We shall all be shouted at if he does not.' He stepped back, a hand on Kate and Andrew's elbows to move them back too. The coach edged forward. 'I shall see you later, Mama. Enjoy the ball. You too, Irene.'

Kate stood and watched the landau gather a little speed as it moved closer to the Assembly Rooms. 'Richard!' called a young female voice. 'Yoo-hoo!'

A coach full of several young ladies and two older ones pulled up. The latter were chaperoning the former, of course. Young ladies didn't go out without a chaperone. Only young women did that. Common women. Women who were never addressed by their betters with any degree of politeness. Women who didn't merit the designation of *Miss* before their names. If she had worked in his mother's house, she would have addressed her as *Dunbar*. If Mrs Hope had bothered to address her at all.

'They're my cousins,' Richard said. 'And two of my aunts. Should I introduce you to them too?'

'I dinna think so,' Kate said tightly, all too aware that his cousins' eyes were fair popping out of their pretty heads. 'Come on, Andrew,' she muttered, stepping out into the roadway and walking along in front of the crowd. She didn't stop until she had rounded the corner of Castle Street and then only because Andrew called to her not to go so fast, he couldn't keep up.

'I'm sorry,' she said, stopping dead. Following on behind, Richard had to put his hands on her shoulders to stop himself from crashing into her. Angry with him, herself and the whole world, she shook him off. Andrew looked from her to Richard and back again, offering a very tentative 'We've no' seen all the illuminations yet.'

Kate bit her lip hard enough for it to hurt. 'I think maybe we should head for home now, Andrew.'

'Must you?'

'Aye,' she said, looking at Richard for the first time since the encounter with his mother and Irene Steele – and that carriage full of his cousins and his aunties. 'We must.'

'Don't go home yet, Kate. Please.'

When she threw him a warning glance, he dug into his pocket and handed Andrew a coin. 'Go and buy us some hot chestnuts from that stand over there, Andrew, will you? We'll wait for you on the corner of this lane along here.' He pointed it out. 'See where I mean?'

As Andrew made his way across Castle Street, Richard's eyes followed him. 'He's managing very well on his built-up shoe, don't you think?'

'I think a lot of things.'

Richard's eyes came back to her face. 'I'm sorry. I'm really sorry that happened.'

She shook her head as though trying to rid herself of a persistent fly. 'Dinna tell me lies, Richard. Dinna tell yourself lies. You made that happen. Why did you do that?'

He propped himself against one of the new gas lamp-posts set at intervals along the edge of the pavement, ran a hand through his hair and blew out a long and noisy breath. 'I don't know, Kate. I really don't know.'

'You don't know?' Her voice rose in incredulity. 'If you thought you were in trouble wi' your parents before…well…I wouldna like tae be there when they ask you why you were out on the town wi' a lassie who works in an oyster cellar.'

'You are so much more than that, Kate!'

'Will your parents think so? Why in the name of God did you introduce me to your mother, Richard?'

'It was an impulse. I got carried away. Maybe I thought I could make everything work out.'

'Things dinna work out just because we want them to. I learnt that an awful long time ago.'

'I want you not to think like that. I want to be able to make you not think that way!'

'Och, Richard!' She threw one hand up, indicating the illuminations that surrounded them. 'This is lovely. But it's no' real. It's make-believe. That's no' actually a beautiful butterfly up there, it's nothing but a trick wi' glass and light.'

He took a step towards her, his hands curling into fists at his sides. 'It's a lot more than a trick, Kate. Somebody made this happen. Somebody had a dream and worked hard to make it real.'

'You're a dreamer,' she said, gazing sadly up at him. 'And this has been a dream I've been dreaming with you. All summer long. Maybe it's time for us to wake up, Richard. Especially after what's just happened with your mother and Miss Steele. Maybe it is time for us to part.'

'I can't do it, Kate.' He was studying her intently. 'I won't do it.'

'Richard, you're a gentleman and I'm not a lady. That's all there is to it.'

'You look like a lady in that dress.'

'Maybe. But your mother could tell as soon as I opened my mouth that I wasna one.'

'You are a lady, Kate,' he said passionately. 'In every way that matters. And you're intelligent and kind—'

'None o' which will matter to your mother. You must know that too. For God's sake, Richard! Gentlemen who keep mistresses are supposed to be discreet about it. And we have tried so hard all summer long to be discreet. So why on earth did you introduce me to your mother?'

His mouth set in a firm line. 'Because I wanted her to see you as Miss Dunbar. As the charming and lovely Miss Dunbar in her pretty frock with her clever wee brother beside her. With her

clever wee brother who's going to George Heriot's. The same
school I went to.'

'We dinna ken yet if he's going to get in.'

'Of course he will. Have faith in him, Kate. Have faith in me.'

For a moment she studied him in silence. Then she asked him
her question again. 'Why did ye introduce me to your mother,
Richard?'

He looked her straight in the eye. 'Because I want my mother
and my father to know who you are when I tell them that I'm
going to marry you.'

CHAPTER FORTY-SIX

'You're staring at me as though I'm no' quite right in the heid, Kate.'

'That's because you are no' quite right in the heid.' Her voice was as sharp as broken glass. 'How could you and me be wed?'

He raised his eyebrows. 'Not perhaps the sort of response a man hopes for to his proposal of marriage to the girl he loves.'

'You haven't proposed to me. You've told me you're going to marry me. And you're talking nonsense, Richard. Ye ken fine I'm no' good enough for you.'

'You have that the wrong way round, Kate. It's me who's not good enough for you. Only I'm hoping you'll stoop, hold out your hand to me and say yes. Please say yes, Kate. Please don't keep me waiting any longer to hear you say the word either. I can't stand it.' He smiled at her. 'I really can't.'

She could hear Ella Balfour's voice in her head. After a few drinks she'd tell anyone her story.

Promised me marriage, didn't he? And I fell for it. Should ha' known the minister's son would never marry a lassie like me. The wee shite swore on the Bible the bairn wasna his either.

Kate shook her head, trying to shake that buzzing fly away too. It refused to leave. 'Are you asking me to marry you so that tomorrow at the Old Physic Garden I'll let you lie with me?' she demanded.

A look of horror flashed across his face. 'How can you think that about me, Kate?' Taking her hand in his, he pulled her round a high wall and into a mews and repeated his impassioned question. '*How can you think that about me?*'

'Because it happens all the time to girls like me,' she said flatly. 'And I'm remembering what Mrs Henderson said after you wrote what you wrote on the slate—'

He interrupted her. 'I remember what she said too, Kate. That the words I had written were sacred, never to be used unless they are genuinely felt and meant. Sincerely, and from the bottom of one's heart. Never to be used cynically by privileged young men who always get what they want and have no conscience as to how they do so. And I'm asking you again, after this summer, after everything we have been to each other over these months, do you really think I'm that sort of a man?'

'No,' she said, moved by his words. 'I ken fine you're not like that. But I'm scared, Richard.'

'Och, Kate,' he said with melting gentleness, 'I know you are—'

She shook her head. 'No. You don't know, Richard. You really don't.'

Ye dinna ken the half o' it. You think I'm innocent and untouched and I'm not. I'm soiled and sullied. That's why I've taken so long to make up my mind. Because if I become your mistress I'll either have to fool you and cheat you and make you think I'm still a virgin or I'll have to tell you the truth. I don't want to fool you and cheat you, but if I tell you the truth you might reject me, thrust me away from you. That's what I'm really scared of.

Those unexpressed thoughts were followed by another. His mother was scared too. Scared he had got himself entangled with a girl from the wrong side of the bridges. Scared there was going to be gossip and scandal. Scared he wasn't going to make the good marriage she and his father thought it was so important for him to make. Scared that the rigid and unforgiving social code by which people like the Hopes lived their lives might mean her losing her son. Oh, God Almighty, Kate thought, I can't be responsible for that!

Taking a firmer grip on the hands he held, Richard backed her up against the wall of the lane. He did it hard enough to dislodge her straw bonnet. Tied in a bow, the broad ribbons which secured it under her chin had already worked their way loose, sending the bonnet askew, angled to one side of her head.

'Listen to me,' he said urgently. 'I do understand how scared you are. But you don't need to be. I'll look after you. I'm asking you to marry me because I love you, Kate. Because I love you and want to spend the rest of my life with you.' Releasing her hands and raising his own, he pushed the bonnet off. Her smooth hair offered no resistance and in a matter of seconds he had her head uncovered and was cupping her face. 'Now I'd like an answer to my proposal. As soon as possible, if you please. I require you to say yes, of course. The alternative answer isn't acceptable to me.'

'You canna marry me, Richard.' She wrapped her fingers around his wrists. 'Your parents and your relatives and your friends would never accept me as the right wife for you. Never.'

'You're exactly the right wife for me. Look how you've whipped me into shape as regards my studies. Once my parents find out it was you who made me do that you'll definitely be in their good books. Besides which, we don't need their permission to get married.'

'What if they cut ye off wi'out a shilling? What would we do then?'

'Get married and hope they'll come round to the idea eventually. Which they will. Once they find out for themselves what a lovely girl you are. Bright and clever and kind. Clean and fresh and pure.'

Clean and fresh and pure. Oh, dear God. 'And what will they say when they find out that I'm a lassie who works in an oyster cellar wi' an uncle who—'

'With an uncle who what?' Richard asked when she skidded to a halt in the middle of the sentence.

'Never mind. That's no' what I meant, anyway. What I meant was how would we live if your parents cut you off?' Why was she asking him that? This was never going to happen.

'I'm asking you to marry me and all you can think about is money, Kate?'

She stared at him for a few seconds. It was shadowy here in the lane but there was enough light spilling in from the illuminations and the brightly lit street at the end of it for her to be able to see him clearly. He was so handsome. So young too.

He might be older than her in years but he was much younger in experience. He had no real idea what life was like for people outside his own class. He had absolutely no understanding of how important money was. How could he? He had never been short of it, couldn't know how the lack of it governed your life and ground you down into the dirt.

All at once, Kate couldn't bear it any more. Couldn't bear seeing with such clarity how wide the gulf was that separated them from one another. Couldn't bear knowing the only sensible course open to them was to part. Couldn't bear him thinking that somehow the two of them could marry and live happily ever after. Couldn't bear standing here with him for one moment longer.

'I have to go now,' she said, breathless with distress. 'I have to.' She pulled his hands away from her face. 'If Andrew hasn't been served yet I'll send him back to you with the money you gave him.'

'For God's sake, Kate. I'm not going to miss a sixpence.'

'That's the point,' she cried. 'That's the whole bloody point, Richard!'

'I don't know what you mean.'

'Och,' she said, 'I dinna suppose you do!'

'Leave him where he is and let him buy the chestnuts, Kate. There was quite a crowd round the stall. It'll take a while. Please stay here with me for the moment. I need you to tell me why you're so angry with me.'

'I'm not angry with you. I'm sad.' Sad enough for tears to well up. When he saw them, he reached for her, ready to take her into his arms.

'No,' she protested, trying to fend him off, but not trying so very hard. This might be the last time he would hold her in his arms.

'Don't fight me,' he murmured as he enfolded her into his embrace. He spared one hand to stroke her back and pressed his lips against her temple. 'Cry,' he commanded. 'Cry all you like.'

Instead, she sniffed the tears back. 'Tears dinna help onything. I've tellt ye that afore.'

'Practical Kate,' he said softly. 'Always so practical.'

'One o' us has to be.'

'You think I'm such a dreamer?'

'Aye. You and me getting wed is a dream, Richard. Nothing but a dream.'

He slackened his hold on her, put one finger under her chin and tilted her head up. 'Is it one you would want to dream, Kate?'

'Of course I'd *want* to, Richard. How can ye doubt it?'

'Know where we are, Kate?'

'Edinburgh.'

'Very funny. We're at the back of my house.' His grip on her tightened. 'No need to run away. No one's going to see us here.'

'Servants' and tradesmen's entrance? Where I belong, then.'

He gave her a long-suffering look. 'My entrance a lot of times over this summer. When I've come sneaking back home from the Cowgate. I've decided I'm not going to sneak home any more after I've been seeing you. I've also decided that before this year is very much older I'm going to be walking up to the front door with you on my arm.' His face lit up. 'I suppose the first time we do that you'll be my bride. I'll have to carry you over the threshold.'

'Richard,' she urged. 'Try to imagine what would happen if we went off and got ourselves wed.'

'In Greyfriars Kirk. That's where I'd like us to tie the knot,' he put in, adding, with the air of a man making an embarrassing confession, 'Have an affection for it from my school days. Unless you absolutely want to get married in the Tron, of course. That's where you go to church, isn't it?'

'Richard,' she said again, despairing of ever making him see sense.

'Greyfriars or the Tron?'

'It doesna matter!' she cried. 'It's never going tae happen! Richard, your parents would *never* accept me. I'm a girl who works in an oyster cellar off the Cowgate. I live inside the South Bridge. Be realistic, Richard!'

'Maybe they won't have to know all of that. Not if you go and stay with the Hendersons for a wee while first. You could be married from there. As though they're your guardians or something.'

'You think your parents won't still want to know everything about me: where I was born and who my parents were? Are you expecting the Hendersons to tell them a pack o' lies, Richard?'

'I don't know,' he said after a spiky little pause. 'I don't know, Kate. I haven't worked all of this out yet.'

'Ye havena worked any o' this out.' She glanced towards the street. 'Andrew's bound to be getting served by now. We canna talk about this in front o' him.'

'Then we'll talk about it tomorrow in the Old Physic Garden.'

'This is a dream, Richard. This is never going to happen.'

'You said that before, Kate. About this being a dream.' He was gazing intently at her. 'So I'm asking you again: is it a dream you would want to dream?'

'D'ye no' ken?'

'Is that a yes? Is that yes, Richard, I will marry you?'

'Och, Richard,' she burst out, at the end of her tether. 'Of course I'd *want* to marry you! D'ye no' ken that by now, ye big daftie?'

Seconds later she was once more being backed up against the wall and having a series of darting little kisses planted along her mouth. 'Kate's going to marry me,' he said, excitement leaping and dancing through the words. 'Miss Catriona Dunbar's going to marry me!'

'Shout a wee bit louder,' she suggested. 'I'm no' just sure the *whole* o' Edinburgh heard ye.'

'I want the whole of Edinburgh to hear me. I want the whole world to hear me. I want the whole world to know you're going to marry me.'

'I'm not going to marry you—'

'Haud your wheesht,' he commanded, and reinforced the command with another series of kisses. 'Dream the dream with me, Kate,' he urged. 'Shall I tell you how it's going to be once we're married?'

'Can I stop you?'

'No. But I'll be quick, because I know you're worried about Andrew and we've got to get back to him soon. So here goes. You and I will have a really nice house, Kate. Wherever you fancy. In the New Town, or maybe down by the Forth somewhere, if you would like that better. We'll have a big comfortable bedroom – oh,' he groaned, 'with a huge soft bed and a fire we can sit by in the winter.' He groaned again. 'Or maybe we'll take the covers off the bed and lie on the hearth rug and make love to each other all night long. After that or before that we'll have the bath brought in and you can soak for as long as you like in front of the fire. How am I doing so far? Can you see all this?'

'I can,' she whispered, as entranced by his words as she was by the dreamy expression on his face. 'That's the trouble.'

'There's no trouble in you being able to see it, Kate. We need you to be able to see it. We'll have a lovely parlour too. Where you can sit looking out of the window watching the world go by or reading all sorts of books or having your friends to tea. You'd like all of that, wouldn't you? I'm exactly the right sort of husband for you, you know.'

'Modest, aren't you?'

'Always.' He grinned at her. 'We'll have an account with the Hendersons and you can buy any book you want from them. Read all day long if you want to. Learn *hoo tae ken aboot everything*.' His grin widened. 'Only I'm giving you fair warning now that I'll expect you to put your books down sometimes. When your husband requires you to pay attention to him.'

'Is that right?'

'That *is* right. Although I think I can guarantee you will derive as much enjoyment from those occasions as your husband will.'

He was as hard to resist as he always had been. 'What occasions would those be?'

'Tell you tomorrow. When we're all by ourselves in the Old Physic Garden. Now then, let's go and find Andrew. We'll put your bonnet back on first.'

'Richard...' she said, standing there like a wee bairn as he lifted her hat back onto her head and untied and re-tied the ribbons of the bonnet into a neat bow under her chin. 'You ken fine what my answer has to be.'

'Indeed I do,' he said, and moved his hands to her shoulders, resting them on the soft velvet of the lovely little blue spencer. When she tried to speak again, he placed a finger against her mouth. 'No more words, my love.' His eyes were warm. 'Only dreams. Dream the dream with me, Kate. Please.' Dipping his head, he kissed her. 'Now, let's go and find Andrew.'

CHAPTER FORTY-SEVEN

'I dinna think you're listening tae me, Kate.'

'Of course I am. You were talking about the lady carrying the boat in her arms.' As they walked together down Niddry Street, Kate reached out and ruffled her brother's hair. Reassured by her and Richard's behaviour after they had met him at the chestnut stall that whatever had been amiss between them was now resolved, Andrew had been chattering away nineteen to the dozen all the way home. 'I doubt ye'll no' be able tae get to sleep tonight for thinking about the illuminations.'

'Och, but that would be a nice reason tae lie awake, Kate.'

'Aye,' she agreed. 'Although maybe ye will fall asleep quickly and dream about them instead.'

'That would be grand too. I'd like that fine,' he said as the two of them rounded the corner into the Cowgate.

Kate was glad that Peggy Henderson too had been as enthusiastic as Andrew about the illuminations. When they had changed their clothes in her bedroom a few moments before, Kate hadn't been required to say anything very much. Part of her had wanted to, desperate to blurt out the amazed words *He's asked me to marry him, Mrs Henderson!* Another part of her had kept silent.

It was late and there were only a few customers left in The Pearl Fisher. Behind the bar drying some tankards, Michael Graham looked up and across the tavern at his niece and nephew.

'Do you want a drink?' Kate asked Andrew. 'Some milk to wash the chestnuts down?'

'Had a jolly evening, have we?'

'It was rare,' Andrew said, so pleased and excited he was forgetting to be nervous of his uncle. Kate was immediately uneasy when Michael Graham smiled at Andrew in response, and when he listened for a few moments to his descriptions of the illuminations. Slipping in behind the bar and her uncle, she busied herself with fetching the cups of milk.

She soon realised why Michael Graham had gone to the trouble of playing the kindly uncle. 'Drink up now, laddie,' he told Andrew, and had the cup out of the boy's hands as soon as he did. 'And away tae your bed. Your sister'll be along in a wee minute. Mind ye dinna wake your auntie as ye ging past her door.'

The excitement of the evening beginning to overtake him, his eyelids drooping, Andrew went without a murmur. Kate dunked the two cups from which she and Andrew had drunk their milk in the wooden washing-up bowl, hastily dried them and hung them and the cloth back up on their respective hooks. 'I should go to bed too.' She found her way barred.

'Should ye no' soon be going tae young Mr Hope's bed, Kate?'

She couldn't think of anything she wanted to say to him. Apart from: 'I'm needing tae get past.'

'And I'm needing tae ken when ye're going tae reel him in.'

'It's late,' she said. 'I'm no' prepared to discuss this right now.'

'Drop the airs and graces, miss,' he growled, stepping forward and gripping one of her wrists.

'Let go of me.' All that got her was a tightening of the fingers that had her wrist pinioned. It hurt, but she wasn't going to let him see that. 'Dae ye ken whit Richard Hope would dae tae you gin I tellt him how you've ill-used me?'

'Ye never would tell him that,' came the murmured response.

'Aiblins I already have.'

'He'd have had a go at me lang syne if ye had. The daft bugger still thinks ye're pure and innocent, am I no' right?' He lowered his voice. 'When dae ye spread your legs for him, ye wee hure?'

'Don't you dare call me that!'

His hated features settled into lines of comic surprise. 'Come off it, pet. It's a hure's game you've been playing wi' young Mr Hope all summer lang. Time for us baith tae collect.' He was peering into her face. 'Hang on a wee minute,' he said slowly. 'Ye've no' persuaded him tae set ye up somewhere, have ye?'

She stayed silent for a moment too long.

'Shite,' Michael Graham exclaimed, letting go of her hand, 'that *is* whit ye've done!'

Released from his punishing grip, Kate found the pain not diminishing but expanding, shooting up her arm and down into her fingers. The aching intensity of it kept her where she was, unable for the moment to do anything else but remain a prisoner of her own body, trapped by the pain this man had inflicted on her. For the last time. *For the last bloody time!*

'Aye,' she cried. 'That is what I've done! And he's mair than happy aboot it! He loves me! I'll be going tae live wi' him as soon as the toun clears efter the king's visit and we can find rooms! And you'll no' be able tae tell his family that he's ruined me! I'll hae ruined masel! And I dinna care! It'll get me and Andrew away from here!'

'Keep your voice doon,' hissed Michael Graham.

Kate glanced round the tavern. 'They're a' tae blootered tae be bothered.' She looked back at her uncle. She hadn't meant to tell him any of this but it was out now and she didn't see what he could do about it.

'So he loves ye? Och, is that no' awfy nice? Whit'll happen

when I tell him whit a dirty wee slut ye are, Kate? That'll likely break his heart, eh?'

'I'll tell him it was you wha made me that.' Kate lifted her chin. 'He'll *go* for you!'

'He's strong enough,' Michael Graham said coolly. 'But I canna think he has my experience wi' his fists. I could break his nose wi' one punch, Kate. Or his jaw,' he added, with the air of a man already pondering where he would strike. 'I wouldna fight clean, either. He would. A gentleman, is he no'? I'd have him lying battered and bleeding on the floor afore he kent whit had hit him.'

The picture was too hideously vivid for her to be able to deny it. Her face must have been betraying what she was seeing in her mind's eye.

'Lassie, lassie,' her uncle said, with a smile that made her shiver. 'Gin you're sensible it's never going tae come tae that. Once young Mr Hope has you safely installed in these cosy wee rooms, I'll call on ye frae time tae time – shall we say once every week or twa? I'll no' be greedy. Efter all, I'm only looking for something tae keep me warm in my old age. It'll be security for you too, pet. Keep me sweet and ye'll ken I'll no' tell his family whit their boy's getting up to wi' a trollop in the Old Town.' The hated voice hardened. 'Or tell young Mr Hope a whole heap o' filthy stories aboot you.'

His family already knows about me. She managed not to say the words out loud, not sure whether they would hurt or help.

'I'm thinking I'll keep that one in reserve, Kate. Ye can fool him into thinking he's the first tae shed your shanks – aiblins ye already have – but I'm sure I'd be able tae convince him he's in a long, long line. Or at least plant that wee seed o' doubt in his mind. Will he still love ye then, wee Kate?'

Her hand and arm were tingling now, pins and needles

prickling up and down from her fingers to her shoulder and back again. Willing the sensation to pass, she stared at her uncle. *Keep me sweet.* She knew he wasn't talking only about money. She knew too what role was assigned to her now.

She should crumple in the face of his threats, agree to do whatever he wanted her to do, allow him to control and pollute her life as he always had done. If he had his way, he would taint and spoil everything. This glorious summer, the most wonderful days, weeks and months of her life, would be distorted into something ugly, misshapen and horrible.

'Is it no' time we locked up?'

Michael Graham looked past Kate to his wife, standing in the doorway to the tavern with her nightcap on her head and enveloped in a blanket. 'Chrissie. I thought ye'd gone tae your bed, pet.'

'That blasted bairn woke me up when he came in. Clattering a' ower the place.' Chrissie Graham's eyes flickered without interest over Kate. 'You get away tae your bed too,' she said roughly. 'Right now.'

Richard was famished when he woke on Sunday morning, ready to do justice to a huge breakfast. Deciding discretion was the better part of valour, he lay in bed until he was sure everyone had left the house. It wasn't difficult to work out when that happened. His cousins and aunts didn't do anything quietly.

Hearing the front door close at last behind their excited chatter, he wasted no time in slipping on his dressing gown and leather slippers and going downstairs to the dining room. With a bit of luck, there would be something left for him to eat. With all that talking going on, maybe his cousins hadn't managed to scoff everything. The servants were clearing up the debris by the time he got there.

'Won't get in your way,' he promised Jamie and the two maidservants who were clearing away. 'Allow me to fill my plate and I'll just sit here at the end of the table.'

'Shall I make you some fresh coffee, Master Richard?' asked Jamie.

'That would be most acceptable,' Richard said, taking a couple of sausages and some scrambled eggs from the silver chafing dishes on the sideboard and depositing them on his plate. He found a clean fork, walked over to the table and sat down.

Hearing Jamie make an odd noise, he looked back across at him. The other young man's gaze was fixed on the open door of the dining room. Richard's father was standing there.

The master of the house gave the order to Jamie. As the sole male servant in the room, it was only he who was worthy of his attention.

'Leave us,' Edward Hope said.

CHAPTER FORTY-EIGHT

Richard opened his mouth to speak.

'Wait,' warned his father. Not until Jamie had closed the double doors behind himself and the two maidservants did Edward Hope walk forward, pull out the chair next to Richard's and sit down.

'*Pas devant les domestiques?*' Richard queried, with a somewhat superior lift of the chin. 'Does it occur to you, Father, that a house's servants almost certainly know more about a family's business than the individual family members do?'

'It occurs to me, Richard. The proprieties must nevertheless be observed.' Edward Hope and his youngest son had always got on well, which made the question the former put to the latter now – and the tone of voice in which he asked it – all the more pointed. 'What the devil possessed you to introduce the girl to your mother? Not to mention to do so in front of Irene Steele?'

The girl. He could not allow Kate to remain that. 'I take it you are referring to Miss Dunbar, Father – if you are speaking of the young lady whom I introduced to Mother and Miss Steele yesterday evening.'

'Get off your high horse, my boy,' came the robust response. 'This girl is no lady. Am I not right?'

'She is to me. And I'm going to marry her, Father.'

For a moment the only sound in the room was that of the ticking of the huge clock fashioned in the form of a Grecian temple which stood on the high mantelpiece; until Edward Hope leant forward, took the plate and fork out of his son's hands and placed them on the dining table.

'Richard,' he said. 'I require an honest answer to this question. Is the girl going to bear you a child?'

Colour flooded Richard's face. 'No!' he burst out. 'She is innocent, Father. Untouched by any man. Including me!'

'Oh, Richard,' Edward Hope said, shaking his head in cynical disbelief, 'have you really been taken in by that? It's the oldest trick in the book!'

'No, Father, you're wrong,' Richard cried, shaking his head in turn. 'She is innocent. If you knew her you would not say that, Father. You would not!'

His father studied him for a moment before leaning across and laying a hand on his shoulder. 'I had not thought you still so innocent, my boy. Love her, do you?'

'With all my heart,' Richard said passionately. 'With all my heart, Father. And I am going to marry her. I would rather have your blessing but if I cannot have it I shall go ahead without it.'

'You are prepared to break your mother's heart to do so?'

'I would never wish to do that. I would never wish to hurt Mother.'

'If you marry this girl, you will, Richard. Make no mistake about that. You know how much your mother wants you to make a good marriage.'

'But, Father, you don't understand! Marrying Kate would be a good marriage. Oh, Father, she's beautiful and she's kind and it's her who made me study this year.' He smiled. 'Licking me into shape. That's what she called it. Told me I had to stick in at my studies.'

'Then she is one of the clever sort.'

'You are determined to think badly of her!'

'Tell me something, Richard. Your mother tells me the girl was well and fashionably dressed. That she had a young boy with her, also well clad. Who paid for their clothes, Richard?'

'I did, Father.'

'Well,' Edward Hope said, with a raise of the eyebrows which made him for a moment look very like his son, 'I think in reality I did, Richard. Perhaps you might like to ponder that thought.'

'You are threatening to cut me off?' Richard's chin went up again.

'If I have to do that in order to bring you to your senses, I will. Be under no illusions about that.' He stood up. 'I shall excuse your presence at dinner tonight. Your cousins are consumed with curiosity as to who the mysterious young woman was they saw you with yesterday. A gentleman does not make either a young lady or even a young woman the object of gossip, Richard. Remember that.'

Leaving the chair on which he'd been sitting pulled out from the table, Edward walked across to the door. 'I expect your attendance at the Caledonian Hunt Ball at the Assembly Rooms on Monday night, as I expect you to come with us to the Theatre Royal on Tuesday night to see *Rob Roy*. On both occasions you will, of course, act like the gentleman you are. You will turn away any questions about the young woman and you will bestir yourself to be charming to Miss Steele, your mother, your aunts and your cousins. Is that understood?'

'Not going to lock me in my room on bread and water then, Father?'

'That,' Edward Hope pronounced, 'is unworthy of you. And of me.'

'I love her,' Richard said. 'And I am going to marry her.'

'Over my dead body, Richard. But we shall speak of this later. Until we do, you might like to consider this. You talk so easily of the love you claim to feel for this young woman. What of the love your mother feels for you, her youngest child? Does that mean nothing to you? What of the duty you owe your mother, who has given you years of care and devotion? Are you prepared to throw all of that away for the sake of a summer flirtation?'

'Kate is so much more than that, Father! So much more! I *love* her!'

'So you keep saying.' Edward Hope's voice was very dry. 'The sort of love of which you're speaking can be a very ephemeral commodity, my boy. Bear in mind that it often does not last. Keep her as your mistress for a few months if you must. But for God's sake keep her out of sight of respectable society.'

CHAPTER FORTY-NINE

Ten minutes later Richard stormed out of the house, fizzing with rage. *Love can be a very ephemeral commodity. Keep her as your mistress for a few months if you must.* Why were the middle-aged so fucking cynical? Had they never been young? Had they never been in love?

Leaving the dining room seconds after his father, Richard had taken the stairs two at a time, grabbed a clean shirt and thrown on the clothes he had thrown off the night before. Instinct sent him striding towards the North Bridge. Instinct and need. He needed Kate.

Only Kate could make this right. Only Kate could give him the comfort he craved.

The oldest trick in the book. How dare his father accuse her of that? She was so sweet and fresh and innocent. It simply wasn't in her to do something like that. Kate Dunbar was as honest as the day was long and in a few minutes' time he would be with her – where he belonged.

As he turned the corner onto the North Bridge, he found himself engulfed by a flood of chattering, cheerful humanity. Pressing himself against the wall as he watched them wheel right into Waterloo Place, he realised they must be going up Calton Hill, the vantage point for so many of the events of the last couple of weeks.

Forced to stop to allow the noisy crowd free passage, he took stock of what he was doing and where he was going. Kate had agreed to meet him at the Old Physic Garden as soon as she could get away, at two o'clock this afternoon. She had specifically asked him not to call for her at The Pearl Fisher. Richard knew why. She didn't want her aunt and uncle knowing the two of them had arranged to meet in private.

Surveying the hundreds of people streaming across the North Bridge, he realised he had better respect Kate's wishes. It wasn't even eleven o'clock yet, which left him with three long hours to fill. Going back home wasn't an option he favoured. After his argument with his father this morning, the servants were probably gossiping enough as it was.

He would walk, that's what he would do – back along Princes Street and up the Earthen Mound to the Old Town. Once he got there he would take the most circuitous route possible to the Old Physic Garden. His feelings needed movement. He was far too restless to simply find a tavern and sit there until it was time to meet Kate.

With so many people heading for Calton Hill, Chrissie Graham had decided for once not to open for business this Sunday morning. Her husband had just suggested to her they go up Calton Hill too. 'Something a bit different, Chrissie, eh? We could be back here for six, ready tae open up for the evening. Want tae come efter ye've seen the laddie off, Kate? We could meet up wi' you somewhere.'

'No, thank you,' Kate said, her voice cool.

He winked at her. 'Other fish tae fry, eh?'

'I'm locking this hale place up tight as a drum,' Chrissie warned. 'Gin ye're back afore us, ye'll hae tae bide in the street or the close.'

'No' if I tak the key tae the vault.'

'There's nae problem aboot that,' Michael Graham said expansively. 'We can trust Kate wi' the key, Chrissie.'

She met her uncle's dark and scheming eyes, her own schooled to give nothing away. What a fool he was to think she would ever bring Richard back here. What a fool he was to think she had no option but to fall in with his plans. Today she had her own.

'A sheet of paper, Kate?'

'Please, Mrs Henderson.' The two women had just waved Andrew and the Gunns off. 'And the use of a pen and ink. I promise not to delay you and Mr Henderson long.' For the Hendersons too were going up Calton Hill, promising to be home by five o'clock at the latest, well before Andrew was due back from the boat trip.

After a laborious ten minutes, Kate asked Peggy Henderson to seal the paper she had now blotted and folded and to keep it for her in a safe place.

'That's all you want me to do, Kate?'

'For the moment, Mrs Henderson, if you please. There may come a time when ye'll have tae open it, but no' yet.' Kate hesitated, knowing she would cause alarm if she asked the bookseller's wife to read the letter should anything happen to herself or Andrew. She'd have to trust she would do so if – God forbid – those circumstances should ever arise.

'This is all very mysterious, lass. Are you all right?' Peggy added. 'You look a wee touch pale.'

'I'm fine, Mrs Henderson,' Kate reassured her, already on her way to the door of the bookshop. 'And I'll no' hold you and Mr Henderson back any further.'

Standing in front of Ramsay Gardens, gazing over the chimney pots of the New Town towards the Firth, Richard moved at last. He'd been away in what Kate – and his grandmother – would have called a *dwam,* going over in his mind the events of this summer, which would in a few short weeks draw to a close. It had been the most wonderful summer of his life.

He mentally corrected himself. The most wonderful *spring* and summer of his life. He had found Kate in the spring and he had been with her throughout the summer. If he had his way, if she said yes, there would be so many springs and summers for them to enjoy together.

Taking the steep brae up to the Castle Hill, barely noticing the incline, he glanced at the site where the scaffolding had collapsed. It had been cleared away remarkably quickly. People had wanted to forget the accident as soon as possible, sweep it out of sight, fearing, like Kate, that it was a bad omen for the success of the royal visit.

Apart from the downpours that had dogged it, the whole event had gone off well. It had only a few days to run now, the king being scheduled to leave Edinburgh this coming Thursday. Richard had privileged information on that. George IV would embark not from Leith but from Port Edgar, to the north and west of Edinburgh. The Earl of Hopetoun was to host a huge farewell breakfast for him, his entourage and, by the sounds of it, half of Edinburgh. Richard had been invited but hadn't the slightest intention of being there.

Sauntering down the dizzyingly steep stone steps that plunged from the castle into the Grassmarket, Richard walked across it and up the Vennel, another stepped path. It led to George Heriot's, his old school, and soon to be Andrew Dunbar's school. He knew the lad would get in. It was a foregone conclusion.

Richard paused for a moment, remembering himself as a scholar. He and his friends had got up to some high jinks here. The Vennel had always been the place where disputes were sorted out, boy to boy, without the masters needing to be involved.

Passing some impressive remnants of Edinburgh's city walls, Richard walked through to the Wark, the original school building. A grand Renaissance palace, he'd been taught that the architect who had designed it two centuries before had borne the same name as Scotland's greatest hero, William Wallace. He went into the quadrangle and stood for a moment, remembering, before about-turning and carrying on through to Greyfriars Kirkyard.

He must be getting old. He could feel the peace today, the sense of being at one remove from the busy world outside the graveyard's gates. Yet he and his friends had got up to some mischief in here too. He grimaced, thinking about how they had lifted exposed bones – femurs for preference, naturally – and fenced with them. The callousness of youth. He grimaced again, this time considering the bodies that had been and continued to be disturbed in this place.

Perhaps that was why he was also aware of an eerie atmosphere underlying and intertwining with the peaceful one. Or perhaps that was because he knew the Covenanters had been imprisoned here. If the memory of their sufferings in defence of the right to worship God in the manner of their choosing wasn't enough, many of the gravestones bore the traditional Scottish funereal symbols. The skull and crossbones. A coffin. A glass egg-timer through which the sands of time ran. *Memento mori.* Remember you must die.

Remember you must live, he thought. *Remember you must live.* He didn't think he could do that unless he had Kate by his side. If he had to sacrifice his comfortable life to do that, then so be it. Purposeful now, he directed his steps towards the Old Physic Garden.

CHAPTER FIFTY

The Old Town was eerily quiet, making it seem oddly unfamiliar. How many times had she walked past the bookshop, across the High Street and clattered down Fleshmarket Close? It must be hundreds. Yet today she felt as though she were undertaking a journey through unknown territory, one for which she had no map, no compass and no sense of whether or not she was heading in the right direction.

There was a Latin term she had heard Mr Henderson use. *Terra incognita.* That's what this part of Edinburgh she knew so well felt like today. Unknown territory.

Richard was waiting for her, wearing the same clothes he'd had on last night and leaning back against the gates of the Old Physic Garden. He stood with both arms outstretched and hooked over the curved wrought-iron – all rust removed and freshly painted in glossy black – of the gates. He had one leg drawn up behind him, his foot laid flat against one of the iron railings. He looked up, and the familiar long, slow smile spread across his handsome face. She ran to him and his arms came off the gates and around her.

'Oh,' she cried on a little gasp, 'your hands are cold!'

'That's because I've been standing in the shade for so long,' he murmured into her hair. 'I've been waiting here for ages.' Compounding the offence, he wrapped his arms more tightly around her, his chilly fingers touching her breasts and making her shiver. 'An hour, at least. And before that I spent all morning stravaiging about the town.'

She edged herself out of his embrace. 'And afore ye did that did ye have a fight with your parents?' she demanded, and urged him on when she saw him hesitate. 'The truth, Richard. The truth canna hurt us. As long as we baith ken it.' Oh God, how she hoped that was true.

'My father,' he said. 'He did the dirty work.'

'What did he say?'

'You don't want to know, Kate.'

'But I do,' she insisted. 'Forbye I can probably guess. Your father likely tellt ye that ower his deid body is his son going to marry a girl frae the wrang side o' the bridges.'

'Were you there? That's exactly what he— Oh!'

'Surprised that oot o ye, did I?' she asked with a rueful twist of the lips.

'You're too clever by half, Catriona Dunbar.' He took hold of her hands. His own were warmer now. 'I told my father that too. How clever and beautiful and kind you are, how sweet and fresh and innocent too.'

'I'm no' exactly recognising this paragon o' all the virtues as myself, Richard.' Kate's voice was very dry. 'I'm also guessing that these supposed virtues o' mine didna do much tae change your father's mind. The truth,' she reminded him. 'We're no' wanting anything but the truth here. Ye didna change your father's mind, did ye?'

'No. So that means we'll have to get married without my parents' blessing.'

'We canna get married at all, Richard. I won't be the person who comes between you and your family.'

'If I get my way, you will be my family. You and Andrew. I've got it all worked out, Kate. Do you want to hear what the plan is?'

She studied him for a moment. He was all rumpled and crumpled, his black hair in its usual tousled disarray. He cocked his head to one side and gave the searching look back to her. 'What do you see?'

'The man I love.'

'That's good. Am I also the man who's convinced you to marry him?'

She shook her head. 'It canna be, Richard.'

'Kate,' he said urgently. 'I was in Greyfriars Kirkyard this morning. There are all these old gravestones there and they have this Latin inscription on them. *Memento mori.* Know what that means? *Remember you must die.* And I stood there and looked at those Latin words and thought, no, what we all should do is remember that we must *live.* Do you understand what I'm saying, Kate?'

'*Remember you must live.*' She nodded in agreement. 'It's a grand sentiment.'

His smile was like the sun coming out. She remembered thinking that before, when they had first stood together in the Old Physic Garden, back when this whole adventure had begun. A strange sense of calm settled upon her, giving her the sense that nothing could touch or threaten them here. All would be well as long as they were inside the black gates and the protective embrace of the garden's walls; and what would be would be.

'Ye ken that poem by Keats you really like, the one about the Grecian urn?'

'What about it?'

'The last two lines,' she said. 'Beauty is truth, truth beauty – that is all ye know on Earth, and all ye need to know. That's a grand sentiment too, Richard.'

'You'll get no argument about that from me,' he said. 'Now, come into the garden.'

* * *

They were standing close by the garden wall, next to one of the espaliered pear trees, and he was holding her so tightly she had to issue a laughing, if muffled, protest. 'Let me go before you crack my ribs!'

'No,' he said, although he loosened his grip a little. 'I'm never going to let you go, Kate. You know that, don't you?'

I know you think that now. She didn't express the thought out loud, only stayed where she was with her head against his chest, listening to the solid thump of his heart.

I wish we could stay like this for ever, standing in this sunny garden listening to the bees buzzing and smelling the perfume of the flowers and plants. I wish I could always be in your arms, safe and warm and loved.

'Are you thinking about my brilliant plan?'

His brilliant plan was that he would get himself a position as assistant and demonstrator to one of his professors. That way he could continue to study for his medical degree and earn enough money to support himself and Kate, maybe even make a contribution to Andrew's keep at the Hendersons.

'I'm thinking about your brilliant plan,' she confirmed. She wasn't going to tell him what she was thinking about it: that it would involve him in bodysnatching, that he would have to enter the clandestine world of Edinburgh's night and the people who lurked in its shadows and dark corners – the world Michael Graham inhabited. It would never be the one where Richard Hope belonged, not if she had anything to do with it.

'What are you thinking now, Kate?'

'That you should unlock the door to the summer house.'

'It's not raining.'

'No. But I think we should go into the summer house all the same.'

'Not before you give me an answer to the question I asked you last night.'

'Richard. Haud your wheesht and unlock the door of the summer house.' Do it, she thought. *Do it now before I lose my nerve!*

'You don't want to wait till we are wed, Kate?'

'Do ye no' want to make love to me, Richard?'

CHAPTER FIFTY-ONE

'So they did fit it out as a *pleasant garden parlour*,' Kate said, taking in the long cane sofa and armchairs gathered round a small, square table fashioned from the same material. Its pale colour contrasted well with the blue and cream checks of the thick cushions which made the chairs and sofa look so inviting. 'There are even pictures on the walls.'

Richard accorded those barely a glance. 'Not so good as the drawings our friend Mr Geikie does. There's a sink too, and running water,' he added, his eyes drifting over a gleaming brass tap above a decorated porcelain basin. 'There's a water butt round the back, isn't there?'

'You should know. We've stood there often enough.'

'I'm always looking at you when we're round there, not anywhere else. Do you have any idea how beautiful you are?'

She didn't reply, only stood by the cane sofa smiling at him.

'I fear you are too beautiful for me to be able to resist you, Kate,' he told her, his voice husky with emotion and desire. 'You're sure you don't want to wait till we are wed?'

'Certain sure.'

He ran a hand through his hair. 'I must confess I'm not so certain sure where to begin, Kate.'

'Dinna try telling me ye havena done this afore,' she said, her smile growing impish. 'Wi' more than one lassie, I'd jalouse.'

'One or two,' he admitted.

'Or maybe three or four?' Her voice was warm and teasing, making him feel despite this interchange as though it were he who was the inexperienced one and not her. She drew her fingertips across the sofa's long cushion. 'Should we pull this onto the floor?'

He lifted the low cane table out of the way to make space and turned to find she had already begun to shift the cushion. He took the other end and together they dropped it onto the floor so that they each stood at one end of their makeshift bed. While Richard was wondering which of them was going to make the first move, knowing it really ought to be him, she came up with another practical suggestion. 'Aiblins we should take our shoes off?'

'Aiblins we should.' He had slipped his feet out of his shoes within seconds. She sat down on the edge of one of the cane chairs and set about unlacing her old battered boots.

'Allow me.' He was already kneeling on the edge of the cushion in front of her, swaying from side-to-side because it was so deep and soft. Steadying himself and looking up at Kate, he saw that, for the first time since she had suggested coming into the summer house, she seemed less than self-possessed. She seemed scared.

So the teasing was an act, her way of hiding her natural nervousness of what they were about to do. Richard's desire was tempered by huge tenderness now, and that was good. He would hang on to these gentler feelings, use them to hold himself in check. This was their first time together and her first time ever. He had to make it special. Her hand was on his, trying to stop him from unlacing her boots. 'You shouldna be doing this for me.'

'I've been dreaming about doing this for ages.'

'Really?' She sounded doubtful but she took her hand away,

letting him unlace and remove one boot before starting on the other.

'Really. Ever since that day you showed me around the inside of the South Bridge and I caught a glimpse of your striped stockings. Never knew I liked red and white stripes so much till I saw them on your legs.'

Placing her boots to one side, feeling himself bounce on the thick cushion of the sofa as he leant over, Richard steadied himself again. Circling her ankles with his hands, he ran each one up those striped stockings, pushing her skirt and petticoat up to the garters that secured them a few inches above her knees. She seized his hands with her own.

'No?' he queried, glancing up at her. 'Are you saying no, Kate?'

'I dinna ken whit you're going to do.'

'Touch you,' he told her, hearing his voice thicken. 'I think you will like it. It will also help make you ready.'

'Make me ready?'

'To receive me,' he explained. 'My fingers touching you will make you wet. And thus I shall not hurt you when the time comes for me to enter you.'

Colour flooded her cheeks. Wrapping one arm around his neck she buried her face in his shoulder. 'Och, Richard,' she murmured. 'Och, Richard...'

He wondered if she knew she might have to endure some pain when her hymen tore. Should he warn her of that or hope he could carry her through it?

He took his hands from her thighs, wrapped his arms about her waist and spoke into the tumbling waves of her hair. 'If I touch you in any way you do not like, you have but to say so and I will stop.'

'Will you?'

'I promise.' He spared one hand to comb his fingers through her hair, tugging free the red ribbon that was confining its exuberant auburn waves today, tossing it in the direction of her boots. 'Perhaps you will first permit me to look at you. I want to see your hair spilling down over your breasts. Your naked breasts,' he added in a whisper. 'I've been dreaming about seeing them for such a long time.'

It took a moment. She was shy, as she was entitled to be. As he held her against him, waiting and hoping for her to conquer that shyness, his eyes went to a cabinet set against the wall of the summer house. A pile of folded towels lay on one of its shelves. Nothing left to chance: in the case of a sudden downpour, the king's physician would have been able to dry himself off.

When the time came – or a little before it – he would need one of those towels to place beneath her, for the blood. He was going to make Kate bleed. Awed by that, Richard redoubled his grip on her. She struggled against it and he let her go.

The way she looked at him then took his breath away. She was nervous still, yet teasing and loving too, gaining confidence in herself and the power she had over him. 'You like undoing laces?'

'All at once it's become one of my favourite occupations.'

'Am I permitted to undress you?'

His breath caught in his throat. 'When it's your turn.'

'You have done this before,' she murmured against his cheek a moment later. For her bodice now was loose enough for him to have pushed back its fronts and slipped it down to her elbows.

Untying the bow that secured her chemise, he sent it the same way, exposing her breasts. Her arms pinioned by her bodice and chemise though they were, he saw the instinctive move to cover herself up, as he saw her abandon the attempt, fighting her innate modesty so his eyes might feast on her nakedness.

'Your breasts are every bit as beautiful as I'd imagined them to be, Kate,' he murmured. 'High and round and beautiful. May I please touch them?'

She nodded her consent and he reached out to draw his fingertips under each breast and over one lovely nipple. It sprang into life.

'I'd better touch the other one too, hadn't I?' he asked, still speaking in a soft murmur. 'Wouldn't want you falling over. That's a lovely wee sound you just made, Kate. Such a lovely wee sound.'

When he lowered his head and kissed each nipple in turn, she made some more lovely wee sounds, tilted her head back and threaded her fingers through his hair. After a moment he allowed one hand to return to her knee. 'All right?' he whispered against the curve of her breast.

'All right,' she murmured in return.

He slid his hand further up her leg. 'You know where my fingers are headed?'

'I'm no' that daft.'

He laughed and raised his head. They kissed. His fingers reached their destination. She jumped...and sighed.

'It feels nice?'

She answered him not in words but in the adjustment of her posture.

'Am I to take that as an invitation?'

'Dinna ask sae many questions.'

When she came, breathless and panting, she snapped upright, seeking to replace the power of his hand with the strength of his arms. He wrapped them around her, filled with a fierce joy that he had brought her to such a pitch of pleasure.

By the time the excited breaths which were stirring his hair had begun to slow down, he was laughing at her. 'I take it my efforts met with your approval, madam?'

She sighed into his hair. 'Oh, aye, Richard. Oh, aye...'

'Plenty more where that came from.' He slid one hand under her hair and caressed the nape of her neck. 'If such is your pleasure, my love.'

'What about you?'

'What about me?'

'You should have some pleasure too.'

'I'm having lots of pleasure.' He planted a series of butterfly kisses on her lips, travelling from one side of her mouth to the other. 'Watching you receive pleasure at my hands is giving me so much pleasure, Kate. I'll have even more if you'll permit me to undress you fully.'

She coiled her arms about his neck and spoke soft words into his ear. 'Only if I get to do the same to you.'

'As naked as Adam and Eve,' he murmured as they knelt facing one another on the mattress of the day bed. 'Do you know the old question, Kate? *When Adam delved and Eve span, who was then the gentleman?* When we are naked like this we are simply Richard and Kate. I beg your pardon. Kate and Richard. I should put you first.'

She smiled at him, rose up onto her knees, leant forward and kissed him. His high and intelligent forehead. Each eye in turn. His nose. Each cheek in turn. His chin. His mouth.

'Finished with my fisog?' he murmured against her own mouth.

'Not yet.'

'Must be my turn to kiss you soon.'

'In a moment,' she said, and proceeded to take what breath he had left away.

'I-did-not-expect-that,' he managed, and stayed her busy hand. 'But I think we had better stop there.'

'We're going to stop?'

'We're going to head in a different direction.' He slid his hand between her legs.

'That feels gey like the same direction.'

'Are you complaining?'

'No. Oh...no... I'm no' complaining. You're making me ready again?'

'You're a quick learner. Let us lie down next to one another. Permit me to do one thing first.' He reached up for a towel.

'Am I ready now?' she whispered a few moments later.

'I'd say so.' He dipped his head and kissed her. 'With your permission, then, my love? Don't be scared. I'll be as gentle as I possibly can.' He moved so that his long body was above hers. 'Don't be scared,' he said again.

'I'm not scared, Richard.' She threaded her hands through his hair. 'How can I be scared when I'm with you?'

CHAPTER FIFTY-TWO

'I did not know,' she whispered. 'I did not know there was such pleasure to be had in the world.'

He captured the fingers that were smoothing his hair back from his face and pressed a kiss on the heel of her hand. 'Nor I, my love. Nor I.'

She gazed up at him. They were lying together on their temporary bed, she on her back and he on his side with one arm about her waist and his head and shoulders raised. 'It was not like this for you with those other lasses?'

'What other lasses?' he asked, smiling down at her. Then he grimaced. 'I was so transported that when the moment came when I should have pulled out I found I could not do it.'

She drew a circle with the tip of her index finger in the springy hair of his chest. 'I'm glad you didn't.'

'So am I. But we should perhaps get up now and then you can...' He paused, and she guessed he was trying to formulate what he wanted to say as delicately as possible.

She saved him from having to spell it out. 'In a minute,' she said, thinking of the clean cloth and the small bottle of vinegar she had brought with her in the pocket of her apron. 'I know what I have to do.'

It was not too late, even now. She could plead embarrassment, ask him to dress and leave the summer house before she cleaned herself up and got dressed. Being him, he would probably want to help her but if she insisted, he would leave her to do it herself. 'Can we please stay like this for a wee while longer?'

He pressed a kiss against her forehead. 'A wee while longer it is. Are you cold?' She felt the movement as he tilted his head back to look up at the shelf where the towels were. 'I could fetch some of those to put over us.'

'I'm not cold. Not while I'm lying here like this with you.'

'And it's warm outside today.'

'Aye,' she agreed. 'It's warm outside today.'

'A beautiful day. We shall lie together on so many days like this, Kate. So many days.'

She gazed across his bare chest to the windows of the summer house. He had opened them when they had come in and, as she watched now, she saw a bee buzz in through one of them and out through the other. On the other side of the glass, two red butterflies fluttered past. A beautiful day.

We shall lie together on so many days like this, Kate. Would they?

'I think perhaps we should get up now, my love.' Richard coughed. 'Shall I fill the sink with water for you?'

It still wasn't too late. She could wrap the towel around herself, wait till he had drawn the water and then ask him to wait outside. He would do that. He was a gentleman and he would understand she might be embarrassed if he stayed.

He wanted so much to believe she was innocent and untouched. It was important to him. It would be easy to fool him. It would be so much kinder to fool him, to allow him to hold on to this lovely idea of his that she was a maid, pure and clean.

It would also start their life together with a lie, put dishonesty at the very heart of it.

Kate sat up, rose onto her knees and made no attempt at concealment.

His eyes realised the truth first. Through them, she observed the stages he went through: momentary confusion; the urge to deny what he was seeing – or not seeing; his eventual acceptance of the truth.

'You have not bled.' His voice was very flat, and carefully expressionless.

'No,' she agreed. 'I have not bled.'

Something flashed across his face then, something he was unable to hide.

'It matters so much to you that I was not a maid?'

'You are saying it should not?'

'I'm not saying anything. I'm only asking you a question.'

'One to which I don't have an answer right at this moment.'

'I think you've just given it to me,' she said sadly. 'Will you please wait outside? I shall be with you as soon as I am ready.'

CHAPTER FIFTY-THREE

Richard was standing staring at the sundial when she emerged ten minutes later, his arms folded and his head bent. It snapped up as soon as she pulled the door of the summer house shut behind her. 'Do you want to lock the door? I have tidied everything up and put the cushion back on the sofa.'

'You should have called me to help you with that.'

'It's done now.' She stepped across to one of the garden's stone benches. 'I have rinsed the towel through. I shall drape it over here and hopefully Mr Gunn will think someone else has keys and has been in here. Hopefully also that there was a rain shower today and whoever it was used the towel to dry themselves off. I could take it away with me, wash it properly and return it but I dinna see how I would explain to Mr Gunn what I had been doing with it in the first place.'

'Kate,' Richard said. 'Come here.'

She did not move. She only shook her head.

'Then I shall have to come to you.' His hand was on her shoulder, spinning her round. She braced herself for the reproaches and the wounding words. Those were not what she got.

'What I wrote on the slate – what I have told you many times since then – still stands. My feelings for you haven't changed, Kate. Nothing that has happened here today has changed those. Except to make me love you even more.'

'Do you really mean that?' Her eyes were ranging over his face, trying to find the truth behind his words.

'Yes. I still love you, Kate. I still want to marry you.'

'But you're disappointed in me. Am I no' right?'

'I could never be disappointed in you, Kate.'

'The truth,' she reminded him. 'We're needing the truth here.'

'All right,' he said unhappily. 'I am disappointed that I'm not your first lover. Maybe it was naïve of me to think I could be. Although I cannot believe there have been many before me.'

She had to moisten her lips with her tongue before she could speak. 'One, Richard. Only one. And he was never my lover.'

'What was he, then? *Who* was he?'

'I do not think you need to know that,' she said. 'I do not think you need to know anything about him.'

'I need to know one thing. I need to know whether you loved him more than you love me.'

'*Loved* him?' she repeated, frowning at this unanticipated reaction. 'I *hate* him, Richard. I always did and I always will.'

'Yet you lay with him? I don't understand—' He gasped. 'Are you telling me you were unwilling? Dear God, Kate! Did he force you?'

'Aye,' she said. 'He forced me.' She felt a single tear slide down one cheek. Richard raised a finger and blotted it, his hand not quite steady. Then he stepped forward and enfolded her in his arms. She pressed her face against his chest and drank in the warmth of his skin, the freshly laundered smell of his shirt, the strength of his arms and the sense of his love for her. Could that love really be strong enough to allow him to cope with this? Oh, please God, let it be so.

'Who is he?' came his voice from above her head. 'Who is this brute who did this terrible thing to you?'

'Why do you need tae ken?'

'You need not concern yourself with why I need to ken.'

'I dinna want you to land yourself in any trouble. I dinna want you to get hurt.'

'I'm not going to be the one who gets hurt, Kate,' he said grimly. 'You can depend on that. Give me his name.'

'He's moved on. I dinna think he's in Edinburgh any more.' She was glad Richard couldn't see her eyes. 'You wouldna know him.'

'I *will* know him. That's something else you can depend on. His name, if you please. And any idea you might have of where he went. Was he a patron of The Pearl Fisher? Would anyone there know where he might have gone?'

'I'm not giving you his name, Richard. Will you let me go? I'm all hot.'

She pressed her hands to her burning cheeks.

'You surely do not seek to protect him?' he asked as he dropped his arms.

'Richard,' she said, 'this happened to me four years ago. Five,' she corrected.

'Which is it, Kate?' he demanded. 'Four years or five years? Oh God, were you only fourteen?' She saw him draw the next logical conclusion. '*It went on for a whole year?*'

Oh God, this would be too much for him, she knew it would. And this wasn't even the truth, only a very small part of it. 'I couldn't stop him, Richard. He was too strong. I tried, Richard! I tried so hard! But he said he would hurt Andrew if I didn't give in to him—'

'Bastard,' Richard said, reaching for her again. '*Fucking bastard.*' He did not apologise for swearing in front of her. 'That makes me even more determined to make him pay for what he did to you.'

'It's over and done with now.' She shook her head against his chest. 'No' something I want tae think about any more. No' something I want tae talk about any more.'

'You couldn't bring yourself to tell your aunt and uncle what was happening? Mr Graham would have sorted the bastard out, I'll be bound.'

'Richard,' she cried, 'leave this be! Please leave this be!'

'How can I when someone who did this awful thing to you is still walking about and hasn't paid for what he did? How can I leave this be, Kate?'

'Because you have to! Because you canna fix everything that's broken in the world. Everything's no' going tae come right just because you want it tae come right. And because I'm asking you tae leave it be,' she finished, her voice breaking. 'Because I'm asking you, Richard.'

He looked distraught. 'I can't bear the thought of you being hurt like this, Kate. Thinking of you suffering for so long. I can't bear it!'

She wrapped her arms about his waist. 'It's over, Richard. In the past. I found a way to make him stop. He's got nothing to do with you and me, Richard. He doesn't matter. As long as you dinna think badly o' me because o' it.'

'Think badly of *you*? Oh, Kate, of course I don't! *Oh, Kate!*' he said again, and now it was him whose eyes were too bright.

She drew his unruly head down onto her shoulder. 'It's over, Richard. What matters now is the future.'

'On that at least we can agree, Kate.' When a nearby church bell tolled the quarter-hour, he lifted his head and gave her the ghost of a smile.

'What else did your father say this morning?'

'That's not relevant.'

'I think it is. Tell me the rest o' it, Richard.'

'He suggested I take you as my mistress.' His mouth tightened.

'Which will apparently be all right as long as I keep you *out of sight of respectable society*.' His tone of voice made it clear he was quoting his father's exact words.

'Aiblins he's right.'

Richard's mouth tightened. 'We're going to be married, Kate, and there's an end to it. Everything open and honest and above board.'

She was too tired to fight this battle now. 'What else did you father say?'

'Not much. Except that he wants me to squire my cousins and my aunts around town until the king leaves on Thursday.'

'Then that's exactly what you should do. Try tae smooth things over. We can see one another again on Friday or Saturday, once all the excitement is over.'

He shook his head. 'Too long without seeing you, Kate. Especially after today.' His voice softened. 'I want to scoop you up and look after you now.'

'And how would ye do that?' Kate asked.

'Give you lots of hugs and kisses and feed you sweets and oranges,' he said promptly.

She laughed. 'That sounds nice. Would you read me poetry too?'

'Any poet in particular?'

'Any and all o' them,' she said. 'But that'll need tae wait a while. And now I think you should go home.'

It took some coaxing and cajoling but eventually she persuaded him to it. 'I'm walking you back to The Pearl Fisher first,' he said. 'Don't bother arguing with me about that.'

'I won't. Only as far as the bottom o' Niddry Street, though. I dinna want my uncle and aunt tae see ye.'

He put his hands on the back of her neck, under her hair. 'D'you not think they might be able to guess who you've spent the afternoon with?' His black eyebrows rose. 'As long as they don't guess what we've been up to we'll be all right. I want you out of The Pearl Fisher, Kate. As soon as possible.'

'I want that too, Richard.' She wrapped her arms about his waist for one final hug. 'I want that too.'

CHAPTER FIFTY-FOUR

She was waiting for them, sitting on her little trunk outside the locked gates of the tavern. 'Whit the devil are you up to?' demanded Chrissie Graham as she stepped in from the Cowgate.

'I'm leaving,' Kate said as she rose to her feet, adding with studied sarcasm, 'Didna want tae go without saying goodbye. Someone's coming tae help me carry my things.' The gods had smiled on her. Moments after she had left Richard she had bumped into one of the printer's apprentices and she had asked him if he and his friend could come to The Pearl Fisher for six o'clock.

'Whit d'ye mean, you're leaving, ye daft wee cow?' Chrissie jabbed a finger towards the tavern. 'Ye'll get in there and ready yersel tae start serving.'

'No,' Kate said calmly. 'I won't.'

Chrissie Graham stepped forward, her hand raised. Her niece caught her arm in mid-air. 'You've struck me for the last time, Aunt Chrissie. You've used my brother and me like slaves for the last time.'

'I'll ging tae the constables!'

'And say what?' demanded Kate. 'That for four years you've worked me like a dog and never paid me a penny piece in wages?'

'Chrissie,' Michael Graham put in. 'Let her go, eh?'

'Let her go?' Chrissie whirled round to her husband. 'Whit are ye on aboot, Michael Graham? If she goes, I'll hae tae pay some other slut tae work here.'

'Ye dinna understand, Chrissie. She has to go. Although no' before she tells us where she's going tae be.'

Cool and composed, Kate looked at Michael Graham. 'Oh, I dinna think so.'

His eyes narrowed. 'We have an arrangement, wee Kate.'

'No, we dinna. Ye can forget aboot that.'

'Is that right?' he asked. 'And here's another question for ye. How hard dae ye think it's going tae be for a man wha kens this toun like the back o' his hand tae find ye?' The familiar sneering smile was on his face. 'Dinna be daft, pet.'

'Ye might think better o' coming anywhere near me gin I tell ye that it'll be me wha gings tae the constables. I've already written a letter tae them and left it wi' someone for safe-keeping. Gin onything happens tae me or Andrew the watch'll find oot what you get up tae in the middle o' the night at Greyfriars Kirkyard.'

Chrissie Graham wheeled round to her husband. 'Michael Graham!' she cried. 'That trade pays good siller! How come I've never seen ony o' it?'

'Money,' Kate said in disgust. 'Can you never think o' anything else?' Her eyes ranged over her aunt. 'There's so many things ye dinna notice because all ye care aboot is siller. Ye dinna even see whit's going on right under your nose.'

Michael Graham stepped towards Kate. 'No' another word, miss,' he growled.

'I'll say whit I want tae say.'

He took another menacing step towards her but at that moment the light from the street was blocked by the figures of the two printer's apprentices.

'Everything all right, Kate?' one of them asked.

'It will be in a wee minute.' She returned her attention to her uncle and aunt. 'Aiblins I should tell ye this in private, Aunt Chrissie.'

Chrissie Graham's eyes flickered contemptuously from Kate to her husband and back again. 'Ye really think ah didna ken?'

Rosy-cheeked from the sea breezes, smiling all over his face, Andrew was swapping stories of the day with the Hendersons. They were in the flat above the bookshop and Peggy had insisted he have a drink and something to eat before he changed out of his good clothes and returned to The Pearl Fisher. The bell that connected with the bookshop door jangled.

'I'll go,' Nathaniel said.

Unlocking and opening the street door a moment later, he blinked in surprise when he saw who was standing there. 'Miss Catriona? Do I know your friends?'

'Mr Henderson, please tell me if this isn't convenient. Although I dinna ken whit I'll dae if ye say that.' She gave him a nervous smile. 'Is it all right if Andrew stays with you and Mrs Henderson from tonight? And could you maybe let me stay here a wee while too?'

Nathaniel swung the door wide. 'Come away in, lass. Will you bring the trunk upstairs, young gentlemen? And who's this?'

'It's the cat,' Kate said, glancing a little desperately at Jack, now winding himself around her ankles. 'He's followed us up the street.'

'Well,' Nathaniel said, 'he'd better come in too.'

There was a soft knock at his bedroom door. Standing at the window gazing out at the darkening city, no longer sure how long he had been there, Richard swivelled round. 'Come in.'

An outdoor lantern in one hand, Jamie came into the room, closed the door quietly behind him and walked across to where Richard stood. 'Your father's compliments, Mr Richard, and he'd be obliged gin ye would come wi' me right now.'

'Is someone ill? Not my mother?' he asked, guilt and alarm

bouncing him out of the confused torpor in which he'd spent most of this evening.

The other young man shook his head. 'Naebody's ill. But I'm tae ask ye tae make all possible haste. The maister also wants ye tae dae that wi'oot waking the rest o' the household. Use the back stairs, he said.'

Following Jamie down those, Richard automatically turned right when he reached the bottom. Jamie grabbed him by the sleeve of his dressing-gown. 'No' that way, Mr Richard. We're going oot tae the stables.'

'The stables? What the fuck's going on, Jamie?'

'I've nae idea, sir. Will ye please just make haste?'

Following the other young man through the dark and quiet kitchens and out over the cobbles of the mews, Richard blinked as he stepped into the stables. Several of its lamps were lit and three middle-aged men stood in a semicircle facing the door. Brendan the coachman. Edward Hope. Michael Graham.

Michael Graham? 'Mr Graham? What are you doing here?' Then, as a terrifying possibility occurred to him: 'Is aught amiss with Kate?'

Her uncle gave him no answer, simply kept looking at him. Richard strode across the stable's well-swept stone floor and seized the man by the shoulders. 'For pity's sake, Mr Graham. If there is something wrong with Kate, you must tell me. Is she all right?'

Shaking him off, Michael Graham took a step back. He looked Richard up and down. '*Is there aught amiss with Kate?*' he repeated. '*Is she all right?* Well may ye ask, young master. You ken better than ony o' us whit's amiss wi' my niece.' His dark eyes flickered to Edward Hope before coming back to rest on his son's anxious face. 'You've ruined her, you young blackguard. That's what's wrong with Kate.'

CHAPTER FIFTY-FIVE

'Well?' demanded Edward Hope. 'Is what this man says true? Have you ruined his niece?'

Richard looked at his father. Then he looked at Michael Graham. 'She told you?'

'Aye, she told me. Couldna help but tell me. The lassie was fair beside herself when she got back to The Pearl Fisher this afternoon. Nae bloody wonder. She was a maid this morning. Now she's ruined. How will the poor girl ever find a husband if this gets oot?'

Richard stared at him, trying to take it all in. He could understand she might have lied to her uncle about not being a virgin, unable to bring herself to tell either him or her aunt what had happened to her. He couldn't understand any of the rest of it.

The lassie was fair beside herself. Kate had seemed calm enough when they had parted at the foot of Niddry Street. In the few yards from there to The Pearl Fisher she had become so distressed?

There was also her concern that her uncle and aunt shouldn't know she and Richard were spending the afternoon together. She'd been adamant about that. For her then to immediately tell her uncle the two of them had lain together didn't make sense.

'Richard,' his father said. 'I asked you a question. Have you ruined the girl?'

'She'll no' find herself a husband without a dowry, that's for sure,' blustered Michael Graham.

'Ah,' said Edward Hope. For a moment there was no sound in the stable save the snuffling of the horses. When Richard's father spoke again, his features had acquired a cynical cast. 'So now we come to the heart of the matter. How much?'

'How much?' spluttered Michael Graham. 'You tell me how much a young lassie's innocence is worth, sir. Young gentlemen like your son think they can play fast and loose wi' girls like my niece. It's no' right, sir, and it's no' honourable.'

He hadn't taken her innocence. Someone else had. He could nip this in the bud right now with a few well-chosen words. Only she had kept what had happened to her secret for so long. In the midst of his own distress and confusion, Richard found himself remaining silent.

'How much?' Edward Hope said again.

Michael Graham drew in a breath. 'One hundred guineas.'

'Fifty,' Edward Hope said. 'Don't even think of coming back for more.'

'What if my niece is with child?'

'Fifty guineas is a tidy sum.' There was steel in Edward Hope's voice. 'So I repeat: don't even think of coming back for more. Don't think of spreading this story abroad either.' He looked at Michael Graham. He looked at the neatly stowed rack of horse whips. Finally, he looked at Brendan, big and broad and powerful, stronger even than Michael Graham and certainly much fitter than him.

Brendan returned his master's gaze. He too surveyed the Hope household's unwelcome visitor – as he might have looked at a nest of rats infesting his stable and disturbing his beloved horses. 'Any time, Mr Hope, sir,' he said in his lilting accent. 'You'd only have to say the word.'

* * *

Richard walked along the line of stalls, giving each beast a clap in turn, pausing when he reached the mare at the end and sliding one hand in under her warm mane to rest his fingers on the silky neck beneath it. He was aware that Brendan was studying his back, aware too of the coachman's silent sympathy.

'I cannot believe she knows anything about what's happened here tonight, Brendan. She loves me.' His voice sounded rusty, as though he hadn't used it for a while. He coughed to clear his throat. 'I know she does.'

Soft-footed though the coachman was, Richard felt the big man approach him, lay a hand on his shoulder. 'Maybe that's true, sir. But the want of money can make people do terrible things. The root of all evil, as the Good Book says.'

Richard wanted to deny that with all his might but the words wouldn't come out. So he stood there with his hand on the horse's warm neck and the Irishman's big hand on his own shoulder until at last he found something to say. 'I should let you get to your bed, Brendan.'

'God bless you, Mr Richard, I'd be happy for you to stay here as long as you like.'

'But?' Richard asked, his voice dull.

'But your father told me to tell you whenever you were ready that he's waiting for you in the library.'

Edward Hope walked across to a small chinoiserie cabinet, opened it, took out a decanter and two crystal glasses and poured out a generous measure of brandy for himself and his son. 'Here,' he said, handing one glass to Richard. 'Medicinal purposes. And sit yourself down.'

'She loves me, Father,' Richard said as he obeyed that gruff instruction, too confused and upset to want or be able to hide his feelings from his father. 'I know she does.'

'Richard,' Edward Hope said, taking his own seat at the opposite side of the library fireplace, 'do you not see now how she and her uncle must have had this planned from the beginning – from whenever it was you first met her? I'm sorry, my boy, but I'm going to have to be cruel to be kind. I think you have to treat this unfortunate episode in much the same way as you might view one of the illnesses of which you are learning. As a canker to be cut out. Cut it out, Richard, and make a clean break.'

Richard took a great gulp of brandy, feeling the warmth as it slid down through him. Kate as a *canker to be cut out*. Their love affair *an unfortunate episode*.

'Distraction too, Richard,' his father said, his voice full of sympathy for his son. 'You will come to the ball tomorrow night and attend the other planned events. That will help.'

'Father, I don't think I'm in the right frame of mind—'

His father leant forward. 'For your mother's sake? Who continues to be upset by what happened on Saturday night but who knows nothing of this evening's events. Shall we agree to keep it that way?'

Richard took another slug of brandy. 'Whatever you say, Father.'

When father and son emerged from the back stairs onto the first floor landing, Edward Hope, like Brendan, clapped Richard on the shoulder. 'Things will look better in the morning, my boy,' he said, soft-voiced so as not to wake any of his sleeping guests. 'They always do.'

'Kate,' came an enquiring female voice. 'Are you awake now, lass?'

Turning her head on the soft pillows, Kate saw Mrs Henderson peeping round the edge of a door.

'I've brought you some tea and toast. Sit up and I shall lay this over your knees.'

Kate gazed at the tray being placed on the counterpane in front of her and stuttered out a protest. 'You shouldn't be serving me, Mrs Henderson.'

'Why ever not? Don't worry about your brother, by the way. He's downstairs in the shop helping Nathaniel, who called first thing this morning on that skinflint of a saddler to tell him Andrew won't be going back there.' Peggy straightened up. 'Now then, do you want me to go and leave you in peace or would you like to talk?'

'You've both been so kind to us,' Kate said, her voice not quite steady.

Peggy patted her shoulder. 'Drink your tea. I find it always helps me when I'm a wee bittie upset. Look,' she said, turning to look at the open doorway, 'you have a visitor. Our new friend Jack.'

Jumping up onto the high bed in one graceful leap, the ginger-and-white tom padded over the covers, sniffed the edges of the tray, accepted a tickle under one ear from Kate, and returned to the foot of it. He circled several times until he had softened his chosen space to his precise requirements, curled up and allowed his eyes to close.

'We could do worse than take a leaf out of his book,' Peggy said. 'Food, drink, humans who admire them and a warm and soft place to sleep. That's all cats ask out of life.'

'Ye dinna mind that he's here, Mrs Henderson? I couldna really stop him. He followed me up the hill.'

'I don't mind at all. Eat your toast and drink your tea while they're both still hot, my dear. *Would* you like me to leave you alone or do you want me to stay?'

'Could you please stay, Mrs Henderson? There is something I should like to ask you.'

* * *

Richard had tossed and turned all night, falling at last into a heavy sleep only as the dawn came up. He was pulled out of that uncomfortable slumber at eleven o'clock, finding Jamie leaning over him and shaking him by the shoulder.

'What?' he demanded, shooting bolt upright.

'Ssh,' enjoined the under-footman. 'Mr O'Sullivan says we've tae keep this quiet.'

'Keep what quiet?'

'No' so loud, Mr Richard. There's a young boy waiting tae see you in the stables. Name of Andrew Dunbar. Mr O'Sullivan says you'll understand.'

'Move back, Jamie.' Richard's legs were already over the side of the bed. 'I'm getting up.'

'Gin ye're going oot, ye'd best tak your riding coat, Mr Richard. It's raining again. Fair pissing doon.'

Walking across the North Bridge beside Andrew, the boy dressed in his new clothes and wearing his built-up shoes, Richard was glad of the downpour. It made conversation difficult. All he knew so far was Andrew's excited 'Kate and me have gone to stay with Mr and Mrs Henderson, sir. We're going to live with them for ever! And Kate says can you please come to the bookshop?'

Now Richard was even more confused than he'd been last night. Holding the big black umbrella that Brendan had thrust into his hands above his head and Andrew's, he crossed the High Street. By the looks of it, everyone had taken cover from the elements. Despite the weather, the bookshop door stood a little ajar. As he and Andrew approached, it was swung wide. Kate was standing there, wearing the dress he had bought for her.

CHAPTER FIFTY-SIX

They were alone in the bookshop, the door closed now against the rain. The other members of the Henderson household had retreated upstairs. An occasional cough or the sound of footsteps was the only evidence of their presence in the same building.

Kate had expected Richard to take her in his arms as soon as they were alone together. She hadn't expected him to remain on the other side of the big table like a polite stranger. 'Will you not take your coat off?' she asked, confused by his stiff demeanour and his unsmiling face.

'I'm not sure it's worth it. I may not be here for very long.'

'Richard,' she asked, growing more puzzled by the moment, 'what on earth's the matter? I thought you'd be pleased that we were here. I didn't expect you to come over today but I wanted to let you know as soon as I could that we had left The Pearl Fisher.'

'For pity's sake, Kate.' He ran a hand through the dark waves of his hair. 'Don't pretend you don't know!'

'Richard, I don't know what's upsetting you, I really don't!' She began walking round the table towards him but he barked out a 'Stay where you are!' and one hand shot up, palm outwards.

Fear stabbed at her heart. 'Richard,' she cried, 'please tell me what's wrong. I really have no idea what's wrong!'

'So it would be news to you that your uncle came over to

Castle Street last night and dunned my father for money to compensate for me having *ruined* you?'

Dumbfounded, Kate stared at him for a moment without speaking. In the next instant, comprehension dawned. *Oh, dear God.* She might have known Michael Graham would try something like this. 'Did your father give him any money?'

'Och, Kate,' Richard cried, the air of cool condescension vanishing. 'Can you at the very least stop pretending you don't know all about this?'

She opened her mouth to protest again that she really didn't but he spoke over her, rattling the words out. 'You owe me that much at least, Kate. *Some* honesty. How much of the fifty guineas did you get? Was it equal shares? That should be enough for you to pay the Hendersons for your bed and board for quite some time. I suppose you're going to tell me it's a simple coincidence you and Andrew have come to stay here the very day after your uncle screws fifty guineas out of my father?'

'Yesterday. We came yesterday. Fifty guineas?' she queried, astounded by the sum.

As though he could not bear to look at her, he tilted his tousled head against the end of a tall bookcase and turned his gaze towards the rain falling out on the High Street. 'Tell me one thing, Kate. Was this planned right from the beginning? Or did you perhaps like me a little? Maybe as much as the wee flower I gave you in the Old Physic Garden?'

She was instantly transported back to that bright day, could see him handing her the bluebell and herself taking it from him. She had thought then that this could lead to nothing but heartache. Had she been right? Had the Fates decreed their love affair should end here and now, on a wet Monday morning in the Hendersons' bookshop?

His riding coat had three little capes falling from its shoulders.

Fawn in colour, the material had darkened in places to brown in response to the rain that had fallen on it, despite the big black umbrella now furled and propped up to one side of the shop door. Mrs Henderson had taken it out of his hands and put it there, well away from the books— And Richard stopped staring out at the driving rain.

'Brendan says the want of money can make people do terrible things. Tell me he's wrong, Kate. Please tell me he's wrong!'

She stared at him, distraught. How could he even think she'd been involved in this? The answer came hot on the heels of the question: because of what Michael Graham had done and said last night; because she had never given Richard the slightest inkling of how she felt about her uncle. There could be little doubt either that Richard's father believed her to be part of the plot. He would have influenced his son's reactions too, that son who stood before her now, so terribly hurt by what he believed to be her betrayal of him.

The only way to change this would be to tell him the truth, the whole of it this time. Nothing less would do. She knew what would happen then.

I could break his nose wi' one punch, Kate.

A gentleman, is he no'? I'd have him lying battered and bleeding on the floor afore he kent whit had hit him.

Horrific though the vision was, the scandal that would ensue would be much worse. He was Mr Richard Hope, not just well-off but gentry, kin to the Earl of Hopetoun, weel-connecktit to lots of other important folk, coming out in a year's time to be a doctor. She was Kate Dunbar, a lassie who worked in an oyster cellar, her people a tavern-keeper and a grave-robber.

If the story got out – as it would – folk would react in different ways. Good people like the Hendersons would feel sorry for her. Others would condemn her, assume she must have invited her uncle's attentions. Many would devour the tale with relish, gaze at her with malicious or lascivious eyes.

Few would have any respect for her. She'd be in the gutter for the rest of her life, the worthless wee slut her own aunt thought her to be. Especially if Michael Graham, with his reputation as a genial landlord, presented her as a flighty little trollop, making up slanderous stories about him to cover her own loose morals.

Richard's family would be horrified, and the shame would attach itself to them too. Dreamer that he was, he might give them and everything else up for her, in which case there would be nothing for the two of them to do but sink into the murk of the Old Town. The university probably wouldn't let him back in to finish his degree – and Andrew could forget about George Heriot's.

Or she and Richard could run away, start life afresh in another town – London, maybe. The tiny spark of hope in Kate's breast was extinguished almost as soon as it flared into life. They would have no money, no friends to help them, and for her to leave Andrew would be like tearing her heart out – as it would be for Richard to leave his family—

'*Is* Brendan right?' he demanded. 'That the want of money makes people do terrible things?'

He had put the words into her mouth. Or perhaps they'd been put into his by those unseen and uncaring Fates, swooping and diving around them. All she could salvage from the wreck was to send him back to the solace of his family and his studies. She spoke before she lost her courage.

'I'm afraid he is,' she said, wondering how she could sound so calm when her heart was shattering into a hundred pieces. 'I'm sorry, Richard. I really am very sorry.'

He bowed his head, raised one hand to his face and pinched his nose between his thumb and his index finger. 'What if you have conceived a child?'

'I dinna think that's very likely. It never happened wi—' She caught herself.

Richard raised his head. 'With the other men you've lain with?' he queried. 'Was the story about the one man forcing you true in any particular, Kate?' He was already at the bookshop door, stooping to lift the umbrella. 'Goodbye,' he said in a clipped, tight voice. 'I hope you find whatever it is you're looking for.'

He was gone, leaving her blinking at the speed of his departure. Rushing forward to the door he had left open behind him, she saw that he had almost reached the corner of the North Bridge. Striding out of her life for ever. She curled her hands into fists, pushing her fingernails into the soft flesh of her palms. Forcing herself to stay where she was and not go running across the wet cobblestones of the High Street after him. How could she let him go? *How-could-she-let-him-go?*

He was carrying the umbrella by his side, the big daftie, allowing the rain to pour down on him. She could call after him about that, use it as an excuse to stop him. She could run up to him, bring him back to the bookshop and tell him the truth... But that was the one thing she could not do. For his own sake, she could not.

She had to let him go. *She couldn't let him go!*

If he turns round, she thought. If he only turns round, I'll run out into the rain and tell him the truth and somehow keep him safe, somehow make it all right. If he only turns round.

He made it onto the North Bridge before he stopped, invisible hands clutching at his heart. He had checked his progress for the merest instant before he had rounded the corner onto the bridge, willing her to call out to him. If she'd done that, he'd have run back through the rain to her, told her he'd forgive her if she only told him she really did love him. Even now, even after what had happened, he'd have been ready and willing to forgive her. No question about it. But she hadn't called out.

His body went to the ball that evening. His mind was elsewhere. He'd been so distracted that Jamie and his father between them had to coax him into his evening clothes as though he were a child being encouraged to dress himself for the very first time. The noise and the crush when he got there allowed him to retreat even further into himself, his aching heart and his puzzled brain striving to work out what had happened.

He'd been so sure that Kate loved him as much as he loved her. If she'd wanted money she could have come to him for it, and she must have known that. He couldn't make any sense of this. His thoughts roamed over the events of the summer, all the precious memories that were now tainted by the events of the last twenty-four hours.

It was only as supper was announced that Richard realised that this afternoon in the bookshop, he hadn't actually asked Kate the most important question of all.

Do you love me, Kate?

He stopped dead in front of the double doors into the supper room. Two footmen – with absurd flashes of tartan on their livery, of course – were throwing them open. His father, who had never been far from his son's side this evening, turned. 'Best move out of the way, my boy. The king has to go in first.'

Richard didn't hear him. *Do you love me, Kate?* Of course. It was the only question that mattered. If she said yes, then nothing else did. He swung round, ready to race down the stairs and out into George Street, and found himself face-to-face with His Majesty King George IV. 'Excuse me, please,' Richard said politely. 'I have to go somewhere.'

The men around the king froze into astonished silence. One of them was Richard's illustrious relative, the Earl of Hopetoun. Flashing a warning that Richard didn't see, he laughed. 'Impetuous youth, sire,' he said to the king. 'I think that's what we're witnessing here. May I present Mr Richard Hope?'

The king smiled. Richard smiled back, an automatic response. 'His Majesty and I have already met,' he said, and made as though to pass him and his entourage.

'The king decides when you will leave his presence,' came an urgent mutter in his ear. 'Not the other way round.'

Richard looked at the man who had spoken. He didn't recognise him but he presumed he was a courtier. That would be the word. Like the other gentlemen present, he was swathed in tartan. Next to him and similarly attired stood the Lord Advocate of Scotland.

Richard looked past both men to the supper room. It too was festooned in tartan, its long tables covered with white linen tablecloths on which a lavish feast was laid, footmen waiting to serve it. So much fuss. So much money spent. So much luxury for people who already wallowed in it. So much false praise and sycophancy lavished on the unprepossessing man who stood in front of him. And why was it that in this modern world one was expected to bow the knee to someone whose right to reign over others derived not from his own character, personality or abilities but was merely to do with who his ancestors had been?

'Sir,' Richard said, directly addressing the king, 'do you have any idea of the poverty and degradation in which many of your subjects in Edinburgh live? Or of how well-nigh impossible it is for them to pull themselves out of the muck and filth? Or of how they might feel if they could be here in the Assembly Rooms tonight and see you and these fawning courtiers rolling about in luxury like pigs at a trough?'

* * *

They were at the back door of the Assembly Rooms: Richard, his father, the Earl of Hopetoun and the Lord Advocate.

'What in the name of God possessed you, Richard?' asked the Earl. 'Edward,' he demanded, turning to Richard's father. 'Can you explain your son's behaviour?'

Edward Hope shook his head and laid a hand on Richard's shoulder. 'Is he in trouble?' he asked the Lord Advocate.

'For insulting the person of the king?' replied that gentleman. 'It's treason, Edward. Rank sedition. I cannot see we can avoid a warrant being issued for his arrest. There were too many witnesses to what he said.'

'No need for that, surely,' said the Earl. 'If his father guarantees there will be no repetition?'

The Lord Advocate thought for a moment. 'Get him out of Edinburgh for a while.' He inclined his head in indication of Richard, who stood among them staring into space. 'There's bound to be a ship leaving from Leith tonight or tomorrow morning. Make sure he's on it!'

CHAPTER FIFTY-SEVEN

You have not bled. That was what he had said to her two months ago in the summer house of the Old Physic Garden. For the last few weeks she had been saying those words to herself. Now that a second month had passed, there was only one conclusion to be drawn. What to do about the situation was a more complicated matter.

Busy serving in the bookshop, Kate was turning over the various possibilities in her mind and realising there were not too many of them. Some she immediately ruled out. Going to Richard's father as the girl his son had ruined had already been tried. Besides which, if she did that, Mr Hope might tell his son of her condition.

She could not bear that. Hurt though he was, wounded by what he thought she had done to him, he would nonetheless feel an obligation to her, especially if she carried the child to full-term and gave birth to his son or daughter.

There was of course the possibility that she might not. The baby might die inside her before it grew very much older. Aiblins that would be the best thing that could happen. Yet instinct had her laying a protective hand on her stomach.

She could ask Mrs Henderson for help but that was another choice she had to rule out. She had made a promise to Peggy Henderson – as Richard had too – and neither of them had kept it. How could she go to Mrs Henderson, see the disappointment in her face that Kate had let her down?

There was the other possibility, of course. She could kill the baby growing within her womb, snuff out this life before it had properly begun. She knew who would help her do that.

It was all arranged. Tomorrow, while Andrew was safely at school, she would go to Ella Balfour's dingy room in the Cowgate. Ella had said Kate could spend the rest of the day lying in her bed getting over it and be up again and back to the bookshop by the late afternoon. Neither Andrew nor the Hendersons need ever know anything. Kate had told them she wanted to smooth things over with her aunt by spending the day at The Pearl Fisher.

Asleep in the truckle bed at the foot of her own, Andrew was snoring gently. Confused as he was by why Richard Hope had disappeared from their lives, he must never know what she was going to do tomorrow to Richard's baby. He must never know that his sister had killed her own child, his nephew or niece, her and Richard's son or daughter. Only God should have the power to take a life.

Dream the dream with me, Kate.

No, she responded silently. Get out of my head. I don't want to hear your voice.

I don't want to hear your lovely voice. Mellow as a russet apple. I don't want to hear it!

Dream the dream with me, Kate. A nice house with a garden, a spacious bedroom with a big, soft bed. A fire to sit by in the winter. A window to look out of and watch the world going by. Andrew going to school every day. Herself with her feet up on a stool reading a book. Caring for and playing with her happy, laughing babies.

The cat was purring at her feet. Distressed beyond reason,

fighting for breath, Kate sat up and reached for him. 'There's nothing else for it, Jack,' she murmured brokenly. 'I've got to be able to work and pay my way. No other choice,' she said again, and buried her face in his warm fur.

'This is it?' Kate took the beaker Ella was handing her.

'Aye, this is it. It tastes bloody awful, so it's best tae drink it doon in one go. Then I'll gie ye some whisky tae sip.' Ella lifted the second beaker she held. 'That'll take the taste away and make ye a wee touch tipsy, forbye. That'll help.'

Kate lifted the beaker to her lips, took an experimental sniff, lowered it again in instinctive reaction and pulled a face. 'It smells bloody awful too. Is this going to hurt, Ella?'

'Ye'll have a gey sore stomach once it starts working, Kate. Soon efter that ye'll get the feeling that'll send ye tae the chanty.' Swinging round, she pointed to the chamber pot in the corner. 'Ye'll be on there for a wee while, I should think, until it all comes awa'. Your guts'll still be girning but ye can lie doon until ye feel better.' She reached out with her free hand and smoothed a lock of Kate's hair back from her face. 'Best no' tae delay, lass. Just dae it, like.'

'You'll no' leave me alone, Ella?'

'Of course I'll no'. Soon be all over. Then ye'll be richt as rain. Drink up, now.'

Her eyes on Ella's sympathetic face, Kate raised the beaker to her lips.

PART THREE

Autumn-Winter, 1824

CHAPTER FIFTY-EIGHT

They had been able to save neither the mother nor the child. Saddened as ever by the loss, Richard gazed down at the two pale bodies. The nurse had wrapped the badly underweight baby boy in a scrap of clean linen and placed him in the crook of his mother's arm. She looked little more than a child herself.

'If only she had been able to preserve her innocence for a year or two longer. Until she was more able to withstand the rigours of labour.'

'Lord love you, Dr Hope, sir, I don't imagine she had much choice in the matter. I knew her. She lived close-by the hospital. Her father is a brute.'

Richard turned to her, wide-eyed. 'You cannot mean that her own father was responsible for her condition?'

The nurse shrugged, saddened but resigned. 'It happens. More often than many of us would like to think.'

He knew it did. Why he was being so naïve about it, he wasn't sure. He had seen enough of the squalid side of life over the last two years to have few illusions left about his fellow man – and woman, sometimes. After a year aboard one of His Majesty's ships of the line as a surgeon's mate, he had come here to London and managed to secure himself a houseman's position at St Bartholomew's Hospital.

He wasn't qualified but when he'd walked in here off the street he'd found one of the senior surgeons was an Edinburgh man and more than happy to take him on. 'Only one year short of an Edinburgh degree with experience in the Royal Navy? Come away in, laddie.'

There were, Richard had discovered since, lots of Scottish doctors in London, several of them at Bart's. Quite ironic, that. The hospital lay hard by Smithfield market, where Edward I, the Hammer of the Scots, had ordered William Wallace put to death in the most prolonged and painful manner possible. Scotland's greatest hero had been butchered here, in the most literal sense of the word.

Richard had never yet run into Torquil Grant, though that was hardly surprising. He would be attending to wealthy ladies and gentlemen, encouraging their hypochondria and pocketing the handsome fees. A houseman at Bart's didn't move in those circles.

Both at the hospital and during his stint in the Navy, Richard had learnt about the structure of the human body; what diseases, ailments, guns, knives, violence and accidents did to it; and he had also learnt a great deal about human nature. He had discovered much about himself too.

Like how he really did not want to believe that a father could force himself on his own daughter – because of what the nurse had said, he supposed. People who found such impulses unnatural and repugnant didn't like to think other people not only succumbed to them but actively relished them. It was always more comfortable to block out the unpleasant side of life. He should know.

He was a past master at that, had worked hard at it since he had left Edinburgh two years before. Blocking *her* out. Blocking out the sights and sounds and smells and emotions of that summer he had spent falling ever more deeply in love with her.

At first he had thought it was going to be impossible to rid himself of the pain and hurt. Lying on his bunk sick as a dog from the rocking of the ship and sick at heart because of his memories of Catriona Dunbar and her betrayal of him, he had thought he would never be happy again.

In time – because it was either that or sink into paralysing melancholia – he found a strategy. He worked hard and he played hard. When he discovered that playing too hard led to a sore head, regrets and twinges of conscience, he made up his mind to concentrate on the first half of that equation. Besides which, he was always skint these days. Walking the wards didn't pay much, what paltry spare cash he had going to fees for anatomy classes rather than the pleasures of life.

That evening, in his austere but clean room high up under the eaves of the hospital, he found that the fate of the young girl and her baby he had lost during the morning was preying on his mind.

What a life she must have led. Raised in squalor not merely physical but of the mind and spirit too. Preyed on sexually by her own father, more than likely from an early age. Dreadful. Unimaginable. Unthinkable. Only, as the nurse had said, it happened – and therefore had to be thought about.

What chance was there for a girl like that to make something of herself and have a happy and useful life? Not much. None now. Her short and unhappy sojourn on this Earth was over.

Her fate was by no means unique. Knowing the squalor of the London slums as he now did, Richard was aware of that. He would not – could not – make any excuses for her brute of a father. He had, though, often pondered how hard it must be for anyone to lead a decent life when they were obliged to live in such filthy and overcrowded conditions.

Edinburgh was no better than London. Nor, he imagined, was any other city in the so-called civilised world. Like all of them,

London offered visitors and citizens alike magnificent public buildings and palaces, gracious neo-classical avenues and verdant green parks and pleasure gardens.

Yet within a mile of these glories you found mean little alleys full of prostitutes and cut-purses and begging children dodging around piles of human ordure and rotting rubbish. No clean air, no clean water. If one person got sick, the infection would spread to twenty others, and then twenty more.

Exactly like Edinburgh, Richard thought, the medical textbook he'd been studying resting unheeded on his drawn-up knees. He had no table or chair in his little pigeon loft here. Like himself, the hospital was always skint too. Hospitals generally were, no money to spare for anything that was not strictly necessary – or on show to the richer and more influential of its benefactors.

If he wanted to sit rather than sleep or stand gazing out over the rooftops of Smithfield, he could do so only on the edge of his narrow and not very comfortable bed. The thought took him back again to Edinburgh, to his bedroom at home. He hadn't appreciated the luxury of what he'd had there, that was for sure. In touch with his parents again – this time he'd told them where a letter from them might find him – he'd had an impassioned missive from his mother the week before, begging him to come home. He had to make a decision about that soon, his contract at Bart's very shortly coming up for renewal.

He longed to go home. He missed his parents, he missed Brendan and Jamie and the other servants, he missed the house on the corner of Castle Street and Princes Street, he missed the view of Edinburgh Castle from his bedroom window, he missed the university, he missed the bustle of the streets and he missed the people of Edinburgh. Most of all – God help him – he missed Catriona Dunbar.

In his more honest moments, when he was tired or sad as he was now, he was willing to admit to himself that he had never been able to get her out of his heart or his head. A callow youth, that's what he had been. Both she and her uncle had seen him coming – and yet something about this still didn't ring true. He had been so sure Kate had loved him as much as he had loved her – as much as he still did love her.

Alone in the silence of his room, Richard succumbed to a groan. He was a hopeless case, a stupid fucking idiot. If he didn't pull himself out of this melancholic stupor very soon he would be at it again: trying to find reasons for what she had done to him, trying to justify her actions.

Like the child-mother whom he hadn't been able to save this morning, Kate too had led a difficult life. Working like a slave amid the stink and heat and gloom of The Pearl Fisher, at the beck and call of her aunt all day long, hoping against all the odds to secure a better future for herself and her wee brother.

He himself had been the means to an end for her, Richard supposed. Could he blame her for seeing him that way? That difficult life of hers had been immeasurably different from his own comfortable one. His time in London had allowed him to see that, as he hadn't been able to see it before.

Oh, Christ Almighty, but she had hurt him so much, wounded him to his very soul, which might be a melodramatic way of putting it but was nothing less than the truth. Perched on the edge of his bed, Richard leant forward, clutching the top edges of the textbook he had long since stopped pretending to read and peering over it to the bare floorboards. 'You nearly finished me off, Kate,' he muttered. 'How could you do that to me? Especially after I offered you marriage. Would it have been so awful to have married me without my family's money behind me? I thought you loved me, Kate. I really thought you loved me.'

He would stop this in a minute. For his own good, he knew he had to. Doctor's orders, he thought wryly. Take a tincture of Feverfew once *per diem* and eschew painful reminiscing. Ah, but he only had to close his eyes and she was there, her bright, beautiful hair blowing in the breeze and a smile in her beautiful blue eyes that was for him alone. Or so he had thought.

There was the rub. He still couldn't believe Kate hadn't loved him as much as he had loved her. When she had given herself to him that day in the Old Physic Garden, when the two of them had knelt naked and unashamed before one another, it had seemed so true, so honest.

There was the way too she hadn't pretended to be the untouched virgin he had believed her to be. Looking back on it now, he realised how easily she might have fooled him. She would only have had to ask him to leave the summer house while she cleaned herself up.

Yet she had made a deliberate choice not to fool him. Why had she done that? If he hadn't still been so pathetically playing the gentleman when her uncle had come to the mews that night, their heartless little plan wouldn't have worked.

Heartless? Not Kate Dunbar. He still couldn't believe that of her. His mind was filled with pictures of her. Handing oatcakes to the Gunn children. Throwing herself with such joy into learning how to read. Taking such pleasure in her wee brother's progress. Being so entranced and moved by the verses of Burns and Shelley and the other poets to whom he'd introduced her.

He could well believe Michael Graham might not be in possession of a heart. He had naively thought him so affable. A clever act. He could see that now. Yet he could also see that Kate had never seemed very well-disposed towards her uncle. She'd all but shrunk away every time the man had come near her—

Richard straightened up so abruptly the textbook on his knees fell to the floor. For a moment he stared into space – and then struck himself on the forehead with the back of his hand. Dolt! How in the name of God had he managed to be such a fucking dolt!

Grimly, he sat there and put it all together. It didn't take long. By the time he'd worked it out, he realised his decision was made. He was going home to Edinburgh.

It was strange coming back, as though he had been away for a lifetime rather than a mere couple of years. His experiences in those two years had matured him, he knew. He had become a man. Yet in some ways he still felt like the boy he had been when he had first met and fallen in love with Kate.

He travelled by sea, the same journey the king had taken two years before, although without the accompanying flotilla and on a cargo boat, for cheapness. It was a fine way to come home, all the same. Having Lindisfarne and Bamburgh pointed out to him by a helpful and knowledgeable sailor, he stood on deck for hours on the last evening of the week-long voyage, long after it had grown dark, allowing the ship to bear him ever closer to home.

Up on deck again at first light the following morning, he found himself gazing in awe at the Bass Rock with its astonishing cliffs and profusion of seabirds. Walking round from starboard to port, he saw Berwick Law. How often had he gazed at its distinctive pyramid shape from the North Bridge?

As the vessel rounded the corner into the Firth of Forth, the skyline of Edinburgh began to reveal itself. Arthur's Seat. Salisbury Crags. Calton Hill. The castle. Crowning its volcanic ridge, the doughty fortress looked as magnificent as ever. It was a Monday morning in November, crisp and cold but sunny and bright too, the sky an impossible shade of blue, the few clouds in it as white as freshly laundered sheets. Filled with the melancholic joy of the returning exile, Richard could feel his emotions soaring and dipping in equal measure as he walked down the gangplank at Leith. He was home.

CHAPTER FIFTY-NINE

He was standing on the corner of the North Bridge and the High Street and he was scared out of his wits. He was looking at the Hendersons' bookshop, that was what was doing it.

How the hell did he even know she was still there? He had hoped so much that she was. Devastated though he had been by what for so long he had seen as her betrayal of him, he had still wanted her to be somewhere safe. Now he was realising he might have been making an awful lot of assumptions.

One of those had been that she would have used her share of the fifty guineas her uncle had dunned out of his father to help pay for bed and board for her and Andrew at the Hendersons'. Now he was sure she had never seen any of that money.

Richard's brain raced through the other possibilities. What if she'd swallowed her pride enough to stay with the Hendersons temporarily before looking for employment elsewhere, perhaps at a rather more respectable tavern than The Pearl Fisher or even at one of the grander hotels on Princes Street? She could have worn the dress he had bought her, minded her *p*s and *q*s when she spoke and secured herself a good position.

Or she might have married.

Disliking that last option intensely, Richard forced himself to consider it. As he gazed up at the first floor windows from which they had watched the king travel up the High Street, he remembered the skinny young man who'd had a definite fancy for her. Maybe she'd married him. He'd been a Radical. If he'd been true to his principles, he wouldn't have cared one whit about Kate's family background.

He was never going to find out anything unless he screwed up his courage, walked across the road and went into the bookshop. He found a moment to be grimly amused at himself. Over the last two years he'd seen and dealt with all manner of hideous illnesses and horrific injuries. Yet here he was back in Edinburgh, scared to walk into a bookshop. Then again, maybe he shouldn't be tackling it first.

Taking the High Street diagonally, averting his eyes from the bookshop windows, he plunged down Niddry Street. A moment later he was in the Cowgate, blinking as he remembered always having to do when he stepped from the sunshine into the underground close.

The smells were exactly as he remembered them: fish, alcohol, tobacco and unwashed humanity. As his eyes grew accustomed to the gloom he saw that the look of the place hadn't altered much either. Except that the woman busy over cooking pots behind the bar wasn't Chrissie Graham.

'It's ower early,' she said, looking Richard up and down. 'A fine young man such as yersel is surely no' needing a drink at this hour? It still wants ten meenits till noon.'

'I'm no' wanting a drink,' he said, feeling himself slip back into the patois of the Old Town. 'It's Mr Graham I'm after.'

'Who?' demanded this new landlady of The Pearl Fisher. 'Och, Michael? Him and Chrissie are long gone, moved up in the world, ye might say.'

'Can ye be a wee bittie more precise?' Richard asked.

She could. A few moments later he was walking up from the Cowgate through Old Assembly Close. Go right through, almost to the High Street, but if he saw Kirkwood's printing house he'd gone too far. Those were his directions. Graham's Tavern. He was there.

Richard paused for a moment outside, giving its exterior the once-over. Graham's Tavern. Not so lyrical a name as The Pearl Fisher but it looked a lot more prosperous, its windows clean and their woodwork and the big double entry doors freshly painted. His mouth tightened. His father's money had allowed the Grahams to move up here.

There had been a higher cost, and he and Kate had paid it. Richard stepped into the tavern just as the bells of St Giles began to peal twelve o'clock.

'You're quick off the mark, young sir.' Coming forward to greet this prompt customer, Michael Graham, smartly dressed and full of professional bonhomie, stopped short. 'Well, well, well,' he said, 'if it isn't young Mr Hope.'

'It's *Doctor* Hope to you, Graham,' Richard replied, insisting on the title he had earned over the past two years as he seldom did.

'Dae ye tell me that?' Michael Graham's dark eyes ranged over him, taking in Richard's shabby caped riding coat and the threadbare trousers and waistcoat beneath it. 'No' treating wealthy patients, I see. And it's *Mister* Graham tae you, laddie. I used tae aye get one out o' you before, ye young whippersnapper.'

'That was when I was too wet behind the ears to recognise the cut of your jib, you bloody unnatural bastard.'

There was the sound of footsteps coming into the tavern, several sets of them. Richard didn't turn his head. Michael Graham looked past him to the newcomers. 'Good-day, gentlemen. You're welcome as ever. I'll be wi' you directly.'

'Not a problem here, Mr Graham, is there?' asked one of the four men who'd come in, all of them shooting curious glances at

Richard as they had perforce to walk round him, as he stood in the middle of the wooden floor.

'No problem here, sir. No problem at all.'

'Your good wife is well today, we trust?' asked another of the men as they slid into one of the booths set round the wall.

'Very well, thank you. I'll be bringing you a fine hot plate of her partan bree in a wee minute.'

'Shouldn't you ask them if that's what they want first?'

Michael Graham's head swivelled back round to Richard. 'I ken whit they like. They're a' regulars. All fine upstanding citizens, too. The Lord Provost himself takes his meridian in Graham's Tavern.'

'And what would all these fine upstanding citizens think if they knew how you had ill-used Kate, I wonder?'

Michael Graham adjusted his position so his back was to his customers, lowering his voice so they wouldn't hear his next words. 'The slut was aye willing. Mair than ready tae spread her legs for me.'

Richard's hands snapped into fists. With a supreme effort of will, he kept his arms hanging loosely by his sides. Not yet. Not just yet. He wanted an admission of guilt first. Not because he had any doubts about that. Simply because he wanted Michael Graham to acknowledge the evil he had done to the defenceless and innocent young girl Kate had been.

'You've already been tae renew your acquaintance wi' the wee hure, I take it.'

'Don't you *dare* call her that.'

Michael Graham pulled a mocking face. 'If the cap fits. Now get out afore I throw ye out. Or call the constables tae dae it for me.'

'I'm terrified,' Richard said in the coolest of voices. 'You forced yourself on Kate. Violated her time and time again. And you're not even man enough to admit it.'

A slow, leering smile slid across Michael Graham's face. 'No' man enough? I was man enough wi' her, all right. Took her whenever I wanted her. *However* I wanted her. Never paid any attention tae a' that begging and pleading for me tae stop, either. When a woman says no, she means yes, everybody kens that. I'd jalouse I had the dirty wee trollop mair times than you ever did. What of it?'

It was his casualness that did it, the sheer bloody lack of any shame or remorse. Richard's right hand went back, the better to power the blow. Michael Graham wasn't expecting it.

As his fist smashed into Graham's nose, Richard experienced a brief moment of primitive joy. The man reeled backwards, roaring in pain. Hitting the edge of a table, he bounced off it and fell in an untidy sprawl of arms and legs to the floor. The four men in the booth were on their feet, staring in open-mouthed astonishment at this eruption of violence.

Richard spared them the swiftest of glances. 'You'll be supping your partan bree soon, gentlemen. Just as soon as I'm finished here.'

Michael Graham was rolling about on the floor, blood gushing from his nose, cursing and swearing and screaming in pain. His wife came running through into the tavern. She too stared open-mouthed at Richard. He was waiting for his opportunity.

It came in seconds. Thrashing around in pain, Michael Graham's legs were flailing, as floppy as a rag doll's.

Richard took aim and kicked. Michael Graham screamed. 'The-punishment—' his now breathless but triumphant assailant grunted before he waded in with a second vicious kick 'should-fit—' a third and final kick, the hardest of the lot 'the-crime.'

He turned on his heel and walked out without a backward glance, leaving the Grahams' customers staring in incredulity at their host.

'The punishment should fit the crime?' asked one of them. 'Like to tell us what the young man meant by that, Graham?'

CHAPTER SIXTY

'Your servant, Mrs Henderson,' Richard said, making her a deep bow as the bell on the shop door jangled behind him. 'I am sorry if I have startled you.'

The bookseller's wife slid off her high stool. 'Mr Hope. It is a long time since we have seen you.'

'Indeed. I trust I find you well.'

'Very.'

'Your husband too?'

'Nathaniel is also very well. Yourself, Mr Hope?'

'I too am very well.' Richard ran the hand that wasn't hurting like buggery through his hair. 'Now we have the social niceties out of the way, I'd be obliged if you will tell me where I might find Kate.'

From her position of authority behind the counter, Peggy Henderson surveyed him with the steely gaze he remembered so well. 'Why do you want to find her, Mr Hope?'

'Och, Mrs Henderson,' Richard said, 'why do you think?'

'You still claim to love her?'

'I *do* love her.'

'And pray tell me how you can possibly know that she feels the same?'

'I don't. That's why I need to find her and talk to her.'

'Do you think this is wise? Do you think you are going to find the same Kate you left behind two years since?'

'Has she married? Please,' he added, seeing Peggy Henderson hesitate, 'if she has married, for God's sake tell me quickly and put me out of my misery!'

'She has not married.'

'Is she affianced to someone?'

Peggy shook her head. 'Not that, either.'

'Then please tell me where she is, Mrs Henderson.' With a leap of the heart that mixed joy in equal parts with trepidation, he pointed upwards. 'Is she upstairs? Please, Mrs Henderson, tell me where she is and, if you please, do so now.'

A faint smile curved Peggy Henderson's lips. 'I see you have not changed very much, sir.'

'I have changed enormously.'

'Yet you are still passionate and impetuous. You still want what *you* want. Despite what anyone else might want.'

'You know for a fact that Kate will not want to see me?'

'No,' Peggy Henderson admitted, 'I cannot in all honesty tell you that I do. But do you know how much you hurt her, Mr Hope?'

'I do indeed, Mrs Henderson,' he said gravely. Impatient though he was to see Kate, the question was a fair one and it merited an answer. Besides which, this determined little woman was the gatekeeper barring his way to Kate. He had to get past her. 'I did her a great injury and I should like, if I can, to put that right.'

'A great injury?' Peggy Henderson's lovely eyes widened.

'Yes. I did not understand how her life had been. I did not understand how different it was to my own privileged one.' The bookseller's wife was still looking startled. 'What did you think I meant?'

'I had no idea what you meant, Mr Hope.' The widened eyes went to his right hand. 'You seem to have suffered an injury yourself, sir. May I see to those grazes for you?'

'They are of no moment. I shall attend to them myself later.'

'What if I were to tell you that Kate is well and happy enough and that it would not help her in any way for you to come back into her life? That it would only cause her distress to see you again?'

The door bell jangled again. A skinny delivery boy with a mop of blond hair and who must have been stronger than he looked strode in and deposited a large box on the counter in front of Peggy. 'That foolscap paper ye've been waiting for, Mrs Henderson. Can ye sign for it, please?'

He had left the door open behind him. It allowed the sounds of the street to enter the shop. Snatches of conversation. The rumble of cart wheels. Richard was reminded of another occasion when he and Peggy Henderson had stood together in the bookshop like this – when she had again been the gatekeeper and he the one who sought and was denied entry. He hadn't taken no for an answer then. He wasn't going to do so now.

'Kate is happy *enough*?' he queried as soon as the delivery boy had left. 'What does that mean?'

Peggy Henderson slid the box of paper to one side and surveyed Richard over the counter. 'I beg you, Mr Hope. Leave well alone. What's in the past should be allowed to remain there.'

'Is she living with you and Mr Henderson – and Andrew, too? How is Andrew?'

'He's well and enjoying his studies. He is walking well.'

'You have continued to buy him the special shoes as he grows?'

'Yes. Mr Hope – or is it Dr Hope now? – I do not mean to be unkind but nor do I think there is any purpose to be served in our continuing to converse on the subject of Kate and Andrew. Please leave, sir.'

'I cannot do that, ma'am. Pray tell me why Kate is only happy *enough*.'

Peggy Henderson looked at him. Her mouth began to form her answer. The bell on the shop door jangled for the third time.

'Peggy, my love,' came an exuberant male voice. 'Our wee lass and I have had a most wonderful walk!'

CHAPTER SIXTY-ONE

Richard looked at Nathaniel Henderson, flushed and bright-eyed as he manoeuvred a perambulator into the shop. Stepping forward to hold the door open for the man, he glanced down at the occupant of the baby carriage. A laughing child somewhere more than a year old, it – she? – was sitting up and holding out her arms to him. She wore a lacy bonnet but underneath it Richard could see a tendril of red hair.

Red hair and green eyes. The child had red hair and green eyes.

He looked up to find that Nathaniel Henderson was staring at him, the cheerful expression his face had borne a moment ago now guarded in the extreme. His wife had lifted the flap of the counter and walked forward into the shop. Bending down, she released the restraints that secured the child in its perambulator and lifted her out. Holding the little girl close to her, Peggy Henderson retreated to the counter, pressing herself up against it. She had become very pale.

'Please go,' she said in an anguished whisper. 'There is nothing for you here. Nothing you can do here. Nothing you have any *right* to do here!'

Richard too had paled. He could feel the blood draining from his face. 'I beg you, Mrs Henderson. I have the right to at least one thing and that is the truth. Is Kate dead?'

'Yes,' Peggy Henderson said.

'No,' said her husband.

The two of them looked first at one another and then at Richard. He could feel himself swaying. Through the haze, he was aware of Nathaniel Henderson gripping him by the elbow and guiding him to one of the chairs set around the big table in the middle of the shop. 'Miss Catriona is alive and well,' he said, his deep voice very gentle. 'Sit down before you fall down, man, and I shall fetch you a brandy.'

'And then tell me everything,' Richard managed.

'And then tell you everything,' Nathaniel Henderson agreed.

'No!' his wife protested.

'He has to know, Peg. He has a right to the truth.'

'Only if Kate agrees. Some of this story is not ours to tell, Nathaniel.'

The bookseller drew in a breath. 'Very well. Mr Hope, will you please wait here while I go and enquire of Miss Catriona if she will receive you?' His long fingers were already wrapped around the door handle.

'She lives close by?' Richard asked eagerly.

'Very close. Pour him a brandy, Peg.' He threw his wife the most rueful of smiles.

'I think he's going to need it.'

* * *

Obediently sipping his brandy – he didn't really want it but it gave him something to do while he waited – Richard sat and watched Peggy Henderson play with the child who had to be his daughter. *His daughter!* My God. She was beautiful. He couldn't take his eyes off her.

Minutes later, his daughter's mother walked into the bookshop. She was beautiful too, exactly as he remembered her.

'Kate,' he said, rising to his feet and depositing the still almost full glass of brandy on the big table.

'Richard,' she responded, her voice very cool. His eyes

narrowed. Perhaps she was not quite exactly as he remembered her. Her hair was cut fashionably short, for a start. The auburn waves had become a riot of curls, adorned with only a narrow blue ribbon.

She was dressed like a lady, and although he knew this was absurd after two years, he could not help but be disappointed she wasn't wearing the clothes he had bought for her. Her dress was dark blue and in the height of fashion, as was the Paisley shawl in shades of blue and cream that fell gracefully from her elbows.

It was not only what she wore that made her seem different. Her manner was as cool as her voice had been when she had pronounced his name. She seemed disinclined to say anything else. Nor did she make any move to offer him her hand. All of this he would have been a fool not to have expected. He wasn't sure what to make of the aloof air. Above it all. Disinterested and uninterested.

'How are you, Kate?'

'I'm well, Richard. You?'

'Fine.' Dammit, this was a replay of the conversation he'd had with Peggy Henderson, an empty exchange of social courtesies. This was Kate he was talking to, Kate whom he had loved and lost, Kate who was the mother of his child. Awed all over again by the existence of that child, he turned and gazed at the little girl.

'What is her name?'

No answer. He turned and looked at Kate again. 'Her name, Kate? What did you call her?'

'Peggy and Nathaniel are her parents. You should ask them.'

'Belle,' the bookseller supplied, filling the awkward pause which followed that statement. 'Her name is Belle.'

Richard hadn't taken his eyes off Kate's face. 'That's a lovely name.'

'I'm so glad you approve.' She adjusted her shawl.

'Kate...' he said, reaching out an imploring hand she seemed not even to notice. 'Don't be like this, Kate.'

'If you have something to say please say it, Richard,' she said crisply. 'Then we can all get on with our day.'

'*All get on with our day?* Dammit, Kate, I've only this morning returned to Edinburgh. And I've only this minute discovered that you and I have a daughter!'

Something flashed in her blue eyes then. 'No, we don't. Belle's surname is Henderson, Richard. She has nothing to do with you and she has nothing to do with me!'

'She has your hair and my eyes! She's the image of both of us!'

Responding to the raised voices and the mounting argument, the child in question began, quite suddenly, to cry. Watching Kate as she glanced over at the little girl, Richard saw the cool and indifferent mask slip completely.

'Aiblins I should take the wee one upstairs, Kate,' Peggy Henderson said.

'Then you and I may talk.' Richard spoke quietly, Kate's obvious distress gentling his voice and his temper.

'What would you and I have to talk about?' she demanded. Now he could hear anger. Not a cool and aloof Kate, after all. Thank God. *Thank God!*

'Lots of things. I could tell you what I've been doing over the past two years and you could return the compliment. Tell me about your life now.'

He was aware of a step change in the atmosphere. It was there in the way Peggy Henderson, the child in her arms, paused on her way to the stairs. It was there in the still watchfulness of Nathaniel Henderson. It was there in the emotions that chased each other through Kate's troubled eyes. 'You want to know about my life now?'

'Very much.'

'You're sure about that? Certain sure?'

'Certain sure,' he repeated.

'You might not like everything you hear.' She raised her russet eyebrows and he saw in the gesture a flash of her old sense of humour. 'You might not like *anything* you hear.'

Unwelcome and unbidden, Richard heard Michael Graham's voice in his head. *If the cap fits.* Please God, he thought, let this not be what I think it's going to be. Striving for nonchalance, he shrugged. 'So be it.'

'Then come with me,' she said.

She led the way, and it was a short one, only round the corner and a few hundred yards along South Bridge Street. She stopped at the last close before the roadway went over the Cowgate. They were standing between a dressmaker's and a haberdasher's.

'You have rooms here?' Richard asked, his eyes travelling up – and down – the building.

'You find that ironic?'

'Don't you? Given that the foot of this building abuts The Pearl Fisher? The life you lead up here would seem to be very different from the one you led down there.'

She murmured something he didn't quite catch.

'What was that?'

'Nothing. My aunt and uncle no longer run The Pearl Fisher.'

Or maybe not. He realised now that was what she had just said.

He was sure now he knew what was coming next but he would not pre-empt it. 'I know your aunt and uncle are no longer down there. Less than an hour since I paid them a visit in their new establishment in Old Assembly Close.'

That had startled her. 'Why did you do that?'

'I wanted to pay my respects – particularly to your uncle. In fact,' Richard continued, 'I paid my respects to him with so much vigour that I am pretty sure I left him with a broken nose.'

Kate's mouth formed a shocked but silent 'Oh.' She recovered herself quickly, once more the imperturbable young lady. 'I wondered what you had done to your hand.'

'Didn't think you'd noticed.'

'I noticed. Why would you want to break his nose?'

'Do you mind if I answer that up in your rooms? I also left him threatening to call the constables out on me – and that was before I kicked him – three times – in the balls. Excuse my vulgarity. So I'm thinking that perhaps I shouldn't be standing out in the street for them and everyone else to see me.'

She was still trying to hide her reactions, but he was beginning to discern them all the same. 'I can see you're real feart at the prospect o' being apprehended by the forces o' law and order.' She sounded at last like the girl he remembered.

He raised his eyebrows at her. 'Having to answer questions would be inconvenient all the same. I'd rather answer yours and put some of my own to you.'

'Gin I were you, I'd save my breath for the climb. We're three floors up a turnpike stair.'

'Nice and airy,' he commented a moment or two later, not at all out of breath. 'May I?' he asked, indicating the window of the very pleasant parlour into which she had ushered him.

'Please do,' she responded with detached politeness. 'The view towards the Firth is what particularly recommended these rooms to us.'

Richard walked over to the window. 'The view is indeed very fine, Kate. But I have spent the last week at sea and this morning sailing up the Firth so I know what it looks like.' He turned his back and propped himself against the window sill. 'You said *us.*

Since I am assuming Andrew now lives with the Hendersons, I am wondering if I am going to be allowed to ask with whom you live.'

She looked him straight in the eye. 'I live with Amelia Drummond and Ella Balfour, who acts as our maid. They're both out at the moment. Our mornings are generally our own. Time to do our chores and run our little errands. You remember Ella Balfour, don't you, Richard? I'm sure you remember Miss Drummond, too. Sisters under the skin. I believe you once made that observation about her and Ella.'

'Ah,' he said, folding his arms and crossing his legs at the ankles.

'Our afternoons and evenings we devote to our friends. They are equally devoted to us. They are all fine gentlemen,' she added. 'Fine gentlemen who like Amelia and I so much they are willing to pay handsomely for the privilege of spending time with us.'

She was reminding him of a sailor lighting the fuse of a cannon. Only, immediately after setting the taper to the wick, any sensible sailor would bow his head and wrap his arms around it, shielding himself from the noise and force of the explosion. Catriona Dunbar stood there proud and straight, waiting for all hell to break loose – and ready and willing to face it down.

CHAPTER SIXTY-TWO

'You see, Richard? I have everything I ever wanted now. Nice airy rooms with a wonderful view. Good food to eat, lovely clothes to wear. I can see Andrew and Belle whenever I like and I have good friends in the Hendersons and the members of the Midweek Club. And I have my books.'

She gestured towards the shelves that lined one wall of the room. 'I have bought each and every one of these with my own money. The pleasant life I live now is all paid for with my own money.'

'Money that you make from selling yourself?' He pushed himself up off the window sill.

'I was the only commodity I had to sell.' She lifted her chin. 'You were going to keep me once, as I recall. Is what I am doing now so very different?'

She was on the receiving end of an unfathomable look. 'I wanted to marry you, not merely *keep* you. Why in the name of God did the Hendersons not try to stop you from doing this?'

'You have no right to apportion blame,' she said hotly. 'Certainly not to Peggy and Nathaniel. They didn't know what I had done until after I had done it.'

'When you only live a few hundred yards away from them? I find that hard to believe, Kate.'

'I dinna care whether you believe it or not, Richard,' she snapped. 'It's the truth. Edinburgh's like that. You must ken that as well as I do.' She pressed her lips shut, hoping he wouldn't have noticed her spurt of anger. She had to send him away and she had to remain calm while she did it, give him no inkling of how she now felt about him.

That was hard to do. She had thought him lost for ever. Over the last two years, through all her vicissitudes and sacrifices, it had been in an odd way some shred of comfort to believe she and Richard Hope would never meet again. That way there could never be any question of things turning out differently from the way they had done – never any reminder of what might have been.

There had been days when she had thought she might die of unhappiness. The day she had seen him stride round the corner onto the North Bridge and walk out of her life. The day she had so very nearly killed her unborn child, halting on the very brink. The day she had handed that child over to Peggy Henderson, telling her through a curtain of tears that Belle was hers now, that Kate would never make any claim on her daughter. The day she had taken her courage in both hands and asked Amelia Drummond if she might call on her one morning for a private talk.

The decision she had made that day hadn't turned out so badly. She had been determined not to be a burden on the Hendersons – more of a burden than she had been throughout her pregnancy – and she wasn't. They wouldn't take any of the money she offered them towards Andrew and Belle's support so she gave it in clothes and toys and treats instead.

Her life was what it was and what she had made it. If at times she loathed what she was doing, at other times it had its consolations. She knew Peggy and Nathaniel were distressed by the choice she had made and, despite her best efforts to convince them otherwise, continued to blame themselves for not having prevented her from stepping onto the path she now trod.

How could they have, when she had stolen out of their house one night leaving only a note telling them not to worry about her? When she had returned briefly a week later she had already crossed her Rubicon. Fearing condemnation, she had found only sorrow for her and boundless loving-kindness. They continued to demonstrate that to her, Andrew and Belle. They continued to maintain the illusion to Andrew that his sister worked as a seamstress for the dressmaker's on the ground floor of the building in which she lived.

What she needed to do now was send Richard Hope away – for good, this time. She might have expected him to have left of his own accord. Yet so far he had taken her dramatic revelation of how she earned her daily bread rather more calmly than she might have imagined. Aiblins she was going to have to shock him into a reaction strong enough to make him go and leave her in peace. That was what she wanted, wasn't it? She clasped her hands and addressed him with ridiculous brightness.

'Was there something else, Richard? My time does cost money, you know.'

Oh, that had worked. She could see his anger in the darkening of his eyes. *Green, velvety pools deep enough to drown in...*

'Kate,' he said. 'Stop it. This isn't you.'

'Oh, but it is. This is who Kate Dunbar is now.'

'I don't believe that.'

She did her best to give a nonchalant shrug. In reality she wasn't sure how much longer she could maintain this air of cool disdain. Go, she thought. Please just go.

I can't bear to have you here. Not when I know there's no future for us. Not when I know you're standing there judging me. I've been here before and it nearly killed me then. I canna do it again.

'Would you please go away?' she managed, wondering how she could sound so calm and neutral when so many emotions were whirling up inside her. Practice at not allowing the men who paid for her time and her body to get anywhere near her heart and her mind, she supposed. 'I have things to do.'

'Lying on your back for any number of men to make free of you requires so much preparation, Kate? Oh,' he said, 'I beg your pardon. Now you are so much in command of your life, I should probably address you as Miss Dunbar. For,' he continued, 'I am finding it quite hard to think of you as the Kate I knew.' He laughed, but there was no joy in the sound. 'I once knew a girl called Kate. She was beautiful and good and kind. Fresh and innocent as an April morning. Do you by any chance know where I might find her, Miss Dunbar? Do you have any idea where's she gone?'

For a moment they looked at one another. Then she spoke. 'You never knew me when I was fresh and innocent, Richard. And it's only one man at a time. Usually the same one for a few weeks or a few months, only the ones I choose, too. Turned your friend Torquil Grant down back in the summer. He was in Edinburgh on a visit and thought he might spend some of it with me. I have to tell you I took enormous pleasure in telling him exactly what I thought of him. And now I think you had better leave. I do not believe you and I have anything more to say to one another.'

'Not even about our daughter?'

'We have no daughter. The Hendersons have a daughter. A daughter who has two loving parents who would do anything for her.' She smiled. 'As well as a big brother who adores her.'

'Does he know he's really her uncle?'

'That's none of your business. Good morning, Richard.'

She whirled round, heading for the door out onto the stairs, assuming – praying – that he would follow her. When she realised he was indeed behind her, she felt herself slide into a pit of despair. Had there really been a part of her that was still so desperately naïve she had thought he might be able to take all this in his stride? Swallowing the pain and bitterness, she flung open the door.

'Go,' she said. He didn't move. 'Go,' she said again, plucking at the sleeve of his riding coat. 'Please just go!'

He looked at her. He tilted his head back and looked over her head to the window on the stair. He bent his head and looked at her again.

'No,' he said. 'I won't go. Not unless and until I get a straight answer to a straight question. And then only if the answer's the wrong one. Here it comes, Kate. It's preceded by a statement. When I realised what I was going to find out about you this morning I was stupid enough to think I wasn't going to be able to say this. Now I find I can't stop myself. I still love you. More than ever. So what I have to ask you is this, Kate – and the question's been a long time coming – do you still love me?'

CHAPTER SIXTY-THREE

His lips twitched. 'You're staring at me as though I'm no' quite right in the heid, Kate. Reminds me of the old days. You used to do that rather a lot, as I recall.'

'I think you truly must have lost your wits this time.' She spoke so differently now, her accent still clearly of Edinburgh but her words precise and crisp – although she had slipped back into her old voice once or twice during the course of this conversation. He was hoping he wasn't fooling himself by thinking that, despite her apparent composure, that might be an unconscious indicator of the strength of her emotions at seeing him again. 'You cannot seriously mean what you just said. You cannot seriously feel the way you say you do. Not after what I have told you.'

'Don't try to tell me what my own feelings are, Kate,' Richard said, finding the strength of *his* emotions tossing him from amusement to anger. 'How the devil would you know what I feel?' His voice shook. 'Nor would you know that I have been to hell and back over the past two years. Knowing what a *dolt* I was. Remembering every day how badly I treated you. How *stupidly* I reacted that day in the Old Physic Garden and afterwards. How cruelly, too. Telling you I was disappointed not to be your first lover. Believing you and your uncle had plotted together against me. Believing it could be possible that a girl like you would act in such a fashion.'

She raised her hands to her face, pressing her fingertips against her lips.

'Say something,' he instructed. When she lowered her fingers to her chin, he saw that it was trembling. His mind clear, his way ahead plain, he knew he wanted to step forward and steady it with his own fingers, knew also it was far too soon to do that.

They both had a bridge to cross here, one he was still in the process of building.

He was praying to God she would meet him somewhere in the middle.

'You are too hard on yourself.' Her voice was little more than a whisper. 'You were convinced that I was innocent and untouched. When you found out the truth it is not to be wondered at that you were hugely distressed, as you were when my uncle went to your father and claimed you had ruined me.'

'While you were keeping from me something that would have distressed that poor, naïve boy I was even more. Weren't you, Kate?'

She looked so much the young lady, in her pretty blue gown and paisley shawl and short, curly hair. Stepping back into the lobby of her house, he kicked the door shut with his foot. 'Will you please come through to your parlour where we may see one another more clearly?

'It was your uncle who ruined you,' he said once they got there. Grimacing at the word, he decided to call a spade a bloody shovel. 'I know now that he raped you, Kate. Over and over again. Violated you in every possible way.'

Something flashed deep within her eyes. 'In every way you can imagine, Richard. There was no degradation to which he did not subject me.'

'And you did not tell me because you were scared I would be disgusted.'

'Aye,' she said. 'And because I was scared too that you might confront him. He promised to leave you battered and bleeding. Said you were a gentleman so you wouldn't know how to fight dirty. Said he could break your nose with one punch.'

'He said that?' Richard tilted his head first to one side and then the other as though in evaluation of her words. 'Seems only fair that I broke his nose this morning, then. It was me who left him battered and bleeding, Kate. Evidently I've learnt how to fight dirty.'

Leaving the subject of Michael Graham, the man no longer of the least interest to him, he went on. 'Belle is yours and mine, isn't she, Kate? You named her for the bluebell I gave you. Am I right there too?'

'Aye,' she said again, her voice cracking. 'Belle is our daughter.'

Not cool and detached at all – but he had refused to believe she was. He longed to take her in his arms and comfort her, but he still wasn't sure whether she would permit him to do so.

'You haven't answered the most important question, Kate. Do you still love me?'

'Don't make me answer that one, Richard. Please.'

His blood ran cold. 'Because the answer's *no*?'

'The answer has to be *no*, Richard. Can you not see that?'

For a moment they stared at one another – until she burst out into a torrent of speech, the precise accent evaporating. 'Och, but I canna say that, Richard, I canna! Dinna look so hurt. Please dinna look so hurt. Of course I still love you! Only I didna want tae tell ye that because there's no use in me telling ye that! I'm a fallen woman now, Richard, that's what the world calls me. If it was so important tae ye before that I was pure and untouched, well I'm gey sullied now. I truly am a hure now, Richard, that's what I am. Naebody forced me this time. I've chosen to be a hu—'

He couldn't stand this any longer. Striding towards her, he replaced her fingertips with his own and stopped her from saying the word a second time. 'I forbid you from using that word about yourself, Kate Dunbar. Do you hear me? I forbid it!'

Her eyes widened in shock, whether at his words or his touch he wasn't sure. 'It's the right word,' she protested. 'It's the right word, Richard.'

'If you're a hure then so am I, Kate. I've probably lain with more women than you have men.' He grimaced. 'Especially in the last two years.'

'It's no' only a matter o' how many people ye lie with. It's about doing it in exchange for money. It's about doing it without love.'

'My point exactly,' he said grimly. 'And I think I heard you say you still love me.' He adjusted his grip on her chin, tilting her face up to his. 'If you meant it, say it again,' he commanded.

'Richard...'

'Try taking a deep breath. I find that usually helps.'

She took a deep breath. 'I still love you, Richard Hope.'

'And I still love you, Kate Dunbar.'

Her eyes were brimming with tears. 'Then God help us, Richard. God help us both!'

CHAPTER SIXTY-FOUR

'Think I know a good method of drying these,' he murmured before gently kissing each of her eyes. He progressed to her forehead, her nose, her cheeks and her mouth. Butterfly kisses. Gentle and tentative. Asking a question and asking permission. She was giving him no answers as yet but he felt her relax, enough to pose an old question herself.

'Finished with my fisog?'

'Won't ever be finished with your fisog. Or any other part of you. I love you. Did I already tell you that? And that nothing you've told me makes any difference to how I feel about you?'

She sniffed. 'I'm not having you thinking you're *forgiving* me here.'

'Wouldn't dream of it. Let he who is without sin cast the first stone. You'll have to put up with me being wildly jealous, though.'

'Are you?'

'What do you think? I'd like to break the noses of each and every one of your gentleman friends. Or at least kick them down that turnpike stair out there, have them bounce off the wall all the way to the bottom. And you're going to have to disappoint your current paramour.'

'I already have. Sent him off with a flea in his ear two weeks ago. He was beginning to bore me. As the actresses at the Theatre Royal say, I'm currently resting between engagements.'

'So he's not likely to turn up later on today? Pity. I was quite looking forward to kicking somebody down the stairs.'

She gave him a speaking look. 'Nobody's likely to turn up later on today. I was being economical with the truth earlier. Amelia's off playing the lady at a big house in Fife while her young gentleman friend's parents are away and Ella's gone over there with her.'

'We're on our own, then? *Resting between engagements*,' he mused. '*He was beginning to bore me.*' His lips were twitching again. 'What did the poor devil do to offend you so much?'

Kate's features relaxed, like a girl confiding a secret to her best friend. 'Kept buying me awful scent. Horribly sweet and cloying. I've gone back to lemons.'

'Thought I'd detected that. Horribly sweet and cloying, eh?'

'Enough to set my teeth on edge. Yeuch!' she said. 'And thrice yeuch. What's so funny?'

'You are. This whole situation is.'

'Absurd, more like.'

She had a smile on her face now. It grew into a grin. He answered it – and suddenly they were laughing together, whooping with merriment, so transported by hilarity they soon had to hang on to one another for support. It lasted for several minutes, stopped as abruptly as it had started and left them standing staring at one another, all amusement fled.

'Kate?' he said, not knowing what he was asking. That was a bloody lie. He knew exactly what he was asking. She went up on tiptoe and placed an admonishing finger against his lips.

'No more words now,' she murmured. 'We'll talk afterwards.'

They made it to her bedroom. Just.

Lying together in one another's arms, Richard turned his head and pressed a kiss against her hair.

'I suppose you're going to tell me ye dinna like me having my hair short.'

'You suppose wrong. I think it's lovely. It makes me want to do this.' He lifted one hand and ruffled the shining auburn waves. Catching the hand as he took it away again, she pressed a kiss on his palm.

'Your hair's longer than mine now.'

'I haven't had the time, inclination or money to go in for fancy haircuts. We have plans to make.'

'Do we?'

'We most certainly do.'

'You make them, then.'

'Why?'

'Because I have missed the sound of your voice so much. I want to hear it again.'

He adjusted his hold on her, only enough to bring her in closer to him again. 'You like the sound of my voice?'

'I *love* the sound of your voice. I always did. Right from the beginning when you helped me up off the floor at The Pearl Fisher and I thought to myself that you had a voice as mellow as a russet apple.'

'*As mellow as a russet apple*,' he repeated, and pressed another kiss into her hair. 'I love you, Kate Dunbar.'

She raised her head to look at him, and what he saw in her eyes made him hold his breath. He knew she wasn't making him wait out of coquetry. He knew it was fear that made her hesitate to say again what only extreme emotion had dragged out of her earlier. When he saw her take her courage in both hands, he wanted to cheer her on.

'I love you too, Richard Hope.'

They smiled into one another's eyes, kissed, and made love all over again.

* * *

'About these plans. We obviously can't live here. We're going to have to find somewhere else. The only trouble being that I don't have very much money at the moment.'

'I have money.'

'Mmm.'

Kate arched her eyebrows. 'I'd forgotten how stubborn you can be.'

'That's rich, coming from you. If I'm the kettle, you're certainly the pot.'

She came up onto her elbows. 'Did your parents cut you off because of me? Is that why you have no money?'

'I cut myself off.' He looked up at her from the depths of her white pillows. 'After I was obliged to leave Edinburgh two years ago I decided it was high time for me to make my own way in the world.'

'Obliged to leave Edinburgh because of me?'

'And speaking rather too frankly to the king.'

'What did you say?' she asked, her eyes widening.

'Tell you later. Don't you want to hear about my exciting adventures on the high seas as a surgeon's mate?'

'Good experience for a doctor?'

'Indeed. Even though I spent a lot of time at the beginning being sick myself.'

'Mal de mer?'

'The very same. Excepting only toothache, the vilest of minor ailments. Lie down again so that I may tuck these covers about us both.'

She settled on her side and turned in towards him. 'What have you been doing since you stepped back onto dry land?'

'Working in a London hospital. St Bartholomew's. Living there too. One of the housemen.'

'Does that mean you're Dr Hope now?'

'More or less. I could certainly start practising. Although I would like to formally complete my studies. Do my final year and get my MD. That'll have to wait for a wee while, I think. I need to earn my living.'

'Could you maybe combine work with study if you got a post as houseman at the Royal Infirmary?'

'I'd have to be unmarried if I wanted to apply for a resident's post at the infirmary. It's a requirement.'

'You are unmarried. Unless there's something you're not telling me.'

'No,' he said, 'I'm still single.' He was giving perhaps a little too much attention to his self-imposed task of pulling the covers up around them both. 'Although not for much longer, I hope.'

'I think we've had this conversation before,' Kate said lightly. 'About two years ago by my reckoning.'

'I didn't get the answer I wanted back then.' He stopped fussing with the blankets and lay still beside her. 'I'm hoping I'm going to get it now.'

'What about your parents?'

'Who I choose to marry is my business. Especially now they're no longer supporting me.'

'Have you told them that?'

'I haven't seen them yet. If I'm going to make my peace with them, they'll have to accept my plans and accept you. As my wife,' he added carefully, reaching for one of her hands.

'There are several people who know what I've been doing over the past year or so. Your friend Torquil Grant, for a start.'

'Erstwhile friend.'

'Who might well take malicious pleasure in telling your parents and everyone else who might be interested how I've been earning my daily bread.'

'In which case we shall be the scandalous Mr and Mrs Hope. Received socially only by bloody Radicals, revolutionaries and the *demi-monde*. Which isn't going to stop me from becoming an eminent doctor and a professor at the university. Eventually. Once the scandal's died down. What do you say, Kate? Will you have me?'

'Richard,' she said, studying him with worried eyes, 'you know this cannot be. The scandal would *never* die down. All the reasons I had for sending you away two years ago still stand. Including that the university might not even let you back in to complete your degree, which could rather get in the way of you becoming an eminent doctor and a professor at the university.'

'We won't let it. As long as we're together, we'll ride out any storm. What do you say, Kate?' he asked again. 'I know I'm not much of a catch at the moment but I will be. I'll make you proud of me, I promise.'

'Not much of a catch?' She raised her hand to his face, traced round the line of his jaw. 'You're the man I love, Richard, the man I've never stopped loving and the man I always will love. But I'm not going to let you marry me. We shall live together and we shall do so as discreetly as we possibly can.'

He sat up, shaking his untidy head. 'Not enough, Kate. You shall be my wife and I will be your husband. And there's an end to it.'

She sat up too. 'Do not think I am not honoured by your proposal, Richard. Please dinna think that!'

'Then accept it. Say that we shall be Mr and Mrs Hope.'

'No. Although wouldn't we be *Dr* and Mrs Hope?'

'Aha!' he said triumphantly. 'I think you're weakening.'

'And I think you're on a hiding to nothing. I also think we have to go and see Peggy and Nathaniel. They'll be concerned about us.' Her eyes were still anxious. 'And wondering what we might be thinking about Belle.'

'When it comes down to it, she is our daughter, Kate. Not theirs.'

'She's been their daughter almost since she was born. It would be so cruel to take her from them now.'

'Could you bear not to have her with you?'

'I've had to bear it.' She bit her lip. 'Sometimes my arms have felt so empty.'

He reached for her. Holding her close, he rubbed his chin across the top of her head. 'We'll think of some way of doing this.'

'Hard to see how without someone being dreadfully hurt.'

'We'll do our best for that not to happen.'

They lay for a moment in silence before Kate spoke again. 'After we've called on Peggy and Nathaniel I think you should go over to the New Town and see your parents.'

'You'll come with me, Kate.'

She shook her head. 'No, Richard. It's going to be enough of a shock to have you turning up on the doorstep. Think of their feelings.'

'All right,' he said reluctantly. He glanced across at the window. 'Soon be dark. That's good. I'm less likely to be seen.'

'You really think the constables might be looking for you?'

'No. Don't think he'd want to have to explain why I thumped him one, do you?'

She lifted his hand and kissed each grazed knuckle in turn. 'My hero. My valiant knight.'

'My fair damsel,' he countered.

'No longer in distress.' She smiled up at him.

'After I've been to see my parents I'm coming straight back here.'

'Of course you are.'

'Our first night together,' he said gently. 'Our first time falling asleep together and waking up together. The first of so many, Kate.'

'Aye,' she agreed, and raised her face for his kiss.

CHAPTER SIXTY-FIVE

Marjorie Hope couldn't take her eyes off her youngest son. Luck had been with Richard. When Jamie, beaming all over his face, had shown him into the dining room, his parents had been eating alone, entertaining no guests this evening. Uncertain of what his reception would be, despite his mother's pleading letter, Richard had been moved beyond measure when his father had stood up and silently clasped his son to his breast.

'You're home, my boy!' Edward Hope said, his voice breaking. 'You're home at last!'

His mother had risen from her chair at the other end of the table and almost fallen to her knees, so great was her emotion. Rushing to prevent that, Richard had found himself locked in an embrace with her too, her tears falling unchecked onto the capes of his riding coat.

Now he had been relieved of that coat and was sitting at the table with his parents, all three of them clustered around one end of it.

'You'll take a glass of claret,' Edward Hope said.

'Thank you, Father.' Richard turned and smiled his thanks at Jamie, already approaching with a fresh glass and a decanter.

'And you'll give us the whole story?' his father asked. 'Where you've been and what you've been doing?'

Richard took a deep breath and began at the beginning.

The landlord of Graham's Tavern was in agony. A local quack had strapped up his nose, relieved him of half-a-crown and prattled out the old saw about time being the best healer. Peering with professional interest and some awe at his swollen and bruised testicles, the man had said the same about them. Much fucking use he had been. Michael Graham muttered an even uglier curse.

Chrissie had banished him to the kitchen so he wouldn't frighten the customers with his face criss-crossed with bandages. So here he was stirring the soup like a woman, brooding on what had happened at noon. Chrissie was in a hell of a black mood, worried the story would spread and affect their trade.

The only thing currently giving Michael Graham any comfort was the certainty that Richard Hope would have got his comeuppance by now. He only wished he'd been there when the arrogant young pup found out that his lady-love really was a hure now. She might be high-class but she was still a slut.

Michael Graham frowned – and winced. Christ, he couldn't even move his fucking face. He stood up, intending to fetch himself some whisky for the pain. Stumbling as he rose to his feet, he grabbed the edge of the kitchen table, knocking it against the wall. The lath and plaster shook in response, the vibrations passing through to the offices in the next door building, occupied by Kirkwood's Printing House.

Through there, on a desk covered with loose papers, a careless clerk had left a candle burning.

Richard had been talking for an hour now, offering information, answering his parents' questions, asking his own about how the wider family and the members of the household were doing. His parents had established that he was well and he had established that they and everyone else were fine. He hadn't yet got on to what he really wanted to tell them.

Kate had suggested he didn't do so at all tonight but he had disagreed. He wasn't going to deny her and he wasn't going to deny their daughter. Ready to mention both of them at the start of this conversation, he had thought better of it when he had seen how drawn and tired his mother looked.

That she had missed him and worried constantly about him over the past two years was obvious. Yet there had been no reproaches, not a single one. Humbled by that, Richard was leading up to his revelations, hoping they wouldn't prove too much of a shock for her.

Jamie knocked and entered the room without waiting to be instructed to do so. 'Something wrong?' Richard asked, glancing up at him.

'It's Mr O'Sullivan, Mr Richard. He's been hovering out there in the lobby for the last twenty minutes and he says he canna wait any longer to see you!'

Richard looked at his father. Edward Hope laughed. Making a sweeping gesture with his arm, he told Jamie to bring Brendan in. Rising to his feet and going to meet him, Richard found himself being swept up into the big Irishman's embrace in his third hug of the evening.

'You're home, sir,' Brendan said. 'You really are home! And I thank God and his Holy Mother and all the saints for it!'

Releasing him just before Richard's ribs cracked, Brendan was unashamedly wiping his eyes. 'Excuse me for my familiarity, Mr Richard, sir, Mrs Hope, Mr Hope. I'm just so happy we've got the boy back home!'

Edward Hope's smile stretched from ear to ear. 'It's fair to say we're all pretty happy about that, Brendan.' His eyes slid to the tall windows. 'What is that light flickering out there?'

As one, Richard and Brendan turned to look. Richard gasped. Brendan spoke. 'It's a fire, Mr Hope, sir. The Old Town is on fire!'

CHAPTER SIXTY-SIX

Thanking God for it, Richard found Kate and the children and Peggy Henderson in the bookshop, some distance away from the fire raging a few hundred yards further up the High Street.

'Where's your husband, Mrs Henderson?'

'He went to see if he could help.' She was wringing her hands. 'Oh, I am so worried about him!'

'He'll be fine, Peggy,' Kate said, slipping an arm about her friend's shoulders.

'I shall shortly make sure of that,' Richard said. 'In the meantime, I want you all to go with Brendan, who is waiting outside with the coach. He will drive you back to my parents' house in the New Town and out of harm's way.'

Kate shook her head. 'No, Richard. Besides which, we are in no danger here.'

'Besides which,' added Peggy Henderson, 'I'm not leaving the bookshop. There are already tales of thieves taking advantage of the confusion being caused by the fire.'

'I would still wish you would go to my parents' house. They are ready to receive anyone I might send them. Anxious to help.'

'That is very good of them,' Kate said gravely. 'But Peggy and I are not going anywhere at the moment, Richard. Not unless and until we are forced to. What was that?'

'I was merely observing that you are the most stubborn woman I have ever met.'

Kate folded her arms. 'Pots,' she said crisply. 'And kettles. I don't suppose I can talk you out of putting yourself in harm's way?'

He grinned at her. 'You don't suppose right.' Planting a smacking kiss on her mouth, he headed for the door, turning when he got there. 'At least promise me the two of you will stay in here and keep the bairns safe.'

'Bairn, singular,' Andrew said. 'I'm coming with you.'

'No,' Kate and Peggy Henderson protested in unison.

'Aye,' Andrew said in return, throwing Richard a very challenging look.

'Hello, Andrew,' Richard said. 'Good to see you again.'

'I'm hoping I'll be able to say the same,' responded the tall youth walking towards him. 'Currently, I'm reserving judgement.'

'I don't blame you,' Richard said. 'But shall we agree to discuss this after the event? And in the meantime, shall we promise the ladies that we'll look after each other? And that we won't run into any burning buildings?'

Andrew Dunbar was surveying him with that measuring gaze Richard remembered so well. It would be small wonder if this young man, no longer a boy, were finding him wanting. Richard imagined he knew quite well what the circumstances of his sister's life were. 'Are you back to stay?'

'Yes,' Richard said. 'Now all I have to do is persuade your sister to marry me. She's proving a wee bit stubborn about that. Maybe you can help me make her see sense.'

'You want to marry Kate?'

'More than anything,' Richard said, sure he could discern a subtle change in Andrew's expression. 'But you and I can discuss this later. There's currently a fire to be fought.' On impulse, he stuck out his hand. 'Are we both on the same side, Andrew?'

Kate's brother took a moment. Then he said, 'Aye,' and put out his own hand to shake Richard's.

Kate glided across the floor to give them both a swift hug. 'No running into any burning buildings, then. As promised. If you two hurt yourselves, you'll have me to deal with.'

'Now there's a threat to have us shaking in our shoes, eh, Andrew?'

Outside, it was as bright as day, the flames from farther up the street lighting up the Old Town and the night sky above it. Brendan sat at the reins of the coach; Jamie stood beside it. There was a whoosh and a fierce spluttering, and they all turned to gaze at the source of the noise.

'Like a volcano,' Andrew suggested. 'The way the sparks and the flames are shooting straight up.'

'Aye,' Richard said. 'Which means there's hardly a breath of wind. Perhaps the fire can be contained. Do we know where it broke out?'

'According to someone I just spoke to, in the Old Assembly Close,' Jamie supplied. 'Maybe in Kirkwood's printing shop but he wasna exactly sure.'

'Hard to tell, I imagine,' Brendan commented. 'Looks like it's already spreading, still night or not. Right then, Mr Richard, what are we doing?'

'I don't know why you're asking me, Brendan,' Richard said equably. 'Although I really would like you to hold yourself ready to carry away Mrs Henderson and Miss Dunbar,' his voice softened, 'and wee Belle.' He ran a hand through his hair. 'The two ladies are currently refusing to go anywhere. Jamie, Andrew and I shall go up the road. This is Andrew, by the way. Although you may all remember each other.'

After nods and smiles were exchanged, Richard saw that

Brendan's face was troubled. 'Could the young man not stay and hold the horses, sir, and I'll come up the High Street with you—' Even before he'd finished asking the question, one of the horses reared up, whinnying and white-eyed.

'There's your answer, Brendan. It's only you who'll be able to keep the beasts calm. We'll see you later.'

Crossing South Bridge Street, they had to take evasive action to avoid the streams of people carrying furniture and all manner of household goods into the Tron Kirk, the doors of which stood wide open.

'Trying to save what they can,' Jamie observed.

As they walked further up the High Street, Richard laid a hand on Andrew's shoulder. 'Over there. Has to be Mr Henderson.' Silhouetted against dark buildings by the light of the leaping flames, the bookseller's lanky silhouette was unmistakable. They hurried up to him.

'What's this?' Richard asked, seeing he was carrying a heavy box that seemed to be full of printing paraphernalia.

'*The Courant*'s office is on fire. We're trying to salvage as much as we can.'

'Thought *The Courant* was a rag of a newspaper,' Andrew said cheerfully.

'It is. But I'd still defend to the death its scribblers' right to publish and say what they think. If that means helping save some of their equipment, then so be it.'

Andrew reached out for the box. 'Shall I take this down to the bookshop?'

'Aye, lad,' Nathaniel said. 'Then come up and get another box.' As he, Richard and Jamie stood and watched Andrew go, Nathaniel spoke again. 'That'll keep him away from the flames too.'

'Good idea. How *is* the fire to be prevented from spreading? Everything's packed in so close here.'

'They're calling for volunteers to take a hose from one of the fire engines up onto the roof of an adjacent building that is not yet ablaze.' Nathaniel Henderson looked from Richard to Jamie. 'Are you two young bloods game?'

'Try stopping us!' Jamie checked himself. 'That is, I mean, if you're all right wi' it, Mr Richard.'

Nathaniel Henderson offered Richard a wry smile. Returning it, he extended his hand first to Jamie and then to the bookseller. 'Under the circumstances, I think simple first names all round might be appropriate. What do you say, Nathaniel?'

'I say *aye*, Richard. Your friend's name being?'

'Jamie,' offered the owner of the name.

'Place your hand above ours, Jamie,' instructed the bookseller. He laughed. 'Like the three musketeers. All for one and one for all.'

'And all for Edinburgh,' Richard said. 'Let's get on with it.'

'Mr O'Sullivan thanks you very much for the offer of coming inside but says he cannot leave the horses.'

Ushering Kate back into the bookshop, Peggy closed the door one-handed behind her. 'It cannot be very pleasant being out there with sparks and ash flying about.'

'It isn't,' Kate said, shaking what might have been pieces of burnt paper from her hair. In Peggy's arms, Belle reached out to try and catch them as they fell to the floor. Kate smiled at her. 'Everything's a game with you, wee lass, eh?' When the little girl reached out both hands towards Kate, Peggy handed her over.

'Kate,' Peggy said, 'will you not accept the offer of going across to the New Town and take Belle and Andrew with you? If he can be persuaded to it when he comes back with the next box?'

'Do you really think I'd be welcome there, Peggy?'

'Mr Hope did say his parents were anxious to help. A calamity such as this can change people, Kate.'

'Only while the calamity lasts, I imagine,' came the cynical response.

'At least take Belle and go along to your own house. It's further away from the fire. Go out the back way, through onto the turnpike stair and down to Niddry Street. That should protect you a little from the sparks and the smoke.'

'Not unless you'll come with us, Peggy.'

'I have to stay and guard the shop.' She smiled. 'Nathaniel's beloved books.'

'Well, if you have to wait here, we're waiting with you. Is that not right, Belle?' she asked the alert child in her arms. 'Look,' she said to Peggy, 'the flames are reflected in her eyes.'

Peggy looked as instructed but her face was troubled. 'You'd both be safer along the road.'

'We're safe enough here,' Kate insisted. 'And we're not going anywhere without you.'

The fire was spreading. Immense confusion accompanied it. Fire engines were being brought from all over the city and as faraway as Leith but there seemed to be no one in overall control to direct them to where they would be most useful. There were plenty of volunteers ready to assist, men and women both. Desperate to help, they were not always sure what to do for the best. Those who had offered to climb up onto the roof found themselves doing so without hoses, only the promise of them being got up to them very soon. A few took ropes up with them, pausing only long enough to wrap those around their bodies.

People were pouring out of Old Assembly Close and Old Fishmarket Close, fleeing their homes as the fire began to run back from the High Street towards the Cowgate, devouring everything in its path.

A gasp went up from the watching crowd. Starkly visible against the red, white and orange of the flames shooting skywards, the men with the ropes had reached the roof of the building that so far had managed to resist the inferno. Three of them were noticeably taller than the others.

An old man in the crowd spoke to his neighbour. 'Gey precarious up there, I'm thinking.'

'Aye,' came the response. 'Those brave souls are taking their lives in their hands.'

CHAPTER SIXTY-SEVEN

'Please take Belle to your house, Kate. I shall endeavour to persuade Andrew to follow you thither. Please, Kate,' Peggy said again, a visible shiver running through her short frame. 'I have this terrible sense of foreboding and I know I shall only feel better if you and the children are safe.'

'We're safe here, Peggy. And I'm not leaving you on your own.'

'I'm not on my own. Mr O'Sullivan is outside.' The two of them were taking it in turns to run out to see if the coachman wanted anything. He had just accepted a drink of water for his horses, jumping down from the coach to raise the largest basin Kate could manage to carry under their noses.

She had stayed to exchange a few words with him, recognising he was champing at the bit as much as the big beautiful animals of whom he clearly thought so much. Anxious to be doing something, he had admitted to Kate that he knew no one else would be able to keep the horses calm in the face of the fire – its roaring and crackling growing ever louder – and the frantic human activity going on around them.

'I need to keep them calm, miss,' he'd said. 'For I'm thinking I might be needed to ferry folk to the infirmary before too long.' Tipping his hat to her, he had sent her back indoors lest any of the thousands of glowing orange sparks drifting down from the night sky should fall on her.

Repeating his comment to Peggy now, Kate wrapped her arms

about herself. *Ferrying folk to the infirmary.* There were bound to be people hurt tonight, aiblins even loss of life. She thought back two years to the collapse of the scaffolding at the beginning of the king's visit. *That's not what they expected when they woke up this morning, is it?* That had been Richard's question about those who had died or suffered appalling injuries back then.

Not Richard nor Andrew nor Nathaniel, please God. Let none of them be hurt. Nor that nice under-footman from Richard's parents' house, nor Mr O'Sullivan the coachman, either. It was a matter of seconds before Kate's prayer extended itself. Oh, dear God, let no one at all be hurt tonight.

The watching crowd gasped. A man on the roof way above their heads – one of the three tall ones – had stumbled. He was swaying from side to side now, arms flailing like a windmill as he fought to regain his balance. Mesmerised by his struggle, the crowd held its collective breath. When he at last straightened up, his arms returning to his sides, everyone starting breathing again. Until someone pointed out how close the flames were coming to the building on which men stood.

'The wind's getting up,' Kate said, peering through the panes of glass in the bookshop door.

'Are you sure?' Peggy asked. Belle had finally fallen asleep again. She lay now in a makeshift bed made out of a drawer and two cushions.

'I'm afraid so. Oh, thank God! I think this is Andrew coming down the road now.'

Peggy flew to join her at the door. 'Where?' she demanded, following Kate's pointing arm. 'I can't see him.'

'He's with a couple of men and women and two or three bairns.'

They were huddled together, cowering from the sparks and ash swirling down through the atmosphere. Kate swung the door open and ran out into the street. Brendan O'Sullivan had already reached the little group.

'They've been burnt out,' Andrew said. 'And the Tron's full to bursting. Can they take shelter with us?'

'Of course they can,' said Peggy Henderson, standing in the doorway behind Kate. 'Come away in now. Do you have any word of our own menfolk, Andrew?'

'No,' he said, and crossed his fingers behind his back so the lie wouldn't count.

'We need some hoses up here,' Richard bellowed down to the street. 'And we need them now!'

'They're coming!' yelled a voice from below. 'Let your ropes down!'

'About bloody time,' said Jamie. 'Eh, Mr Richard?'

'Richard,' came the correction. 'We have an agreement, remember?'

'Right you are, *Richard*,' Jamie said. 'Tell me something. Why have we been risking life and limb up here for the past hour when that bunch down there canna even get some hoses up to us?'

'Because we're no' quite right in the heid?' Richard suggested.

'That'll be it,' Jamie said cheerfully. Nathaniel Henderson grinned at both of them.

The bookshop was full to bursting now. They had taken in as many as they could. Peggy and Kate were offering refreshment and sympathy, both of them calmed and soothed by having something useful to do. Some of their unexpected visitors were saying very little, others wanted to talk, tell their individual tales of escape.

Further up the High Street, some families had managed to bring out a few pathetic sticks of furniture. Standing by those, they stood transfixed, watching their homes and their lives going up in flames. Livelihoods, too, were being lost: businesses, shops, taverns and ale-houses.

In Graham's Tavern, the wooden benches and tables were beginning to smoulder. Any minute now they would ignite. The kitchen was already on fire.

'We're no' going wi'oot the money box,' yelled Chrissie Graham.

'Of course we're no'. I'll ging for it.'

'Whit, and pit some o' it in your own pooch while I'm no' looking?'

'Come wi' me, then,' her husband snapped.

Together they fought their way through the kitchen to the wine cellar. The bottles of spirits within it were rattling in the intense heat, their contents beginning to froth and boil. When Michael Graham pulled open the door of the cupboard, they exploded, shattering into a thousand pieces. His damaged face took the full brunt of the vicious shards of glass. Reeling back, screaming in agony, he careered into his wife and they both went down. The trickling whisky and brandy found the flames and the whole place went up.

The hoses were no use. They were full of holes. All the men on the roof were cursing and swearing now. 'Should somebody not bloody check these things *before* there's a fire?' demanded one of them. Soaked by the escaping water, they were all wet, angry and dispirited by not having been able to do what they had come up here for.

'We'd best go back down,' Richard said.

'Aye,' Nathaniel agreed. 'Take care, everyone, it's gey slippy now with so much water lying about.'

* * *

'Is it a judgement on us, miss? Is that why this dreadful thing has happened?'

'Only if it's a judgement on us for having overcrowded houses that are too closely packed together,' Peggy said, hearing the question. Kate crouched down beside the questioner, an old woman who was sitting with her back against one of the bookcase ends, a girl of about five asleep in her lap.

'For myself,' Kate said gently, 'I dinna believe that the Almighty would pass judgement on his people in this cruel way.'

'You're young. When you've lived as long as I have you'll know that God can be cruel.'

'Some people can be cruel.' Kate glanced up at Peggy. 'Others can be kindness itself.'

'Like yourself, lass.' The old woman reached up and touched Kate's cheek. 'Like yourself.'

God can be cruel. She didn't want to believe that. Surely He or Fate or whoever or whatever it was that determined these things hadn't given Richard back to her only to take him away so soon? Although she hadn't spoken of it again, Peggy's feeling of foreboding was weighing heavily on Kate too. Her friend was usually such a practical woman, not given to flights of fancy.

For a moment, Kate felt herself overwhelmed by fear, paralysed into inaction. She had to summon up every ounce of mental strength she possessed to conquer the feeling. She had work to do here. The people sheltering in the bookshop – who had lost their homes and most of their possessions on this terrible night – needed her support, compassion and encouragement. With a silent instruction to herself to calm down, Kate rose to her feet.

At the very same moment, the bookshop door opened. At first she thought a band of sweeps were coming in. All these three lacked were the lum hats. One of them grinned at her, a flash of white teeth made even more dazzling by the contrast with his black face. The other smiled at Peggy.

'Hey!' protested Richard as she flew into his arms. 'I'm filthy. Not to mention drookit. We all are.'

'I don't care,' Kate cried. 'I don't bloody care! The three of you are safe and that's all that matters.'

'Aye,' Nathaniel Henderson said, his blackened arm around his wife's shoulders. 'We're safe.'

CHAPTER SIXTY-EIGHT

'I'm not going into your bed, Kate. I'm absolutely filthy.'

'So am I now, so does it matter?'

It was nine o'clock in the morning and they had come along to her house – battling the still-rising wind all the way – so they might get a few hours' sleep. The fire, thank God, seemed at last to have been brought under control – though another way of looking at it was that the flames had nothing left to burn. The devastation of the two closes that had been its cradle was total.

Volunteering to go at first light to see what he could find out, Andrew had returned with the news that Queensberry House down in the Canongate was to be opened to accommodate the burnt-out families who did not have relatives elsewhere with whom they might stay. The Royal Infirmary too was opening its doors, in its case to the families of the casualties who had been transported to the hospital during the night.

Brendan had played his part in that. Rendezvousing at the bookshop ten minutes before, Richard had asked him and Jamie to go across to the New Town and tell his parents he was well and unharmed and that he would call on them later in the day.

'I could offer you a bath,' Kate told Richard now.

'Could you? I wouldn't think there would be any water left in Edinburgh.'

'We have a water tank,' she said proudly, pointing towards a door in the corner of the kitchen where they stood. 'It's in there.'

'How do you fill it?'

'By means of a few sixpences to a few wee ragamuffins who run up and down to the well for us. So would you like to bathe?' She eyed his tall frame. 'It's going to be a bit of a squeeze, mind.'

'I'll squeeze. Tell me where the bath is and I'll fetch it.'

'In the same cupboard as the tank.' She passed an experimental hand over what remained of the fire in the kitchen range. 'There's enough warmth left here for me to heat up at least some of the water.'

'Perfect,' he said, already lifting a hip bath out of the cupboard. 'Is here all right?' he enquired, setting it down on the kitchen floor.

'It's fine there.'

'You're not even looking.'

She swung round from the range, one large pan in each hand. 'Whatever you do is fine by me.'

He smiled at her over the bath. 'Pity it's not big enough for two.'

'Aye,' she said, and felt herself slump like a puppet whose strings had been cut. 'Och, Richard, I thought…I was so worried that…'

'Wheesht,' he said, stepping round the bath and taking the pots from her. 'It's over now and we're both safe. Everybody's safe.'

'Everybody we care about. We dinna ken if other folk have been so lucky.'

Hastily depositing the pans on a dresser, he reached out a sooty hand to wipe away the solitary tear sliding down her cheek, then laughed softly. 'Now I've turned you nearly as black as me. You'll have to have a wash too. Better yet, why don't you get in the bath before me? I used to dream about giving you a bath, you know. Not quite under these circumstances, I have to admit.'

'We'll both have to give each other a bath, I'm thinking. Your hair's going to need to be washed too. Probably my own as well to get rid of the smell of smoke.'

He smiled back at her. 'Ladies first.'

'Do you mind if we make love later, Kate?'

'No,' she said, her mouth curving as she climbed into the bed beside him. 'I don't mind. I was thinking you might possibly be a wee bit tired.'

'Are you laughing at me?'

'Would I dare?'

'Oh, you'd dare,' he said, his words slurred with fatigue. 'Isn't it supposed to be bad for you to go to bed with your hair wet?'

'Can't be helped,' she said with a yawn. 'Desperate situations require desperate remedies.'

'I loved you washing my hair. Found it very erotic.'

'We'll have to do it again sometime, then. When we're not so tired.'

'Mmm. Come here,' he mumbled, slipping one strong arm under her shoulders. 'I need you close to me. Did I tell you that I love you?'

'You did,' she said, snuggling into him.

'Did you tell me that you love me? Did I say that right?' he enquired sleepily.

'You did. And I do. Love you, I mean.'

'And you'll marry me?'

'We'll discuss that later.'

'Yes is the answer, Kate...' His words trailed off, and within seconds they were both asleep. Not even the wind battering against the casement window, whipped up now into a gale, could disturb them.

CHAPTER SIXTY-NINE

Out in the smouldering ruins, those small pockets of fire that it had been judged safe to leave to burn themselves out continued to flicker. Occasionally the vicious November wind caught the flames and whipped them up as though in a reminder nobody needed of the fury with which the fire had raged during the night. They soon subsided again. Or most of them did.

Throughout the town, exhausted men and women took shelter from the gale. Despite the wind's best efforts, the smell of acrid smoke hung heavily in the air. There were few, as yet, who had the stomach to go and gawp at the ruins. Others who might have done so were kept away by the weather. There would be plenty of time to stand and stare at the destruction once the wind had died down.

A few of those who sought to profit by other people's misfortunes were out and about, moving through the deserted closes and wynds. There wasn't anything to be had from the burnt-out buildings but elsewhere there was the odd little treasure to be found.

His trouser pockets jingling with the silver he had found in a purse that must have been dropped during a headlong flight from the flames, one looter decided his haul was enough. He would walk back up the High Street and head for home. Then something caught his eye. Something high up.

Tilting his head back, he gazed far above his head at the

wooden steeple of the Tron Kirk. Flames were shooting out of it. He didn't hesitate. Thieving was one thing. This was another. He threw his head back and yelled.

'Fire! Fire! Fire!'

Drugged with sleep – not enough of it – Richard grunted a protest as Kate shot out of bed. 'Come back,' he mumbled. 'I'm already cold in here without you.'

'Something's happening,' she said. 'Out on South Bridge Street. Richard, I thought I heard somebody shout "Fire!"'

'You were dreaming. Or having a nightmare. Come back to bed.' When she didn't respond, he sat up, his brain dull with tiredness. Kate was standing at the window, bracing herself on the sill by the heels of her hands, neck craned so she could peer along the street.

She whirled round. 'Richard, there *is* another fire. I can see the flames. They're coming out of the steeple of the Tron Kirk.' Her hands flew to her face. 'Oh, Richard, the bookshop's only across the road!'

He took her hand as they ran along South Bridge Street, dreading what they might see. Despite the stormy weather, a crowd had gathered. Their attention was fixed on the steeple of the Tron and the firemen who were attempting to scale it.

Wondering where their enormously long ladders had been last night, thinking briefly of his own roof-scaling exploits, Richard found the time to reflect that the men up there certainly didn't lack courage, though the flames were beating them back now, the wooden steeple well ablaze. The lead of its roof and clock face was melting like wax. As he watched, he saw the minute hand fall from quarter to the hour to half past it, before slithering to the ground in one molten piece.

Fighting his way through the growing crowd watching the attempt to save the Tron, Richard didn't bother saying *Excuse me*, he simply forced his way through and pulled Kate behind him. They came up against a platoon of soldiers, their rifles held in front of them, blocking their path.

'Too dangerous to go any further, sir,' one of them said. 'Take yourself and the lady back the way you came, if you please.'

'We have to get through!' Kate cried. 'We have family and friends in the bookshop on the corner.'

The young red-coated trooper glanced over his shoulder. 'Buildings along this side of the street are fine, madam. No cause for you to be concerned—'

The noise that interrupted him was horrific: shearing, splintering, tearing wood. Gazing in horrified fascination up at the church steeple, Richard saw it began to move, separating itself from the building below.

'Back,' yelled the young soldier. 'All of you get back!'

Kate wasn't listening to him. Or not hearing him. So swiftly Richard was unable to react in time, she let go of his hand and ran forward. Poised to follow, he found his route barred by three of the soldiers, closing ranks on him.

'This is madness, sir. Do you not see what's happening up there? The steeple's going to fall at any minute!'

'I must get through!' he shouted. 'You must let me through!'

Two of them passed their rifles to their comrade, and moved to seize his arms. His heart thumping so hard he thought it might burst out of his chest, Richard saw Kate was almost at the bookshop door. The next second, his eyes were drawn once more up to the steeple of the Tron.

This was it. More shearing, splintering and tearing. Then it fell, plunging down, down, down to the street below.

CHAPTER SEVENTY

The bookshop was ablaze within seconds, planks of burning wood from the steeple sticking obscenely out of the windows they had broken. Through those, Richard couldn't see Kate but did make out Nathaniel's tall figure. He looked as if he were moving about, stacking books into boxes.

'Let me go.' Richard ground the words out. '*Let me go!*' Had Kate made it into the bookshop before the steeple fell? The amount of debris that had landed in front of the shop made it impossible to tell. Frantic with anxiety, using a strength he hadn't known he possessed, he wrenched himself free of the restraining arms.

Approaching from the High Street and the North Bridge, a small knot of people had gathered at the corner. 'Round here!' someone shouted. 'There are people at the upstairs windows!'

There in seconds, Richard felt his whole body weaken with relief when he saw the two women standing at either end of the parlour windows. Andrew was with Kate and Peggy Henderson had his daughter in her arms. Between Kate and Peggy he could see billowing smoke. He couldn't tell whether it was rising up from the floor below or if the first floor was on fire. Not that it mattered. All that did was getting them all out of there.

'A blanket!' he yelled. 'Has anybody got a blanket? You must jump,' he called up. 'And we will catch you. Mrs Henderson,' he said, stepping forward so he was directly under the window, 'you must lower Belle to me. But we need someone to hold her while I catch you and Kate. Andrew, do you think you can lower yourself out – drop down the wall? I shall be waiting at the foot to steady you.'

Andrew shook his russet head. 'I'm no' going first. Belle and Kate and Aunt Peggy should be afore me.'

Kate placed her two hands on her brother's shoulders. 'Did you not hear what Richard said, Andrew? We need you to hold Belle. We cannot ask a stranger. She is already upset. She needs the reassurance of familiar arms and a face she knows and loves.'

Andrew looked for a moment at his sister. Then he drew in a deep breath. 'All right.'

The ensuing manoeuvre was accomplished without mishap, leaving Andrew and Richard standing together on the High Street gazing up at Peggy Henderson. 'As soon as you like, Mrs Henderson,' Richard said, raising his arms towards the window.

'You will not let her fall, Mr Hope?' She gave him a very sweet smile. 'That was a stupid question, was it not? Make ready, sir.'

He shifted his position, ensuring his arms were aligned with Peggy's as she lowered the child down. 'Now,' he said. 'Let go now, Mrs Henderson.' His heart was in his mouth as he caught his daughter and handed her to Andrew. 'There. We have her. Now we shall have you and Kate.'

Peggy Henderson shook her head. 'I must find Nathaniel first. He is downstairs in the shop.' She let out a little laugh. 'Trying to save his precious books.'

'Mrs Henderson,' Richard said, horribly afraid he could discern flames behind her, not only smoke. 'Peggy. You must not go downstairs to the shop.'

'There I must disagree with you...Richard.' Once again, she gave him that sweet smile. 'I must go to my husband. My place is by his side.' In the space between one moment and the next, as though by some magician's trick, she vanished from sight.

Richard moved along to where Kate stood above him. 'You now,' he said. 'Don't give me any arguments about that.'

Even as he spoke there was a noise like rumbling thunder. The parlour was on fire, licking, leaping flames shooting across the room, drawn out through the open windows by the force of the gale. Within seconds the whole outside of the building was a roaring wall of fire. 'Get out of there, Kate!' he yelled. 'But don't go downstairs into the shop!'

'Where, then?' she called back. 'The turnpike stair's full of smoke!'

'It's the only way you can go. Put a cloth over your nose and mouth! Soak it in water if you can do that quickly. Make all possible haste, Kate! We'll meet you round in Niddry Street!'

The fire had taken hold now. Finally admitting defeat, Nathaniel turned to make his way upstairs and found one of the bookcases crashing down in front of his feet. It was already well alight. The books spilling out from it fell open. As he watched, he saw the corners of the pages curl up and catch fire.

'Nathaniel!'

'Go back, Peg.' Studying her where she stood in the doorway, he looked and sounded quite calm. 'I'm not sure I can come to you. I should have come upstairs sooner, should I not? I beg your pardon for that, Peg. I really do.'

'You were trying to save the books. I understand, my love.' She made a graceful gesture with one upraised arm. 'I'm afraid my way back upstairs is already barred by fire and smoke.'

Surrounded by flames, the bookseller cocked his head to one side, looking for all the world as if he were debating a political point or discussing the merits of a poet or novelist's latest offering. 'You didn't get much of a bargain when you married me, Peg, did you?'

'You couldn't be more wrong, Nathaniel. I got the best bargain of my life.'

'And I would walk through fire for you, my love,' he said, and did.

So they were locked in one another's arms when the voracious fire, the wind, and a merciful providence caused the ceiling above their heads to crack and fall. It dropped with a roar, raising a storm of sparks and fragments of burning paper. As the echoes of its collapse died away, there was no sound at all in the bookshop save the crackling of the flames.

Kate was at one of the box windows on the second floor, which overlooked Niddry Street. There were other faces there too, pale and frightened, everyone jostling for position at the open casement.

'Kate,' Richard called up. 'Can you not go through into the bridge and so make your way out?'

'We've tried. Every door is locked fast. And the stair is full of smoke.'

'She mustn't go through the smoke,' Andrew said, clutching his niece to him. 'Smoke can kill you.'

'Then you must jump, Kate,' Richard said, striving to sound not at all concerned about the height from which she was going to have to do so. 'There are some gentlemen here with a blanket, standing by and holding it securely. You first, if you please.'

'There are children here. They should jump first. Forbye they're all scared to do it.'

'Then lead by example,' he called up. 'Show them there's nothing to fear! We shall catch you. I promise we shall catch everyone! Feet first,' he instructed, gazing up at Kate. 'Legs together and jump!'

He watched her climb up onto the sill, steadying herself with both hands against the window frame. Poised to do it, gathering her courage, she reminded him of another occasion: when she had shown him around the South Bridge and stood at the top of a flight of crumbling and hazardous stone steps with her lantern raised, lighting the way for him so he would not stumble.

She had been a beautiful beacon, a modern incarnation of the warrior queen with the hair like flame. Whether she'd somehow, magically, heard his thoughts inside her own head Richard didn't know, but she smiled down at him and edged forward. She looked quite calm. She was going to jump and they were going to catch her in the blanket. She would be safe, and out of the fire.

And then the growing panic of those standing behind her at the window erupted into movement. Beyond rational thought, two of them clambered up onto the window sill, pushing Kate forward. She was falling, not jumping, the two other people falling with her.

Three falling bodies. One blanket. It was an impossible task.

'Don't try to talk,' Richard said hoarsely. He was kneeling beside her, Andrew standing behind him with Belle in his arms. 'You have to save your strength.'

'Is that me...under...doctor's orders?'

'Yes,' he said crisply, although he was alarmed by how faint her voice was. 'As soon as we get a stretcher, I'll get you out of here and we'll take you to my parents' house where I can examine you properly. Isn't that right, Andrew?'

'Aye,' Andrew said stoutly. 'Exactly right.'

The doctor in Richard was indeed at work, his eyes ranging over her body. The blanket had partially broken her fall but she had come down hard. He knew that. He had heard that. She could have some pretty severe internal injuries. But her head was all right. There was no actual wound there, only a few inconsequential cuts and bruises. To be sure, she was going to have some swelling and discolouration on her right temple, but that was nothing.

Her blue eyes were clear, her gaze as direct as ever. Richard snatched up her hand.

'Always loved your hands,' she murmured. 'Healing... hands...'

'Save your strength, Kate,' he said. 'You must save your strength.'

She said something else. Not catching it, he looked across at Andrew.

'Something about Aunt Peggy and Uncle Nat,' the boy supplied. His face crumpled. 'Something about them waiting for her on the other side.'

'Promise...me...something...' Kate breathed.

'Whatever you want,' Richard said. He bent forward, straining to hear. *Look after Belle and Andrew for me. Promise me.*

'Of course, Kate. Although you'll be looking after them both yourself just as soon as we've nursed you back to health.'

She smiled up at him. Such a smile it was too: warm and loving and ready at the drop of a hat to start teasing him. 'I love you...Richard Hope...'

'And I love you, Kate Dunbar. Always have, always will. But don't speak any more now. You must save your strength.'

'Wheesht...' she murmured, 'and...kiss...me...'

Could his breath carry his own strength into her? Could life and vigour be passed on in a kiss as gentle as thistledown? He tried – oh, dear God in Heaven, how he tried!

As he lifted his head, he saw her gaze go to Andrew and Belle, heard her murmur words of love, each harder to make out than the last. Tears running unchecked down his face, Andrew lifted his niece so her mother could kiss her. Then Richard took Belle from him so he could lean forward and very gently kiss his sister on the cheek. And when Andrew lifted his head, Richard saw that the light in her eyes had begun to dim.

'Don't leave us, Kate,' he begged, no longer able to deny what was happening. *'Please don't leave us!'*

'You'll...see me again...one day...'

'In my heart and in my head for ever, Kate,' he said brokenly. Her voice was so low now he could hardly hear her but he thought she said something about needing another promise from him.

'Anything,' he said. *'Anything!'* Adjusting his hold on Belle so he wouldn't squash her, he leant further forward, straining every nerve and sinew to hear Kate's words. *'Remember?* What is it I've to remember, my love?'

He heard her answer quite clearly, saw the last gleam of light fade from her eyes. And then she was gone.

CHAPTER SEVENTY-ONE

He sat cross-legged in the middle of the carpet in his parents' drawing room, a sleeping baby cradled in the crook of his left arm. His right arm was curled protectively around the shoulders of a skinny boy whose age was hard to distinguish under the layers of soot and grime which besmirched each member of this most curious of *tableaux vivants*.

As she stood in the open doorway, Richard's parents turning to look beseechingly at her, it occurred to Irene Steele that the French term was a misnomer. The baby was asleep, and Richard and the boy were as still as statues. Even the bedraggled cat the boy was clutching wasn't moving.

Both Richard and the boy had their eyes trained on the central window. Neither of them altered their position in the slightest as Irene walked into the room. Flanking Richard's parents where they sat on upright chairs between two of the room's tall windows, anxiety etched into their faces, Jamie and Brendan and two of the maids looked on.

Marjorie Hope extended a hand to Irene. The other clutched a sodden handkerchief. 'He will not speak,' she murmured. 'Oh, my dear, what are we to do?'

'Let me try,' Irene murmured.

'A chair?' asked Richard's father, he too speaking in a low voice. Irene raised a hand in refusal, walked across the carpet and crouched down.

'Richard?'

'Irene.' He spoke politely, as though he were acknowledging her at a party or assembly, although he did not turn his head towards her. She glanced past him at the boy. A few strands of hair had shaken off their soot. When she saw the blazing red hair Irene realised where she had seen him before. He too had not broken his focus on the sky visible through the window.

'Let me take the baby, Richard.'

His arm tightened around the child. 'No, thank you, Irene. I promised her mother I'd look after her.'

Irene glanced up at the Hopes. Mrs Hope had her handkerchief to her eyes.

Mr Hope made a gesture which implied *go on, keep trying.*

'The baby must be heavy, Richard. Especially since you've been holding it for such a long time. I shouldn't say *it,* should I? Boy or a girl, Richard?'

'A girl,' he said. 'Her name's Belle.'

'That's a pretty name.'

'Yes,' he agreed, and turned to look at her. 'Belle is my daughter, Irene.'

'And her mother?' Irene asked, hearing Marjorie Hope gasp.

His chin had begun to tremble. 'Kate…' he began. 'Her mother is… Her mother was… Her mother is Kate, Irene. You met her once.'

'I remember meeting Kate, Richard. We shall talk about her later, if you like, but now I think we should all stand up and you and the young man should go and get cleaned-up and then have a lie down. Or maybe you both need something to eat first.'

'His name's Andrew. I'm going to look after him from now on too.' The ghost of a smile danced along Richard's lips. 'I expect it's more the case that he's going to look after me.'

'You can both look after one another,' Irene said. 'Stand up now, Richard. You too, Andrew. Would the cat perhaps drink some milk?'

Jamie came forward. 'I'll take him to the kitchen, if you like, Andrew. Will ye let me do that? Or aiblins ye could come along wi' me?'

Andrew looked at the young man, seemed to be considering the idea.

'Mrs Hope,' Irene said, 'although it seems a pity to wake her, I think Belle must have a bath before she is put to bed.' She turned with a smile to the worried-looking maids. 'Perhaps the girls might like to do that?'

'I need to be with Belle when she wakes up,' Andrew put in. 'She might be scared if she doesn't see anybody she kens.'

Marjorie Hope stood up. Everyone turned to look at her, even Richard. She came forward to stand in front of her son, and she spoke without hesitation. 'I shall bathe my granddaughter myself.' She turned to Andrew. 'You should perhaps come with us, young man. Once the baby is asleep you can go and see how your cat is faring. He will be in safe hands until then.'

A single tear slid down Richard's soot-streaked face. 'Thank you, Mama. I think you will need an apron.'

'I'll carry the wee lass for you, Mrs Hope,' said one of the maids. 'Since I've got my apron on.'

'That is very good of you,' Irene Steele said. 'Let her have the baby, Richard.'

He did so without demur. Then he looked at Irene. 'What should *I* do, Irene? I think you said something but I have forgotten what it was.'

'You should have a bath and a sleep, Richard. That's what you need right now.'

'A bath is what I need?' For the second time, a faint smile

curved his mouth. Then his face clouded over. 'I can't say the words I need to say, Irene. I can't say them!'

'Oh, Richard,' she said, 'you don't have to say anything you don't want to say. Give yourself time, my dear. Give yourself time!'

He shook his head. 'Time's stopped. I was there when it did.' His eyes were overflowing with pain. 'Kate's dead, Irene.' He gestured towards Andrew and his daughter. 'Our lovely Kate is dead. We've lost her. Oh, Irene, we've lost her!'

The tears came in a flood then, both from him and from Andrew. Jamie moved to put a hand on the boy's shoulder, as did the maid who wasn't holding Belle. Standing next to the other girl, Marjorie Hope gently cupped her sleeping granddaughter's soot-blackened head. Irene took both of Richard's filthy hands in hers and Edward Hope and Brendan O'Sullivan placed themselves on either side of him, each laying a hand on his blackened shoulders.

They all stood together, enveloping those who had lost Kate in their care, compassion and love.

EPILOGUE

It was April, but he was glad of the warmth of the library fire. The spring was proving to be sunny but chilly. Professor Sir Richard Hope stretched his long legs out on the hearth rug and tilted his head back against the smooth green leather of his favourite wing chair. His hair was white now, but he had as thick a shock of it as he'd always had. He also had his fair share of the aches and pains associated with advancing years but, ach well, that was only to be expected.

His mind was as lively as ever, a faculty appreciated both by his colleagues at the university, the medical students who stopped pretending to be bored when they attended his informative and humorous lectures, the Liberal Party of which he was a stalwart supporter and the members of the many committees on which he had sat. There was still much to be done and absolutely no room for complacency, but he liked to think he had done his bit to help improve public health and hygiene in this city he loved so much.

The door opened and a pretty red-haired girl popped her head around it. 'Grandpapa? I'm not disturbing you, am I?'

The professor bestowed a smile of great warmth upon his granddaughter and beckoned her into his inner sanctum. 'Not disturbing me at all.'

'I thought you might be thinking some of your great

professorial thoughts,' she said mischievously, the crinoline of her emerald green gown swaying as she approached him. She sank down gracefully on the leather stool beside his chair. Ah, the supple joints of youth. These days the professor could only envy them and realise how much he'd taken them for granted while he'd still had them.

'Impertinent young madam,' he said equably. 'How's my favourite girl this evening?'

The young woman's face took on a determined look. 'Needing your help to persuade Papa and Mama that I should be allowed to study medicine at the university. Now that Miss Jex-Blake and her friends have blazed the trail.'

'You know your parents are not against it *per se*,' the professor said. 'Despite the fact that they have some committed supporters among us at the university, Miss Jex-Blake and her friends did not have an easy time of it. Don't forget that riot at Surgeons' Hall two years back.'

'Because some male students were trying to prevent the women from attending a lecture? That was ridiculous!'

'Totally. But it was also unpleasant, uncomfortable and potentially even dangerous. Your parents are concerned about you having to face the same kind of nonsense, arising out of unthinking prejudice and sheer stupidity though we know it often does.'

The girl's fierce expression softened. 'Aunt Irene is very proud of you, you know, Grandpapa. Because you are so much in favour of education for women, and also of extending the suffrage to our sex.'

'It has always seemed to me preposterous that one half of the human race should deny basic freedoms to the other,' the professor said. 'Apart from the considerations of morality and fairness, it's such an appalling waste of potential. Have you had a letter from your Aunt Irene?'

The girl nodded. 'From Venice. They are very much enjoying their trip and send you their love. The next letter will be to you, she says.'

Richard smiled. He counted Irene Steele and her long-time companion among his closest friends. He'd spent many convivial evenings with the two women over the years. It was they who had convinced him to accept his knighthood. Given that he wasn't much of a monarchist, he'd been reluctant to do so until they had persuaded him that the honour was as much for the university, the Royal Infirmary and Edinburgh as for him.

He was a man who had many friends and whose friendships knew no boundaries. To him, class or age or gender did not matter. Neither did lack of formal education nor lack of money. What he valued in his friends was an enquiring mind and a generous heart.

When he had needed help, it had often been under the humblest of roofs where he had found the greatest compassion and kindness. Ah, but despite that those years after the fire had been so bleak, the future stretching out in front of him seeming to offer only the constant pain of what he had lost.

He had kept going for the sake of those who loved him and whom he loved in return, and because of Kate's dying words to him. *Remember you must live.* That was the last thing she had said to him, the last promise she had asked him to make to her. It was a grand sentiment. For her sake, he had done his best to follow it.

His eyes went to the two framed drawings that hung side-by-side above his desk and, between two bookends of its own, the most prized book in his extensive library, an old edition of the collected poems of Robert Burns.

A young man bent over a table, studying. A young woman carrying two wicker baskets, her glorious rippling hair and calf-length skirts flaring out as she turned to smile at the artist. A year after the fire, he had sought out Walter Geikie, asked him if he could draw her from memory and found the young artist already had done a sketch of her.

Her granddaughter and his knew the story. 'You think of her often, don't you, Grandpapa?'

'Every day,' the professor said. 'You're very like her, you know.' He smiled. 'Beautiful and kind and clever and never afraid to speak your mind.'

'I know, Grandpapa,' the girl said gently. 'You've told me that before.' She put her hand on his knee and he laid his own over it.

'I shall speak to your parents,' he said after a few moments of companionable silence.

'Thank you, Grandpapa. Now we've got that settled, my brothers have asked me to persuade you to come to Stirling with us on the train on Saturday.'

'I fear I'm getting a bit too old for picnics, my dear.' He pulled a face, mocking himself. 'At my age, getting down onto the grass is one thing and getting back up off it quite another.'

'No one is ever too old for picnics,' the girl said. 'We'll all help you get back up again. Besides which, this is something more than a picnic. We shall be gathering at the foot of the monument – which I know for a fact is somewhere that is very dear to your heart.'

The new monument in honour of William Wallace on the Abbey Craig just outside Stirling was indeed close to the professor's heart. He and his daughter and son-in-law had been amongst the most vociferous campaigners in support of its being built. They had also contributed generously financially and encouraged others to give what they could to the fund set up to pay for it.

Tall and dramatic, the Wallace monument was visible from

miles around, testament to a groundswell of renewed national pride among Scots of all ages and backgrounds. It also indicated, so the professor thought, what long memories his fellow countrymen and women had. Scotland never forgot her heroes.

And there was a new – or perhaps revived – idea circulating. The prime minister himself had articulated it at a meeting in Aberdeen the year before. If, Mr Gladstone had said, Ireland should be granted home rule, then surely it could not be refused to Scotland. The professor doubted he would see that in his own lifetime but he was intoxicated by the idea that his children or grandchildren or even great-grandchildren might.

So it would be grand to go to Stirling with his grandchildren on Saturday, enjoy seeing that all the fire and passion he felt for Scotland had been passed on to the younger generation. But he should protest a little first, of course. 'Och, you don't want an old man like me with you.'

'One, you're not old, and two, of course we want you with us. The boys say the prettiest girls always appear out of nowhere when you're around. Can't resist your distinguished good looks and charm.'

The professor laughed. 'It's you who're the charmer. What now, lass?'

For his granddaughter had stood up and was tugging at his hand so he would stand up with her. 'I want you to come and dance with me.'

'Me?' He laughed again. 'When you must have an army of young men vying for that privilege?'

There was a gleam of mischief in the girl's blue eyes. 'I need to practise for the army of young men,' she said. 'So I won't fall over my feet when I dance with them and make a complete and utter fool of myself.'

'So that's the way of it,' he said, allowing her to pull him to his feet and lead him onto the polished boards of the library floor. And there, while she exuberantly supplied their musical accompaniment, the eminent professor danced the dance that some of the more dour members of Edinburgh society still considered rather racy: the waltz.

And as he danced he found his thoughts drifting to days long gone: to a dimly lit and smelly oyster cellar, with a fiddler in the corner striking up a lively tune, and his own eyes meeting those of another beautiful, red-haired girl, the smile on her face for him and for him alone.

He was humming a waltz to himself the next afternoon as he stepped out of the Royal Infirmary after a morning of leading ward-rounds. Nothing like having the young medical students hanging on your every word and laughing at all your jokes.

Coming out onto Infirmary Street, impulse took him down Robertson's Close to the Cowgate. Pausing beneath the single exposed arch of the South Bridge, he studied the stone wall to his right. The underground close was blocked up now, had been for years. He supposed very few people even knew there had once been a community living and working inside what looked now like blank walls. Odd how things got buried and forgotten about.

Retracing his steps, he began walking up Niddry Street. For years he had avoided it, the pain of Kate's loss sharp as a sword. Now, with the wisdom of old age, he found he could choose to dwell on the memories of standing with her in the close at the foot of the brae and blowing kisses to her from the top of it. Precious moments, precious times.

Emerging onto the High Street, he wondered about walking along South Bridge to see if Andrew were about. He was an esteemed antiquarian book-dealer now, and a grandfather himself. Remembering he'd mentioned when Richard had dined with him and Rebecca last week that the two of them were going off together on a book-buying tour of Fife, the professor found himself obeying another impulse.

Cut in two halves now by Cockburn Street, Richard considered the precipitous steps of Fleshmarket Close. It held happy memories. In his younger days he had often walked nimbly up or down those steps, remembering standing on them with Kate. These days the smooth slope of the street was easier on his arthritic joints. On the way down he passed the building that housed *The Scotsman*. The newspaper was an august and respectable journal these days.

Standing for a moment on Waverley Bridge, he paused to admire the view. The castle stood proudly on its rock as it had done for centuries and would do for centuries to come. Edinburgh looked as wonderful as it always did. His heart swelled with pride as it always had done.

His eyes dropped to the glass and wrought-iron canopy of the railway station.

Was there any other city in the world that had named its main railway terminus – that symbol par excellence of the modern age – after a novel of romantic, long-ago history? That was Edinburgh for you – always two dramatically different sides to every story.

Waverley's criss-crossing ribbons of railway lines carried passengers and goods west to Glasgow, north to Aberdeen and south to Berwick-upon-Tweed, Newcastle, York and London. The professor loved travelling by train, and had been as far as London on several occasions, attending medical meetings and conferences. Amazing it now took mere hours to do a journey that had once taken a week.

Progress and change. He had seen so much of it over the course of his life: in politics, in medicine, in public attitudes. He sometimes wondered what the Hendersons would have made of it all. He smiled, suspecting that pair would have rejoiced in what had been achieved and immediately fallen to a discussion of what still needed to be done.

Progress and change. Yet, although things did get forgotten about, nothing was ever really lost. It was always layer upon layer. What was buried or hidden left some essence of itself. Take the Old Physic Garden, which had vanished long since beneath platforms and tracks and trains. The ground it had occupied was still there – and he could remember exactly where that was.

Obeying his third impulse of the afternoon, he walked down into the station. As usual, it was all hustle and bustle: men, women and children hurrying hither and yon. Others stood puzzling out destination and arrival boards. Others again enjoined their travelling companions to hurry up as they made for the cab stance where horses, coaches and drivers stood waiting for fares.

The professor made his way serenely through it all. He came here now and again, a silent pilgrimage of which he never spoke to anyone. He'd sometimes thought about telling his granddaughter that here, once upon a time, there had been a beautiful garden where a boy and a girl had kissed and tarried and fallen in love.

Just a lad and a lass. Just Richard and Kate walking through the town.

He smiled again, and came to the spot where, as he had taken pains to work out after the railway station had been built and so drastically altered the lie of the land, the gates to the Old Physic Garden had once been – and stood there, remembering.

Remembering himself making fun of the doctor in George IV's entourage who had wanted to revisit the haunts of his student days. What was it he said to Kate? Something about the man having studied here *about a hundred years ago*. The impertinence of youth.

The memories stabbed at his heart. If only he could have been standing here now with Kate by his side. A lad and a lass journeying through life and growing old together. He had remembered he must live. He had lived a good, full life and, he hoped, a useful one – but he hadn't had Kate. Only for one sweet moment. Och, but what a glorious moment it had been!

That summer had made him who he was today. She had done that, transforming a thoughtless young man into one who cared deeply about his fellow men and women and the world in which they all lived, a man, too, who realised that one person could make a difference. If he had made something of his life – and he hoped he had – it was all thanks to Kate Dunbar.

Startled out of his absorption by the fierce puffing of a locomotive, Richard looked up. The engine stood at the platform behind the cab stance. Like billowing summer clouds the white smoke it was throwing out rose to envelop the bridge that led passengers leaving the station out onto Market Street and across the road to Fleshmarket Close.

In the midst of those white clouds stood a red-haired girl. She was smiling down at him, and as her mouth curved into a smile, he fancied he could hear the words she spoke. *Is that you, Richard Hope?*

The locomotive chuntered out of the station, pulling its carriages off to Glasgow. When the clouds of steam cleared, she was standing right in front of him.

Hello, old man.

She was wearing the dress he had bought for her half a century ago and her glorious auburn hair was threaded through with a simple blue ribbon.

'Kate?' he asked. 'Is it really you?'

Who else would it be?

'Have you come for me?'

Looks like it, does it no'? She was looking at him in the way he remembered so well, warm and loving and ready at the drop of a hat to start teasing him.

'Are you laughing at me?'

Would I dare? The smile on her lovely face widened. Especially wi' you having become such an eminent and distinguished man.

'Oh, you'd dare all right. But what are we going to do about me being so old and you being so young?'

We're going tae start again. As different folk but the same folk, if ye ken what I mean.

'So that *is* how it works!'

Aye. That's how it works. As long as you're prepared tae come through into the Old Physic Garden wi' me. We get tae spend some time here first. Are ye ready tae come wi' me, Richard?

'I'm ready. Och, Kate, I'm more than ready!'

'He just fell,' said the middle-aged lady passenger. 'I noticed him standing here. Think he was talking to himself, actually. But then he gave this big beaming smile, and fell.'

'He was certainly talking to someone,' put in a railway porter. 'I was round the corner here and I heard him.'

'But there was nobody near him,' said another passenger, crouching down by the body of the elderly, well-dressed man.

'Is he dead?' asked the lady passenger.

The other passenger tried for a pulse. 'Seems so. I'm afraid we must check his pockets to see who he was.'

'How very sad for his family. What a shock this will be for them.'

'Yet he's smiling,' said the porter. 'He looks happy. At peace.'

'So he does. That may be some consolation to his relatives. I certainly hope so.' The lady passenger lifted her head. 'Can anyone smell lemons?'

The aches and pains were gone, his joints supple again. The stoop he'd acquired with age had vanished and he stood straight and tall, drawn up to his full height. Thrilled by the rush of youth and vigour coursing though his body, he tugged a lock of hair forward. It was black and glossy. Glancing down at himself, he saw that he was dressed in the fashions of his youth.

'Come away through, then,' Kate said. She was holding one of the gates open. It was as black and glossy as his hair and behind her he could see the paths and the flower beds and the summer house. The air was fresh and clean and a little breeze carried the scent of the flowers to him. Bees buzzed, and a thrush sang its song to the morning.

'Do I get a kiss?' he asked.

'Aiblins,' she said, tilting her head to one side, a gleam of mischief sparkling in her beautiful blue eyes.

'I'd say there's no aiblins about it.' Stepping forward, he put his lips to hers. They kissed, pulled back and smiled at one another. Then they joined hands and together they walked through the gates, past a clump of nodding bluebells, and into the garden.

AUTHOR'S NOTE

In Edinburgh's Waverley station, opposite the taxi rank and close by the war memorial, there is a plaque on the wall. Placed there by the Royal College of Physicians of Edinburgh, it marks the site of the Old Physic Garden.